ALSO BY ROBERT EVERSZ

Gypsy Hearts

Shooting Elvis—A Nina Zero Novel

Killing Paparazzi—A Nina Zero Novel

Burning Garbo—A Nina Zero Novel

ROBERT EVERSZ

Digging
James
Dean

A Nina Zero Novel

Simon & Schuster
New York   London   Toronto   Sydney

SIMON & SCHUSTER
Rockefeller Center
1230 Avenue of the Americas
New York, NY 10020

SIMON & SCHUSTER and colophon are registered trademarks
of Simon & Schuster, Inc.

Excerpt from "Dinosaurs of the Hollywood Delta" by Gerald Costanzo from Nobody Lives
on Arthur Godfrey Boulevard: Poems, American Continuum Series, copyright © by BOA
Editions. Reprinted with permission of the author.

For information about special discounts for bulk purchases,
please contact Simon & Schuster Special Sales: 1-800-456-6798
or business@simonandschuster.com.

Designed by Karolina Harris

Manufactured in the United States of America

10 9 8 7 6 5 4 3 2 1

Library of Congress Cataloging-in-Publication Data
Eversz, Robert.
    Digging James Dean : a Nina Zero novel / Robert Eversz.
        p. cm.
    1. Zero, Nina (Fictitious character)—Fiction. 2. Women photographers—Fiction. 3. Ex-
convicts—Fiction. 3. Paparazzi—Fiction. 4. Los Angeles (Calif.)—Fiction.
    PS3555.V39 D54 2005
    813'54—dc22
                                                                            2004052596

ISBN 0-7432-5015-X

For Sandi, Donna, Marcus, and Sabrina; without trouble life acquires little wisdom but with a little wisdom life acquires less trouble.

In times of plenty
they arrived from everywhere
to forage among the palmettos
of Beverly and Vine, to roam
the soda fountains and dime stores
of paradise.

GERALD COSTANZO
"Dinosaurs of the Hollywood Delta"

Digging
James
Dean

ONE

I WAS SITTING behind a cup of coffee in Café Anastasia when the girl with the lavender-colored glasses walked through the slab of light at the front door, looking for a woman wearing a black leather jacket and rhinestone nose stud. The glasses looked good on the girl but she couldn't see past the blunt line dividing sun and shade and dropped her head to peer over the top of the rims. I knew she searched for a woman in a black leather jacket because she had called twenty minutes before and I wore a leather jacket that day, as I do every day when the temperature drops below 95° Fahrenheit. I sipped my coffee, the movement of my cup drawing her eye. She stepped forward, her head tilted self-consciously high, as though aware that she looked good when she held her head high but also afraid that she might trip in the dim light and that wouldn't look good at all.

"You're the photographer works for the tabs?"

"Sometimes," I said.

She took that to mean yes and sat in the straight-backed chair across the table. "They said you'd give a hundred dollars."

I watched the girl over the rim of my cup. I get a few desperate people trying to sell me fabricated information every week and it has taught me to be cautious, particularly of runaways. Her low-slung knit slacks, bare-midriff silk blouse, and calfskin jacket appeared pulled from the racks of name designers. She'd applied the makeup to her heart-shaped face subtly, as though taught by a cosmetician instead of the myopic older sister with a makeup kit who taught me and most of my friends. She'd pulled her hair back in a tight ponytail to conceal that it hadn't been washed in a week and when she'd turned to sit I'd noticed a swath of dirt at the seat of her pants.

"They said you'd give more," she said, "if I saw someone really famous."

"I don't give anything. I buy information, if it's good enough."

"How do I know if you'll buy?"

"You tell me who and what it is."

The girl nodded. She seemed to get it. She glanced over her shoulder as though afraid someone might be eavesdropping, then leaned far over the tabletop to whisper, "About five minutes before I called, I'm hanging out near the beach, just chilling, you know, and I, like, look across the street and there's Chad Stonewell walking into this place on Ocean Avenue, a restaurant, the Italian-sounding one with the valet parking on Broadway."

She had a sense of the melodramatic, at least.

"Chad Stonewell was a big star ten years ago," I said.

"Is he worth more than a hundred?"

"Back in his prime, he would have been worth more than a hundred. Right now, I don't think I can sell his photograph on eBay, let alone to the tabs."

The girl curled up from the table as though I'd just slapped her. "Okay," she said. "I thought he'd be worth something."

"You hungry?" I asked. "Get whatever you want. My treat."

Her eyes drifted to the sandwiches, pies, and cakes in the display case at the back of the café, then snapped back. "I'm fine," she said.

"Who set you up with the tip?"

She flicked the tip of her index finger beneath her eye, obliterating the tear welling in the corner before it could roll down her cheek. "Nobody," she said.

"Somebody told you to call me, say you'd seen Chad Stonewell, isn't that right? Some PR flack?"

"I saw him with my own two eyes." A second tear sprang from her eye. She flicked it from her cheek and laughed. "What's a PR flack? I don't even know what it is."

"Get yourself something to eat," I said. "It's part of the deal. Not your fault Stonewell's star sank."

She lowered her lavender lenses. "You're not just testing me?" Her eyes glimmered with a half-dozen more tears ready with the slightest justification to leap free. "You really aren't interested?"

I guessed her age at sixteen. Maybe younger. She hadn't been on the street long. Crying one moment, laughing the next, subject to the wicked sway of hormones that emotionally cripple most teenagers— the wolves on the street would sniff her out soon enough. She didn't have a clue and even less of a chance. I sucked down the last of my coffee and stood. "You got it right, little sister. It was a test. You passed."

The Rottweiler stood on his hind legs and barked when we stepped from the café. I let him jump his paws to my shoulders, then pushed him down and untied the leash from the no-parking sign. I felt bad about tying him up but the city sanitary codes discriminate against dogs. Can't take one into a restaurant, no matter how well behaved the dog or badly behaved the waiters.

"Aren't you afraid it'll bite somebody?" the girl asked.

I dropped the leash. The Rott leaped the door frame into the old Cadillac convertible I drove, settling behind the wheel like he thought I was going to let him steer. "He's only bit two people in the three months I've owned him," I said.

The girl stood at the passenger door, afraid to open it.

"He bites?"

I pointed to the backseat. The Rott got the message and jumped over the headrest. "Get in," I said. "If he bites it won't hurt much."

The girl slid into the passenger seat, her eyes never leaving the Rott. "A dog that big, it could take your head off."

"He could," I admitted. "If he had any teeth." I started the engine and pulled into traffic. Café Anastasia wasn't far from the beach. With luck Stonewell would be a fast eater and I could grab his photo and be gone within the hour. I asked, "Where you from?"

"Around here."

"Don't lie to me. I hate lies."

"Indiana."

Her face burned red. I proved I was tough enough to intimidate a teenaged runaway, if nothing else.

"How many days you been in L.A.?"

"A couple."

"You sleeping rough?"

She leaned against the passenger door, as far away from me and the dog as possible. Her survival instincts weren't completely dead. "Somebody's taking care of me," she said.

"Doesn't look like they're doing that great a job."

"That's none of your business, is it?"

It wasn't. I curbed the Cadillac at the narrow strip of green that forms Palisades Park, pointed to the public toilets across the grass. "Wait for me there. When I've taken the photo or at least confirmed your tip, I'll drop by to pay you." I dipped into the side pocket of my leather jacket. "Here's a twenty on advance."

She took the money and climbed out of the car.

Before she shut the door I said, "In case you're scamming me and I never see you again, some advice. Be careful who you trust, and never let a man talk you into sleeping with someone for money."

She crossed her arms over her chest, looked away. "I'm not scamming you."

"Good to hear it," I said. "But the advice holds true anyway."

Only one parking valet worked the curb at the restaurant where the girl said I'd find Stonewell and he didn't look overwhelmed by traffic. I hopped out of my car brandishing a cheap folding map. An unwritten set of rules governs the paparazzi biz and one of the most important is never to embarrass informants. Most of my tips come from waiters, waitresses, and parking valets. If I charge into a restaurant, flash attachment firing, I burn my contacts. As I approached the stand I flashed a twenty-dollar bill in my opposite hand, asked, "Can you help me with directions?"

The valet's eyes clicked from map to cash.

I lowered my voice and said, "I heard Chad Stonewell's taking a late lunch."

"I heard the same thing but I wouldn't know for sure," he said, playing along, glancing at the map. "Mr. Stonewell's driver doesn't valet park."

"No reason you should get stiffed. I'll be parked across the street, on Ocean. Give me a salute when you see Stonewell's driver pull out, okay?"

The valet nodded. He was a twenty-something Latino, probably worked two jobs just to get by. The bill changed palms when we shook hands. I didn't know why I was going to so much trouble. Stonewell would never be a nobody—he'd been too famous for too long for that—but he hadn't been in a hit film for almost a decade and despite owning the most famously dimpled chin in the history of motion pictures, his name was rapidly dropping to the bottom of the list of bankable stars. An undisputed champ of big-budget action flicks in the 1980s, when he burst onto the scene as the Bruiser from Brewster, Texas, Stonewell was no longer the first name called when the script called for a brawny kind of action hero, and so the parts that came his way were ones others had already rejected. Hard to get another hit that way, particularly when the rise to fame came on a reputation for invincibility rather than acting talent. Not that I wouldn't be able to sell his photograph after I'd taken it. If *Scandal Times*—the primary tab I worked with—didn't take it, another one would. But I wouldn't get much more than a couple of hundred for it. I'd be lucky if I broke even.

I circled the block a couple of times before a spot opened on Ocean Avenue in clear sight of the parking valet. The girl had needed money, sure, but that didn't mean I was responsible for giving it to her. I hated being played for a sucker even if I'd played myself for one. In prison I'd seen a hundred variations of the same girl ten years after the wolves had found her, hollowed out by drugs and hardened by abuse. Nothing I could do to stop that from happening to her, but I didn't have to contribute to it by refusing to help. Maybe she'd take that hundred dollars and change her life. Maybe a hundred dollars was all she needed to tip her life over to the good. Maybe Stonewell was inking at that very moment a multimillion-dollar contract to star in the Next Big Thing and I'd sell his photograph for a couple grand. One thing about suckers like me, we have hope.

The sun rolled over the lip of sea and the sky darkened to violet before the parking valet saluted and a black Mercedes S430 rolled to the stoplight up the street from the restaurant. I wrapped the 35mm Nikon in a plastic bag and tucked the little point-and-shoot into the ankle of my boot. Stonewell's image hadn't graced the pages of a tabloid in months. He needed the publicity. He was going to kiss the sidewalk at my feet when the first flash popped. I checked the avenue for traffic and jaywalked to the opposite curb. The Mercedes stopped in the space reserved for valet parking. I lingered on the corner next to a blond guy waiting to cross the street at the green. When the driver circled the hood to open the passenger door I pulled the camera from the bag and stepped around the corner. A bodyguard held the door to the restaurant open. Stonewell strode out wearing jeans, sneakers, and a satin windbreaker, the kind with the name of a film emblazoned on the back. The guy with him wore a black suit that made him look like a priest in Armani. They stepped into the shot before they even knew I was there.

"Hey, Chad, give us a smile!" I called, and fired the flash.

That was the only shot I'd need, I thought, Chad Stonewell leaving a Los Angeles restaurant with an unidentified man, but Stonewell shouted like I'd just pulled a gun and the bodyguard bolted from the door. My finger twitched again to get the shot, Stonewell pointing at me, the bodyguard vaulting around his left shoulder. I'd seen the same gesture from other celebrities and knew it meant I needed to jet. I backpedaled for a last shot, turned to start my sprint, and collided into the citizen I'd seen waiting for the light at the corner. I spun to go around him, but he grabbed my arm and hit me with a forearm shot to the jaw. He jerked the camera as I fell, held it over his head to show Stonewell that he'd gotten it, and tossed it to the bodyguard. The bodyguard flipped open the back of the camera and stripped out the film.

"Teach her a lesson," Stonewell said. "Camera, too."

The bodyguard shrugged and windmilled the Nikon on its strap. On the downstroke he dropped his shoulder and smashed the camera lens-first into the sidewalk.

"Again," Stonewell said.

The black-suited man behind him presumably watched, his expression impassive behind teardrop-shaped sunglasses. The Nikon swung in a high arc, taut on its strap. The lens had already shattered and the film compartment twisted open on a broken hinge. The second blow came like the coup de grâce to a corpse. The lens snapped free and rolled like a severed head into the gutter. Had they stopped at stripping the film from my camera I would have accepted the loss as one of the hazards of the trade. Celebrities have bodyguards. Sometimes they catch you and when they do they take your film. Every now and then they might throw an elbow into your ribs or in extreme circumstances wrestle you to the ground. By breaking my camera they had taken the chief tool of my trade and that threatened my survival. I pulled my legs up to my chest and drew the boot cam concealed in my Doc Martens. Nobody paid any attention to me when I stood. Stonewell tapped fists with the bodyguard and said something to the man in the black suit as they stepped toward the car. The citizen returned to the street corner, as though waiting for the light. I leapt forward and swung the point-and-shoot to my eye.

"Hey, Chad, how about a smile?"

The flash popped on a group shot, the black-suited man almost smiling in surprise, Stonewell and the bodyguard gaping like they'd just been caught robbing the bank. The flash momentarily blinded them. I sprang from my shooter's crouch and sprinted for the gap between the driver and the man in the black suit, who stepped back to avoid me, cutting off the bodyguard. The driver just looked on. I wasn't his job. Midblock I cut left onto the 3rd Street Promenade, a walk-street of shops and cinemas three blocks from the beach. They'd pile into the car, I thought, and try to catch me on the streets, probably at Wilshire, where the Promenade ends. I cut left again, toward Palisades Park, got lucky catching a green light at Ocean Avenue, and when I reached the mouth of the pedestrian bridge that crosses over the Pacific Coast Highway to the beach, I glanced back to see the bodyguard hunched three blocks behind, vomiting into the curb. I maintained my stride until slowed by the sand beneath Santa Monica Pier and only then, safely concealed among the pilings, did I begin to wonder what the hell had just happened.

TWO

THE GIRL jittered from one foot to the other near the public restrooms in Palisades Park, her calfskin jacket buttoned against the cold, and every minute or so she stepped to the curb to peer first one way down the avenue and then the other. A dozen yards distant, a slender young man stood against the wood railing that marked the cliff edge, as though he loitered there with no other objective than to enjoy the sweeping night vistas of ocean, pier, and mountains. He couldn't keep his glance from the girl, betraying his not-so-clandestine surveillance to catch her eye and show his palms to the sky as if to ask, "What's up?" When he turned his face toward the railing again the park lights reflected against a scraggly blond goatee waging a battle for survival on his chin. Personally, I didn't think the goatee was going to make it.

"Coming up behind you," I said.

The girl turned quickly. "I thought you'd come by car," she said. "Did it work out? Was he there?"

I lifted the point-and-shoot camera to my eye. The flash burst across a face too confused to know whether to smile or turn away. "He was there," I said.

"Why did you take my picture?"

"I'm a photographer. It's what I do." I pulled four twenties from the side pocket of my leather jacket. "Don't worry, I'm not going to put it in the paper."

She tried out a brave smile. "You kidding? I wish you'd put my picture in the paper. Like maybe then some producer would notice me."

"You want to be an actress?"

"I guess everybody here says that."

I gave her the money, glanced over my shoulder at the young man standing at the rail, said, "Don't let your boyfriend take all of it, okay?"

She pushed the money into the front pocket of her pants. Her pants were tight. She had to push hard. "How did you know he was my boyfriend?"

"Just guessed. What's your name?"

"Theresa." She said the name like it was her own.

"Thanks for the tip, Theresa. Just one more question for you."

She tilted her head to the side, her expression bright and attentive, wanting, it seemed, to get the answer right.

"The guy in the black suit who accompanied Stonewell, you know who he is?"

She shook her head before I finished the sentence. "No, never saw him before," she said.

"That isn't what I asked you."

Her eyes furrowed and she gave her head a little shake. "But you just—"

"I asked if you knew who he was."

"No, I don't, no idea," she lied, stepping back.

I handed her a card with my home and mobile phone numbers, said, "Ask your boyfriend."

"Look, thanks for the money. If I get another tip, I'll give you a call." She turned and took the path toward the pier. A moment later, the boy at the railing decided to walk that way too, still playing the game as though I hadn't made him the moment I walked up.

While I drove the freeways I counted my losses. I'd be lucky to lose half a grand, including a replacement camera and lens, and that factored in selling the photograph, which I wasn't sure I'd be able to do. It didn't matter that Theresa might have lied to me about the guy in the black suit. Frank would know him if he was anybody. Frank knew everybody by sight, name, and reputation. He wrote for *Scandal Times*. Some of his pieces were first-rate investigative journalism, some pure fiction. He was a good writer. The readers never knew which was which.

The staff at *Scandal Times* worked out of a former sewage-works warehouse converted to office space in the San Fernando Valley. The paper offered its devout readership the usual tabloid fare—cloned sheep giving birth to live aliens, as Frank liked to call the perfect story—but had made its greatest mark in the tabloid world by reporting on celebrity scandals, where it was the most authoritative source of rumor, if not fact. I freelanced for *Scandal Times,* giving them first look at everything I shot. They didn't care that I was an ex-con. In fact, they considered it an asset.

I plugged my parking card into the slot and drove into the employee parking lot next to the building. The lot was about a quarter full and as usual people had double-parked the spaces nearest the door, as though a twenty-yard walk would kill them. I read once that if Americans took the first available space when they parked, rather than circling the rows looking for the closest possible space to the entrance, the gasoline saved every year would power 23,468 rocket trips to the moon. I read that in *Scandal Times.* I parked toward the back of the lot and gave the Rott a pat on the head, told him to stay. The only animals the paper allowed in the building were the two-legged kind. He whined and let out a single angry bark.

I pulled the point-and-shoot camera from my jacket pocket and pressed the rewind button as I threaded my way between cars. The Rott barked again, and when I turned to let him see I was all right, a man stepped from the cover of the SUV beside me, a ski mask sheathing his face. I whirled to run but another ski-masked figure popped from the opposite side, trapping me in the narrow aisle between the SUV and van beside it. I vaulted toward the roof of the SUV but the one behind me grabbed my leg and something streaked against the side of my head as he pulled me down. Time skipped a groove and I found myself belly-down on the asphalt, a pair of Timberland hiking boots dancing around my head. Hands rifled my pockets and rolled me over. Someone shouted and the shapes vanished, replaced by a black face carrying a wet, red cloth.

The Rott. He was licking me.

A flash sparked, the light flicking hot across my forehead. Frank Adams knelt beside me, a digital camera gripped in one hand while he felt for my pulse with the other. He said, "You don't mind me taking your photo, do you? This is really too good to pass up. Assaulted right in our own parking lot."

"It was the dog," Hector said, arms crossed below the badge that identified him as the *Scandal Times* security guard. "The second they saw him, they run off." He pointed through the ring of bystanders toward my car, parked a half-dozen rows back. "Look, you can see the glass on the ground. Went clean through the side window. That dog's a hero, I tell you."

"Do you want an ambulance?" Frank asked.

I shook my head and nearly vomited.

"Are you going to live?"

"Hope so," I said.

"Then get closer to the dog." He pointed the lens at the Rott. "Hang around his neck or something."

The Rott licked my face.

The camera flashed.

"That dog may be ugly but he's a natural around a camera," Frank said. "We'll run a sidebar near the back of next week's issue, headline it 'aMazing Mutt Mauls Muggers.'"

I stretched my hand out to Hector. He pulled me to my feet. I held on to my knees, back braced against the SUV, and tried to breathe some clarity into my head. "They weren't muggers," I said.

"*'They could have killed me,'* Scandal Times *photographer Nina Zero said, tears in her eyes. 'And maybe they would have, if not for my heroic hound.'*" Frank moved in for a close-up of the Rott while he improvised. "See, the story just about writes itself."

"I think I'm going to throw up."

"Sure, it can use some polish, but it's not that bad." Frank watched carefully, ready to photograph me if I fell. "You could cooperate a little, give me something quotable so I don't have to make everything up."

I stepped around the SUV and vomited. The crowd of late-night staffers quickly scattered. Someone getting mugged in the employee parking lot was an exciting diversion. Watching the victim throw up wasn't. I breathed through my nose until the wave of nausea passed, then asked for water. The camera flashed again and I looked up at Frank, pointing the lens at me.

"Don't get mad," he said. "You'd take my picture in the same situation. But as your friend and colleague, I counsel you to sit down."

Somebody handed me a bottle of water, said, "Keep it."

"I'm not mad at you for taking my picture." I took a swig, swirled it around my mouth, and spat it out. "I'm mad at you for being such a lousy journalist."

Frank's lips made a little O, as though my remark wounded him. He isn't a handsome man. He's about forty pounds overweight, cuts his own hair, and wears oversized T-shirts and baseball caps to compensate. Making faces doesn't help his appearance.

"This story is bigger than a sidebar," I said.

"You sure you're okay?"

I took Frank's advice and sat down again.

"Because sometimes when people get whacked over the head, they can't think straight for a while."

"I took Chad Stonewell's picture this evening outside a restaurant in Santa Monica."

Frank arched his eyebrows, as if to say, "So?"

"One of his bodyguards stripped the film, broke my Nikon. You know I carry a backup."

Frank nodded, eyebrows still arched.

"I took his picture with the backup and ran."

"And you think Stonewell set this up."

"Sure. Made it look like a mugging."

"Chad Stonewell would kiss my ass to get his photograph in *Scandal Times.*"

"I know."

"Why are you wasting film on him? He's worth maybe a hundred bucks, tops."

"I got a tip from somebody needed money."

Frank stared at me. "Somebody needed money?"

"She wasn't more than sixteen."

"I know, you wanted to help her." Frank glanced pointedly at the dog. "You're a sucker for lost creatures, aren't you?"

The carnival lights of an approaching patrol car skimmed the blacktop. A loud voice told everyone to go back inside, let the boys in blue do their job. I stretched out my arm for a hand up. Frank said, "I think you're better off sitting down."

THREE

THE INSIDE of my skull felt lined in jagged glass when I woke the next morning, curled on the floor beside Frank's desk, a Chicago Bulls sweatshirt for a pillow and extra copies of *Scandal Times* covering me like a hobo's blanket. I've suffered my share of headaches—mostly alcohol induced—but this one disoriented me in a way the others hadn't. I braced my arms against the floor and pushed myself to standing. Frank had left a glass of water, two Tylenol, and a note on the desk. I swallowed the Tylenol, scanned the note. He'd gone to walk the dog, it read.

I couldn't immediately figure out why I'd crashed on the floor. I didn't remember passing out, but then, people who pass out rarely remember it. Two officers from the Los Angeles County Sheriff's Department had taken my statement the night before. I remembered that much. I'd lost a ninety-nine-dollar point-and-shoot camera and hadn't been killed—no need to call out the crime scene technicians to vacuum the parking lot. The officers had given me a case number and a phone contact, advised me to seek medical treatment, and motored off to respond to the next call, less than thirty minutes elapsing between the moment they stepped from the patrol car and the flash of their lights pulling out of the lot. I remembered walking up the stairs to Frank's office after they left. We were going to talk about Stonewell but I couldn't remember if we did.

I searched out the employee restroom and splashed cool water on my face. Blood veined my eyes so thickly the whites disappeared and the irises had shrunk to black dots. The lump behind my ear had swollen to the size of my chin. My face steamed like a hot rock splashed with water, my heart accelerated, and I wanted to smash something, anything, preferably Stonewell. I breathed deeply, through the pain in my head, through my rage, slowing the anger in my heart, beat by beat. My heart swelled as it slowed and my throat tightened. I gasped, inexplicably near tears. I hadn't cried in years. I thought the tears had been burned from me years ago, but that morning, as I stood over the sink, they sprang perilously near the surface. Most of the women I knew cried when sad or angry or just frustrated. Tears came to them as naturally as water. Years before, I'd been arrested and convicted of manslaughter. I never regretted committing the crime but since then I've been more likely to cry stones than water. Maybe what I'd needed all along to make me a more normal human being was a little tap behind the ear.

Frank and the Rott were waiting for me by the desk when I stepped out of the restroom, the Rott wagging his truncated tail so hard he spun in circles, Frank with half of a glazed donut in his mouth. He pointed at a box on the table, said, "Help yourself. The dog's already had his share."

I took a cup of take-out coffee and sat, the Rott quickly finding his spot at my feet. I knew Frank didn't care much for dogs, said, "Thanks for walking him."

"No problem." Frank gulped down the last of the donut and blindly groped for another. "We took a walk in the park. Your dog met another dog, I met the dog's owner. Your dog got a good sniff of the other dog's rear end, I got the owner's phone number. As a matter of fact, your dog and I got along just fine until we started fighting over the donuts." He kicked out, rolled his chair back to the printer, pulled a sheet of paper from the tray, and scooted forward. "You might want to take a look at this."

Frank handed me an itinerary of some kind. I tried to read it but the lines on the page fractured like windblown pieces of a jigsaw puzzle. I closed my eyes, breathed deeply, and when I opened them again the word *Chicago* fluttered to the surface of the page. Frank had booked me a round-trip ticket to Chicago. "What am I doing going to Chicago?"

"We talked about it last night," Frank said, his mouth full. "You don't remember?"

I looked at the paper again. "Tonight? Midnight? I can't possibly make it."

"You really did take a crack on the head, didn't you? We're renting a car in Chicago, driving from there to Fairmount, Indiana. And you've already agreed to go."

I blew ripples across the surface of my coffee, cooling it enough to gulp. A smirk fought to the corner of Frank's mouth. I asked, "Was I conscious when you asked me?"

"Enough to say yes."

"I need permission to leave the state. I can't just pick up and go. Conditions of my parole."

"I already spoke to your parole officer. It's in the works."

I glanced at the donuts, thought something in my stomach might clear my mind. I grabbed one, asked, "What's the story?"

"Night before last, someone stole James Dean."

"He's dead. How can somebody steal him?"

"With a pick and shovel," Frank said. "Broke into the cemetery after midnight, located his grave, and dug down to the coffin. Then they pried open his coffin and stole his bones."

"His bones? All of them?"

"Just some. I don't know which ones yet."

"Anybody else running the story?"

"Our exclusive so far. I got an anonymous phone call yesterday, some kid asking me if I paid for stories. Sure, I said, but it depends what it is. Dumb little bastard told me everything over the phone. We got an appointment tomorrow morning with the guy who's heading up the investigation."

"I don't get it." I dropped the half-eaten donut back into the box and rubbed at my eyes to try to clear my vision. "Sure, somebody stealing James Dean's bones, it's quirky enough to make a good story but it's not front-page stuff and I don't get why it's big enough to fly us all the way to Indiana."

"Because Dean's coffin was broken into by a sect intent on cloning him from the DNA in his bones."

"Really?"

"Who knows anything for sure anymore?" Frank said. "But it's going to make one hell of a story."

■ ■ ■

My parole officer stepped out of a brown Chevy sedan when I neared the steps of my Venice Beach apartment, just as Frank had promised, the tail of her gray suit coat catching in the gap between her shoulder holster and blouse. She took an unhurried moment to free it and then another to smooth the coat over her shoulders before shutting the door with the clipped heel of her black pumps. She always likes to remind her charges she's armed, she once told me; it eliminates the question of authority. She didn't need her authority reinforced, in my opinion. She was a mid-thirties blond who worked out regularly with free weights and trained in judo. If she had a sense of humor, she hadn't shared it with me. When I evoked her suspicions—which was often, and with good reason—she fixed me with a look of such cool fierceness it was like staring down the barrel of a gun. She didn't need the one under her shoulder.

"Thanks for coming out," I said, holding the Rott by his collar. My parole officer was wearing a nice-looking suit, a distinction the dog might fail to grasp in his enthusiasm to greet her.

"I was due for a visit anyway." She tapped a white envelope against her hip as she walked up. According to the terms of my parole, I needed permission to leave the state. By the look of the State of California seal on the envelope, she'd brought the parolee release form that granted it. She offered her other hand to the dog. He licked it. "He looks good. Fully recovered?"

"He limps a bit when he runs," I said. The Rott had taken a bullet a week after I'd found him. "But that just makes it easier for me to keep up with him."

"Your dog looks considerably better than you do." She didn't offer the envelope, and though her sunglasses were tinted to a shade that cloaked her eyes, I knew she stared at me by the tracer lines of heat her glance left on my skin. "In fact, you don't look like you could keep up with a Chihuahua right now."

"I was mugged last night," I said, fingering the bulge behind my ear. "And yes, I filed a police report."

"Don't expect me to pat you on the back for obeying the law if, in fact, that's what you did." She pointed the corner of the envelope up the stairs. "You can tell me how it happened while I look around your apartment."

That was another condition of my parole: at any time of her choosing my parole officer had the right to enter my residence, my place of work, or my car and to search it for evidence of parole violations. I walked her up the exterior stairway to the third-floor landing, keyed the door, and swung it open.

"When you moving?" She stepped over the boxes I'd packed several days before, in an unexpected fit of optimism.

"I'm due out next week."

"Where you going?"

"Don't know yet."

Graves slipped her sunglasses into the side pocket of her suit coat, leaned against the kitchenette counter, and stared at me.

"What?" I said.

"Don't think you can escape by sticking your head in the sand. You knew the consequences when you decided to keep the dog."

My landlord had given me an eviction notice three months before, when I'd found the Rott. The lease didn't allow dogs.

I said, "Right."

"How's your financial situation?"

"Good enough."

"Then get off your butt." She flung open the door to a kitchen cabinet and rearranged the boxes of breakfast cereal. "You need a place to live. You're on parole. You need a place of residence. If you don't have a place of residence, your parole is revoked, understand me?"

I said, "Yes, ma'am."

"Good. Now tell me what happened last night."

I told the story the same way I'd told it to the police, watching her attack the kitchen cabinets first, then the bookshelves, clothes closet, and bathroom. Every time my parole officer visits, she searches the same places in the same way. Ninety-five percent of the time parole officers are searching for drugs. She knew I didn't use any. Given my record, however, a gun wasn't out of the question. She paused once during the search to observe the number of messages beside the blinking light of my answering machine. "Aren't you curious to hear who called?"

I suspected that was one of the tricks of her trade, the parolee gambling the replay wouldn't be legally compromising and playing back drug buys or sex dates. "They would have called my cell if it was important," I said.

She glanced around the apartment one last time, tapped the envelope against the palm of her hand, asked, "How's your love life? Seeing anybody?"

"Nobody. How about you?"

She snorted, the closest she ever came to laughing. As though she'd tell me anything about her personal life. "You're going to Indiana?"

"Small town called Fairmount."

"Notify the local police department when you arrive. They like to know when felons come to town." She pointed the envelope toward me like a finger.

I took it.

"And report back in when you return," she said.

I waited until she reached her car before I played the messages on my machine. My life then was reasonably clean but I expected to hear from my local fence, who had promised to see whether a new Nikon had recently fallen off the back of a truck. The first message was from my mother. I leaned against the wall, then sat down. I hadn't heard from her in six months. I closed my eyes and let her voice wash over me. She and Pop were fine, she said. She wished she could talk to me rather than the machine. She was sorry we'd fallen out of contact, hoped I was okay. I could call tomorrow, if I liked. Pop would be out. She'd be in all day. The next message was from my fence.

I leashed the Rott and eased down the steps, past the flashing colored lights behind the ground-floor apartment's barred windows. I walked slowly to minimize the pain each step jarred into my head. The last time my mom and I had spoken she'd been in the hospital with a broken hip and laceration above her left eye. She'd fallen off the front step, she claimed, but I knew Pop had hit her. He hit everybody. When I was a child, I'd accepted it as one of the laws of life, as certain as gravity. Every man lost his temper, Pop more than most. He hit me one day, my older sister the next, the day after that my brother. If my mother provoked him he'd beat her, too. She never left him. The last time I'd seen her, in the hospital, we'd argued about that. I'd just been released from prison. She probably didn't think I had a right to lecture.

My fence sat three rows high in the stands overlooking the blacktop basketball courts, watching a pickup game of shirts and skins. I tied the Rott to a palm tree and folded a hundred-dollar bill into my palm. The fence nodded once when I neared the steps, giving me permission to approach. Wraparound sunglasses shielded his eyes and he didn't turn his head from the game, seemingly absorbed in the flow of action.

"Still got that dog?" he asked.

I dipped the bill into the side pocket of his black leather trench coat, a liberty he wouldn't have allowed with less regular clients. I told him I did.

"Don't like dogs," he said.

I could have pointed out that most housebreakers and fences didn't. Dogs are bad for business. I thanked him for the service and left with a new, boxed Nikon in a plastic bag.

A neighbor sat perched on the lower two steps when I returned to the apartment building, a mug of what smelled like mint tea warming his hands. The steps overlooked the strip of plants that made his a garden apartment. "You're the one with the dog," he said, his voice friendly and completely unaware of the obviousness of the statement. The building housed the eccentrics typically found in Venice Beach and a few young urban professionals, whose recent arrival was driving up the rents, making it uninhabitable for those making less than six figures a year. With curly gray hair swarming about his head like a cloud and mystic blue eyes that seemed to see everything and nothing at the same time, I guessed my neighbor was one of the eccentrics.

"Not for long," I said, and pulled the Rott to my side. "I expect to be out next week sometime."

"I heard about the eviction notice." He stood as though about to offer his sympathies, but his first good look at my face paused him. His glance lifted just above my head, the tint of his eyes darkening as though an invisible something hovered there and that something was worrisome. "Oh, no," he said.

"Oh no what?"

"Somebody hit you on the back of the head."

"How did you know?"

"Your aura," he said. "Forgive me for not introducing myself earlier. I'm Dr. James Whitehead. I'm an aura healer."

"Oh," I said.

His glance dropped to meet my eyes just long enough to be polite and drifted again to the space above my forehead. "We really have to take care of that."

"Take care of what?"

He raised his hand cautiously and pointed to the side of my head. "Your aura is so badly cracked it's almost separated."

"You can see my aura?"

He nodded, no doubts at all. "You have a lot of anger, don't you?"

"Doesn't everybody?"

"Your aura is so red it's pulsating." He moved his hand lightly over my head and above my shoulders. "Thank God you have some blue in there to compensate. Let's just hope it's enough, eh? A couple days of treatment should tell, a week at the most."

Every day, diviners of Tarot, palm reading, astrology, numerology, and every other variety of psychic seer lined the Venice Beach boardwalk, waiting patiently for customers. I guessed his angle. "I don't have any money," I said.

"We're neighbors. I'll do it without charge." He darted through the door of his apartment before I could object.

Through the crack in the doorway I noticed a battery of colored lights pointing at an aluminum pole. The pole stretched from the floor to the ceiling, squares of what looked like photographs clipped to the metal. Dr. Whitehead emerged from the apartment carrying an antique Polaroid camera. "The sequencing of lights bathing the photograph is what heals the aura," he said, as though it made perfect sense. He framed a close-up and pressed the shutter. The camera spat out a tongue of film and for a moment both of us watched the old but still compelling magic of a photograph emerging from the black.

"What's so bad about having a cracked aura?" I asked.

"That's how the demons get inside your head." He waved the Polaroid to speed the drying. "Through cracks in the aura. And once they're in, they're hell to get out again."

I gave that a moment of thought, asked, "If new demons get in, any chance they'll kill the ones already there?"

FOUR

I SLEPT that night curled toward the window on a red-eye flight into Chicago, woke just long enough to drag my camera bag from the terminal, crashed out again slumped against the passenger window of Frank's rental car. I opened my eyes a couple hundred miles later to the film-strip jitter of telephone poles clipping by. Farmland lined the highway, the fields fallow in midwinter, and the sky hovered, low and gray, above the land. A half mile from the road, grain silos flanked a barn painted Andrew Wyeth red. Awareness returned to me like a series of lights thrown on, one by one. I felt anxious about something I couldn't identify, but my headache was gone and my arms tingled with energy. Sleep cures most ills and it was curing mine. I asked, "Where are we?"

"A few miles outside Kokomo, Indiana." Frank leaned against the door, his head tilted toward the side window and right wrist draped over the wheel, the posture of a man in the middle of a long drive. I reached into my camera bag on the backseat, slid out the hot Nikon, and focused on Frank's profile. When he yawned I released the shutter.

"The Raelians," he said, like the punch line to a Surrealist joke.

I knew community service clubs were big in the Midwest so I asked, "You mean the Rotarians? What do they have to do with anything?"

"Not the Rotarians. The Raelians. They're a religious sect that believes scientists from another planet created all life on earth."

I figured he was just talking, trying to stay awake. I said, "That doesn't sound so screwy. In fact, it sounds almost normal."

Frank glanced away from the road to judge whether or not I spoke seriously. "When that guy hit you on the head, did it turn your brain into cottage cheese?"

"You know what I heard the Scientologists say?"

"That's it, first hospital we pass, I'm committing you."

"A hundred billion space aliens were kidnapped in ancient times, brought to Earth, and blown up with hydrogen bombs." Dr. Whitehead had told me that the day before. "We can't see them, but that's the reason we're all so screwed up, because we're infested with the souls of murdered space aliens. And those murdered space aliens? They're not very happy about being murdered, which is why they insist we can't be happy either, until the Scientologists chuck 'em all out. Compared to that, the idea of alien scientists sounds almost sweet."

"The Scientologists aren't cloning themselves, at least, not yet. God help us if they find a way to bring L. Ron Hubbard back."

I remembered what Frank had said the day before, his claim that a group of cloners had broken into James Dean's grave. "That's what the Raelians do? They're cloners?"

"They say we're all clones of alien scientists. It's their religious duty to clone themselves, a point of honor." He stretched the word *honor* around a wry smile.

"Little harder to do than say, isn't it? It's not like you can go out to the local electronics store, buy yourself a do-it-yourself clone kit."

"The Raelians have one thing not even the most sophisticated research labs can produce." He jutted his chin toward my abdomen. "Wombs. Hundreds of them, donated by volunteers culled from the sect." The face of James Dean flashed by on the right, appended to a town-limits sign welcoming us to Fairmount. At first sight, the town didn't present itself as more than a few grain silos, vacant fields, and real estate signs. "This first piece needs to be visually compelling—desecrated grave sites, spooky shots suggesting aliens in the cemetery, that sort of thing. We're going to ride this story for a couple issues, whether it's true or not."

I didn't have a problem with that, not then. I glanced out the window. Fairmount was a farming community, not more than five thousand people in the town itself, and like most farming communities the only structure of any size in what passed for downtown was the bank, a Victorian-era brick building two stories tall topped by an onion-domed turret, as though the architect's steady and sober Midwestern vision had suddenly slipped into Slavic fantasy.

The town marshal worked out of a two-room office around the corner from the bank, close enough to come running in the event someone wanted to rob it or just needed help with their deposit bags. His uniform—a snappy green number with triangular arm patches and big gold badge—clung to a slim, muscular build, the type of beautiful young body most men lose in their thirties. Portraits of his wife and abundant children on the wall framed him like a halo. I knew by the family photos that I'd left L.A. far behind; no officer of the law in L.A. would leave photos of his family in plain sight. Too dangerous. I'd thought towns like Fairmount existed only in old Hollywood, as fictitious backdrops for Jimmy Stewart movies. He stood from behind his desk when we entered his office and without waiting for an introduction said, "You must be the reporter from *Scandal Times*."

Frank stopped dead still, his eyes widening in mock wonder, and asked, "How did you know?"

"We don't get a lot of strangers this time of year, not until spring, when the tourists come. The lady, now," he said, nodding at me, "I suspect she'd probably be your photographer."

I looked at him through the Nikon's viewfinder. "Lucky guess. What was it gave me away, the camera?"

The marshal laughed at the remark as though he truly thought it funny and introduced himself as Tom Tuchman. "Just call me Tuck," he said. "Everybody else does, whether I like it or not." His vehicle was parked outside. Maybe we'd like to drive out to the crime scene? He could brief us on the status of the investigation on site, answer any questions we might have while we took a look firsthand. Neither Frank nor I were accustomed to such hospitality from the law and mostly kept our mouths shut as he drove the streets of Fairmount, afraid that if we said anything, he'd change his mind about cooperating and drop us on the highway leading out of town. Wisely or not, I refrained from disclosing, as my parole officer demanded, that I was a convicted felon serving out my

parole under the guidance of the California Department of Correc-
tions. Given the peacefulness of the town, he might be shocked to
meet a real criminal.

James Byron Dean's grave lay in a small tree-lined cemetery at the
edge of a field that may have grown corn in the summer but in
February stretched frozen and bleak to the horizon. His name and
the brief dates of his existence had been engraved into a stumpy
block of polished beige granite mounted on an unpolished granite
pedestal. Behind Dean's name the headstone had been painted white,
like a single page in the Book of Judgment. The headstone was neither larger nor smaller than those surrounding it, nor was its position within the cemetery in any way privileged. As a monument to
one of the most famous figures of the twentieth century, a symbol of
beautiful but doomed youth not just to his generation but to suc-
ceeding ones as well, the grave site was a bit underwhelming.

Tuck kicked at the edges of a gently packed mound of dirt in front
of the headstone, the entire grave site fenced by the yellow tape that
marked it as a crime scene. "By the standards of a big city like Los
Angeles, the theft of a couple bones might not seem like the crime of
the century, but around here it's pretty big news." He pointed to the
surrounding fields. Near the western horizon a pale silver light glimmered through the haze; sunset, or what passed for it during a
Midwestern winter. "As you can see, we're pretty isolated out here.
They came on a Sunday night, about midnight, maybe a little later,
figuring everybody would have done their visiting over the weekend.
As a matter of fact, the robbery wasn't spotted until the following
afternoon." He sidestepped to the headstone and sat on his heels.
"See this red stuff here?" He pointed to five puddles of congealed
wax on the headstone's granite base.

I lay on the frozen grass for a low-angle shot of the marshal, his
finger pointed ominously toward the headstone. "It's candle wax,"
he said. "They set five red candles on poor Jimmy's headstone, probably part of some Satanic ritual, before they broke the earth. The
ground is pretty well frozen here, so they came well equipped. It's not
as though they had a bit too much to drink, suddenly decided to go
digging for souvenirs." He stepped over the crime-scene tape and fin-

gered through the mounded earth until he uncovered a long splinter of wood. "Whoever done it took the time to fill the grave back in but they couldn't do anything about the grass. When I found pieces of wood mixed in with the dirt, I knew they'd broken all the way through to the coffin."

"What bones they take?" Frank cupped his reporter's notebook in his left palm, pencil tip poised to record the reply.

"The entire set of bones from the left hand were picked clean as corn by a crow. The right foot, too. Two ribs, five vertebrae, some small bones from the neck, I forget what they're called, hyoids or something, both femurs, a tibia, and five teeth." Tuck palmed dirt over the piece of coffin he'd uncovered and stood. "I asked a doctor to come out from Marion. Don't know what the right word is for what he did. An inventory, I guess. That's how we learned what was missing. He said digging up a corpse was common in Satanic rituals."

"That was smart, getting the doctor to examine the body, but did you ever stop to think the people who lit these candles might be setting a trap for you?"

Tuck dug a white handkerchief from his left hip pocket and used it to wipe his hands. "How so?"

"Simple misdirection," Frank said. "It's pretty obvious, isn't it? They want you to think it's witchcraft because that's what they know you'll expect to see. Everybody knows devil worshippers are more likely to steal the skull than the bones of the hand or foot." Frank turned to me and winked. "How about a picture of the marshal here, next to the headstone?"

"Already got it," I said.

Frank turned a serious look on Tuck, asked, "What do you know about cloning?"

"Not much," Tuck said.

"Did it occur to you that Mr. Dean's grave might have been robbed by a rogue sect of cloners, intent on artificially reproducing a new copy of the actor?"

Tuck smiled, thinking the big-city reporter was making fun of his small-town gullibility, but when Frank didn't acknowledge the joke his grin turned more wary. "I'm familiar with the kind of stories *Scandal Times* likes to print." He knew he was being had, his grin said, it had just taken him an extra moment to figure out how. "Given my druthers, I'd be talking to reporters from the *New York Times* or *Chicago Tribune,* but I know that's never going to happen. Fairmount's just not big enough."

"A hundred million eyes," Frank said.

Tuck looked up, wondering what that had to do with anything.

"That's the number of eyes that scan the *Scandal Times* headlines at the supermarket checkout counter, and this is a front-page story for us, not something we'd bury like the *Times,* on page forty-two between ads for men's underwear."

Tuck folded the handkerchief, taking care to get the creases right, said, "I get your point, and I sure appreciate you taking the time to come out here. If you want to get down to the truth of it, those bones are a major part of who we are as a town, and to have them stolen, even just some of them, it hurts like the dickens. The more press we can get, letting people know what happened, the better. How you cover the story is your business. My job is to tell you the facts. And right now, your guess is as good as mine."

"So it could be cloners."

"Could be Satanists. Could be kids from one of the towns around here, playing a prank. Could even be some unholy combination of the two. About the only thing we know for sure is whoever did this has a taste for cola-flavored soda pop."

Frank scratched the back of his head with the eraser of his pencil, glancing through his notes for context. "How the hell do you know that?"

"Found a thirty-two-ounce cup from McDonald's buried about halfway down. Back in 1955, when they buried Jimmy, the nearest McDonald's was in Des Moines, and they sold cola by the bottle, so I suppose whoever took the bones left the cup."

"A soft-drink cup," Frank repeated.

"Thirty-two ounces." Tuck craned his neck to the side to see if Frank thought that important enough to write down.

"This cup, it have any fingerprints?"

"Oh sure, I pulled a clean set. The dirt in the grave picked up the oils so well I didn't even have to use powder, could see the prints the moment I picked up the cup. 'Course I used powder and tape anyways. But for the prints to be any good to us I need someone to match 'em against, which at the moment I don't."

"Should be easy enough to interview the employees at the local McDonald's," Frank said, "find out if they remember anybody came in that night."

"You're right, should be easy enough, if I could come up with a good definition of *local*."

Frank looked at the marshal as though he suspected he wasn't just mentally slow but completely stopped. "How about the one in Fairmount? Is that local enough?"

"Fairmount doesn't have one. Not big enough."

"The next town over, then."

"You seem like an educated man." Tuck stepped back over the crime-scene tape. "How many McDonald's outlets you think there are within, say, an hour's drive from here?"

"Five?" Frank guessed.

"That's a good guess," Tuck said. "Why don't I just show you?"

A map of Indiana, punctured by colored pins, covered the far wall of the back room in Tuck's office, opposite a television set, VCR, and ink jet printer perched on a rickety metal stand. Blurred black-and-white photographs surrounded the map and spread to the adjacent walls on both sides. Tuck ushered Frank around the table in the center of the room, stacked at the moment with videotapes, and asked, "How many pins do you see?"

Frank nosed up to the map and did a quick count. "Looks like about a hundred."

"Over a hundred, and each pin is a McDonald's outlet." He pointed to a cluster of pins in the middle of the state. "About fifty are in Indianapolis. I'm saving those for when I'm really desperate. That leaves me fifty or so franchises spread out in all directions, not to mention the time it takes to go through the surveillance tapes."

I changed lenses, my hands working blind while my eye wandered to the images taped to the wall. The photographs mostly depicted young men holding what looked like large soft-drink cups, shot in the smudged black and white of a video surveillance camera. I asked, "These photographs on the wall, they're your suspects?"

"Not exactly suspects, no. Just the ones I'm trying to keep an eye on." Tuck pointed to the cassettes on the table. "I'm still collecting tape from most of the franchises."

"Suspects or not, how are you identifying them?"

"Anybody buying a thirty-two-ounce soft drink the night of the crime."

"Looks like you're focusing on teenaged boys," Frank said.

"Not focusing, no," Tuck said. "Just happens that most everybody in McDonald's between ten and midnight is teenaged and male, at least around here. I haven't looked specifically for any cloners, but you'll have a better idea what those look like." He showed the palm of his hand to the wall. "You want to take a look, tell me if you see any, be my guest."

I clicked the shutter on his gesture and when I lowered the camera, thinking I'd taken the shot I'd wanted, I saw a face I recognized. I stepped up to the wall and examined the photograph pinned to the right of Tuck's shoulder. A young man stood at the counter, accepting change from the cashier, his purchase concealed in a take-out bag. He wore jeans and a denim jacket buttoned against the cold. The quality of the photo was so poor I could barely make out what looked like a scraggly blond goatee. I asked, "Who's this guy?"

Tuck glanced at the photograph and pointed to the next one in the series, which began another row down. "Somebody I'm not looking at too hard. He's with a girl. I'm not interested in couples that look like they're dating."

The second photo snapped from the tape caught the young man as he lifted the bag and turned away from the counter. The woman with him couldn't resist a brief glance at the surveillance camera before she followed him out. I'd seen the same young man or one just like him loitering by the railing in Pacific Palisades Park, and the girl at his side, glancing up at the camera, looked like Theresa, the girl with the lavender-colored glasses.

FIVE

BEN WAS framing the new deck to his trailer, the Rott camped at his side, when I coasted the Cadillac into the cul-de-sac across the way. The trailer was a new Fleetwood single-wide, perched on a bluff overlooking the ocean from the sliding glass door in the living room and Temescal Canyon from the new deck. He'd lived half his life behind the wheel of a Los Angeles County Sheriff's Department patrol car and since retirement prided himself on his developing skills as a handyman and part-time dogsitter. The trailer, at the end of a lane landscaped in palm trees, bougainvillea, and birds-of-paradise, did not stand out among the others; everyone in the neighborhood took good care of their homes, rooting them to the land with decks, car porches, and brick foundations. The Rott galloped forward at the sound of my engine, standing on his hind legs to greet me the moment I stepped out of the car. I let him get in a few good licks before I pushed him down, told him to behave himself.

"Damn dog's been moping ever since you left," Ben said, wiping his palm on the side of his jeans before offering his hand. "Stole one of my shoes this morning. Found him under the trailer, slobbering all over the thing."

"Good thing he has no teeth or I'd owe you a new pair."

"Got a minute to lend me a hand?"

He'd framed the deck on the ground and needed me to lift it onto the support posts, then hold the frame in place while he set the T-braces and bolted them down. He'd broken his collarbone some months back, about the same time the Rott had been shot, and still had trouble lifting things. We hoisted one end onto his shoulder, then I circled around to lift the opposite end.

"Have a good trip?"

He was just making conversation.

"Good enough," I said. "Made some money, at least."

"Anytime you make some money, that's a good thing." Ben had a blue-collar attitude toward money; its supply was not inexhaustible and so you grabbed what you could without being greedy and tried to hold on to it. He pulled a ratchet from his hip pocket and fit the end over the head of the bolt. "You're getting kicked out of your place at the end of the month, aren't you?"

"That's what the landlord says."

He tightened the bolt, asked, "Found anything yet?"

"Haven't found anything, no, not yet." I didn't want to tell him that I hadn't started looking, not beyond a closed-eyed glance at the classifieds.

He moved to the next post, slid the bolt into the hole, said, "I heard about a cabin up Malibu Canyon. The place isn't very big, but there's lots of land around for the dog to run."

"Sounds ideal," I said.

Ben nodded, tightening the bolt.

"Probably a lot of people would love to rent a place like that."

He nodded again, concentrating on the bolt, said, "Probably."

"Then why waste our time?" I said.

He circled to my side of the frame and set a T-brace onto the nearest post, glancing at me from beneath the brim of his baseball cap.

"I'm a convicted felon," I said. "My current landlord is throwing me out for violating the lease. Lee Harvey Oswald had better rent references."

"Don't forget the dog."

"What about the dog?"

"Landlords don't care for them, particularly."

I shifted the weight of the frame on my shoulder, trying to get comfortable. "We'll get a room in a flophouse, somewhere that takes ex-cons and dogs."

Ben reached over with his free hand, gave my shoulder a little squeeze. "Let's give this place a look, just to see what you're missing."

The cabin in Malibu lay near the end of a narrow dirt road that scaled down a hillside grove of oaks, the ground lanced by late-morning sunlight. I caught glimpses of glass and wood as we rolled past in Ben's old Chevy Blazer, then forest intervened and I lost sight of anything but trees until the main house emerged, a hand-built, ramshackle wood and glass structure perched above a creek. The owner stepped outside before Ben turned off the motor, having heard us drive up, a concept I did not immediately grasp after my time in the city. He looked a few years older than Ben, wore jeans, a red-checkered shirt, and sported an old-fashioned handlebar moustache white as the freshly barbered hair on his head. He greeted Ben with a handshake and shoulder slap. His hand, rough with calluses and boney-strong, didn't boast when it shook mine, taking into account the strength of my own grip and matching it. "You must be the lady paparazzo," he said.

"Got a dog and a criminal record, too," I said. "But I don't have leprosy, not yet anyway."

His smile had more warmth to it than I had a right to expect. He offered his hand to the Rott, waited for the introductory sniff, then pulled the dog to the side of his leg and stroked him with the authority of a man accustomed to animals. "As long as you don't have a hard place in your heart for old cowboys, we'll get along fine. So why don't we wander up to the cabin, see if it suits you."

The walk wasn't more than a few hundred yards, but he moved slowly, his legs broken, he admitted casually, a half-dozen times over the years. He'd worked most of his adult life as a stunt coordinator for Hollywood, getting his start on the John Wayne cowboy films of the 1960s because he knew how to fall off a horse well enough to get up again for take two. I glanced back at Ben, who heeled the Rott to his side and winked at me as though it had all been a good joke. Again I felt the odd sensation of a simultaneous burning and swelling in my throat, and if I didn't know myself better, I would have thought I was about to burst into tears. They'd met on a film set, the owner told me, Ben hired to work traffic control. They both liked bourbon and bad jokes and had found a way to test their wide tolerance for both at one bar or another every month for the past ten years.

The cabin had been built in the shape of a pentagon, windows on all five sides framing views of the surrounding forest. Redwood shingled the exterior walls and a narrow deck circled the entire structure, widening at the back, where a couple of lawn chairs had been set up to enjoy the view of the creek that trickled down canyon. The Rott immediately went on patrol, nosing the base of each oak before marking it as his own. He had a lot of trees to cover, and I imagine he felt some anxiety, wondering if he had enough in his tank to mark them all.

The owner keyed open the front door and I stepped into a studio-sized room, a small corner walled off with just enough square footage to fit a shower stall and toilet. The cabin wasn't any bigger than my place in Venice and the rent was higher, but the view of trees on all sides compensated. Had the owner bothered to advertise or list the cabin with an agency, he could have asked for twice the rent and still had his pick of tenants. The cabin never should have been offered to me. I didn't deserve it and I certainly didn't deserve having an old stunt cowboy for a landlord. Given my history and place in society, I belonged in a studio apartment with barred windows, leaky plumbing, and views of a freeway on-ramp. But the Rott took to the place like he'd been a country dog before he met me and if I didn't deserve it he did. I said I'd bring first and last months' rent plus a security deposit the following Monday, move in by the end of the week if it was okay with him. He didn't ask for a credit report or a reference from a previous landlord. Ben vouched for me and that was enough. I thanked him as we drove out of the canyon.

Ben glared at me over his shoulder, as though daring me to make something big out of it, said, "For what?"

"For standing by me, I guess."

"The way I look at it, I'm acting purely out of self-interest. I don't get you and your dog settled into a place soon, I'm likely to have a couple of permanent houseguests." He reached out, gave my shoulder a squeeze. "I like the both of you, don't get me wrong, but I don't want to share my bathroom with a girl and a toothless Rottweiler."

I didn't expect to see the girl in lavender glasses when I cruised Palisades Park early that afternoon, nor when I walked the 3rd Street Promenade, the Rott leashed by my side. The drifters, runaways, and just plain lost who gather outside the shops and cinemas to beg spare change from the crowds know me by my dog, and those who are sane enough to remember know that I'm willing to pay cash for information. Most homeless like dogs more than people. Even those who lost their minds long ago relate to animal warmth. I asked everyone I encountered whether they'd seen a couple of teenagers hanging around, one a boy struggling to grow a blond goatee, the other a girl who favored lavender glasses. The paper I worked for wanted to do a story, I said, and was willing to pay. One of the skate punks said he'd seen her, but I think he was just trying to scam some cash out of me. I returned to my apartment no wiser and ten dollars lighter in change.

The landlord had thoughtfully taped a copy of his eviction notice to the door, reminding me I had until the end of the month to vacate the premises. He'd secured the notice to the door with duct tape and encased it in clear plastic as a safeguard against the elements. It was the tenth such notice he'd taped to my door. The apartment smelled of dog, girl, and unemptied trash when I stepped inside. I left the door open to air out the room. The message light on my answering machine blinked methodically in the corner.

I dropped my travel bag onto the floor and flicked the play button on my way to the refrigerator. The Rott knocked me against the kitchen counter in his excitement to get to the refrigerator before me, as though he believed he could open the door without my assistance, help himself to dinner. The first several calls hung up in rapid succession, as though someone couldn't believe she'd dialed a wrong number but would get it right with one more try. I nudged the Rott aside with my knee and pulled the hamburger from the bottom drawer. The voice that followed the hang-ups didn't sound familiar at first. The voice sounded thin and trembly and when it apologized for all the time we hadn't spoken, recognition stilled me. My brother was speaking. I hadn't heard his voice for five years, not since the night I'd been arrested for manslaughter. He preferred to tell me this in person, he said, and was sorry that I'd have to hear this on an answering machine. He cleared his throat and then he told me that my mother was dead.

SIX

MY MOTHER'S body lay partially enclosed in a cardboard box placed atop the table of a mortuary viewing room. A single, hooded lightbulb cast around her head a soft skirt of light that faded to darkness just beyond the table edge. She suffered a massive stroke, my brother's recorded voice had said. She died before she reached the hospital. He didn't know when or where the funeral would be held. I could drop by the funeral home if I wanted to view the body. He gave me the address and viewing hours, again said he was sorry, and hung up. She died the night after she'd called me, sometime before my flight to Chicago. That we might have been moving toward reconciliation will haunt me for the rest of my life.

I approached the body in a slow, dull dread, eyes cast down to the toes of my boots shuffling on the cut-pile carpet. I did not need to see her death to heal, to move on, to achieve closure, or to engage in any of the emotional processes the feel-good doctors of our time have told us are necessary for a healthy psyche; when I lifted my head just enough to glimpse her face, the sight of her death burned into my heart and cauterized the hole at one stroke, a wound that would not kill me outright but would never heal, never completely, that would linger and ache with each contraction of tissue and pulse of blood.

I stood at the edge of the table and forced myself not to turn my head or close my eyes, but to stare, unblinking, into the fact of her death. Looking at her dead face was not like a mirror; facing her death was not like facing my own death. It was far worse. When I was a child, I believed in my mother above all people and all things. She had given me life and had done her best to protect me from the rages of my pop, often taking blows meant for my back. I believed in her far more than I ever believed in the distant God of a non-churchgoing family. The year I committed the criminal acts that would later imprison me I stopped believing in her. She lived with a man prone to unpredictable, violent rages, a man who had beaten not just her but every member of the family. My older sister had run away from home when I was just six years old, unwilling to submit herself any longer to his fists. My brother had taken his beatings as a lesson and though he still cowered before the old man he now beat his family, too. My mother could have left him. She held a job at the local Kmart, worked as a cashier. She could have supported herself. But she was terribly afraid of being alone, more afraid of loneliness than of her husband's rages and brutality. And so I stopped believing in her. But once you truly believe in something, vestiges of that belief remain, no matter how many and loud the protests to the contrary.

A violent trembling gripped and shook me by the spine. I grabbed the edge of the table for support and gasped for air. I expected to grieve. I expected tears and sorrow. But I didn't tremble with grief. I trembled from rage. It wasn't the cheap cardboard box that my pop had chosen to display the body, a final slap at her dignity, nor was it the thin mortician's gown that covered her shoulders when a moment of thoughtfulness and decency would have consigned her to the incinerator in a favorite dress. I expected pettiness from my pop. It wasn't his pettiness that so enraged me. Despite the haphazard attempts of the mortician to conceal it, a dark crescent surfaced from beneath the sheen of makeup above her cheek, hanging by its hooked tip at the inside corner of her left eye and spreading, purple and black, toward her ear. I'd seen her marked like that before, after Pop had hit her. Did her eye bear the mark of his fist when she'd called me? Is that why she had reached out to me after months of silence? Had the blood clot that killed her been unloosed by the blow that blackened her eye? The air rasped from my lungs and throat as I hyperventilated, the sound rough and ragged, like the barking of a dog. Had my father shown his face at that moment, I would have gone for his throat. A hand gently squeezed the slope of my shoulder, and a woman's voice said, "Mary? It's okay. It's okay."

I traced the hand back to the face of a stranger in a dark gray skirt-suit, her eyes lit by fear and compassion as she repeated my birth name and her assurances. The color of her green-flecked eyes seemed vaguely familiar, as did her strawberry-blond hair, which curled inward, once at her neck, like a breaking wave. The wear of gravity had slackened her skin and time had coarsened it, obscuring who she once had been to me, but when the corner of her lip turned in a timid smile, I recognized through the mask of years the face of my sister. I called her name, Sharon, and she nodded.

"I thought you were a stranger when you first came in." She pointed to the chair in the darkest corner of the room, where she had been sitting. "I almost didn't recognize you. God, what's it been, twenty-plus years? The last time I saw you, I don't even want to think about it. You were, what? Six years old? My baby sister. And your hair, it was blond, fell halfway down your back. God, you were such a cute little girl."

"Times change," I said.

She fingered my hair, examining the color and, perhaps, just wanting to touch me. It occurred to me that I should hug her, but it had been so long since I'd seen her it would have been embracing a stranger and I was still too near my rage; I still wanted to hit someone. I stepped back to put some distance between us, made it seem like I wanted to look at her more fully. She had the manicured look of someone who took good care of herself, but beneath the makeup the years on her face did not look to have been easy ones. "Funny," I said, "in all my memories of you, I see this really tall girl looming over me. But you're really kind of tiny."

She hooked her hair over her ears, gave me the same appraising look I'd given her, said, "And I remember you being much shorter, too." She laughed and covered her mouth. A look of panic darted her eyes to the side and her weight shifted from foot to foot. "You don't know how many times I wanted to come back, see how you were doing. God, at least a hundred. But I couldn't do it, no matter how much I wanted. You know why?"

I nodded. I knew. It made me no less angry, but I knew.

"I swore I'd never see him again and I've kept my word. Did you see the shiner he gave her? Did he have to beat her all the way to her grave?" She laughed again. It was a nervous little laugh, as though what she said frightened her. "Maybe I'm exaggerating. Maybe she fell when, you know, when she had her stroke. I guess that's what she had. That's what Ray told me anyway. Maybe she hit her eye like that. When she fell. If she fell." She rocked from side to side, feet arched in low-heeled gray pumps. "I don't know nothing no more, been away from the family so long."

"No, I think he hit her," I said.

The fact of it lay heavily in the room. I turned away from my sister and looked again at my mother. The makeup didn't conceal her scars. A sliver of skin still divided one of her eyebrows, which never completely healed from the blow that split it. She had taken stitches in her lip once, when I was a child, and the dotted pattern of it still marked her. Her face did not look peaceful in death.

It looked scarred.

SEVEN

WHAT DO you say to someone you haven't seen for twenty-four years, who even during the years you knew her was nothing more than a large, mysterious person who doted on you one moment, ignored you completely the next? I remember adoring my sister as a child, in the hero-worshipping way children have with much older siblings, and I remember after she'd run away from home how long I'd hoped for her return, and I also remember forgetting her, slowly over the years, when that return never came, her image fading to the shadow of someone I loved but never really knew. The years buried that childhood love and longing, and as I stared at my sister over a cup of coffee in the local Denny's restaurant I wondered whether I could ever recapture those feelings or whether they were any more alive than bones buried a quarter century ago.

She'd bounced around since leaving home at the age of sixteen, living at first in a commune near San Francisco, she said, then moving gradually up the coast until finally settling in Seattle, where she currently worked as a real estate agent, selling homes to an upper-middle-class clientele in the exclusive Belleview district. She'd lived something of a wild youth and though she wasn't particularly proud of all the things she'd done, times were different then. She laughed at herself—in fact, she seemed to carry on a continuous and critical inner dialogue with herself as she spoke—and said she'd become the straightest, most respectable person she knew. Her hands lay clasped together on the table, knuckles white with strain, as though holding them together cost her supreme effort and would, if she relaxed her grip, fly about the room in unfettered gestures. She liked it in Seattle, she said, enjoyed hiking in the rain forest or taking a boat onto Puget Sound. She caught herself boasting about all the things she liked to do and laughed self-consciously. "It's not like I get out near as much as it sounds," she said. "I'm working most of the time, and when I'm not working, something else always seems to come up. Plus you have to realize most people look for a new home on the weekend. I wish I had the time to do all the things I like to do, rather than what I gotta do to pay the rent. How about you? Do you still live in the area? What do you do here?"

"I'm down in Venice Beach," I said. "I'm a freelance photographer, working mostly for the tabloids."

"Tabloids? You mean, like the papers by the supermarket cash register? That kind of thing?"

"That kind exactly."

She glanced down at her hands and nodded as though trying to decide whether that was good or bad. From the evasiveness of her glance I guessed she concluded the latter. "Does that pay anything?"

"Sometimes yes, sometimes no." I shouldn't have said anything more, because it felt as though I was trying to justify myself. She was the one who disappeared. I didn't need to justify myself to her. "Last month I cashed a check for twenty grand."

Her lips bowed outward in a silent *wow*. "Just for taking somebody's photo?"

"More or less. It was an exclusive. But that's a rarity. Most months I make considerably less than that."

"What do you do with the money?"

"Put it in the bank."

"You should put half that money into something safe, like a money market fund, save up to buy a place of your own. No better investment than real estate." She leaned back in the booth and laughed, her hands briefly flying apart before she tracked them down like errant children, waving in the air between us. "Listen to me, I'm giving you a sales pitch. It's just that I've had to learn the hard way about these things. You ever been married?"

"Once, and briefly," I said.

"My second husband worked in a bank, and he may have been

lacking in some ways, but he really knew his way around invest-
ments." She told me all about him, their mostly happy eight years
together in Seattle. He'd wanted children and she couldn't have any.
They'd broken up a couple of years ago and she'd suffered the kind
of midlife crisis that hits many women from their late thirties on:
she'd devoted too much of her energy caring for her husband and
didn't have a career that would support her. She took some courses
in real estate, got a job, and was doing so well she swore she'd never
get married again, because men always break your heart. Her first
husband, a butcher by trade, was so promiscuous that when women
walked into the store asking "Where's the beef?" they weren't talking about the meat inside the display case. The marriage lasted two
years. I let her talk, because it seemed something she liked to do. She
was telling the story of her life and it didn't matter so much that her
style was so breezily impersonal she could have been talking to her
beautician or the stranger on the bar stool next to her. Twenty-four
years is a lot of time to catch up on and I don't suppose I should have
expected her to confide in me as a sister.

When she paused to signal the waitress for more coffee I asked,
"What do you know about the funeral?"

"Ray told me it's tomorrow morning, at the funeral home."

"Want to go together?"

"I'm not going," she said.

"You flew all the way down here and you're not going?"

I must have put some anger into my voice because Sharon sat
rigidly back in the booth as though slapped and said, "First of all, I
didn't fly down. I was already here when I heard."

"Why did you come down then, if not for family?"

"Private business," she said, like it was none of my concern. "And
second, I lit a candle for her in church this morning."

"You're religious?"

"Religious enough to hold my own ceremony. A private one. I
meant it when I swore I'd never see the old man again. I'm not going
to dignify his so-called grief. I'm not going to cry in front of him, not
ever again."

I remembered my pop slapping me to the floor, then taunting me,
You gonna cry now, go running to your mommy? I remembered
rushing to hit him and how he allowed my fists to flail against his

chest before he trapped my arms in a bear hug, kissed me on the cheek, called me Poppy's little girl. I said, "You think I'm not gonna want to take a chair to his head the moment I see him?"

Something in the way I phrased the question got her attention. She looked up at me, her eyes suddenly inquisitive. It was the first moment I sensed that in some way I interested her. She asked, "Did he beat you, too?"

"He hit everybody."

"Looks like you developed some armor." She cocked her head and appeared about to say something that cut through the bullshit, but hesitated long enough for caution to blank it out. "But just because I'm not going to the funeral doesn't mean we won't see each other again. I don't fly out until Monday. I'm staying with an old friend, Anne Chambers. Do you remember her?"

I shook my head.

"No reason you should." Her voice ascended a couple of octaves and sweetened at the edges. "You were so small! Well, Anne and I have kept in touch over the years. I'm staying with her and her husband while I'm here."

"How about lunch tomorrow, after the service?" I suggested. "I don't expect I'll be the most popular face with Pop and Ray. Maybe you'll want to hear how it went. I know I could use a little support, even after the fact."

Again, an inquisitiveness came into her eyes before caution—or just timidity—glossed it over. Maybe she feared emotional closeness. Given our family, I couldn't blame her. "I'd love to," she said, drawing out the last word. "It's been so long since I've seen you I want to spend as much time together as we can." Her smile was so sweet but completely false that I wondered, *Why is my sister lying to me?*

I stopped in a church on the drive back to my apartment. I didn't even know what kind of church it was until I sneaked through the door, sat at the outer edge of the back pew, noticed lit candles on altars along the walls leading to the main deal in front. The Catholics used candles as symbols of prayer, I remembered that much. Catholic or Protestant, it made little difference to me. Sharon and I hadn't gone to church much as children, just once or twice a year when our mother's guilt at raising us as heathens overwhelmed her. Still, my sister's religious conversion shouldn't have surprised me. The church offers consolation to those whose lives are troubled, and my sister must have needed that consolation during the early, difficult years of her independence. I think my mother would have attended church more regularly if not for Pop's hard-assed opposition to becoming part of the Bible-thumping set, as he called it. He sulked those rare times we did go to church and sometimes broke into one of his characteristic rages, and then one of us would bear the mark of it for weeks.

I crept forward, skirting the edge of the pews, until I sat next to the candlelit painting of a woman praying. A brass plaque identified the portrait as St. Anne. I stared at the image, trying to remember my mother's living face, and summoned no more than snapshots torn from the flow of time and stashed haphazardly away. Her face appeared in the background of my childhood memories, constantly present, but never in focus, as though I'd always taken her for granted without ever precisely looking at her. I thought I should pray and tried reciting the Lord's Prayer, but I'd never properly memorized it and stumbled over the lines about debts and trespassing. A Catholic prayer might have been more appropriate but I hadn't been exposed to any, except in the abbreviated form cited in films when someone is getting ready to die, and couldn't remember past *Hail Mary, full of grace.* An old man walked by, dressed in black, a white tooth of cloth at his neck. I said, "Can I ask you a question?"

The old man planted his cane to the floor and pivoted around it, his shoulders bowed toward his chest, and he carefully lowered himself onto the pew in front of me, the grip of his hands on the cane easing the strain on his legs. "You don't mind if I sit, do you?" As though he needed my permission. He turned to stick me with a curious look, his rootlike fingers lacing the cane's wooden curve. "I'm Father Morales. I haven't seen you here before, have I?"

"First time." I pointed to the portrait of the saint to my right. "St. Anne, who was she?"

He leaned back to better see who asked a question with such an obvious answer. "The mother of Mary, the grandmother of our Lord Jesus Christ."

I nodded, said, "Guess that's how she got to be a saint."

"She became a saint by living a holy life and because she led a holy life the Lord chose her for a holy task. She proves herself to us every day by answering our prayers. Do you have any children?"

He was a kind old man, his eyes like antique bottle glass, and traces of Aztec or some other ancient Indian lineage rounding the edges from his face. I didn't want to laugh at the absurdity of his question. In his world, women were born to marry and have children. I doubted many of his parishioners knew the kind of life I'd led. "No sir," I said.

"Well, your mother had you and her mother had her. If they prayed to St. Anne, she listened. She's the patron saint of pregnant women." His hands flexed against the cane and he pushed himself up. "You're always welcome here as a guest or to make the Church your home." He gave me a little wave of his hand and shuffled toward the front of the church.

I moved to the railing before the altar to St. Anne and thought about my grandmother, who died early in my teens, and though I didn't believe then in any specific afterlife, I thought of my mother in her mother's arms and that image gave me a small moment of peace. I dug through my pockets for a few dollar bills, stuffed them into the slot before the altar, and lit two candles. As the candles flamed into life I wished fervently that my mother and her mother before her find peace and grace, in whatever form they might now reside, even if their sole remaining residence lay in my own heart. It was the only prayer I felt capable of giving. I watched the candles burn, and when the church began to fill for evening mass, I said my thanks to the place and left.

EIGHT

THE TERM *funeral home* is one of the great unchallenged oxymorons of our time, as though calling a place home where dead people are embalmed or cremated could warm the chill of death. The services were held in a wood-paneled chapel with cushioned pews, vaulted ceilings, and a stained-glass window depicting a sun that either was rising or setting, depending on your philosophical view. A simple wooden cross hung above the altar, present for the faithful but inconspicuous enough to be ignored by the agnostic. My mother may have called herself a Christian but hadn't been to church in twenty years, and so it was her fate to be memorialized by a rent-a-pastor who stood at the podium and mouthed platitudes about the glories of heaven, never having been there himself and never having met the woman he eulogized. He knew nothing about her except her name and the names of a few of her surviving relatives, which he read from a slip of paper clipped to the podium, and he recited a brief, personal story about how she rose at dawn every morning to feed her husband breakfast before he left for work, to demonstrate, I suppose, what a kind and loving woman she'd been. Not so curiously, the list of surviving relatives did not include my name or the name of my sister.

The chapel was large enough to accommodate two hundred mourners, and twelve people showed up to see her off, hardly filling the first two pews. Two of my father's pals from the machine shop accompanied him on one side, and my brother's family lined up on the other. Our neighbors from down the street, Jackie and Bob, and four of my mom's co-workers at Kmart sat scattered along the opposite pews. I arrived late and sat alone in the back row. My mother had been cremated. The small pine box that held her ashes rested on a table beside the altar, lit by a baby spotlight hung from the ceiling and framed by two small arrangements of gladiolas. My mother's name is Gladys. The flowers were a nice touch.

Death had done for Gladys what she had never been able to summon the strength to do for herself. She had married Pop at the age of seventeen and lived with him for over forty years. She had not left him once during those years, not for a night to escape one of his drunks or for a day to reclaim her dignity after he had beaten her, nor had I ever heard her threaten to leave him. She remained faithful to her wedding vow, neither loved nor cherished, poorer rather than richer, for the worse far more than the better, and always in sickness, the psychological sickness that for inscrutable reasons bound her to him like the loose chains of a willing slave. I could have more easily forgiven her had she not tried to bind her children with those same chains. Death released her from her marriage vows and so I released her from any responsibility for the marks those chains left on me. I tried to remember the good, the earnest and enduring love I always felt for her, and I hoped she had forgiven me for burdening her life before she passed. It hadn't been easy for her to have a convicted felon for a daughter.

I might even have forgiven Pop had he not hit her again, in the final days of her life. Had the blow that blackened her eye loosened the clot that cut the flow of blood to her brain? I didn't know how the law viewed it but I considered that to be murder. I stared at the back of his bull neck, his hair cropped closely around a bald spot, ears pinned closely to the side of his head like those of a fighting dog, and imagined how difficult it would be for an executioner to kill him, having no neck to fit a rope and no heart to pierce by firing squad. Even the chair might juice him more to monstrous life, like Frankenstein. But the hook of black beneath my mother's eye had looked more than a few days old and so the direct cause and effect of blow and murder could never be established in a court of law or even in the court of my own heart.

But I didn't want him to get away with hitting her that last time, not for any of the times he'd hit her or other members of our family, and imagined, as the pastor read from scripture, how I might wait for him outside the chapel doors after the service ended. I wouldn't hit him, not then, but I'd finally tell him what I'd been thinking the years I'd spent in court and prison and during the less than a year of freedom I'd so-called enjoyed since my release. He'd take abuse from me no more at the age of sixty-two than forty-two and he was still strong enough to break me in two, but he wouldn't catch me, and then, and then, and then the fantasy imploded because no matter how much I wanted to I couldn't imagine hitting Pop, even though, once when driven to a sort of madness, I'd put a gun to his head and ordered him to leave his own house and even I didn't know whether I would have pulled the trigger had he not left. But I couldn't imagine hitting him, not sitting those twenty rows back in the chapel where someone who never knew my mother eulogized her, and I realized then that I was doomed to live with my rage at him because I'd never let it go and I could never give it back to him either.

The pastor finished his eulogy with a solemn glance at the cathedral ceiling and asked everyone to bow their heads in prayer. A strange hacking noise interrupted the silence and turned the pastor's startled glance to the left front pew, where my father sat, his head in his hands. The pastor cleared his throat and stepped away from the podium to allow him a moment to regain his composure. But the noise that poured from my father grew more alarming, as though his heart and lungs squeezed out his throat, and the effort of disgorging them was slowly strangling him. For a moment, I believed justice was being done and the old bastard was keeling over with a heart attack, struck dead by a rightfully vengeful God, but as I watched him shake uncontrollably, my own heart pounded at its cage of ribs, aware that for the first time in my life, I witnessed my father crying.

"You sure he wasn't just choking on a loose tooth?" my sister said over lunch at Denny's. "The man I knew had no tears in him. No pity, no remorse, no grief over any of the damage he caused."

"I thought he was having a heart attack or something." Rain, blown by the wind, swirled against the window, blurring the view of the parking lot into a smudge of blacktop and colored fenders. "He was crying like he'd just lost everything he had in the world. Like he was out of his mind with grief."

"Self-pity, more likely."

"He fell flat on his face."

"You're kidding," Sharon said, meaning, too good to be true.

Pop had lurched forward from the pew, Ray grabbing at his elbow too late to steady the old man as he pitched forward and struck his head against the carpet. "I think he was trying to get up, to walk to the table where they put her ashes, and he just collapsed."

"Don't tell me you feel sorry for him." The look of disgust on my sister's face washed away in nervous laughter.

Did I feel sorry for him? I had rushed from the chapel, the air in my lungs burning like salt water, and taken refuge behind the rear fender of the Cadillac, parked at some distance from the other cars in the lot. No matter how hard I breathed I felt as though I suffocated, and then, my system perhaps still disoriented by the blow I'd taken to the head a few days before, I vomited on the pavement, again and again, until nothing expelled from my stomach except the air I couldn't breathe into my lungs. "I don't know what I felt," I said. "I went to the funeral expecting to want to kill him."

She looked at me, waiting for an explanation. I couldn't give her one. I had been so angry at my father for so many years that I couldn't cope with pity and I wondered if, beneath all the scar tissue, a little love still flowed for the old man, like an underground stream buried beneath a mantle of earth and granite. That thought had driven me out of the chapel as though the devil had my tail.

"Really rocked your world, huh?" Sharon laughed as though she might have been joking but I sensed my sister always laughed after speaking an unpleasant truth, as though truth made her nervous. She had no reason to be nervous around me. I suspected she was just a nervous person and her fidgety gestures and frequent laughter proved that she wanted to please, wanted only to be liked. Considering the number of times my pop beat hell out of her when she was growing up, maybe that wasn't so surprising a defense mechanism. She talked again about her life in Seattle, repeating many of the details she'd told me the day before, and this time I heard the rehearsed inflections in her story, as though she'd memorized it by frequent telling. She talked nonstop through lunch, setting up such an impassable barrier of chatter that I stopped listening. I don't think she realized she was such a boor. I gazed out the window at the rain and tuned her so far out, thinking instead about the little studio in Malibu and how much I was going to enjoy living there, that I didn't realize she was asking me something until she called my birth name.

"Earth to Mary Alice Baker, you anywhere in the galaxy?"

"Of course, I'm right here," I said, wondering what I'd missed.

"So can I stay?"

"Sure," I said, without knowing exactly what I'd agreed to.

"Great." Her hands flew open for a brief moment of freedom before she caught them again and clenched them together on the table. "Anne and her husband are fighting like cats and dogs right now and it's really best I don't stay another night because not only can't I get a decent night's sleep with all that yelling I think it's better for them too, you know? It's such a strain to have houseguests when you're fighting, believe me I'm talking from personal experience here. Remind me never to get married again, okay? Besides, I really really should see Venice Beach before I go, I mean, it's only like world famous so it would be a shame to drive all the way down, have a long-lost sister living right on the beach, and not visit her place, right? I mean, am I right?"

"My apartment isn't very big," I said.

"I've slept in some pretty small places," she said, and laughed again. "You'd be surprised."

"Then you're welcome to stay," I said. "I only have the futon but we can sleep on it together. Like sisters."

"Like sisters," she repeated. "I'd like that."

NINE

THOUGH IT seemed a waste of energy to clean a place I was going to be evicted from at the end of the month, I didn't want my sister to see me for the slovenly creature I often am and went into a frenzy of cleaning the moment I stepped through the door of my apartment. The Rott tried to bite the broom and jumped his front paws on the counter to help me clean the kitchen sink. When I splashed water on his nose he ran off to hide in the bathroom, where he warned me with a bark that someone was coming up the stairs.

"Oh, this place is tiny," Sharon said, poking her head through the open doorway. She wore the same charcoal-gray pantsuit from the day before, carried a gold canvas bag labeled *Virsace* and a battered gray suitcase. Her glance settled on the short stack of boxes against the wall that I'd packed in a fit of optimism that I'd actually find another place to live. "Are you moving in or out?"

"Out," I said, wiping off my hands and stepping forward to kiss her cheek. "The landlord doesn't like dogs."

"Well, fuck him then." Sharon giggled and covered her mouth with the back of her hand. She pointed to heavy security bars striping the only window in the room. "You got a problem with crime in the neighborhood anyway, right?"

"It's the beach, you know?" The security bars had been installed by the landlord so long ago they'd rusted shut permanently. "Urban beaches are always high crime areas."

"Then I'm glad you're moving out." She zippered open the bag's side compartment and pulled out the latest edition of *Scandal Times*. "You know I looked for your name but didn't see it anywhere. Did I buy the wrong paper?"

"I changed my name." I pointed to the photo credit beneath the shot of James Dean's headstone that ran on the front page. "I pretty much go by Nina Zero now."

"What kind of name is that?" She laughed at the rudeness of her question and said, "I mean, you have to admit it's kinda weird, why Zero?"

"Just where my life was at the time," I said.

"Like maybe you were starting from zero?" Sharon looked at me with a sense of understanding I never expected from her.

"That's right," I said.

"I know what that's like." She nodded and laughed. "I must've started from nothing a half-dozen times in my life. Maybe they can call us the Zero sisters. Or you can be Nina Zero, and I'll be Lotta Nothin'."

She laughed and this time I laughed with her. She pointed to the headline, "RIP Rip-Off—Cult Cloners Dig James Dean." "Hey, all this shit about space-alien cloners stealing the body of James Dean, is that true?"

"Sure, in the same way that Bigfoot and the Loch Ness Monster are true." I watched over her shoulder as she flipped through the pages. The edition had hit the supermarket checkout stands that morning. It was the first I'd seen it.

"There's one born every minute, that what you're saying? Hey, your photos are all over this thing!" She pointed to another shot, this one of a fake skull I'd used to double Dean's, half covered with dirt as though rising from the grave. "So if it wasn't cloners, who do you think did it?"

"Teenagers, probably."

"What makes you say that?"

"It's just the kind of thing kids do, playing around with death and the devil," I said. "Plus I got a call last week from a teen, a runaway from Indiana. I get calls all the time, tips coming in about celebrity sightings, that kind of thing. Then when I'm in Indiana I see a picture of this same girl and her boyfriend, caught by a surveillance camera the night Dean's bones were stolen."

"What girl?" Sharon flipped from page to page, looking. "I read the whole thing and didn't see anything about a girl."

"The paper thought cloners would sell better than teens."

"Made it all up, huh? You sound like con artists."

"I'd rather think of it as entertainment."

"So's three-card monte," she said, and laughed. "This girl—what's her name?"

"Theresa."

"You ever heard of the Church of Divine Thespians?" She didn't laugh this time, her attention taken by flipping the news pages.

"Never. Who are they, some new cult?"

"Just something I read about, musta been another paper, the *Enquirer* or something." She pointed to another photograph, this one of the Rott. "Hey, that's your dog, isn't it? You were mugged in a parking lot?"

"I took a picture of somebody didn't want his picture taken."

Sharon ran her hand along the paper, flattening it. "Wow, how exciting. It's almost like my baby sister is a detective."

"Sure, a detective whose job is to invent the truth."

"Isn't that what the cops do all the time? Make up shit to convict people?" She folded the paper back into the side compartment of her purse and asked, "So where's that famous beach everybody's always talking about?"

Sharon seemed less skittish and chatty the more time we spent together, and as we walked the Venice Beach boardwalk at sunset she seemed content to silently watch the human freak show that makes the place Southern California's second leading tourist attraction. She no longer recited stories about her current life but spoke impulsively, inviting conversation. In prison I'd learned that people use stories as defense mechanisms. Those who preferred to keep relationships distant and superficial told nothing about themselves except shopworn stories that bored any listener after a few tellings. My sister's playing the energetic saleswoman was nothing more than that, a thin coating of armor that protected her from unwanted intimacy. Maybe we'd broken through that. She must have been feeling my same yearning for family. She didn't have to spend the night in my apartment. Real estate agents make good money. She could have chosen to stay in a motel.

We dined that night at a Mexican place on Rose Avenue within walking distance from my apartment. Walking distance meant I could drink, a freedom I celebrated by claiming my fair share of two pitchers of margaritas. We talked about what we remembered about each other, our memories as different as our ages had been. I remembered watching her sneak out of the house late at night to meet boys, and she asked if I remembered the abandoned Nike missile base in the hills outside of town, a favorite party spot. The location had haunted my young mind, I said, until years later I'd gone there to raise a little hell myself. I thought she was going to mention something else about the base, something particularly memorable that had happened there, but she swerved suddenly into memories of teaching me how to read and our games of hide-and-seek. She sometimes felt like a mother to me, she said. Midway into the second pitcher she asked, "I forgot, you ever marry, baby sister?"

"Once," I said. "An English paparazzo with legal problems. It was a green-card marriage. I wasn't supposed to care for him. But I did. We were only married two weeks."

"When was this?"

"Last April."

"So the wounds are still fresh." Her words slid together, alcohol dulling her tongue.

"I should have gotten over it long ago. I mean, it was only two weeks, right? And he'd lied to me about everything, right from the start. Even now, I don't know whether he ever truly cared for me. They fished him out of Lake Hollywood one night. He'd been working both sides against the middle in a celebrity blackmail scheme and so they beat him to death."

"That's fucking awful." Sharon stared at me, pity and awe softening the focus of her eyes. "I wondered, you know, why you dye your hair like that, wear black all the time. You're in mourning."

"No, I looked like this before."

She reached across the table to finger the strands of my hair, the alcohol making her more impulsive, just as it made me less guarded. "I bet your hair is still blond, just like it was when you were little, just like my Cassie."

"You have a daughter?"

A truthfulness came into her eyes, what seemed the urge to confess something important. I'd seen the same look from her at our first reunion, just before she'd returned to trivial chatter. "Well, not a daughter exactly. A stepdaughter. Cassie. The daughter of my second ex-husband."

"How old is she?"

"Nine." Her eyes glistened. She reached for a napkin before the first tear fell.

"You must miss her," I said.

She pressed the napkin to her eyes and nodded. "My ex, fuck him, I couldn't care less. But I miss Cassie. I wish we could have stayed together, for her sake. And of course I have no legal rights as her former stepmother so I hardly ever get a chance to see her."

I wondered whether I should reach out and hold her hand, try to comfort her. The mention of her daughter revealed an emotional depth I hadn't suspected. Maybe that was one of the reasons I couldn't cry. I didn't care deeply enough for anybody. Maybe the most compelling reason to have a child was to have someone to care about so deeply that she could break your heart, like I'd broken my mother's heart. I leaned forward and laid my hand over my sister's on the table.

"And now it's too late to have another child, or at least really fucking difficult." She pulled her hand from mine and fumbled through her purse, strung on the back of her chair. "Mom's death started me thinking about what would happen to Cassie if I ever kicked. I mean, it's gotta happen sooner or later, right? Her old man's an asshole. I can't trust him. I want to make sure she's taken care of." She unfolded a sheet of paper, scrawled to the margins in a careless hand, and laid it on the table. "Will you be my witness?"

"To what?" I leaned forward, struggling to decipher the words in the dim light.

"That I'm of sound mind and body." She laughed as though there might be some doubt to that. "It's my last will and testament. Somebody has to act as a witness for it to become legal. I read how to do it at the library yesterday."

I scanned the document, making out a scribbled word here and there in the dim light. Her daughter was the only beneficiary listed. A straight line three inches long had been drawn across the bottom-right corner of the page, above the words *Witnessed by.* "Of course I'll sign it for you," I said.

Sharon was quick to set a pen next to the document. I signed my name and dated it, never imagining how such a simple gesture could so completely change the trajectory of our lives.

I rose after dawn the next morning, careful not to wake Sharon, who slept curled at the edge of the futon, blankets tucked over her shoulder. The Rott waited impatiently at the door while I stumbled into my running sweats and shoes, letting out a low bark to hurry me along. Sharon dug herself further under the blankets and lay still again. I dashed off a quick note directing her to the coffee and anchored the note with a spare set of keys in case she woke and wanted to step outside for air.

The Rott and I had become accomplished running partners in the few months we'd been together, and though he lost his sense of discipline every now and then, particularly when encountering other dogs, I could pretty much let him run off the leash with confidence that he'd heel when commanded. The night with my sister hadn't turned out badly at all, and by the end of it, curled by her side on the futon, half drunk and giggly, I had begun to remember what it had been like to have a big sister. Her language coarsened in direct proportion to the number of margaritas she drank and the chatty real estate saleswoman stripped away to someone darker but also more familiar. A runaway at age sixteen, her life couldn't have been an easy or sheltered one.

She'd begun to curse our pop during the walk home, using language I hadn't heard since my release from prison. I didn't want to talk about him anymore, I'd said. To hate someone gives that person power over your life. I didn't want to give him that power anymore. I wanted, finally, to be free of him. I told her that I was having problems remembering Mom. I could remember isolated moments, like snapshots stored in memory, but couldn't see her move or laugh anymore. We prepared for bed telling stories and when Sharon mentioned the smell of Mom's home permanents I suddenly saw her as clearly as a Super 8mm movie, bent over the kitchen sink, massaging the vile-smelling liquid through her hair. Sharon and I had fallen asleep giggling.

I followed the run with ten minutes of stretches a few yards from the high-tide line, then returned to the apartment an hour after I'd left it. Sharon had awakened in my absence and straightened the blankets over the futon. The keys were gone from the kitchen counter. I cast a quick glance at the note she'd left before I closed myself into the bathroom to shower. *Out to get juice,* she'd written. *Back soon.* When I emerged from the bathroom she hadn't yet returned and so I puttered about the kitchen, preparing a fruit plate to share for breakfast, until I noticed the blinking red light on my answering machine. I pressed the play button and instantly recognized the voice. "Hi, remember me? It's Theresa," the girl with the lavender glasses said, her voice falsely cheerful. "Listen, I have something really important to talk to you about, something that could be—"

The message ended midsentence. I played it a second time, glancing about the apartment as I listened for any clue in the background noise to where the girl could be found, and noticed that my sister's suitcase was gone. Maybe she wanted to load it into her car, then come back for breakfast. Maybe she wanted to sit on the beach and go through the things she'd packed. That she'd taken her bag proved nothing.

I waited out the hour and part of the one that followed before I allowed myself to realize that the girl in the lavender-colored glasses wasn't going to call again and my sister wasn't coming back. I searched the apartment for some clue to her leaving and found under the bottom-right corner of the futon my spare set of keys and a note scrawled on the torn half of an envelope. *Some day you'll understand,* the note read. Maybe she'd returned from her walk and, still not finding me home, had decided to leave. Did my morning run take so long? Did my absence so offend her that she decided to return to Seattle without saying good-bye? Someday I'll understand what? That once again she'd run away?

I shouldered my bag and headed for the bank to collect the money I'd need to secure the lease on the cabin in Malibu. It served me right, I thought. Dysfunctional was an understatement when applied to my family. Sharon may have been justified in running away from home, but she'd left behind more than an abusive father. I was only six years old when she left. No matter what her reasons, she had abandoned me to the same fate she'd escaped. It shouldn't have surprised me that she'd left without bothering to say good-bye. She hadn't really ever cared about me, not then and not now.

I pulled my personal organizer from my bag as I approached the teller window, intending to purchase a cashier's check big enough to cover renting the place in Malibu. It felt lighter than usual but I didn't think anything about it until I unsnapped the cover. My checkbook was missing and the slot where I kept my California driver's license was empty.

"How may I help you?" The teller was a young Latina, her round face open but serious.

I tore open my bag to see if it had somehow fallen free of the organizer, said, "My checkbook, it was right here."

"You mean you lost it?"

"I don't know, I mean, my identification is gone, too."

"Could you have left them at home?"

I shook my head. I never stored them separately from my organizer. The top of my ATM card poked from its slot. When I pulled it I noticed my hands were shaking. "Can you tell me how much money I have in my account?"

The open look in her face closed to one of suspicion. The bank probably warned her against situations like mine, a dodgy-looking woman coming up to her window and making claims that can't be substantiated. "I need to see identification," she said.

"But it's missing," I said. I wasn't mad at her. It wasn't her fault. "It was here last night and now it's gone."

"Do you know your PIN?"

The personal identification number to my account. Her tone of voice suggested she doubted I did, that she doubted I even had a legitimate account. I could use the automatic teller machine to check my balance. I stuttered out an apology and hurried out of the bank. Three ATMs lined the bank's street-side wall. I inserted my card, tapped out my PIN, and selected "balance inquiry" from the menu of services. The five-digit number that flashed to the screen hit me like a blow to the womb. I had less than three hundred dollars remaining in my account. Someone had just robbed me of nineteen grand.

TEN

BEN **FOUND** the Rott panting at my side that sunset, exhausted from an afternoon chasing seagulls while I stared at the breaking waves. Since the morning I had careened between rage, disbelief, grief, and depression, and the tensions between those emotions crippled me. I hadn't moved from my spot in the sand for hours, except to push the Rott when he stopped the chase long enough to sit between me and the view. He'd always been sensitive to my moods, one of the reasons we got along so well. He did his best to cheer me up, and when he saw I wasn't going for it, he pursued other interests.

"Sorry about your money," Ben said, settling into the soft sand next to me. I'd told him over the phone what little I knew about the theft of my money, timed not so coincidentally with my sister's disappearance. "Funny you didn't see it coming."

"What was there to see?"

"Somebody your sister's age doesn't come from nowhere." His glance both faulted and pitied me. "If she stole from you, she's probably stolen from a lot of other folks."

I thumped the Rott on his side, said, "You think because I did time I'm supposed to have some kind of radar for other criminals? Or maybe we have some special handshake we give one another, like we're part of some secret society?"

"I think it's more like a gut feeling. I made you the moment we met, didn't I?" The smile he tried failed to work and so he dropped his head to pinch the sand between his boots. "Well, I got no right to second-guess. That's a hell of a thing to do to somebody, sister or not."

"We're sisters, all right," I said. "Sisters in a screwed-up family. How was I supposed to know she was going to scam me? I hadn't seen her in more than twenty years. I'd always looked up to her. How was I supposed to know she'd rip me off the day after our mother's funeral? I've never met a better liar in my life. You should have seen the tears in her eyes when she was talking about her imaginary step-daughter."

"Why imaginary?"

"Part of the setup. The second she began to cry she asked me to act as a witness to this will she'd just drawn up. Said she wanted to make sure her stepdaughter was provided for. The whole thing was a lie. The will, the daughter, everything. The day we met I told her I'd just cashed a big check. She wanted my signature so she could practice forging it."

"The stepdaughter could be real, though."

"The stepdaughter is a fiction."

"You don't know that for fact, do you?"

"What the hell difference does it make?" Talking about it made me mad and Ben's contradicting me made me mad at him, too. "My sister is a liar. She lied about everything."

"Liars never lie about everything," Ben said.

"My sister's the exception."

"You could predict her if she was. Just take the opposite of what she said. That's almost as good as telling the truth."

I thumped the Rott hard on his side, said, "I'll remember that the next time I see her." The Rott stood, shook off the sand, and circled over to Ben's side. I'd offended him, anger tainting even my gestures of affection.

"Liars lie about one thing, tell the truth about the other, and you never know which is which." Ben wrapped his arm around the dog's neck, rubbed the top of his head. "If you'd get over that stubbornness of yours, maybe you'd understand I'm making a point. What's your sister's name?"

"Sharon."

He looked at me like I was an idiot. "Her last name."

I started to say "Baker," our family name. But of course she'd been twice married and divorced. Had she kept her married name? Her second husband, the banker, what was his name? She never mentioned it.

"Where does she live?"

"Seattle."

"You see a letter with her name and address?"

"Of course I didn't."

"A driver's license?"

"What, I'm going to ask my sister for ID?"

"You even see her car, look at the license plate?"

"I understand what you're telling me." I didn't know her name or where she lived, whether she had married or not, was childless or the mother of a criminal brood. I knew nothing about my sister except that she was a liar and a thief. "She stole my boot cam, too," I said.

Ben thought about that in his usual measured way, asked, "What's a boot cam?"

"A little camera I keep in my boot when I'm on assignment. That way, if something happens to my primary camera, I have a backup."

"I get it. Like a boot gun."

"It only cost a hundred dollars. Big deal, right? At least she left me the big Nikon."

"You report what happened to the police?"

"Not yet."

"You going to?"

"She's still my sister," I said.

"That doesn't mean she doesn't belong in jail."

"Sure, but I don't want to be the one to put her there."

"She abused your hospitality, stole your checkbook and your driver's license, forged your signature, and took you for nearly every dollar you had in the bank. If you saw her right now, what would you do?"

"Drown her, probably."

"Still the vigilante at heart, I see."

He pushed himself to his feet awkwardly, knees cracking with the movement, and dusted the sand from his backside. "Come on, we'll go together," he said, and extended his hand to pull me up.

■ ■ ■

Ben was a good friend, probably better than I deserved. After we reported the theft he took me to dinner at the Galley, a steak and seafood joint in Santa Monica that looks something like a tiki bar designed by Captain Nemo, with blowfish lighting fixtures and year-round Christmas lights threaded through the thatched-roof booths. Ben ordered a bucket of clams and a beer and I ordered cut lime and salt to go with successive shots of bar-brand tequila. After the third shot Ben said, "You keep drinking like that you won't be too happy to see the sunrise tomorrow."

"I don't think I'll be happy tomorrow no matter what," I said. "So why not concentrate on getting happy here and now?" The owner-bartender dropped by when I signaled for another shot. I bit into a lime, licked the spread of salt on the back of my hand, and flung the tequila down my throat.

"Any chance the bank will give your money back?" Ben asked.

"Not much."

"I thought they were insured against fraud."

"She's my sister. Who's to say I didn't give it to her?" I waved at the bartender before he returned the bottle to the shelf. "The fact that I'm a paroled felon doesn't dispose them to be generous. If I ask for my money back, they'll investigate *me* for fraud. But if the police arrest my sister and she cops a plea or they convict her and meanwhile the money doesn't turn up anywhere, then there's a chance I might be quote compensated unquote after the bank completes its review."

"Don't hold your breath, in other words," Ben said.

"Why not? If I hold my breath I'll die and won't have to worry about it anymore."

The bartender returned with the bottle and told me he'd be happy to stand there and pour until I drank myself unconscious, or he could just leave the bottle until I was too drunk to pour for myself, when he'd come over again and help me fill the glass. I think he was being sarcastic. I asked him to pour two shots and promised to wait at least five minutes before calling him over again.

"If you want, I can loan you some money," Ben said.

"You mean the rent?"

He nodded.

"I can't take your money, Ben."

"I'm not asking you to take it. I'm offering to lend it."

I should have accepted his offer with heartfelt thanks but I couldn't do it. I was too proud to accept charity, even in the form of a loan, or maybe I feared that I might have trouble paying him back and that would interfere with our friendship. "Thanks," I said. "It's important to me that you offered. But I just can't take money when I don't know where my next check is coming from. I'll call tomorrow, tell your friend to go ahead and find somebody else."

"Suit yourself." He eyed the bucket of clams coming toward the table and tucked a cloth napkin under his collar like a bib. "Any idea where you're going to find another place?"

"Lots of people sleeping on the street in Venice. Always room for one more." I watched him pry apart the clams one by one, dipping chunks of sourdough into the broth, and drank myself into oblivion in near record time. He ate through my increasingly drunken rant without complaint. We both liked to drink every now and then, and when drunk we ranted about what bothered us. The distances make Los Angeles a lousy town for drinkers; one of us had to stay sober enough to drive, and the one who stayed sober listened to the other rant. When Ben let me off in front of my apartment I thanked him for agreeing to be the designated listener that night.

"I didn't agree to nothing." The dome light clicked onto his mock-grim smile. "You didn't give me the chance to drink more than a couple beers. If we'd stayed any longer I would have needed to drag you out by your heels."

I thought about leaning across the seat to give him a peck on the cheek but figured I'd just fall onto the floorboard if I tried. A quick walk with the Rott along the boardwalk sobered me enough to shower and then sleep without the room whirling about my head, but I was still a little drunk when the Rott let out a low warning bark at five that morning. I counted two sets of footsteps before the door shook with a full-fisted knock that provoked a retaliatory fit of barking from the Rott. I shushed the dog and pulled myself up to a peephole view of black uniforms and billy clubs. Black uniforms meant LAPD. I cracked open the door until the security chain engaged and asked them what they wanted.

The officer nearest the door, a wary-eyed Latina, scanned the space between the door and jamb, then met my eyes. "Mary Alice Baker?"

I nodded.

"Can you open the door, please? We'd like to talk to you."

I'd received visits from the police before. Every few months the call went out to round up the usual suspects and because of my record I was near the top of the list. I knew better than to fight it. I asked her to give me a minute to dress and lock the dog in the bathroom. They'd probably ask a few questions and then leave. I bolted enough ibuprofen to dull the edge on my hangover in case I was wrong.

And I was wrong.

"Could you collect your identification and keys and come with us, please?" the Latina officer said when I unlatched the chain and opened the door.

"Am I under arrest?" I asked, shocked.

"Not at this time," she said.

That hardly filled me with confidence.

"Can you tell me where I'm going and why?"

"You're wanted for questioning."

"Oh, well that explains it."

I don't think she noticed the sarcasm.

The black and white was double-parked in front of the apartment. They didn't bother to handcuff me, but at the bottom of the stairs the Latina officer told me to stand with my feet at greater than shoulder width and to place the palms of my hands on the roof of the cruiser. Her frisk was brief but efficient. She opened the rear door to the prisoner compartment and told me to watch my head getting in.

"Will I get a phone call to my lawyer?" I asked.

"You'll have to ask the detectives that," she said.

"What about my dog?"

She cast a wary eye through the partition.

"I'll need someone to feed him, take him for a walk."

"You'll have to ask the detectives that, too," she said.

ELEVEN

THEY TOOK me to the Hollywood station, a low brick building on the corner of Wilcox and Hollywood Boulevard, swinging the cruiser through the lot to a rear entrance reserved for officers, prisoners, and special guests like me. The prisoner containment area was relatively quiet at that hour, just one drunk cuffed to a long wooden bench running the length of an open-air bullpen. The Latina and her partner handed me over to the duty officer, who told me to sit in a chair along the wall in a tone of voice that meant stay out of the way. The last time I'd been taken to the Hollywood station, after an arrest on a parole violation, they'd cuffed me to the bench with the drunks. I was moving up in the world.

The detective who claimed me from the duty officer a few minutes later looked like the human equivalent of a walrus, his massive chest and belly leading his feet as he waddled through the bullpen. He opened the door to a small room with beige metal walls, centered by a square wooden table with chipped edges. He motioned me toward the chair facing away from the door and sat at the opposite end of the table. The chair he'd offered me was a reject from the bullpen, one leg shorter than the other three and the seat worn to a hard bowl by years of sitting. The detective absently thumbed the fringe of his moustache as he glanced through the contents of a blue notebook, paying no attention to me. He seemed to be waiting. The moustache was a big one; if you stuck a handle into the back of his neck you could have used his face as a push broom.

"Do I have the right to call my lawyer?" I asked.

He looked up as though surprised I'd spoken. "I thought you were here voluntarily," he said. His tone was aggressive, daring me to contradict him.

"Two officers hammered on my door at five this morning and told me to get in the patrol car." I carefully folded my hands in front of me and compressed my emotions into a tight little ball hidden behind my rib cage. Anger doesn't play well with cops. "I wasn't given the chance to volunteer."

He slapped the notebook shut, said, "You're not under arrest. You don't have to tell us anything. You don't want to say anything, don't say anything. You're here because you volunteered to help." He made a big show of glancing at his wristwatch. "If you want a lawyer present I guess we can hold everything until he gets here. Is that what you want?"

"I want someone to take care of my dog," I said.

He pulled his face back as though I'd slapped him. "What does your dog have to do with anything?"

"He's stuck in my apartment without anybody to feed or walk him. I didn't realize I'd be volunteering to come to Hollywood at five o'clock this morning."

"You want to call somebody to take care of your dog?" he asked, wanting to make sure he had it right.

I nodded.

"And if we manage that, will you still want your lawyer?"

Good question. I still owed my lawyer five grand from the last time I'd been arrested and the money I was planning to use to pay him was gone. A detective in a suit from Brooks Brothers strode into the room and shut the door, a gold badge pinned to his belt, just to the side of his zipper. I guessed that meant he was proud of the thing. He seemed young for the badge, no more than thirty-five, and his face looked as fresh and unlined as his suit.

"She wants someone to look after her dog," the one with the moustache said.

"Not a problem." His partner gave me a cursory scan and hitched up his belt, no doubt so I'd notice the badge. "But let's ask a few questions first, okay? We hope to get you out of here so fast you won't need someone to look after the dog."

I said that would be fine. I could change my mind later if the questioning dragged on. The first detective introduced himself as Dougan and the flashy one as his partner, Smalls. Dougan asked the questions while Smalls paced the length of the interrogation room. I got the feeling he had a lot on his mind. Dougan started with the simple ones, like my name, occupation, and address, then asked me to account for my time between late afternoon of the day before to the early hours of that morning. The question confirmed my suspicion that I was one of the usual suspects and nothing more. I figured the interrogation would end as soon as they confirmed my story. Not many ex-cons can present as her alibi a night of drinking with a retired sheriff's deputy. The only problem with my alibi was that it ended before midnight.

"What about the hours between ten last night and two this morning?" Dougan asked.

"Like most honest citizens I was home in my bed," I answered. "Though I may have been a little more drunk than most."

"Can anybody confirm you were there?"

"Just my dog. He'll vouch for me."

I was trying to be funny.

Nobody smiled.

"If your dog can talk, you shouldn't have a problem, then," Dougan said.

Smalls walked out first. Whatever he seemed to be thinking about consumed him. I'm not sure he even heard what I'd said. Dougan promised to let me call somebody about the dog soon and left, careful to lock the door behind him. I'd spent no minor part of my life in similar small and windowless rooms. My brushes with various law-enforcement agencies had taught me how to wait, if nothing else. The only thing I feared was a hangover that, blunted by the ibuprofen, still sent exploratory jabs from the far side of pain. I counted the holes in the acoustical ceiling tiles for a few minutes, then tried to multiply the result by the number of tiles from wall to wall, but that made my head hurt even more. When Dougan and Smalls returned, I was dead asleep, the sign of a clear conscience and bad math skills.

"Can I call someone about the dog now?" I asked, lifting my head from the table.

"In a minute," Smalls said, and this time sat at the table, around the corner to my right. Dougan pushed something small wrapped in a clear plastic bag across the surface of the table. A driver's license of some kind. I squinted, trying to see through the sleep in my eyes. A driver's license from Oregon, issued to someone named Sharon Bogle. The thumb-sized photograph depicted a petite woman with bleached-blond bangs and a face masked by makeup.

"Do you know the woman on this license?" Dougan asked, his voice carefully neutral.

"It's my sister," I said. "At least I think it is."

Dougan glanced at Smalls, who raised his eyebrows.

"What do you mean, *you think it is*? If she's your sister you should know. It is or it isn't."

"Two days ago I saw my sister for the first time in twenty-five years. Her hair was strawberry-blond and she said she was living in Seattle." I poked my finger at the license in the bag. "She wasn't a bleached blond from Oregon in pancake makeup."

Dougan slipped another object from the blue binder and pushed it across the desk with the eraser end of a yellow Ticonderoga pencil. "Can you identify this for us, please?"

The object was similar to the first, except from California, and the face staring back at me from the evidence bag was mine. "It's my driver's license," I said.

Dougan made a note in the binder, asked, "Can you tell us what it was doing in the possession of the woman you identified as your sister?"

"Did you find my checkbook and money, too?"

"Why should we have found your checkbook?"

"Because she stole my ID and checkbook yesterday morning, just before nineteen grand went missing from my bank account."

Dougan's glance was hard and sharp. "You're saying your sister forged your signature and cashed a check on your account?"

"I reported the theft yesterday," I said. "Not here, but the station in Venice. Check it out."

"Give us another couple of minutes," Smalls said, and stood.

"Did you find my money?"

Dougan wedged both evidence bags into his blue binder and joined Smalls at the door.

"My sister's already in trouble, isn't she?"

"We'll make this as fast as we can," Dougan said, and shut the door on their way out.

"Hey, what about my dog?" I called, too late. Not that asking any earlier would have gotten a different reply. They didn't want me making any phone calls, not until they'd finished talking to me, and certainly not when the person I wanted to call to take care of the dog was providing my alibi for whatever it was my sister had done. It seemed pretty obvious Sharon had been unable to resist one last scam before fleeing town. Her luck hadn't held and she'd been caught. The search at her arrest had turned up my driver's license. The police had run my ID through the computer and scored a series of hits. Bingo. Initially, they had to suspect me of being complicit in my sister's criminal enterprise, only they hadn't known we were sisters, and they hadn't heard about the complaint I'd lodged against her. I silently blessed Ben for pressuring me into doing the right thing in reporting the theft. Without that report, my liar of a sister could have blamed everything on me. The police might have believed her for a time. It felt great to do the right thing for once. I was going to have to try to do it more often.

Half an hour later the duty officer poked his head in the door and said I could make my call. I stood and followed him into the detective bull pen, bustling now with plainclothes cops getting an early start on the day. The duty officer pointed to a phone at an empty desk and told me to punch nine to get an outside line. He hovered at the other end of the desk while I dialed.

"I'm guessing they've got you in custody at the Hollywood station," Ben said when he heard my voice. "If this is your one phone call maybe you should tell me what the hell's going on."

"Something to do with my sister," I said. "The police found my ID when they arrested her. So far they've been a little short of talkative. They tell you anything?"

"Not a damn thing, and don't think I didn't ask."

The duty officer leaned forward, said, "Can you complete your phone call now, please?"

"Listen, I've got to go. Can you take the Rott today? He's been stuck inside the apartment since five this morning."

"Happy to do it. He can help me varnish the deck. Hey, those detectives, they working the robbery desk?"

"They didn't say." I thanked him for his help and hung up.

Dougan and Smalls were waiting when the duty officer returned me to the interview room, Dougan's face slack with fatigue but Smalls's still tautly energetic as though he was working his first hour and not pulling a double shift. "When was the last time you visited Hollywood Forever Cemetery?" Dougan began. It took me a moment to recognize the place he meant. Hollywood Forever Cemetery occupied a fifty-plus-acre plot of land next to Paramount Studios, walking distance from the old movie mecca of Hollywood and Vine. Among the celebrity set of the early twentieth century it had been *the* place to be buried.

"Did you see it, for example, last night?" Dougan asked.

"I already told you, I went drinking with a friend last night."

Smalls tapped his pencil, said, "We're more interested in what happened after he dropped you off."

"I already told you that, too. I took my dog for a walk, then showered and went to bed. I was asleep by midnight."

"When was the last time you were there?" Dougan asked.

"There was no last time. I've never been there."

"Never?"

"Never, never."

"But you know the place, what's there."

"It's a cemetery. Dead people are what's there."

Smalls's forefinger inscribed a quick circle in the air.

Dougan spotted the gesture, asked, "Did your sister ever mention Hollywood Forever Cemetery to you?"

"Never."

"You're sure about that?"

"Dead sure."

Dougan and Smalls exchanged glances. Smalls nodded.

"Did she mention anything about her plans last night? Where she was going, what she was doing?"

"Wouldn't matter if she had."

"Why not?"

"My sister is a liar and a thief. How can you possibly think she'd tell me the truth about anything? She ripped me off for nineteen grand. Nineteen grand! You think she's going to leave me her forwarding address? She didn't tell me the truth about anything. I wish

I could help you because I suspect you've arrested her. She belongs in jail. How can anyone with a shred of conscience rob her own sister? You've picked her up, right?"

"In a manner of speaking," Smalls said.

"Did you find my money on her?"

"Not nineteen grand. Not even close."

"That money's mine when you find it. I have no idea what kind of a scam she was running and you know what? I don't care. I hope I never see her again. All I want is my money back. My sister is dead to me."

Dougan leaned forward abruptly, asked, "Why do you say that? Why do you say she's dead to you?"

"Because I have no feelings for her anymore. I don't care how desperately she needed the money. She killed whatever sisterly affection I had for her when she robbed me."

"Try to help us here." Smalls propped his chin on clenched palms, his glance aggressively intelligent. "Why would your sister be in Hollywood Forever Cemetery at two in the morning?"

"Stealing pennies from the eyes of the dead, probably."

"You can't think of any other reason?"

"You don't understand anything I've told you," I said. "My sister is a stranger to me. She could be dancing naked in Satanic rituals and it wouldn't surprise me."

"Why Satanic rituals?" Dougan asked.

"Why not? Why not digging her way to China dressed in a Donald Duck costume? Nothing she does makes any sense to me."

Dougan's eyes rose toward the ceiling, as though my answer exasperated him, then drifted down to Smalls, who subtly tilted his head to the side. Dougan pointed a stubby finger at my chest. "What you said earlier, about your sister being dead to you?"

"What about it?" I said.

"Looks like you got your wish."

Smalls pulled his hands from his chin and looked at me as though I was an extraordinary species of bug. "Your sister was beaten to death last night," he said. "We found her body near the Douglas Fairbanks memorial at Hollywood Forever Cemetery."

TWELVE

I STARED at the back of Smalls's neatly shaved neck while Dougan drove to the morgue. After being informed of my sister's death, I'd answered their questions monotonously, repeating either "Don't know" or "No idea" until I began to doubt the extent of my own vocabulary. I'm not a bad liar, particularly when lies are needed to protect myself or others I care about, but nothing convinces like the truth. I hadn't a clue. The detectives questioned me for another half hour before leading me out the back of the station to an unmarked brown Chevy sedan. They needed someone to identify the body. Neither my brother nor my father could do it—they hadn't seen her since the day she'd left home. I hadn't been able to tell Dougan and Smalls much about my sister but they had revealed even less to me. "What happened to my sister?" I asked when the car stopped at a light.

"Already told you. She was beaten to death." Smalls didn't bother looking back at me from the front seat when he spoke, his mind on other things.

"Why?"

"We don't know. We were hoping you could tell us."

"My sister is a complete blank to me. Her driver's license told me more than I learned in two days talking to her, unless the license was a lie, too."

"The license is legit. The name was one of several she used but I guess you'd call it her legal name. We're still working on a viable address."

"Her name was Sharon Bogle?"

Smalls nodded, watching the street as Dougan accelerated.

I wanted to be helpful, said, "She told me her second husband worked in a bank."

Smalls tipped his head back and shouted a laugh to the roof. "Worked in a bank? Dougy, you hear that?"

"I wonder if he listed that on his job résumé?"

"She told me her first husband had been a butcher," I said.

The cruiser swerved from side to side, Dougan doubled over the wheel and Smalls slapping the dash, their laughter the release of men who'd worked too many hours under too much pressure.

I didn't get it. I said, "What's so funny?"

Smalls breathed deeply to calm himself. "It's been a long night," he said, trying to force the smile from his lips. "We don't mean to be disrespectful to your sister. You really don't know anything, do you?"

"Nothing," I said.

Smalls caught Dougan's eye in the rearview mirror. Dougan nodded. "Your sister's second husband robbed banks for a living. He's in the state pen in Oregon right now. Your sister drove the getaway car on his last job, did three years on the conviction."

He turned his eye out the window.

"The first husband?" I asked.

The smile was gone from Smalls's lips by the time he turned to me and said, "A meth dealer who went off his nut and hacked two people to death in a drug deal down in Texas. They executed him last year."

My criminal record paled in comparison to my sister's. She'd begun her career as a prostitute in Las Vegas, where youth and beauty had served her well enough to keep her out of jail until a couple of birthdays made her a less desirable commodity. By the age of twenty-four she'd been booked in four states on charges of solicitation. In her mid-twenties she learned the arts of check kiting and insurance fraud from a meth-addicted boyfriend and began to rely on her wits more than her body. The bunko squad in Phoenix arrested the boyfriend for selling retirees fictitious memberships in an equally fictitious private golf course. My sister negotiated a deal with the district attorney, aided by medical records that portrayed her as the victim of domestic violence. In exchange for immunity she gave evidence against her boyfriend and soon after the trial married his meth dealer. He beat her badly enough that she required hospitalization on two different occasions, though charges were never filed. She turned state's evidence again five years later, this time to avoid being charged with accessory to murder when her husband used a samurai sword to behead a couple of his dealership's slow-pay accounts.

Dougan and Smalls signed us into the coroner's office and followed an attendant to a room Dougan casually referred to as the meat locker. Pull drawers lined the far wall, each drawer labeled with a case number: file cabinets for the dead. The assistant gripped the handle of a drawer one up from the bottom and braced his feet. The drawer rolled out its contents: a zippered bag made from thick green plastic, filled at the head of the drawer but flat toward the back. The body inside was a short one. The attendant drew down the zipper. The cold white face of my sister emerged from the cocoon of her body bag like a stillborn butterfly.

"It's her," I said.

"This is your sister, born Sharon Baker?" Dougan asked for the record.

"Yes," I said. Since the last time I'd seen her she had dyed her hair black and trimmed it to match the cut in the photo on my license. We looked enough alike, I suppose, to fool an inattentive bank teller. I turned my head from side to side, looking for bruises. A slim cut bisected the brow above her right eye—far too thin an injury to be fatal. "I thought you said she'd been beaten to death."

Dougan tilted his head sharply to one side, cricking his neck. "We found her at the base of the steps leading down to the memorial. Her neck was broken."

"You think someone hit her, knocked her down the stairs?"

"We think a couple of things," he said.

I waited for him to continue. He didn't.

"Can I touch her?" I asked.

Dougan glanced at Smalls.

"Not allowed," Smalls said.

I wanted to smooth the parallel furrows that scored the skin above her brows. She looked worried about what awaited her in the hereafter. I tried to work up sufficient emotion, if not to cry, then at least to have the decency to regret what had happened to her. Whatever her crimes, she had not deserved to be murdered.

"You poor fool," I said.

The attendant sealed my sister in darkness and rolled the drawer shut again, where she awaited the brutal indignity of the coroner's scalpel and sternum saw. With little mystery as to the cause of her death and no family clamoring to bury her body, she'd been placed near the bottom of the pile of corpses awaiting autopsy.

As we walked through the county morgue parking lot Smalls said, "Your sister left a child behind."

"A stepdaughter," I said.

"The records say it's her own flesh and blood."

I nodded. Everything my sister told me was a lie. It wasn't until they guided me into the Chevy's rear compartment that I thought to ask, "My niece, where is she?"

"Records say foster care in Arizona," Smalls said. "Family name is Micklin. Social services in Phoenix should be able to help you find her."

I thought back on what little I knew about Sharon's life. "The kid is from her first marriage? The one to the killer?"

"Don't know the details, but the dates line up."

The engine sparked and the car rocked forward.

"What is she, twelve, thirteen?"

Smalls was looking out the window, already thinking about something else. "Something like that," he said.

What moral obligation did I have toward a niece I'd never met, borne of a sister I'd seen once, with disastrous consequences, in twenty-four years? She wasn't my responsibility. I didn't like my family and the thought of having to deal with an unseen niece disturbed me. If experience was any guide, we wouldn't be good for each other. But I was being selfish and narrow-minded, family traits I'd tried to escape. It may have been too late to develop love for each other but I still owed her respect. If I didn't make a sincere effort my indifference might contribute to the considerable damage already done to her. I wondered what I might tell her about her mother's final days, whether I'd lie or tell the truth. I remembered the sheet of paper I'd signed the day before my sister had been murdered. "Did you find a will with the body?" I asked.

"In her purse," Smalls said.

My niece would learn about me through the will. I'd have to meet her sooner or later. I asked, "Anything else you can tell me about the daughter?"

"Nothing specific, but I can tell you one thing." Smalls looked at me over the seat. "A convicted murderer for a father and a con woman for a mother, the kid must be well adjusted."

THIRTEEN

TWO SECURITY guards stood sentry at the entrance to Hollywood Forever Cemetery when I pulled into the drive, the wrought-iron gates securely closed behind them. The older of the two ambled over to greet me, gun belt clinging precariously to the southern slope of his pear-shaped torso. "We're closed for the morning," he said, bending to peer into the car.

"What's going on?" I asked, curious what he'd say.

"Just a little unscheduled maintenance. We hope to have everything cleared away by noon, if you want to come back then." He glanced up, his eye drawn by something across the canvas top of the Cadillac. The passenger door clicked open and Frank Adams settled his considerable girth into the passenger seat, next to my camera bag. "Thanks for your help, Don," he said, leaning across my shoulder. "Don't forget to look for yourself in next week's issue."

The security guard touched his thumb and forefinger to his cap, said, "Anytime, Mr. Adams."

Like Frank was some kind of big shot.

"How much you pay him?" I asked.

"Twenty bucks and a couple of compliments." Frank pointed to the right, told me to go down one block and turn right again. "He gave me a name from one of the apartments overlooking the cemetery, said the guy saw the whole thing."

Frank had buzzed my cell phone after I'd walked out of the police station, telling me to meet him at the front gates of Hollywood

Forever Cemetery. He didn't know I'd been picked up that morning. "What whole thing?" I asked.

"Somebody staged a raid on the cemetery last night, broke into Rudolph Valentino's crypt. Looks like one of them was killed too, a woman. We're still waiting for the police to contact next of kin, release a name."

"The victim's name was Sharon Bogle," I said.

Frank half turned in the seat, asked, "How do you know?"

"I was the next of kin they notified."

"No shit?"

"None at all," I said, and told him about it.

The eyewitness lived in a third-floor apartment on the avenue bordering the cemetery to the east. Frank buzzed the name on the building directory with the eraser end of his pencil and dipped the leaded tip back to his notebook, intent on taking down my story without missing a single relevant detail. As the elevator doors opened to the third-floor landing he said, "Duplicity, theft, murder, and scandal— I only write about this stuff but you live it."

"Not by choice."

He lifted a ham-sized arm and knocked on the door. "I wish my family would do something interesting, like rob banks and get murdered. All they do is sell used cars and sit around the porch, getting fat and drunk."

The door snapped open to a sixty-something man with a wild spray of gray hair curving around a polished, bald pate and glasses so thick an average-sighted person could have used them for birdwatching. Frank flashed a business card, said, "Frank Adams, *Scandal Times*," and pointed a thumb toward me. "This is our staff photographer."

The man held the card above the top rim of his glasses and ran it past his eyes a letter at a time, then slipped the card into the ink-stained pocket of his off-gray pocket T-shirt. "The whole thing happened beneath my balcony window. C'mon, I'll show you." He led us from the hallway into a studio with broad windows and a sliding glass door overlooking the cemetery. Movie posters and macabre, cartoonish drawings hung haphazardly on the walls and leaned against a drafting table. Frank stopped at the first drawing we passed, depicting a ghoul standing over the body of a woman, an ax in one hand and her head in the other. The drawing looked pulled from the pages of a comic book.

"*Tales from the Crypt,*" Frank said.

The witness tapped a long, yellowed fingernail against the frame and peered at Frank above the rim of his glasses. "You know it?"

"Are you kidding? I've read 'em all. When's this one from, 1950?"

"Fifty-four."

"Don't tell me you're the artist?"

"*Tales from the Crypt* was my first major gig."

Frank slapped his forehead, lurched forward, and shook the man's hand. "Of course! You're Joe Harvest! You drew for EC and Marvel. I should have known right away by the drawing." Frank generally yawned in the face of celebrity, so I first suspected he was being obsequious, hoping to wheedle information from the witness, but genuine excitement surged through his voice as the two discussed the fine points of comic-book illustration. For the first time since I'd met him, he seemed starstruck.

I jiggled the latch at the sliding glass door and stepped onto a balcony not much larger than a door laid flat, the lushly tended grounds of the cemetery laid out before me like paradise. The cityscape between downtown Los Angeles and the ocean was a little short on parkland—not counting the six country clubs restricted to private members—and so by default Hollywood Forever Cemetery was the largest tract of green on the West Side open to the public, even if its chief public was a dead one. The grass rolled to a small lake rimmed by headstones, monuments, and palm trees, and from the center of the lake rose an emerald-green island topped by a columned white temple that could have housed the remains of ancient Greeks—but didn't. Across the lane from the lake an imposing mausoleum done in a more stodgy Greek Revival stood amid the palms, and beyond that, weeping willows, lush Bermuda, and granite markers stretched to the warehouse-like soundstages of Paramount Studios looming over the southern wall.

"It's beautiful," I said, focusing on the island.

"A great place to live if you're dead," Frank said, stepping behind me to the balcony's threshold. "You see that building there?" He pointed to the mausoleum near the lake, its massive, black iron doors festooned with yellow police tape. Two beige sedans blocked the steps to the gates and a black van emblazoned with the LAPD logo straddled the grass to the side of the lane. "Valentino was buried behind those doors."

I framed the scene and took a shot just as a crime-scene investigator stepped under the tape, a white surgical mask strapped across his mouth. "That whole building was his?"

The illustrator snorted and peered around Frank's shoulder. "Just a crypt no bigger than the size of his coffin. They stack them away like boxes in that building, five or six crypts high. Valentino doesn't even have the top bunk. He's hidden away in the corner, about chest-high."

"But he was a major star."

"The most popular leading man of his time, the Sheik of Araby and all that," Frank said. "You'd think he rated more than a shoe-box."

"Valentino died in a hurry, kinda like he lived." The illustrator stepped onto the balcony and gripped the railing for balance, as though afraid of pitching over the edge. "It was probably a good thing he died when he did."

"Why's that?"

"You hate to see the great ones fade away, don't you? You hate to see all that youthful beauty corrupted. Valentino died in his thirties but still, he bloated up like a corpse his last few years and died so broke a friend of his had to donate the crypt. James Dean had the right idea. Live fast, die young, leave a beautiful corpse."

That, I thought, was an easy thing for an ugly old man to say.

"You were home last night?" Frank asked.

"Sure was." The illustrator's glasses slipped down his nose when he nodded and he returned them to their rightful place with a deft, one-fingered push. "I like to work late so I was more or less awake when it all happened."

"What time was that?"

"About two in the morning. I'd just settled into bed when I heard the first noises, big bangs, like somebody whacking something with a sledgehammer, so I jumped up and looked outside." He pantomimed his movements as he spoke, craning his neck left and right. "This part of town, we get a lot of street crime, not all that unusual to hear gunshots, people screaming at each other, sirens, tire screeches, a whole city nightscape of sound." He pointed toward the cemetery. "But the neighbors on this side, at least they're quiet."

Frank and the illustrator flashed ghoulish smiles.

"Who's down there?" I asked. "Other than Valentino?"

"Mostly the early pioneers of cinema, the silent and early talkie stars, like Peter Lorre, Marion Davies, Douglas Fairbanks. Directors like Cecil B. DeMille and John Huston. The stars of the post-silent-film period are mostly in Forest Lawn, near Glendale. That's the real mother lode of celebrity graves."

"So when you looked outside, what did you see?" Frank asked.

"Hardly anything." The illustrator's eyes blinked behind their thick glass shields, as though he couldn't understand it. "Too dark, I guess."

Frank glanced at me. Some eyewitness.

"Okay, then, what else did you hear?"

"Two screams. Terrified, female screams." He opened his mouth to imitate the expression of a woman screaming, then whirled as though reacting to the sound. "So I ran to the balcony again, because the screams sounded like they came from the cemetery." He gripped the railing and leaned his head over the edge, listening in memory to the sounds from the night before. "But that was it, just two screams, and then all kinds of noise, people running, whispers loud as shouts—*hurry, come on,* that sort of thing—clangs and bangs like tools being thrown into a van."

"Van?" Frank asked. "Any idea about color or make?"

The illustrator shook his head. He didn't know.

"How do you know it was a van?"

"It wasn't completely dark. I could make out the shape. But mostly it sounded like a van, you know the ratcheting sound the side doors make when they open and close."

"Hear anything after that?"

"The sirens, of course," he said. "Took the cops a half hour to respond."

"Screams in a cemetery probably didn't worry them all that much," Frank said. "I mean, everybody in there's dead already."

FOURTEEN

SOMETHING THAT looked suspiciously like compassion glimmered in Frank's eyes, veiled by the steam rising from the bright yellow Winchell's Donut House coffee cup he held just below his lips. The baker's dozen box of donuts he'd bought on entering the coffee shop lay reduced to crumbs just beyond his elbows. I'd eaten two to his eleven. The consistency of the dough was light as air, and he'd simply inhaled them. "I'm sorry if I sounded flip about your sister," he said. "If you don't want any part of this story, if you want to back out for personal reasons, I understand."

"I'm not crying about what happened to my sister." I shook my head, hearing how callous I sounded. "It's a shame. I'm sorry it happened. But I didn't love her."

Frank's eyes widened fractionally. I'd shocked him.

"She was a con artist. She ripped me off. Why should I care?"

"What about the old saying, blood is thicker than water?"

"Shit is thicker than water too, but that doesn't mean you should value it."

Frank laughed, said, "And I thought I was unsentimental."

"I am too sentimental. Just not about my family, not anymore, not after they've abandoned and beaten the crap out of me so often. The blood in my family is bad. I care more for my dog, and frankly, I care more about you. You know why?"

"Because we're so good-looking?"

"Exactly." I sipped at my coffee, said, simply, "Because you care back."

Frank rolled his eyes. "You are sentimental." He wet the tip of his thumb with his tongue, mopped up the crumbs still scattered in the box. "Do you care about finding out who did this to your sister?"

"That's different. Maybe I sound cold and uncaring to you, but that doesn't mean I won't seriously damage the creeps who killed her if I get the chance. Okay, so I didn't love my sister. It's still personal, particularly because they were probably thinking it was me they killed."

Frank's thumb stilled en route to his mouth, a fat crumb clinging to the skin. "How so?"

"I think she took a phone call meant for me." I told him about the call from the girl in the lavender-colored glasses.

"Say your sister answered the phone, talked to this girl." Frank remembered the donut crumb and licked it off his thumb. "Let's say the girl tipped her about the action last night at the cemetery. That still doesn't answer the question, why would she go?"

"Money."

"You mean blackmail?" Frank thought about it while he dipped his thumb into the corner of the box for more crumbs. "She wanted to blackmail the grave robbers? Was she that stupid?"

"Stupid in a different way. I told her that I'd made twenty grand on a photograph a couple months ago."

He sucked the crumbs off his thumb. "I get where you're going now. You think your sister wanted something to sell to the tabs."

"Like I said, she was stupid in a different way. Probably thought if I got twenty grand for a photograph, so could she, particularly with a hot tip from one of my contacts."

"That doesn't mean whoever did this was gunning for you. Just means your sister was unlucky or stupid enough to get caught."

"Maybe," I admitted. "But I still get the feeling she took a death meant for me. What if I'd taken the call instead of her?"

Frank pushed away from the table and stood. "You would have taken the shot you wanted and kicked the hell out of anybody trying to stop you." He tossed his crumpled napkin to the table and pushed out the glass doors into the mini-mall parking lot, firing up a cigarette with a silver Zippo the instant his face crested the threshold. When I caught up to him on the sidewalk he said, "I thought we'd drive to an address in Hollywood, interview someone from the Raelians."

"You mean the cloners? That's not a story. It's a joke."

"A joke that sells newspapers." Frank blew smoke through his smile. The Cadillac was parked in a metered spot down the block. He walked slowly, pacing himself to the length of his smoke. "It wasn't easy finding this guy. The sect is based in Canada. But this being Los Angeles, I knew I'd find a representative sooner or later. We got all the wacko fringe groups here. New Age, Old Age, and In-Between Age."

"You can't seriously believe the Raelians are behind this," I said, vaguely angry but unsure why.

"Seriously? No."

"Then why are we wasting time on them?"

"Because it makes great copy."

"My sister just got murdered and you're treating the investigation like a joke?"

Frank gave me a look like I'd just confirmed his suspicions. "I thought you didn't care," he said.

"I care about the truth."

Frank's lips formed an ironic O. "You want to find your sister's killer?"

"Yes," I said, with more conviction than I'd thought I felt.

"You want to find your sister's killer, talk to the police. You want to sell newspapers, talk to me."

"You're right," I said.

"Good to hear you admit it."

"About my wanting to back out of the story."

Frank nodded as though he'd expected to hear as much, said, "It's not the first time we've disagreed about a story."

"I can't play the game this time," I said. "It's too personal."

"No problem. You'll drop me at my car?"

I told him I would and stepped off the curb.

He puffed his cigarette down to the filter, watching me across the top of the ragtop. "Hey, aren't you getting kicked out of your place at the end of the month?"

I nodded, keying the door.

"And your sister stole all your money, is that right?"

"Not all," I said. "She left me about three hundred dollars."

"What with first, last, and a security deposit, that should get you a couple of days in a skid-row flophouse." He cackled like a startled rooster and flicked the cigarette to the curb.

I drove him to Hollywood.

■ ■ ■

The Raelian who greeted us was a tall, tanned, and bearded man whose white jumpsuit with reflective silver trim made him look like a refugee from a 1960s sci-fi flick. He introduced himself as Rood Cirelius, Regional Director of Media Relations, and with polite excitement ushered us into his one-room office in a crumbling courtyard complex off Hollywood Boulevard. Sometime before, the office had been decorated entirely in white, but the wear of years had grimed the carpet, scuffed the walls, and chipped the furniture, and so rather than the shimmering image of modernity the design intended the office now looked merely tawdry. Rood bounded with energy as he directed us to white-leather wing chairs positioned before his desk. Either he was overdosing on health stimulants or despite his title he didn't have many opportunities to meet actual members of the media.

Frank gave him free rein, asking general questions about the Raelians and their interest in cloning. Rood tilted back in his chair as he spoke, looking over steepled fingers to the ceiling as though channeling his responses directly from the extraterrestrials. I observed him through the viewfinder of the Nikon as he spoke, framing the shot around the books prominently displayed on his desk. The titles running along the spines—*The Message Given by Extra-Terrestrials, Let's Welcome Our Fathers from Space,* and *Sensual Meditation*—told me all I really wanted to know about the Raelians. Rood was more than happy to raise my consciousness whether I wanted it raised or not. The movement began in 1973, he explained, when visitors from another planet contacted French journalist Claude Vorilhon while he walked through the woods. Many years before, the space visitors had created the human race from the DNA in their own tissues. The time had come, they told the journalist, whom they dubbed Rael, to establish an embassy, preferably in Jerusalem, and begin official interplanetary contacts. Claiming fifty-five thousand members worldwide, the Raelians were now the largest UFO-based organization in the world, easily outdistancing lesser rivals such as Aquarian Perspectives Interplanetary Mission and the First World Conclave of Light, which were honorable in their intent but suspect in their unorthodox teachings about the history, nature, and intentions of our visitors from outer space. The extraterrestrials were not our space brothers, as so many incorrectly claimed. Rood shook his head vehemently at this heresy. The extraterrestrials more correctly were our fathers from space. That was a key difference, the one that defined the Raelians and elevated them above the dozens of other UFO-based theologies.

"The aliens first visited Rael in 1973?" Frank said as though asking for simple clarification. "A lot of psychedelic drugs going around France then?"

"No more than here," Rood said.

Frank scratched behind his ear with the eraser end of his pencil, said, "No more than, say, San Francisco?"

"Absolutely not. No more than San Francisco."

Frank scribbled the answer into his notebook. "So according to Rael, we're all essentially clones of space aliens, is that right?"

"Exactly right!" Rood lurched forward, elbows skidding to a stop on the dull white surface of his desktop. "And this is why the cloning issue is so fundamentality central to the Raelian philosophy, the—if you'll allow me the phrase—Raelian way of life. We didn't evolute from apes. We descendemated from extraterrestrials. Tell me, which group would you rather claim as your ancestrals?"

"I prefer the apes," Frank said. "But I get your point. Has there been any interest or discussion within the Raelian organization about producing clones from the DNA of famous personages?"

Rood looked lost but vaguely hopeful. "Famous personages? You mean, like, people?"

Frank deadpanned him a look, nodded.

"We've discussed it, but only as a hypothermical issue."

Frank cocked an ear, asked, "Hypothermical?"

Rood flushed. "Hypertheoretical, I mean. You know, talking about what might happen without planning to in fact make it happen. I mean, if you get a chance to bring someone like Albert Einstein back from the grave, why not do it?"

"What about James Dean?"

"Absolutely!" Rood bobbed up from his desk, so excited by the idea he couldn't sit still. "We'd love to be able to clone someone like James Dean. Beautiful, talented young man cut down in the prime of his youth by a tragic accident. Imagine if he could be brought back to life. Imagine the thrill of seeing James Dean perform again, as alive as you or me. All that wonderful charisma and potentiality, saved for humankind!" Rood bowed deferentially toward me, as though expecting my thanks, as a woman, for not saying "mankind."

"And how about Rudolph Valentino?" Frank asked.

"The James Dean of his time," Rood enthused. "Handsome, talented, like Dean cut down in the prime of youth and mourned by millions. Another worthy candidate for cloning."

I imagined the headline Frank would write based on Rood's clueless admission: "UFO Freaks on LSD Clone James Dean." I sensed what was coming next and stood to frame the Raelian in the light bleeding through the courtyard window.

"Would the Raelians be able to, say, extract DNA from the bone marrow of someone like James Dean, enough to produce a clone, at least theoretically?"

"From the bone marrow, you say?" Rood contracted his eyebrows as he puzzled this over, seemingly a little fuzzy on the science. "That's different from our current experimentations, which are with, like, eggs and wombs. But I don't see why not."

"Do you have any comment on police speculation that members of the Raelian sect stole the corpse of James Dean?"

Rood blinked as though the wind had just blown sand into his eyes. "Police? Really? They think that? But why?"

"To clone him."

The expression on Rood's face did not appear to emanate from a being belonging to one of the higher orders of intelligence, which contrasted nicely with the light from the window haloing behind his head. I pressed the shutter and held it down, going into rapid fire.

"Wait a minute," he protested. "I never said we wanted to clone him. You said that."

Frank's glance dipped to his notebook. "You said, and I quote, 'We'd love to be able to clone someone like James Dean.'"

"You put those words into my mouth!"

"Yes, but you swallowed them," Frank said.

Rood sat behind his desk like a man falling from great height and cradled his head in his hands. "You misunderstandimate," he said. "Theoremetically, we'd love to clone everyone. But we have no reason to clone James Dean, not when there are so many other more qualifiled candimates around."

"Such as Rudolph Valentino?"

"Such as Albert Einstein," Rood said.

I watched Frank pen what would be the story's subheadline, "Einstein Next to Be Cloned."

"How far along are your plans to clone Albert Einstein?" he asked.

"But we have no plans to clone Einstein!" The palms of Rood's hands thwacked onto the desktop. "You're twisting everything I say. I was just speaking hypertheoretically. You said someone stole the body of James Dean?"

"Last week in Indiana," Frank said. "Rudolph Valentino last night in Hollywood."

"That sort of thing just isn't our style. Grave robbing sounds like the work of one of the darker cults, not the Raelians."

"What makes you say the Raelians aren't a dark cult?"

"We're not a cult at all," Rood said, offended. "We're the truth." He plucked a copy of *Sensual Meditation* from the short stack of books on his desk and held it up for our inspection. "If you want a glimpse into what the Raelian revolution is really about, we're holding a local seminar based on the teachings of this book next week. Sensual meditation allows Raelians to enjoy sounds, colors, smells, tastes—our entire sexo-sensual environment—to achieve a more intense sexual experiensation and, for the truly advanced among us, to reach cosmic orgasm." Rood looked smugly modest, as though he counted himself among the few.

"Cosmic orgasm?" Frank repeated, unsure he'd heard correctly. "That sounds like something Hugh Hefner would dream up while watching *Star Trek*."

"You have to experience it to truly understand." Rood attempted a soulful look into my eyes.

I avoided it.

"I think I've got everything I need," Frank said, rising from his chair, "Thanks for agreeing to talk to us."

I scrambled for the door but the Raelian, taking advantage of my pause to shoulder the camera bag, beat me to it. "I missed hearing what you thought about our seminar on sensual meditation," he said, his eyes hot and sticky.

"Sounds like a great way for horny men to con women into having free sex with them," I said.

Rood looked shrewdly hopeful. "Does that mean I can put you on the guest list?"

FIFTEEN

THE GIRL in the lavender glasses backed away as though seeing a ghost when the Rott and I found her panhandling that afternoon on the 3rd Street Promenade in Santa Monica, her soft green slacks filthy at the cuffs and mud staining the elbows of her calfskin jacket. The rigors of sleeping rough and eating badly had chapped and reddened her skin. Life on the street is hard on the complexion and even harder on the spirit. She half turned from me, cracked lips parted in shock.

"If you run, I'll catch you," I said.

"You can't hurt me, not here." Theresa glanced at the streams of people flowing past the sign she'd penned to go with the upended baseball cap at her feet.

"Why would I want to hurt you?" I asked.

FUTURE MOVIE STAR NEEDS DONATIONS FOR ACTING LESSONS, her sign read, the handwriting as flowery as a rose garden. I counted fifty-seven cents tossed into the cap.

"I thought you were dead," she said. She pressed her hips against the painted brick wall of the clothing store she'd chosen as her panhandling spot and wrapped her arms around her stomach as though the sight of me somehow sickened her. I'd traded tips with one of the dredlocked skate punks who hung out near Broadway, five bucks to hear that he'd skated past a girl who looked like my description not more than half an hour earlier. A single week had peeled Theresa's veneer of confidence to the raw, frightened, and increasingly desperate girl beneath. I blocked her in with the Rott on one side, my out-stretched arm on the other. I asked, "Why did you think that?"

Her chin dipped into her chest, the breath flitting in and out of her lungs with birdlike speed. "I heard. At the cemetery. Someone had been killed. I thought it was you."

"You're disappointed to see me, then?"

Her head shook a quick denial.

"Did you set me up?"

She shook her head again, this time so violently her shades slipped to the side. She straightened them with a quick, furtive hand. "The woman who died. Was it your sister?"

I nodded.

"I didn't tell anybody she'd be there. It wasn't my fault, what hap-pened. I swear I didn't know they'd kill her. How could I possibly know that?" She gulped her apologies and held her guts like she was afraid of losing them and at the end broke into a sustained fit of sob-bing. On the sidewalk at her feet tears fell like rain. I offered neither reassurance nor comfort, merely watched, like someone waiting out a cloudburst from the dry safety of a doorway.

"You'll have to tell me everything," I said.

She held her breath to stifle the sobs and straightened her back against the wall. "I don't know anything," she said. "My boyfriend arranged everything. I just made the call. I mean, look at me! I'm broke, I haven't eaten in twenty-four hours, I haven't even had a bath in a week." She stooped to pick up the cap at her feet and showed me the change. "Not even a dollar and I've been here for two hours!"

"Where's your boyfriend?"

She cried like a burst of siren, one long wail broken by whooping gasps for air. A few passersby looked but no one stopped. It took her several broken attempts to explain that the boyfriend had abandoned her yesterday morning after an argument, taking every single one of the two hundred and fifty dollars my sister had given them for the tip that had brought her to Hollywood Forever Cemetery and to her death.

I waited her out. No one cries forever.

"How did you know about last night?" I asked.

She shrugged, too self-involved to cooperate.

"Did you know they were going after Valentino?"

"You mean the fashion designer? I didn't even know he was buried there. I thought he'd be somewhere like in Italy."

Her confusion seemed sincere. It's hard to pretend that much ignorance. I asked, "Where did the tip come from?"

"Heard it on the street."

"You make it worse for yourself when you lie." I probably sounded like her mother, assuming she had a mother who cared enough to level with her. "If you're going to lie do yourself a favor and keep your mouth shut."

Vivid patches of red blotched her skin in the colors of high emotion and a look of defiance rose behind the tears welling from her eyes. "I don't have to talk. I don't have to tell you fucking anything."

I lifted the cell phone from my pocket and tapped out an eleven-digit number, keeping her pinned against the wall with the Rott on one side and my arm on the other. "You think I feel sorry for you, you little creep, because you haven't eaten for a few hours? My sister is dead. They broke her neck because of your innocent little tip." A voice picked up on the other end of the transmission and I changed my tone to talk to it. "LAPD Hollywood? Can you connect me to Detective Smalls in homicide?" I swiveled the phone away from my lips while I waited, said, "You're going to need acting talent where you're going, if only to save your candy ass from the sisters in county jail. The cops aren't going to be as gentle as I am in making you roll over on your friends."

She glanced wildly about, as though looking for an escape route. The dog frightened her enough to keep her from bolting, even though he'd done nothing more threatening than try to lick her hand. "I didn't know it was going to be Valentino," she said, her voice breaking again. "I just heard it was going to go down in the cemetery next to Paramount."

"Who told you?"

"The gang breaking in."

The transmission connected to Detective Smalls's voice mail. I pulled the phone from the side of my face and pressed it against Theresa's ear. At the sound of the tone I said, "No message," and disconnected.

Theresa sniffled, threatening to break out the siren again. I didn't have time to waste watching her cry. "I'm either going to be your best friend or worst enemy." I took her by the arm. "Your decision. Pick up your cap."

"Where are you taking me?" she asked.

I took her down to the beach at sunset, a large take-out bag from the local Fatburger stand clutched to her chest. Life was already adventurous enough for Theresa and given the choice between tacos and hamburgers, she chose the familiar. I figured she'd be less likely to bolt weighed down by the bag, and once we'd eaten, she'd have a hundred yards of sand between her stomach and any chance of escape. I shouldn't have worried. The only bolting she intended at that moment was the food. She reversed her baseball cap and attacked the hamburger with ravenous bites, washing down half-chewed swallows with a large cola. I didn't want to ruin her appetite or give her time to think about her options. To distract her I asked about her favorite movies.

She responded with an enthusiasm that matched her appetite. Reese Witherspoon was her favorite actress, followed by Winona Ryder, Thora Birch, and Renée Zellweger. Romantic comedies were clearly her favorite genre, though the plots didn't interest her as much as the characters. She saw every film through the eyes of the female lead, talking about their predicaments to the exclusion of all else. Films were about stars and the roles they played. In that she wasn't different from most actors I'd met—or filmgoers. When she reduced the bag of takeout to empty wrappers I said, "Tell me what happened to my sister."

She cupped a fist to her mouth to suppress a belch, said, "I don't know."

I slipped the cell phone from the side pocket of my jacket.

"I'm not lying." The girl looked at the phone, offended more than frightened. "All I know is what I heard on the radio."

"She picked up the phone when you called?"

"I thought it was you at first."

"What did she say?"

"That you were too busy to meet me, so I should talk to her." She glared over the top of her lavender glasses, as though I shared the blame for what happened. "She was your partner. I mean, didn't she like, call you or something, say what was happening?"

"That's what she said? That we were partners?"

"First thing out of her mouth when I called. Said the same thing when I met her. She carried a little camera, said she was a photographer too, you worked together on things."

"Where did you meet?"

Theresa pointed her chin toward the palisades across Pacific Coast Highway. "Same place we did. By the bathrooms in the park. So was she your partner or not?"

"Not," I said.

"Then why did she say she was?"

"Probably thought there was money in it."

"You mean your sister double-crossed you?"

I nodded.

"Your own sister?"

I nodded again.

"That's so cold it's ice."

"About as cold as your boyfriend ditching you."

"That little fucker. I hope his bus crashes."

"Where did he go?"

"New York, probably."

"Why New York?"

"The theater."

"Ah. Another actor," I said.

"Real actors work on the stage, he said." The girl grabbed a handful of sand, spread her feet wide, and let the grains dribble from the bottom of her fist. "I should have known he was going to run off when he started lying about how easy it is to get cast on Broadway, the rat bastard." She gave her head a disconsolate shake. "And I let him hold the money."

"Which one of you met my sister?"

"I did."

"What did you tell her?"

"Just that something was supposed to go down in the cemetery." The girl grabbed another fist of sand. "I should have known something was wrong. She didn't even know where Paramount was. And that camera she carried? The camera? What a joke." Behind the lavender shades her eyes rolled scornfully. "At least you carry a real camera."

"What did you care as long as she paid you?"

"She was a real bitch about the price. I wanted five hundred."

"Five hundred is a lot of money."

"You would have paid it."

Even a teenaged girl from Indiana could see it.

"I'm a sucker, obviously," I said.

"You're not a sucker. You're just fair." She watched the sand drift from the base of her palm, and after the last grain fell, her eyes slid to mine as though judging whether or not she had fooled me.

"Who told you about the cemetery?"

She said, "Nobody," as though it might be a negotiating ploy, and eyed my hand, curious whether I'd reach once more for my cell phone. I plotted in my mind the moves I'd need to make to pin her face down and feed her a little sand to go with the hamburger. She may have been a shameless liar but she was only fifteen and I had difficulty imagining myself astride her back, beating the truth from her. I remembered what I had been like at her age and how intensely I resented all authority figures, particularly my pop, for whom force was the first, middle, and last resort. I remembered thinking that my turn would come someday, that someday I would be the strong one beating the weak. I could make her learn to hate me quickly if I pushed rather than guided her. She was testing me just then, trying to figure out for herself whether I was just another morality cop telling her what to do or whether I intended to help her. Then again, maybe she was calculating how big a sucker I was. And no matter how much I despised force when I was a teenager it kept me in line, a seemingly sweet and submissive girl until one day I stopped obeying and all hell broke loose. I said nothing. I stared and waited.

"Nobody told *me* anything." She returned my stare with a look of innocence, as though it was my fault for misunderstanding. "My ex-boyfriend is the one who found out. I've seen them around but he's the one knows them best."

"Them?"

"The gang."

"What gang?"

She looked at me like my stupidity was tragic, said, "The gang that broke into the cemetery."

Her use of the word *gang* summoned to my imagination desperate characters and hardened criminals before I realized the difference in our experience could lead to an equal difference in perception. "This gang, who's in it?" I asked.

"Runaways, mostly."

I thought I noticed a glimmer of deception behind her violet shades but in the fading light I couldn't be sure. "So kids, mostly."

"Just because they're kids doesn't mean they can't get involved in some serious shit," she said. By my definition she was a kid too, and the way I'd dismissed them offended her.

I nodded once, asked, "These kids the type to kill somebody?"

The girl picked up another handful of sand and shrugged. "What kid isn't the type to kill somebody anymore?"

Good point. It figured to be kids playing games with death and the devil. Sex alone does not obsess the adolescent mind. Like a positive print and its negative image adolescence and death mirror each other. Teens develop a fascination with death and dying the moment their bodies spring most to life. They dwell on death with all the fervor of romantic love, compelling them to visions of doom and decaying flesh, to contemplate the end of desire when they first begin to feel how unbearable desire can be, the sense of fatal romance drawing them to fights and speeding cars, drugs and cemeteries at night, and other means of courting death.

I played the scene out in my mind, my sister walking into the cemetery before the gates closed, hiding behind one of the monuments until the kids broke into the crypt, the spark of flash when she released the shutter betraying her presence. Could she have been that stupid? If she thought she photographed nothing more threatening than kids on a prank, maybe, but breaking into Hollywood Forever wasn't a prank. The operation required equipment serious enough to crack the metal gates guarding both the cemetery and the mausoleum and then to break into the crypt itself. Why would kids go to the trouble to steal the bones of a movie star idolized by their great-grandparents? "I'm sorry, but this makes no sense to me," I said. "Maybe you're telling me the truth and maybe you're not."

"I'm not lying," she said, her tone sullen.

"Then tell me where I can find them."

"I need money," she said.

I was tempted to grab her by the hair and drag her into the next wave. I resisted. She watched me above the rims of her shades, her eyes sly as a poker player's. "You think I'm a greedy little bitch, don't you? All I want is bus fare back to Indiana. And some money so I can eat along the way. I want to go home, okay?"

I stood, dusted the sand from the seat of my pants.

"You've gone too far to find home the same place you left," I said, and extended my hand to help her up.

"Does that mean you'll pay or not?"

"I won't pay," I said. "But I know a reporter who might."

SIXTEEN

A WARREN of concrete barriers protected the entrance to the *Scandal Times* building, and the iron-gated, steel-reinforced front doors, electronically monitored by a security guard at a control desk shielded in bulletproof glass, could withstand impacts up to but not quite including high-velocity tank rounds, making the newspaper almost impregnable to attacks by terrorists, space aliens, hostile celebrities, three-headed sheep, and other frequent subjects of the paper's sharp and incisive editorial coverage. Some considered Hector, the security guard in charge of entry most nights, the weak link in this impressive chain of defense. Fifty-five years of age, balding, overweight, saddled with a chronic limp from a bad hip, and cheerfully confessing that if ever forced to draw his gun he'd be more likely to shoot his foot than his intended target, Hector was about as intimidating as a ball of wool. He was also one of the paper's most ardent readers and so the most popular guy in the building. When I buzzed for entry he called through the intercom, "Hey, it's the damsel in distress and her heroic hound!"

He met us at the door personally, the most recent issue of *Scandal Times* neatly folded open to the Rott's page-twelve photograph and the article below it, headlined "aMazing Mutt Mauls Muggers," which recounted the dog's attack on the men in terms appropriate to a World Wrestling Entertainment match. My sister had showed me the same article the afternoon she'd come to my apartment. As much as I enjoyed photographing for *Scandal Times,* I didn't appreciate being the subject of its reportage.

Hector offered the Rott his hand to sniff as a way of greeting. "How's the wrasslin' Rottweiler tonight? Bite any bad guys lately?" The Rott licked the guard's hand and leaned against his leg, his way of soliciting a scratch. Hector obliged, pointing to the guest register with his newspaper hand and asking us to sign in.

I signed my name and the time into the ledger and extended the pen toward the girl, who stared at it for several seconds, either unsure of the process or unwilling to play her part in it. "You have to sign in unless you want Hector here to throw you out," I said.

The girl took the pen and moved the tip across the surface of the page. I glanced at her entry before we headed up the stairs, curious to know her last name. Natasha Gurdin, she'd written. I briefly wondered if that was her real name and so I said it aloud while she walked ahead of me, not calling her specifically, just saying the name to see if she'd turn to it. She didn't. Still, the name sounded familiar, though I hadn't a hope of placing it, not with my sieve of a brain and the sight of Frank appearing at the landing at the top of the stairs, a cigarette dangling from his lips.

"Shit, thought I'd have time for a quick smoke," he said, delighted to see me. "Well, you're here so we may as well get this over with." He offered his hand to the girl, who stared at it as though he'd just extended a dead fish on the end of his arm.

"You're the reporter," she said, touching his hand with hers and pulling it away as quickly as politely possible.

"Best damn reporter in the business, I might add," he said, and introduced himself by name.

"I know who you are," she said.

"Another fan, eh?" Frank seemed pleased to be recognized, his disappointment at not being able to sneak out for a smoke momentarily forgotten. He led us through a news bullpen half staffed for the night shift, mostly reporters working late on stories composed from imagination as much as fact, and pointed the girl to a chair across from a desk littered with the remains of Chinese takeout.

The girl swept the seat cushion with her hand and, satisfied that the surface was relatively clean, sat. "I want five hundred dollars," she said.

"I want five million but I haven't a chance in hell of getting it." Frank plunked his elbows onto the table and stared at the girl, a tactic intended to intimidate his source and control the interview.

"No money, no story," the girl said.

Frank heaved a world-weary sigh and pulled a sheaf of twenties from the top-right drawer of his desk. He tossed one to the corner nearest the girl. "The first one's free, just for showing up. The rest you'll have to earn." He slid a reporter's notebook under his pencil. "Let's start with your name."

The girl looked at the twenty, then at the sheaf on Frank's side of the desk, and I thought I could see despair sag at her face, as though she enjoyed little hope of seeing much more than that first twenty. "No names," she said.

"No names, no money."

The girl tried to meet his stare and failed. "Natasha Gurdin." She leaned abruptly forward to snatch the twenty from the corner of the desk.

Frank rolled his eyes. "Right. If you're Natasha Gurdin, I'm Bernard Schwartz."

"Her name's Theresa," I said. "At least, that's the name she used when we first met."

Frank wrote it down, asked, "Last name?"

The girl remained stubbornly silent, staring at me, certain I had betrayed her.

"Theresa's good enough for now. I'm assuming you're a minor, so we wouldn't normally publish your full name anyway. Where you from, Theresa?"

"Chicago." She tried to sound tough saying it, as though she knew people from Chicago were tough and so she had to sound tough, too.

Frank swizzled the pencil's eraser tip in his ear and said, "I'm sorry, what town in Indiana is that?"

"Chicago is in Illinois, not Indiana."

"Indianapolis?" Frank tapped the eraser on his desk while he stared at her, contemplating her origins, or pretending to. "No, too big. Fairmount?"

The girl's eyes widened a fraction, a noticeable fraction.

"No, too small." He snapped the eraser end forward. "I'd guess Logansport or Kokomo."

The girl again stared at me.

Frank leaned back in his chair, kicked his feet onto the desk, and linked his hands behind his head, elbows veed outward like chicken wings. "What you got to tell me, Theresa from Kokomo?"

"I know who broke into the cemetery next to Paramount Studios."

"Great." Frank stifled a yawn. "Who?"

"Some runaways my ex-boyfriend knows."

"Care to be a little more specific than 'some runaways'?"

"Teens mostly. They live up in the hills outside the city."

"Names, descriptions?"

"I only saw them from a distance. They looked like Goths. You know, long black trench coats, black hair all greasy like, big boots, upside-down crosses around their necks, lots of piercings and tattoos."

Frank reached for the pile of bills, airmailed another twenty across the desk. "Why did they break into the cemetery?"

The girl pocketed the twenty and dropped her voice to a melodramatic whisper. "They wanted to hold a black mass, you know, pentangles, blood sacrifice, that kind of shit. They're devil worshippers. They needed some bones."

Frank jotted a few lines into his notepad, said, "And this being Hollywood, they decided to steal the bones of a dead movie star?"

She drew her head back in a bad imitation of surprise. "Wow, you're quick. How did you guess? My ex-boyfriend, he said they told him the mass would be more powerful if the bones of somebody famous was used."

"This ex of yours, what's his name?"

The girl backed against her chair, her face stiffening as though she might refuse to answer, but something that looked like spite flashed in her eyes and she said, "Sean Casey. He's from Logansport."

"Sean have a history of problems with the law?"

"Just shoplifting, marijuana possession. Nothing major. He wants to be an actor, you know? James Dean is his idol. And James Dean was no saint."

Frank dropped his feet from the corner of the desk and leaned as far across the surface as his ample stomach allowed. "He idolized James Dean? Is that why he dug up his grave last week? He wanted a souvenir, some talisman for luck?"

Theresa may have been a talented young actress but she had entered the room prepared to play an entirely different scene, and so the sudden change in performance required iced her. She stared at

Frank as though unable to believe he knew what he knew and uttered a single profanity to express the trouble she found herself in. The look she turned on me, seconds later, so accused me of betrayal I could have mistaken it for hatred.

"He was caught by a security camera with a key piece of evidence later found at the scene," I said. She wasn't my responsibility but I didn't want her to remain ignorant of the trouble she faced.

The girl crossed her right leg over her left and both her arms across her chest as she thought about what that meant. Her look turned defiant and she asked, "What evidence?"

"A thirty-two-ounce soft-drink cup from McDonald's."

"You're kidding."

"A store in Kokomo caught him on surveillance tape."

"Big deal. Lot's of people buy Cokes at McDonald's." Her voice had both hope and scorn in it. She thought she might be able to bluff her way through this.

Frank coughed into his fist to stifle a laugh and said, "Sure, but not many people leave their fingerprints on a McDonald's cup found at the bottom of James Dean's grave."

She stared at the wall.

"Did you drink from the same cup?" I asked.

She shook her head. "I don't eat junk food. Half the girls in my school are twenty pounds overweight because of that stuff."

"Maybe you'll get lucky, then, skate on all charges," Frank said. "Even if stealing the bones was your idea."

"It wasn't my idea. I wasn't even there." The girl darted quick, arrowlike glances at me, as though trying to read my mind. Beneath her affected calm grated the harder edge of anxiety. "The security camera, did it film anybody besides Sean?"

"You mean, were you on camera?"

She nodded.

"Yes," I said.

"All that means is we went out, you know, earlier."

"On the same night he robbed James Dean's grave? You know the law is not going to let this drop. Sean stole an important part of the town's legacy."

"Fairmount?" The girl pursed her lips and blew a scornful stream of air. "The town could give fuck-all about James Dean. He's money to them, that's all. They didn't even like him when he was alive but they all love him now that he's dead, or at least love the money he brings to town."

"What did Sean do with the bones?" Frank asked.

"Threw them in the river."

"Why would he do that?"

"Felt like it, I guess."

"What river?"

"The Wabash. Or maybe it was the Eel. Both of 'em run through the center of Logansport."

"So he throws the bones into the river and less than two weeks later he gets a tip about a planned grave robbery at Hollywood Forever Cemetery. Just a coincidence, right?"

She shrugged as though credibility was the least of her concerns.

"Did they cheat him? Is that why he double-crossed them?"

"He didn't steal any bones," she said, her face bloodred.

"You told me he threw them in the river," Frank said.

"I was just trying to get you off my back."

"You were lying then but you're telling the truth now?"

"Why are you protecting him?" I asked. "Were you with him that night in Fairmount? Did you help him break into Dean's coffin?"

The girl abruptly stood, glanced sullenly around the bullpen, asked, "Is there a bathroom around here?"

Frank pointed to a hallway breaching the far wall, near the stairway. "At the end of the hallway to the right. It's unlocked."

Theresa tilted her chin toward the ceiling and walked away with the studied composure of a fashion model strutting the catwalk. She might have been a liar and a thief but I appreciated her sense of the theatrical.

"She's lying," I said.

"Of course she's lying. That isn't the problem." Frank opened the right desk drawer and waved the sheaf of twenties off the table. "The devil knows I'm not a stickler for truth. The problem is, her lies are too boring to print. Kids playing at Satanism? That story is so trite it wouldn't play in a box buried near the classifieds."

"Maybe she'll invent a better story for you in the bathroom," I said. "Why don't you try to write the truth for a change?"

"If you believe in truth, justice, and the American way you

shouldn't be in this business," Frank answered. "I've interviewed thousands of people and after a while you develop an eye for things. This girl isn't going to tell us the truth. Not now. I'm happy to settle for something I can print."

I thought about the girl's facility for lying and about how she'd walked out of our meeting. Had she needed to answer the call of nature or regain her composure or something else entirely? "I think you'll have to settle for what you just heard."

"Why's that?"

"Because I think she's just done a runner," I said.

SEVENTEEN

ONCE CLEAR of the *Scandal Times* security door I could see the girl trudging resolutely a half mile distant down the boulevard. Tailing someone on foot in the San Fernando Valley is like trying to sneak up on somebody in the middle of a salt flat. As long as they don't turn around you can get away with it, but if they glance over their shoulder you have little alternative except to stick your head in the ground and hope they don't notice the only other thing visible on foot is someone pretending to be an ostrich. I jogged to my car, curious whether she'd run back to the beach to beg more spare change or turn to someone else, to the boyfriend she claimed had abandoned her or perhaps the people she supposedly betrayed. She seemed desperate enough to do something stupid, and though I didn't feel responsible for her, I didn't want to see her thumb a ride with some stranger willing to trade sex for bus fare. But then, I didn't know whether she was truly desperate or just calculating. Her boyfriend hadn't pitched James Dean's bones into the river. He'd sold them to somebody. She might hit up that somebody for money. She might be smart enough to beg or stupid enough to make it sound like blackmail. Liars lie about one thing and tell the truth about the other, Ben had said, and you never know which is which. They also tend to lead short lives, if my sister and husband were any example. I called Frank as I rolled out of the lot and turned left onto Laurel Canyon asked, "Who's Bernard Schwartz?"

"Tony Curtis," he answered, as though every idiot knew.

Then I remembered. Natalie Wood had come from a Russian family in San Francisco. Her name had been Natasha Gurdin. Some director had Anglicized her name. "Natalie Wood costarred with James Dean in *Rebel Without a Cause*. Do I remember right?"

"I was wondering if you caught the reference," he said. "You got the girl in your sights yet?"

"She's on foot a couple hundred yards ahead of me. I think I'll let her run, see where she goes."

"If she contacts the Raelians be sure to let me know."

I cut the connection on his laugh and slid the Cadillac to the curb. Ahead, the girl stopped to consult a bus schedule posted near the traffic light. I glanced at the dashboard clock at the same moment she raised her wrist to check her watch—a few minutes before ten PM. She gazed up the boulevard, then paced behind the bench until at ten past ten a yellow and white RTD bus opened its doors. The girl descended from the bus at the Canyon Plaza shopping center five miles later. She strode between the parked cars in the lot with her chin tilted up and forward as though she fixed a course just a bit higher than the rest of us, turning her head neither left nor right while heading straight for a row of pay phones stationed beside a Blockbuster Video store. She clenched one arm tightly around her ribs and pressed the phone against her ear, rocking from side to side as though psyching herself up for the conversation. The call lasted less than five minutes.

The girl paced out the hour, deflecting the interests of a couple of boys and a curious security guard, and when a battered blue Toyota Tercel approached the curb she sprung into the passenger seat as though making a getaway. I wheeled out behind them, headlights dim until camouflaged by traffic, KXLU student-run radio piping from the Caddy's tin speakers. The Tercel caught the first southbound ramp onto the Hollywood Freeway and hugged the slow lane into Cahuenga Pass, the lights of hillside homes studding the cutout shapes of Mount Olympus and the Hollywood Hills. Past the crest the lights of Hollywood refracted against the smoke and exhaust to cast a glowing sheath above the rim of the city's buildings. The Tercel rode the freeway down to the Franklin off-ramp in Hollywood, followed Franklin east toward the hills of Los Feliz, turned onto first one and then another side street, and sputtered to the parking gates of a two-story apartment building dating from the 1960s. Gilt script running three feet high along the stucco facade spelled out THE PALMS, and accurately enough two of that species flanked the front walkway.

Parked cars lined both sides of the street bumper to bumper. I coasted to the red zone at the corner and cut the engine. The apartment buildings and private homes on the block huddled together like immigrants from different cultures and times, Queen Anne cottages butting against Beaux Arts duplexes that turned aghast windows on California stucco apartments. The brake lights flashed and the Tercel sloped down a short concrete ramp into a parking garage beneath the California stucco. I lifted the viewfinder to my eye, bringing into telephoto close-up the face of the driver ascending from behind the wheel. She wasn't more than nineteen or twenty, gamine-thin and dressed in a stylish grab bag of velvet, paisley, lace, and beads, her blond hair falling past her shoulders and the bangs curving to her jaw like a pair of scythes.

I clicked the shutter and panned the lens across the roof to frame Theresa nudging shut the passenger door, her eyes peering beyond the gates as though she searched for something, or someone. It's difficult to see into night shadow from a lit room. She couldn't see the Cadillac but her look unnerved me. She hadn't bothered to watch her back before. Her escort curved her hand forward in a curt wave. Theresa ducked out of the frame and hustled around the hood of the Toyota, following her escort to a door at the far wall. The door led to an interior courtyard visible through the glassed entrance. I followed their progress up steps ascending beside the deep end of the pool to a rear corner apartment. After they keyed themselves in I strolled up the front path and raised the telephoto lens again to read the number on the door: 2G. The name printed beside the buzzer to 2G read RYAN.

I leashed the Rott and walked him around the block, thinking about the look Theresa had given me that night, and decided I needed to put some distance between us. I made a phone call. When we returned to the Cadillac I tuned the radio to a talk show—some moron spouting political opinions just offensive enough to keep me alert—and waited.

The Rott sensed him first, sitting bolt upright on the passenger seat to give a bewildered bark no more than two seconds before long, bone-white fingers shot from the cuffs of a black leather jacket to settle onto the driver's-side windowsill. I fought the urge to auto-eject through the canvas roof, glanced casually at the ruby-encrusted gold ring circling the hand's thumb, said, "Hiya, Vulch. Thanks for coming."

"Anytime, Nin." The voice, a baritone, spoke softly. "You wanna ask the dog to move over so I can get in the car?"

The Rott whined and hopped into the backseat when I snapped my fingers. I sought Vulch's image in the rearview mirror as he circled the trunk and saw movement more than shape, as though what moved was less than half human and the rest vampire. We'd met shortly after my release from prison. He'd been a friend, mentor, and competitor to my husband, and a man of such shadowy ethics that I'd initially suspected him of being complicit in my husband's death. Some in the trade called him the king of the paparazzi, not that his long and lanky form and penchant for dressing entirely in black looked regal but because he was the best in the business, a man so good at what he did that he'd become a legend long before his goatee and swept-back hair had gone gray. Early in his career he'd been nicknamed the Vulture, Vulch for short, partly because he always seemed there for the kill, but also for his nose—a prodigious, beaklike appendage jutting below ever-present black Ray-Bans. Vulch slinked into the car and pulled a large black case onto his lap, shutting the door so gently I didn't hear the latch click. One by one he flipped the three latches that secured the case's hinged top.

"What's the target?" he asked.

"Why, I'm fine, thanks, considering. How are you?"

I caught a glimpse of his eyes over the side rim of his shades. They were as dark as the rest of him. He extended his hand sideways to shake mine without looking at me, intent on taking inventory of the case on his lap. "I heard about your sister. Your mother, too. My condolences."

"Who told you?" I asked.

He shrugged as a way to let me know it was none of my business, said, "A lot of people you know have a tendency to stop breathing all of a sudden so I'd rather not spend any more time here than necessary." His lips split over yellowed teeth, his version of a smile.

"Death happens to everybody, eventually," I said.

"Sure, but it happens with uncommon regularity around you." He set the case on the floor between the edge of the seat and the dash, the LCD monitor positioned to be read with a downward glance from the steering wheel. "This is a real antique—a digital tracking system. You remember how to use it?"

"Why antique?"

"The new stuff uses GPS and cellular technologies, kind of like a combination cell phone and global positioning device. But you need a laptop computer to use the GPS system. You have one?"

"Not yet."

"Didn't think so. Sometimes I don't think you understand how profoundly technology changed those five years they locked you away. No computer, you probably don't even have a digital camera."

"I hate those things."

Vulch wrinkled his nose, said, "I smell dinosaur." He gave me a quick refresher course on the instrumentation. The system operated on digital transmissions, relaying distance and direction data from a transmitter mounted on the target to the receiver in the case. It was simple enough to read while driving but from what I remembered it took experience to translate the data on-screen to the view out the windshield. Vulch was showing me how to select the transmission ID code when a black van rolled past the line of parked cars on the right and veered to block the driveway leading to the Palms' underground parking. A man dressed in khaki and black hopped onto the sidewalk from the front passenger door and hustled toward the entrance to the apartments. I couldn't get the telephoto lens up fast enough to get a good look at him before the van obstructed my view but in that brief glimpse he looked familiar.

"Is that your target?" Vulch asked.

"It is now," I said.

He observed the van, still as a predator waiting on prey, then turned his head to scan the block behind it. "The target can move at any moment, driver presumably keeping an eye on his side mirror, no windows in the back of the van but could be somebody looking out the passenger mirror, not to mention the possibility of someone watching from the apartments. Know how you're going to do it?" He spoke as though he'd figured it out.

I knew how I was going to try. He handed me the transmitter—a half pound of electronics encased on a magnetic pad—and wished me luck. I said, "You should have the number of a local hospital ready in case luck isn't enough."

Los Feliz is a hipster neighborhood, the kind of place where someone wearing a fez and bowling shirt can walk after midnight without drawing a second look, and so once I cleared the Cadillac I made no attempt to hide my presence on the street. I walked away from the rear of the van, parked to my left on the opposite side of the street. Even if the driver spotted me on the fringe of his side-view mirror he wouldn't consider me a threat. At the corner I crossed the street to the left and dropped behind the bumper of a Hyundai, the last car parked in a contiguous line that ended at the black van. The crawl space beneath most cars is less than a foot high and decreases toward the center of the chassis, but the undercarriage of the Hyundai was barely big enough for the cat that eyed me suspiciously from the left front tire. I bellied under the bumper, stretched my arms full forward, and slithered under the car. For once in my life, I was happy I never reached my girlhood ambition of filling out a C cup.

I couldn't identify the next car in line from my roadkill-eyed view but the ground clearance improved enough to allow me to turn my head. I stretched my hands palms down onto the pavement and pulled them one at a time toward my shoulders, simultaneously pushing with my toes, swimming along the pavement like some strange species of land fish. I kept my eye on the curb, watching the black-on-white house numbers float by, until the curb sloped to street level and I knew I'd reached the driveway to the Palms. Overhead, a tailpipe smoked below a black-enameled fender.

I pulled myself under.

The van offered greater ground clearance than the Hyundai, enough to allow me to turn my shoulders and hips. I rolled onto my back, the van trembling with the low-rev fire of pistons, and looked for a secure spot under the chassis to affix the transmitter. I touched the drive train and jerked my hand away, cursing myself for being so stupid. The drive had heated the metal enough to blister skin. I looked for a concealed surface, someplace secure from jarring. The unit wouldn't do much good scraped off the chassis at the first pothole or bump in the road. The click of a distant glass door echoed between the curb and asphalt, putting a clock on my decision. Footsteps shuffled toward the van—heels and two pairs of soft-soled shoes. A single male voice said, "Remember, no talking inside the van."

I swung my heels to the side and inched my shoulder blades across to the street-side wheel well. The transmitter broadcast its signal through a ten-inch flexible antenna. I extended it and palmed the back of the unit, magnetic pad facing the interior well behind the wheel. Footsteps scraped the curb. I turned my head to a pair of Timberland hiking boots, strapped leather clogs, and Theresa's scuffed brown lace-ups. The van gently rocked as the side door slid open. The clogs and lace-ups leapt out of view. I waited, the magnetic pad hovering above metal, until the van rocked again with the force of the side door ratcheting shut, and when the latch struck the frame I pasted the transmitter to the wheel well. The passenger door snapped open. I pulled my hand away. The van rocketed forward the instant before the door slammed shut. Exhaust sprayed my hair and face. I opened my eyes and saw what passes for stars in Los Angeles.

Vulch slipped out of the Cadillac and pointed to an antenna he'd mounted on the right rear fender. "You're hooked up, wired, and ready to go," he said. "Remember, the range is only two miles, so don't let him get too far in front of you." He'd started the car while I'd been under the van. The LED display flashed numbers in green to my right. I slapped the transmission into drive. Vulch gave me a little salute as I sped from the curb, two fingers to the right corner of his sunglasses. I think he meant to wish me luck. When I looked for him in my rearview mirror he was gone.

I took the first right and glanced at the numbers rolling on the display, six thousand and climbing as I approached the next major cross street. Six thousand what? Feet, I remembered. But how far was six thousand feet? Over a mile? The number of feet to target decreased to five thousand as I accelerated onto Franklin. A cop car turned onto the avenue from a cross street to drag my speed back under the limit and a moment later the traffic light ahead went crimson. The direction to target swung north while I idled behind the black and white and the numbers shot upward as though the van picked up speed. The light greened. The cops in front of me weren't in any hurry, sat behind the crosswalk ten seconds before noticing, hey, look, the light changed, then feathered the gas pedal to a speed five miles an hour below the limit. I watched the distance to target click higher and higher, like the ticker on a gas pump, and when the number seized up at just over ten thousand feet I knew the van had sped out of transmission range.

A sign flashed by on the right announcing a northbound on-ramp to the Hollywood Freeway. The cop car continued straight. I swung up the ramp and already exceeded the speed limit by the time I merged into the right-hand lane. The numbers remained frozen in place. If I'd guessed wrong, the odds of incidental contact decreased to needle-in-a-haystack proportions. I told the Rott to hold on and swerved to the fast lane. The dashboard clock read just past one in the morning. When the speedometer needle topped a hundred the display's numbers jolted back to life, the direction still north by northwest and distance dropping thirty feet a second. At one thousand feet I spotted the van's taillights in the second lane to the right. I pulled into the same lane. The van held at a steady sixty-five down the long slope of Cahuenga Pass into the flickering lights of the Valley, signaled a lane change, and rode the cloverleaf off-ramp to the warehouse district between Van Nuys and Burbank airports. The driver wasn't taking any chances at getting pulled over for a traffic violation, meticulously following every rule in the Department of Motor Vehicles handbook. When he turned off the boulevard and into a nest of warehouses I pulled to the curb. A pair of headlights showing on the street at that hour wouldn't look coincidental. The distance to target ascended slowly, no more than twenty feet per second, and the direction veered to the east. A moment later, the numbers held steady at less than two thousand feet. The van had parked.

I rolled forward, passed the van's position to the east, turned again and again to come at him from the opposite direction. I pulled to the side when the distance dropped to three hundred feet, put the tele-photo lens to my eye, and scanned the warehouse across the street. A chain-link fence topped by razor wire rimmed the perimeter. Twenty yards of blacktop stretched like a no-man's-land between the chain-link and the corrugated aluminum side of the warehouse, a sprawling one-story construction with a sloping tin roof. I panned the lens left, toward a spill of light. The corner of the warehouse hid the light's source. Probably a security lamp. Beneath the spill I spotted the front fender of the van, the light reflecting against glossy black paint like streetlight on tar.

I opened the Nikon's aperture wide and slowed the shutter speed. The car shook with the roar of a jet descending toward Burbank airport, the silver, fishlike belly of the plane floating directly overhead, wing lamps slicing through the liquid night. I waited and watched, calming the Rott—and myself—with long, forceful strokes to his back. I thought about what Vulch had said, that people who know me tend to fall a little short of their allotted three score and ten. He'd been joking but the joke had some truth to it, and for a few minutes I allowed myself to feel like a modern Typhoid Mary. But I'd barely known my husband, having hooked up with him in a Vegas marriage a few weeks before his death. I'd been entirely ignorant of the incendiary photos he'd been taking that led to his murder. I'd learned more about my husband after his death than before it. My mother had died, yes, but everybody's mother dies, one of the reasons life is essentially painful. And my sister's own greed had killed her. The nineteen grand she stole from my checking account hadn't been enough. She'd stolen a tip to a hot photo, hoping to make even more, and she'd been paid with a broken neck. Not my fault.

Had Theresa set me up for a grass blanket, thinking I'd steal into the cemetery to photograph the theft of Valentino? Not Theresa herself—she was only sixteen, after all, not Charles Manson—but someone else, someone older, perhaps the driver of the black van? If true, why had she been reduced to panhandling on the 3rd Street Promenade? Or had she been planted there, with the knowledge that I'd be certain to go looking for her? If she wanted to escape me—or been conscious of the fact that I'd be looking for her—she could have chosen some other spot to solicit money. But teenagers are not entirely conscious and so trying to figure out their behavior requires a balance of rational and irrational thinking. They tread between the rich fantasy world of children and the mundane realm of adulthood until the world kicks reality into their teeth often enough, kicks the dreaminess out of them.

I stepped out of the car to stretch a moment and use the curb behind the rear fender as an emergency toilet. Before I unzipped my pants a figure in black trotted out to the rolling chain-link gate and the van eased away from the warehouse, lights dimmed. I ducked below the fender and crawled toward the wheel, waiting for the sweep of headlights that would flush the Cadillac from the shadows, but the van instead sped in the opposite direction, toward the city. I slipped into the driver's seat, my profile low, careful not to shut the door behind me. The numbers on the distance meter rolled slowly higher as the van motored south, then accelerated when the direction veered to the east. I poked the telephoto lens above the steering wheel and focused on the gate, now closed, and the figure saunter-ing toward the warehouse. When the corner clipped him from view I started the engine and swung the Cadillac a hundred and eighty degrees, gripping the door to prevent it from winging open. I waited until the next block to slam it shut.

I caught sight of the van again as it turned left at a traffic signal to ramp onto Hollywood Freeway south. The green arrow morphed to amber as I approached. I gunned the engine and slid across on red, no more than half a mile behind the van. If someone wanted to push false information it would have made more sense to have Theresa call my cell phone or landline again. But then, maybe that would look too obvious. They knew I'd be looking for her after my sister's murder and they knew where I'd look. But who were they? Not teenaged Satanists seeking cheap thrills in kissing the devil. The driver had moved like a man in his late twenties to early thirties. The van looked no more than a year or two old. Not many teens can afford payments on a twenty-five-thousand-dollar panel van, not to mention rental on a warehouse in North Hollywood. Maybe they recruited teens like Theresa to work for them, runaways or disaf-fected youths looking for a paid adventure robbing graves. That still didn't tell me who they were. Older Satanists, I supposed, interested in holding black masses with the bones of celebrities or some such nonsense. Whoever they were, they killed people, and I had to be aware that young and seemingly innocent Theresa might be bait for a trap.

The van swung east at the interchange with the Ventura Freeway, then signaled its intent to take the Barham exit south. The dashboard clock ticked three AM, and with few other cars driving surface streets at that hour I let the van play out well ahead of me, past the broad, blocky buildings of Warner Bros. Studios and over the vestigial, concrete-coffined remains of the Los Angeles River. I cut my lights as

I crossed Forest Lawn Drive and sped to close the distance, afraid of losing the van in the labyrinth of streets snaking the hillside on both sides of the boulevard. Then the distance began to close a little too fast, the van slowing to turn left onto a canyon road shrouded in trees.

I flicked on my lights, afraid of running off the road as I turned into the shadows, headlamps flashing over a street sign that read LAKE HOLLYWOOD DRIVE.

EIGHTEEN

MOST WHO frequently drive the streets of Los Angeles carry a Thomas Brothers map on the passenger seat, and those who spend more time behind the wheel than in their bed—including journalists and their hyena cousins, the paparazzi—carry one in their head. I didn't need to flip the pages of the map to know where I was; the chaparral-brushed slopes of Cahuenga Peak and Mt. Lee loomed overhead, fifteen hundred feet of undeveloped desert mountain rising from the urban landscape, two of the Santa Monica Mountains that ripple through the center of the city like a spine. On those rare days of rain, water trickles down the southern slopes toward Lake Hollywood, a fenced reservoir that supplies drinking water to the city. Over the saddle-shaped crest the immaculately trimmed grass of Forest Lawn cemetery rolls up the northern flanks, bordered by a chain-link fence to keep out coyotes and other creatures wishing to dig up one or more of the tens of thousands buried in its soil.

The distance to target held constant at two thousand feet as I wheeled the Cadillac up the ridge, the road fringed with oak, eucalyptus, and oleander. The van's direction veered north and the distance numbers plummeted. I knew by the change that the van had turned and stopped. I switched off my lights and slowed to a jogger's pace, windows rolled down to listen to the low thrum of the city in the distance and the crackle of tires over leaves until the unmistakable clunk of a vehicle door shutting sounded from the darkness of a side street. I pulled to the side of the road at Wonder View Drive and signaled the

Rott to stay quiet. I kept a pry bar in the trunk, the closest thing to a weapon I could carry and not violate parole. I went to get it.

Below Wonder View Drive the land canted to the blue-black waters of Lake Hollywood, the city lights spreading beyond like a field of electric flowers. My husband had been murdered there, his body dumped hurriedly into the lake's shallows. I shut the trunk softly and slung the pry bar through a belt loop. A single row of houses perched on the hill to the left of the drive, picture windows dark as sunglasses. I walked the center of the road, footsteps muffled by asphalt, and scanned the darkness ahead. I heard the van before I saw it, the rolling *thwack* of a side door pausing my footsteps at the inside edge of a left-hand bend. Wonder View Drive clung briefly to the mountainside, curling to a dead end at a padlocked gate barricading a Department of Water and Power access road. The van had muscled over the curb to park near the gate, wheels on the steering side dug into the hillside. I counted six heads hustling single file around the barricade toward a dirt road.

I backtracked from the curve and surveyed the hillside, the soft-tipped brush outlined against the darker earth. Someone would remain with the van. I couldn't follow through the gate without passing directly before the windshield. Up the hill two water tanks, painted white, glowed blue in the moonlight. The terrain offered no visible paths but patches of hardpan showed beneath gaps in the brush. I slung the Nikon across my chest and climbed. Sparse rains and constant sun had packed the ground and the footing was simultaneously hard and slick, like gravel spread over concrete. Clear of the water tanks, I circled downslope onto the dirt road, the mountain screening the van from view. A trail branched away from the road to scratch a thin line east through the brush. At the next rise silhouettes bobbed against the night sky and vanished over the ridge.

I cut across the road and onto the trail, chaparral scratching at the legs of my jeans. At every rise I spotted shapes moving along the trail ahead. Two of the figures carried something polelike between them. It took no great leap of deduction to guess where they headed. If celebrity bones were worth their weight in gold, then a little more than a mile around the skirts of Cahuenga Peak lay the mother lode: Clark Gable and Carole Lombard, Walt Disney, W. C. Fields, and

Humphrey Bogart—most of the stars of the post-silent-film era had been buried in Forest Lawn cemetery. The group's target could be one or more of several dozen graves. I didn't intend to stop them. The theft of bones didn't spark my personal moral outrage. I intended to follow them to the site, call the police, and photograph the bust. The carnival display of police lights and fleeing grave robbers would be dramatic enough to sell not only to *Scandal Times* but to the legit press around the world.

The bump and jostle of steps along the hill reminded me of unfinished business I'd tried to conduct behind the Cadillac earlier that night. An outcrop of rock marked the apex of the ridge. I waited until I hiked around it before squatting in the brush. After I finished I heard feet scrabbling for purchase on a patch of loose pebbles over rock. I'd heard sounds before, coming from the group packing through the brush ahead, but this time the footsteps came from the slope behind me. I zipped hurriedly and turned my head in the direction of the footsteps, listening. I counted two people coming up fast, about fifty yards distant. I'd dressed entirely in black and the van lay a half mile from the trailhead. If someone had been watching the hill from the van, they had the eyes of eagles. I slipped the crowbar from its belt loop and peeled the camera strap from my neck. The outcrop jutted a good ten feet from the ground on the downhill side. I crept silently along the wall of rock, feathering my heel to the dirt and softly rolling the foot forward, a kicked rock or cracked twig as potentially fatal as a misstep to a tightrope walker. At the edge of the rock I paused, the crowbar in my downhill hand, the camera on its strap in the other.

While I waited I thought about my sister. Those who followed me had likely been her murderers. What right did they have to decide it was her time to die? They could have taken her camera, tied and gagged her, and left her behind, uncomfortable but alive. They didn't have to break her neck. Maybe I was being naïve, but had she been allowed to live she might have straightened out her life and achieved some sort of grace. Not all lives that go bad have to end badly. My own life had experienced its dark moments but I had some hopes for the future, foremost that I would die a better person. They cut my sister's life at its darkest point and she died a liar and a thief. They damned her, and that fueled my rage.

Tightly controlled rage has always been my best friend in moments of physical crisis and I called on it then, in the name of my sister. Each approaching footstep sounded so crisp I could sense the heavy-heeled impact of boot onto the packed earth, the roll of the boot over crackling grains of sand and gravel, the flex of the toe and soft brush of air as the boot pushed away, each second fragmenting into split seconds that passed as slowly as the seconds themselves. When the six-foot Cyclops strode past my position he seemed to be moving in slow motion.

I let him pass. Had I not lain in wait, prepared to jump whomever and whatever moved past the edge of the rock, the sight of the Cyclops might have terrified the wits out of me. His one eye, a long, telephoto-like lens, protruded from a goggle mount strapped to his forehead, blinding him to both sides, and he tilted his head to the earth then back to the horizon line with each step as though he lacked the depth of vision to track both in the same glance.

The second creature to stride past wore the face of a man, and there was nothing wrong with his peripheral vision. His black-sleeved arms jerked toward his face the moment his head swiveled to my side of the rock. My own arm was already moving by then, the crowbar backhanding the short distance between my shoulder and his chin. He got his left arm high enough to deflect the bar from his teeth but not high enough to clear his head. The bent end of the bar clipped his skull just above the eyebrow and his head jerked sharply away from the blow, feet shooting out from under him as though he'd been clotheslined.

The Cyclops whirled at his partner's stunted cry, one hand deftly flipping the telescopic goggle from his face and the other scrabbling for the zippered gap in his black windbreaker. I swung the camera on its strap like a knight's mace, recognizing the Cyclops's features the moment before the camera body cracked against the side of his head. The blow wrong-footed him and he went down sideways, boots flailing for purchase on the gravel-slick ground before he pitched head-first down the hill. I didn't think I'd done enough damage to keep him down, not like the first one, who stared glass-eyed at the sky. I hadn't liked the way the hand of the Cyclops had snaked toward the gap in his jacket and I didn't think I could leap down the hillside fast enough to deliver a second blow before he pulled and fired what he packed beneath his shoulder.

I bolted while he still skidded down the hillside. I looked back once over my shoulder as I crested the ridge. He stood, one foot higher on the slope than the other, Cyclops eye centered over his face, and pointed something one-handed at my fleeing back.

Then I was over the ridge and gone.

NINETEEN

I MADE an anonymous call to the cops from a box on Barham, notifying the 911 operator that the inhabitants of a black van parked on Wonder View Drive intended to break into Forest Lawn cemetery. The news didn't give the operator heart palpitations. When she asked my name I hung up. I still hoped to photograph the bust, even if the cops would have trouble proving anything more serious than intent to trespass. But the man I recognized beneath the Cyclops eye as Chad Stonewell's bodyguard hustled his crew back into the van faster than I expected, the numbers on the digital tracking unit already on the move by the time I returned to the Cadillac. Once the van began to move, the chance to photograph the bust vanished. By the time it turned right on Barham, speeding toward the freeway, it was just another vehicle on the road. A traffic bust would prove nothing. I didn't bother calling the police again.

The van followed in reverse the same route that had taken it to the fringes of Forest Lawn cemetery. Stonewell's bodyguard had to suspect they were being followed. I wondered which of us played the hunter and which the prey. The Cyclops had been wearing night-vision equipment and trailed the first group by a half mile. The distance between groups might have been part of the original plan, the two men providing backup for the main group. Or the driver could have spotted me from below while I climbed the hill-side and spontaneously decided to take me out from behind. Another possible scenario worried me far more: they might have known I followed them from the start. The trip to Wonder View Drive could have been a ruse designed to trap me, a ruse that failed because of my sex. They lost sight of me when I squatted behind the outcrop of rock. Had I unzipped and let it fly like a man they could have shot me where I stood.

The van ramped off the freeway two exits earlier than expected and sped into the web of residential streets between commercial boulevards. Perhaps they dropped someone off or kept a safe house in the area. I didn't know the neighborhood and couldn't risk following the van down a dead-end street. I coasted to the curb. The numbers switched back and forth on the display, the van heading east, then north, then west, then south, only to reverse course and inscribe the same path in reverse. He was circling the block, I realized, then doubling back to catch anyone trying to follow. The flow of numbers stilled for minutes, as though the van had reached its destination. I suspected they instead lay in wait, trying to flush out their pursuer. The numbers flickered to life again. The van moved due north toward the warehouse, the driver no longer worried, seemingly, about someone on his tail.

The first band of cerulean blue fringed the sky to the east; I'd pulled enough all-nighters to know sunrise was a little more than an hour distant. I needed to get near enough to frame the loading gates through the Nikon's telephoto lens. One of the old, box-shaped Volvo sedans had parked wheel to wheel against the curb down the street. I made for it, back hugging a chain-link fence until a quick sprint and dive dropped me to the pavement behind the rear fender. The van had backed halfway through a roll-up door that yawned open to a dim spill of amber light. Cardboard boxes stacked on wooden pallets blocked a clear view of the warehouse beyond the entrance. The telephoto lens wobbled in my supporting hand as I spun the focus ring, trying to sharpen the image. Nikons are rugged cameras but I doubted that wielding one as a mace was among the manufacturer-approved uses.

I caught the face of the gamine from the Tercel coming around the corner of stacked pallets, the first of six figures, each dressed in black and none looking as though they'd yet bid farewell to their teens. The gamine was shadowed by a boy her approximate age in a black watch cap, and each of the three faces that followed regressed in age until the final figure, that of a strangely familiar-looking Goth girl in black hair and a silver nose ring, who couldn't have been more than fourteen. I clicked the shutter, knowing that even with high-speed black-and-white film the image would be underexposed, the faces shadowed by the light spilling from the warehouse behind.

The group clustered for a moment outside the warehouse, then moved toward the rolling chain-link gate. I'd expected to see Theresa among the faces. I tried to think it through as I watched the teens step past the gate toward the Volvo. If she was nothing more than a confused kid, no more or less naïve than normal for her age, she might have told them about her visit to *Scandal Times*. But the teens continued moving up the street, toward the Volvo, leaving me no time to think about anything except where to run or how to hide.

A flash of movement caught my attention and though what I saw compelled me to keep my eye to the lens my supporting leg began to tremble in anticipation of flight or fight. I yielded to fear—a some-times sensible thing—and ducked behind the trunk. If I ran they might not catch me but they'd know I'd followed from Wonder View Drive. I'd have to settle not only for the shots I'd taken but for the little I understood about what was happening. I'd seen Theresa in that flash of movement, walking toward the side of the van, and though my glance through the lens had been brief and the scene dimly lit, I thought I'd seen something wrapped around her mouth, maybe a gag, and she held her hands clasped in front of her waist as though bound.

Feet scuffed along the pavement some yards in front of the car. Voices, low and dispirited, sounded startlingly near. I bellied down to the asphalt and crawled beneath the Volvo, heart pounding in my ears. To run or fight was much easier than waiting in a space the size of a coffin, unable to defend myself if caught.

"What do you wanna eat?" a boy asked.

"I dunno. What do you wanna eat?"

"I dunno."

"How about Mexican?"

"We had Mexican last night."

The driver's door creaked open and the weight of the driver tilted the car streetside. The car was too old to have four-door automatic locking and from beneath the chassis I noticed the shift in weight as

the driver leaned across the passenger seat to unlock the opposite
side.

"They're going to hurt her, aren't they?" a girl asked.

"Not seriously," another boy said.

A distant motor caught—the van's—and revved a moment before
tires chirped and the sound of the vehicle raced forward. The Volvo's
passenger door clicked open, followed by the two rear doors. The car
settled noticeably with the front passenger, then sagged as the first
two piled into the rear. I glanced over my shoulder at the back
springs, stained rust-orange and sagging with weight. Not a hopeful
sign.

The last two passengers squeezed into the backseat of the Volvo
and the doors slammed shut in stereo. Something pressed heavily
into my back as the motor ignited and sputtered, shaking my body
like the hand of a giant. I craned my neck off the ground and peered
out the corner of my eye; the Volvo had settled on top of my back,
the drive train pressing between my shoulder blades. I exhaled the air
from my lungs and pushed palms against the chassis as the transmission shifted to first. The car ripped at my hands and roared away,
leaving me flattened like a lizard stunned by the windblast of a passing truck. I felt at my lip and watched my finger come away sheened
in blood. I'd been so scared I'd nearly bitten off my lip.

The speed of the van was spinning the meter to a blur when I
jerked open the door to the Cadillac. The numbers continued to gain
velocity as I jetted from the curb. Direction to target read north by
northwest—the Hollywood Freeway. I thought about calling the
cops and realized that not only didn't I have the van's license number, I wasn't sure of what I'd seen or what it meant. Theresa hadn't
been initially kidnapped; she'd gone to them willingly. If I called the
police they'd laugh. The four AM streets were deserted. I floored it.
The Rott jittered back and forth on his forepaws and barked like a
speed junkie thrilling on sheer velocity.

Freeway merged into freeway after freeway, the van heading con-
sistently north against a thickening stream of headlights; the morning commute begins early in Los Angeles, drivers eager to get from
outlying areas into the city center before seven AM gridlock. A stone
began to grow in my heart when the van veered onto the Antelope
Valley Freeway, a route that crosses a pass in the San Gabriel

Mountains and shoots down into the scorched flatland of the Mojave Desert. I could think of no good reason for the van to be transporting Theresa out of the city and one very bad one. The Mojave Desert extends from the San Gabriel Mountains through the southern tip of Nevada, twenty-five thousand square miles of arid wilderness easily accessible to every killer in Southern California and Las Vegas. Nobody knows how many murder victims have been buried in its sand or dumped amid the creosote and blackbush, but every few weeks one hiker or another stumbles over a set of bones scattered by rodents and picked clean by ants.

I lifted the crowbar onto my lap and rubbed obsessively at the metal. The bar wasn't perfectly round; my fingers traced eight ridges, the octagonal shape improving the grip. The van descended from the freeway at Elizabeth Lake Road. I followed it east, toward the network of arroyos flaring from the eastern slopes of the San Gabriels. In the rearview mirror the sun speared bloodred above the distant ridge. The van kicked up a dust devil's plume when it turned off the pavement and onto a dirt road that slashed across the desert floor. I hung back, aware that dust kicked from the tires would rise above the Cadillac like a neon cloud, and rolled down the window to study the terrain. Creosote brush, sage, and the tortured, spiked figures of cholla cacti jutted from a desert floor that sloped gradually toward the foothills. The land provided some cover but little of it more than waist-high. The crowbar warmed to my grip like an old friend.

The van pulled to the side a little more than a mile ahead, the dust cloud thinning and drifting away like a beige stain in the bluing sky. I ordered the Rott to the floor. He obeyed reluctantly. I pulled the lever securing the ragtop and powered it back into the compartment behind the rear seat. Across the sage two bulky figures walked a silhouette of a girl deeper into the desert, away from the van, toward a spot shielded from the road, where what they did to her would not be seen or heard and where what remained of her when they were done would not be discovered unless by creatures that, like them, were expert at digging up bones. I eased the Cadillac forward, careful of the dust, and when the distance to target showed at half a mile I floored it.

At the sound of the Cadillac the one on the right turned a look over his shoulder and the one on the left stuck what looked at that distance like a hand against the girl's ribs. They didn't know my car by sight. I could have been a hiker or hunter, no more dangerous than a cloud of dust on the horizon and gone in another minute. I jerked the wheel. The Cadillac ramped off the road doing sixty miles per hour, all four wheels momentarily airborne before nosing into a flat patch of salt brush. Nobody mistook my intentions after that. The Cadillac bucked violently on landing, front bumper gouging into the brush and the back scraping the dirt as the chassis canted forward and back. I fought to keep the wheels straight and shot more gas to the engine, creosote brush and sage scraping the fenders, rocks kicked by the tires clanging against the undercarriage. The guy on the right kneeled and pointed at the grille. I hit the horn to startle his aim and used the Cadillac's laurel-wreath hood insignia like a gun sight, intending to run him down. I heard the bullet pop a split second before the firing crack of the gun. No reason for caution. I floored it through a prickly pear cactus tall as a man, spine, fiber, and needles spraying on impact.

It takes considerable courage—or stupidity—to stand and fight a four-thousand-pound hunk of charging metal with the momentum to kill you even if you shoot out the driver. The sight of the prickly pear disintegrating must have demonstrated what the same grille would do to a man, because the kneeling figure broke and ran. I twitched the wheel a couple of degrees, intending to shave the remaining gunman from Theresa's side. As the distance closed I noticed a white bandage butterflied across his forehead—he was the one I'd whacked with the crowbar. That made it a grudge match. He pointed the gun at the girl as though that might stop me and when it didn't he turned and fired at the Cadillac, spidering the windshield on the passenger side. Theresa bolted away, hands bound before her. Smart girl. I yanked the wheel. The Cadillac spun broadside and the rear fender swatted the gunman like the tail of a killer whale. He screamed as he went airborne. He should have been happy I wasn't driving a 1959 Caddy, the one with knifelike tailfins.

I turned the wheel in the opposite direction of the skid, dirt pluming as the tires scraped against the desert floor. The car hit a clump of sage and nearly rolled, the two driver's-side wheels coming clear off the ground before bouncing down again. Theresa ran blindly twenty yards distant. Two bullets pinged against the driver's door split seconds before the shots cracked out. I stomped the accelerator and honked the horn. Theresa glanced over her shoulder as she ran, stumbled, and fell. I braked where she fell. She pulled herself over the doorsill. I grabbed a fistful of shirt above her breasts and hauled her face-first onto the passenger seat, eye to eye with the cowering Rott. Her feet jutted almost straight into the air above the headrest as I jetted away, my forearm pressed to her back to pin her down. The Cadillac, solid as a tank, bounced and lurched onto the dirt road. Theresa twisted her legs into the car and buried her head against my side, her body shaking with the force of wild and inconsolable sobbing.

TWENTY

THE WEAKEST point on any tank is its tread; a couple of miles from Elizabeth Lake Road the Cadillac sagged and the steering wheel jerked to the right, the front passenger tire slapping the wheel well at each revolution. I drove on the rim until a cutout appeared on the left, screened by a low ridge and the splayed trunks of a cat-claw tree. I noticed the bullet strikes in the driver's-side door when I vaulted out of the car, two puckered holes toward the front fender that looked like the back end of Siamese twins. The Rott crawled from under Theresa's legs and hopped out to join me at the trunk. I pulled out a bowl and filled it with water, then lifted free the spare tire and jack. The Rott lapped down the water and looked up at me, his expression expectant. I poured another dollop of water into his bowl and his glance turned reproachful.

"Sorry, buddy," I said. "You'll have to wait for breakfast."

He woofed once in protest, then quieted when I gave his head a rub. I warned him to be careful of the cacti because I didn't want to spend half the day pulling needles out of his hide, and when he trotted off to patrol the area I rolled the spare tire to the front. Theresa lay curled in a fetal ball on the seat, hands cradling her face. I touched her arm and dangled the water bottle. "You'll have to pull yourself together and tell me what's going on." I pointed to the digital display beneath the dash. "In the meantime, warn me if you see the numbers start to move."

I knelt to inspect the tire. The stunts I'd pulled while rescuing the girl had inflicted a mortal wound on the rubber, cracking the side-wall until a final bump in the road split and shredded it. I slid the scissors jack under the chassis and cranked until the wheel rose high enough off the ground to accept the spare, then went to work loosening the lug nuts. Theresa's head popped above the dash and she took a long, greedy drink of water.

"They were going to kill me," she said.

I grunted while muscling a lug nut and let that be my answer.

"I didn't think they'd do that. I thought they were cool."

"What did you tell them?"

"That my ex-boyfriend ratted them out to the tabloids."

"You thought they'd be happy to hear that?"

"Grateful, maybe. I mean, it wasn't my fault. I was just with him, you know? It's not like the whole thing was my idea. I was his victim just as much as they were."

I twisted off the last lug nut and pulled the rim free of the axle. "Did you ask them for money?"

"Of course not." She shook her head as though that would have been a stupid thing to do.

"Then why did you call them?"

I lifted the spare onto the spindle, then fingered all five lug nuts onto their bolts. Theresa stared at the top of the water bottle as though it might be a well full of secrets.

"You thought they'd let you join the gang," I guessed.

"Well, why not? I already knew about them." She cast a spiteful glance over the door frame. "You weren't going to give me any money, at least not enough to make a difference."

"Frank wasn't willing to pay for lies," I said. "If you wanted bus fare, you should have told the truth."

The girl's bangs flew away in a burst of air from her lips. "If I told you the truth, they would have tried to kill me."

I tightened the first lug nut, giving her time to consider how dumb that sounded. "Maybe you should tell me who *they* are," I said.

"The people who decide who's going to be movie stars."

"You mean directors, producers, casting agents?"

Theresa leaned out the window and watched me work. "I'm sure some of them belong."

"Belong? To what?"

"The secret society."

"What secret society?"

"The one that decides who's gonna be a star."

It was like talking to a child lost in make-believe.

"I never heard of a secret society like that," I said.

"If you heard about it, it wouldn't be secret, would it?" She arched her eyebrows and cocked her head. Her eyes were green, I noticed. She'd lost her lavender shades in the night. "You're exactly the kind of person they don't want to know about this. I mean, you're paparazzi, right? Do you think they want to see this blasted all over the tabloids? The minute this goes public the whole scheme might fall apart. That's why I didn't want to tell you anything. I was afraid how they'd react."

I so intently listened to the girl, trying to make sense of what she was telling me, that I didn't hear the vehicle moving at speed from behind the ridge, tires spitting gravel, until it was too late to do anything except watch it roar by our position, a blur of black paint and thick cloud of trailing dust. I waited for the red flash of brake lights that would signal they'd spotted us, but the dust settled over the hood of the Cadillac and still the van sped on until the road dipped from view. I leapt to my feet and leaned over the doorsill beside the girl, about to chastise her for not keeping an eye on the display, until I saw that the numbers representing distance and direction stood still as a photograph.

They'd found the transmitter.

Theresa spotted it first, hidden in the brush by the side of the road where the van had parked. It must have taken great patience not to smash the transmitter on the nearest rock when the driver finally found the thing pinned behind his rear wheel. I was glad for his restraint—I didn't have the money to replace it. The girl picked it out of the brush and trotted back to the car. I shut off the display and tossed the transmitter onto the dash. "Tell me about the other kids in the gang," I said.

"I'm hungry." She hugged her arms around her stomach. "We gonna eat soon?"

"Soon as you tell me something makes the trip out here worth my while." I keyed off the ignition and settled against the door frame. "I know you think I'm a sucker. After all, I just risked my car, my life, and my dog to save your skin. Maybe you think it's my responsibility to take care of you. It's not."

The girl stared straight ahead, eyes squinting against the brightening sun. I leaned within six inches of her face to make my point. "I'm a little cranky right now. I didn't sleep or eat last night, I got bullet holes in my car and a shredded tire, not to mention dust in every crack and cranny of my upholstery, and my dog is angry at me because I haven't fed him. If you don't tell me everything you know about these people and what they're doing I'll leave you out here in the middle of the desert."

"Don't get mad at me," she said, as though she wasn't to blame.

"Who else am I going to get mad at?"

She wrinkled her nose, baffled. "You don't think I'm grateful for what you did?"

"Teenagers are never grateful," I said. "It's a universal principle."

"Would you really leave me here?"

"I'd take your shoes with me, too."

The world looked like it was ending in her green eyes and when a single tear slid down her cheek I wanted to take her in my arms and stroke her head. Wanted to, but didn't.

"They're wannabe actors, think they've found the way to be famous," she said. "It's not fair. I was going to tell you anyway and now you think I'm talking because I'm afraid or something."

"I'm tired of being lied to. Just tell me the truth."

I stroked her cheek, once. She nodded.

"How old are they?" I asked.

"About my age, some older, some younger. The Goth, that's this girl looks a little like a vampire? She's the youngest. She's thirteen."

"And the one who picked you up at the mall?"

"Luce? She's eighteen, already been cast in three TV shows."

"When she picked you up, what did you tell her?"

"That Sean was the one betrayed them, not me."

"How did Sean betray them?"

"*Scandal Times* was his idea. He called the reporter, the guy we met last night, after we got to town. To tell him about what happened to James Dean's grave. But he couldn't get any money out of him, the cheap bastard. So when we got this other tip, the one about Stonewell? Sean contacted the other tabs but they said forget it, they weren't interested, until I contacted you."

"I wasn't interested either," I said.

"Sure you were." She dared a small, triumphant smile. "You paid."

"I'm a sucker," I said. "Why Stonewell?"

"It was just something he'd heard."

"Where?"

"From Luce. She was always really cool to us."

"Is she the one who bought the bones from you?"

"Eric did that."

"Who's Eric?"

She stared out the front windshield at the desert warming beneath the morning sun. "The asshole in the van. Not the one you ran over. That was Bobby. They're older than everybody else so they're like the gang leaders."

"What did they pay for the bones?"

"Not enough. That's why Sean was so mad. He said Sven had promised him five thousand but Eric only gave him five hundred. That's why he ratted them out."

"Who's Sven?"

"Sven, short for Svengali."

"Not his real name," I guessed.

"Nobody knows who he is in real life. He just, like, talks to people over the phone. He's the head of this society I was telling you about."

"The one that makes people stars," I said.

She heard the doubt in my voice.

"It really exists! Leonardo DiCaprio, Ryan Phillippe, Kirsten Dunst—they're all members. Winona Ryder was, too, but she messed up. She wanted to, like, break away from them or something and so they punished her by planting drugs in her purse and arranging for her to be arrested for shoplifting." Her eyes flashed in recounting what happened, convinced the story was perfectly true.

"This secret society, it have a name?"

"Of course it does, but you have to be initiated to know what it is, one of those names-that-should-not-be-spoken things, you know, like the Harry Potter books. I think I would have made a great Hermione, don't you?" She showed me her profile, nose tilted to the sky as though playing a smart, conceited little girl. "I mean, if I was a little younger and maybe English? Although Emma Watson—that's the girl who played her—did a really good job."

"This secret society, this name-that-cannot-be-spoken, you think maybe you could whisper it in my ear or write it down on a piece of paper for me?"

"You think I know the name? I never got initiated. They don't tell you the name until they let you in."

"Does your friend Luce know?"

"Oh yeah, Luce is like a priestess or something, I mean, she's not a star yet but they're already grooming her for the big time." The girl turned to me, her eyes flicking little glances here and there, as though she was about to tell secrets, exciting secrets. "This society, you see, they control who gets the breaks necessary for stardom. It's nearly impossible to make it beyond bit parts without their support. That's why so many super-talented actors get, like, nowhere. You go in for an audition, it's all rigged. I mean, you still gotta have talent, but between two talented people? The society member always gets the part. And that's why Eric thought he could get away with screwing Sean and me. Only he didn't know Sean wanted to make it as a stage actor and the society doesn't have so much pull in the theater. And me, I'm hot on Sean so I side with him instead of the society. Then what happens? He dumps me."

"The kids I saw last night, they're all members?"

"They're like the acolytes, you know what I mean? They aren't stars yet but Sven says they'll be stars in the future."

"Tell me about Sven. Did you talk to him?"

Theresa shook her head, responding less to my question than to a thought horrifying enough to pale her cheeks. "Bobby? The guy you ran over in the desert? Do you think you killed him?"

"No, but I don't think he'll walk straight for a while."

Tears welled in her eyes, seemingly from nowhere, and her hands flew to her face to catch a sudden sob. The lightning changes of her emotions amazed me.

"He tried to kill you," I said. "He deserves what happened to him. And if it makes you feel any better it wasn't your fault. I was the one who hit him."

She pulled her hands away from her anguished face, her green eyes rimmed red with grief. "It's not that!"

"Then, what?"

"Don't you see?" she cried. "Now I'll never get to be a movie star!"

TWENTY-ONE

I DROVE Theresa to a freeway Denny's in Palmdale, hoping that her emotional changeability was due in part to low blood sugar. The prospect of food slowly cheered her. By the time we claimed a table for two in the corner of the restaurant she had stopped sobbing and begun to hiccup. Hiccupping was considerably easier on my nerves than the howls and wails that had accompanied us on the road leading out of the desert. When I told her to go to the restroom to clean up a little, she stood and moved to the back of the restaurant like a child-zombie. I left messages at Frank's office and on his cell phone while she washed. He'd know how to find out who owned the warehouse in North Hollywood. He was good at that, checking records, making phone calls, tracking the paper trail.

Theresa looked livelier when she slid across the booth from me. "I'm sorry about your sister," she said. She'd scrubbed her face pink and splotches of water from the bath she'd taken in the sink stained her silk blouse.

I handed her a menu folded open to the breakfast page, said, "I don't hold you responsible for that." If she'd known those people were killers she wouldn't have volunteered for her own execution the night before.

"Can I get anything I want?"

"Keep it under ten bucks, please. I'm broke. I'm having the Grand Slam Breakfast." I poked my forefinger at an entry on her menu depicting a small mountain of pancakes, eggs, and fried meats. I have the eating habits of a python, gorging one day and digesting the next. "My sister was pretty much a mystery to me. She didn't do me any favors, that much is sure."

"She asked me so many questions I was sure she was tabloid."

"What kind of questions?"

"Who was in the gang, mostly. You know, names, hometowns, ages. She seemed real interested in the kids, like maybe she was going to write about these wild runaways robbing graves." She pointed to an even bigger pile of food on the menu. "The Grand Slam Slugger Breakfast gives you everything the Grand Slam does but you get hash browns, orange juice, and coffee extra. Can I have coffee?"

"I'm not your mother. Have what you want."

I shut the menu and glanced around for a waitress. A thin woman with the wrinkled face of a pack-a-day smoker and a name tag that read BEATRICE hustled over. She took our orders, said, "Glad you gals brought your appetites." I asked her to have the cooks mix three eggs with a pound of raw hamburger for the Rott, and after some back-and-forth about whether or not that would be possible she hustled away to place the order.

"I wish you were my mother," the girl said.

Had I been drinking coffee at that moment I might have sucked it down the wrong pipe and sprayed it against the window. "I'm not old enough to be your mother." Confronted by the disappointment in her eyes, I did the math. "Okay, technically I am old enough but I have enough trouble taking care of myself and my dog. The idea of motherhood makes me nervous. Maybe you could instead consider me more like your favorite aunt, the one that lets you do whatever you want as long as you don't hurt anybody. And what's wrong with your own mother?"

She shrugged, said, "Nothing."

"She loves you, I'm sure," I said.

"She doesn't have any time for me, except when she has something to criticize. It's like I'm never good enough for her. Not smart enough. Not talented enough. Not anything enough."

Theresa looked like she wanted to curl up in a ball and hide under the table. I wasn't so old that I'd forgotten what it had been like to be a teenager, my skin on fire with the pain of being, the self-conscious insecurities of learning who I was and more painfully who I wasn't. I said, "Did I tell you I went to prison?"

The revelation drew the girl out of her own problems in one stroke. She stared at me, mouth and eyes gaped in disbelief.

"Four years. It taught me a lot about time. I thought I'd never get out. But one day passed into another, and the next day into another one, and here I am . . ." I pointed to the walls and windows around us. "No bars."

"What did you do, I mean, why were you arrested?"

"Wrong place, wrong time, wrong people." I smiled at the waitress, who stopped by to deliver our coffee thermos. "I'm not trying to scare you, but it wasn't fun. You can't do anything in prison without a guard, inmate, or camera watching how you're doing it. The system tells you when to get up, when to go to sleep, what work to do, what to eat. Do something wrong and you got a guard standing on your neck and a visit with the staff psychologist."

"Sounds like school," she said.

"How old are you? Exactly?"

"Seventeen." She held my gaze for all of three seconds before her cheeks colored to flush out the lie. "Fifteen," she said.

"Three years left on your sentence, then. That may seem like forever to you now, but you haven't learned about time yet."

"You mean, it's like I'm in prison," she said.

"That's right. And just like prison you can run away, but you can't really escape. Even if they don't catch you they won't allow you to live your life because you haven't put in your time. They make you pay your dues. They always make you pay your dues. But the time passes, and if you're smart, when you turn eighteen, you'll be ready for your freedom."

"Eighteen?" She screeched the number as though it represented an age too ancient to understand. "You don't understand. Winona Ryder got her first serious acting role at fifteen. So did Reese Witherspoon. And Brittany Murphy? She was fourteen when she was cast in her first TV series. Eighteen is over-the-hill in this business. If I have to wait that long I might as well be dead."

The teardrops swelled again and I awaited the inevitable moment of opera when she burst into sobs, but her glance darted up and to the side and a moment later two heavily laden plates swung around my shoulder to land on the table before us. She momentarily forgot her failing career as a teenage movie star and dug into her plate of bacon, eggs, sausage, pancakes, and hash browns with the eager determination of someone whose meals had come far and few between the past weeks. We ate in a dedicated, almost holy silence until, about two-thirds of the way through, she started talking about Sven. She'd called Luce from the phone box at Canyon Plaza to confess she'd been duped by Sean and when Luce sympathized by saying Sean had duped everyone, she thought it would be safe to ask to join the society. Luce had been honest enough with her. It wasn't her decision to make, she'd said. But she'd pick her up, give her a place to stay, and ask around to see if it was possible. Sven called less than half an hour after they arrived at Luce's apartment. "I felt totally honored," she said around a mouthful of pancake. "I mean, do you like know how many people Sven talks to in person?"

"I thought you said he called over the phone."

"In person over the phone." She glanced to the ceiling in exasperation that I should be so dense. "Like nobody. I mean hardly anybody. Luce has talked to him, sure, and maybe the others in the group from last night, but he's really selective who he talks to. And he called to talk to me. Because he thought I had a special talent." A dreamy look glazed her eyes and she almost smiled. "That's what he said, a *special talent*. Can you believe that? He called me his lost little lamb, said he was happiest when someone who once was lost was found again."

"His voice, how would you describe it?"

"Soft but really strong, like honey and whiskey mixed together. It makes you a little high just listening to it."

"Could it have been Stonewell's voice?"

"You mean, like Stonewell playing a character?" She wagged her head back and forth. "No way. Stonewell isn't that good an actor and I've never seen him play smart so even a ten-year-old would believe it."

"Sven sounded like an educated man?"

"Not just educated. Cultured. Like he was from England or something, except without the accent. And totally persuasive. I've never met anyone so convincing in my life. I would have done anything for him. He said he had a special future all planned out for me, that I had a special talent so I deserved a special future."

She started to get that teary look again.

"Wake up, girl. The man just tried to have you killed. The special future he planned for you involved a shallow grave in the Mojave Desert."

"He said he forgave me. I believed him."

"Just because he lied to you doesn't mean you aren't what he said you are, that you don't have a special talent. All it means is that he lied to you. The two are different, understand?"

She nodded, her eyes puffy and her lips taut. Some lessons are hard to learn. When I first learned that men would call me special not because they believed it but to get something they wanted from me—usually sex—it broke my young heart. "You told him about me, about my interest in finding out who killed my sister?"

"I told him everything," she said. "Absolutely everything."

Though I'd learned a lot in prison it wasn't an experience I could recommend to an impressionable teenaged girl. As I drove Theresa to the bus station I thought about how she could avoid it. The authorities couldn't legally send her to prison, even if they managed to trump up a grand larceny charge from the theft of James Dean's bones, but juvenile hall would scar her no less than prison. The penal system changes people but for only a small percentage is that change a redemptive one. "You're going to be in trouble with the law," I told her. "No way to avoid that. How serious that trouble depends on you."

She squinted against the bright desert sun as she gathered her wind-whipped hair into a ponytail, asked, "What can I do to make it less serious?"

"How good are you at telling stories?"

She flashed a bright and spontaneous smile. "I love to tell stories."

"You have to get your story straight in your head and stick with it. I'm not a saint, saying you have to tell the whole truth and nothing but the truth so help you God, but the story you tell has to be ninety-nine percent truth. You can get away with one lie, maybe two, but no more. If you try to lie your way through this, they'll catch you for sure. And no way are they going to let you skate on everything, understand?"

The girl nodded and looped a rubber band around the ponytail, her expression almost comically serious.

"The police are not going to let you go without something in return. You'll have to give them Sean."

"They can have that lying bastard on a silver fucking platter."

"No swearing. Cops swear all the time but they hate to hear it from anyone else. You have to play it sweet and innocent. And there's one other thing you can do for yourself, other than get a good lawyer and tell a consistent story."

"What's that?"

"Cry like a baby and beg for mercy."

She smiled, said, "I'm good at crying."

Theresa proved it by breaking into tears again at the bus station when I handed her twenty bucks for food and a one-way ticket to Kokomo, Indiana, routed through Las Vegas. She clung to me so fiercely that I joked about needing the pry bar just to get her onto the bus. She didn't want to go, she said. "What if they return? They might hurt you. You need me to watch your back."

"I need you to get on the bus," I said.

When the driver tooted the horn she peeled away from me and ran for the door. At the top of the steps she waved, a broad grin bursting through her tears, and called, "I promise I won't forget you when I'm famous!"

TWENTY-TWO

THE MOST compelling images from the film I'd shot the night before, spread across Frank's desk in the form of proof sheets, depicted black-clad figures in wide shot walking single file through the spill of light outside the North Hollywood warehouse—good enough for the story's inside pages but hardly fitting for the headline. Every time I zoomed close the image darkened to the color and clarity of mud. I hadn't managed to get a clear shot of Eric, Theresa's abduction, or even the van's license plate. None of the photographs proved anything. However, I did manage some very nicely composed images of cactus flowers.

"I can't track the owner of the van without the license plate," Frank said, examining the proofs on his desk through a magnifying loupe. "I don't have the resources of the FBI or LAPD. I can't order a check of every black Dodge van registered in the county." He picked out one of the wide-angle shots of the gang leaving the warehouse, said, "I can use something like this but only if I have a story and I don't have a story."

"What do you mean you don't have a story?" I was tired and more than a little irritable and I spoke louder than intended. "Teenage celebrity-grave robbers are not a story?"

"If they get arrested, it's a story." Frank stuck a finger to his ear and swizzled it around. "Until then, the Raelians sell more newspapers."

"What about the chase through the desert?"

"Where's the story? A teenager is abducted and then rescued in the middle of nowhere with no witnesses?" He shook his head as though he pitied me. "This guy Sven, who is he, some sort of Swedish mystic? To sell this story I need a face."

"What about Chad Stonewell? He's a face."

"You have no proof he's involved."

"His bodyguard is involved and that's more proof than you have against the Raelians."

"The Raelians love publicity. Any publicity. *Scandal Times* and the Raelians are made for each other. Movie stars, on the other hand, are infamously litigious."

I picked the proof sheets from his desk and returned them to their envelope. "People have called you cynical, vicious, mean-spirited, and the illegitimate son of a crocodile and Komodo dragon but never a coward." I held out my hand for the loupe. "Where's the intrepid investigative reporter I used to know?"

Frank slapped the loupe into my palm, said, "You mean the guy who wrote *The Truth About Two-Headed Sheep* and *Celebrity Kleptomaniacs*? Still looking for his Pulitzer." He sat down behind his desk, the chair squeaking in protest, and opened the top-right drawer. "Are you broke yet?"

"Not yet." I emptied out the right front pocket of my jeans to count the contents. "I still have thirty-five cents."

He flicked his wrist. A check skittered across the desktop. I read the amount. Five hundred dollars.

"Your paycheck for the Raelian shoot," he said.

I folded the check and stuffed it into my jacket pocket, asked, "What if Theresa wasn't the only one?"

"You looking for more runaways to befriend?" The curl of his lip accused me of being a sucker.

"The more the better," I said, going along with it. "Maybe I can start a halfway house. How many teenaged runaways go missing in Southern California every year?"

"How many runaways come to Southern California in the first place? It's an unanswerable question."

"So if some of them disappear, nobody notices."

Frank wadded a sheet of paper and tossed it like a basketball toward the trash basket beside his desk. The wad bounced off the rim and rolled against the wall. "What's to notice? No address, no job, no school. It's like they were never here. But street kids, that's a *Times* story, not something for the tabs."

"If missing kids isn't a scandal, what is?" I asked. "How many dead kids do you need before the story is good enough for *Scandal Times*?"

"Who said anything about dead kids?" A heart the size of a golf ball may have throbbed in Frank's chest but it was still a heart. He sounded as though I'd wounded him.

"Maybe you'll understand the question if I ask it again. What if Theresa wasn't the only one? How about a couple dozen dead kids, shot in the back of the head and buried out in the desert? Is that a story? Or will one or two be good enough?"

I slung the camera bag over my shoulder and strode across the bullpen to call the Fairmount marshal's office. When the answering machine picked up I called Tuck's cell phone. He'd given me the number when I'd recognized two of the suspects on his wall.

"If it isn't the lady paparazzi from L.A.," Tuck said. "You shoot any celebrities since I saw you?"

"None fatally."

He was an easy laugh. Tires thrummed in the background. I'd caught him in his patrol car, probably cruising for jaywalking squirrels and other local delinquents.

"The guy you're looking for is named Sean Casey," I said.

"Whoa, how do you know this?"

"After he broke into the grave he came out to L.A. with his fifteen-year-old girlfriend," I said. "She can testify he broke into the grave, even though she wasn't there herself."

"You know that for a fact?"

"I know that as part of the deal."

"What deal?"

"The deal that I tell her it's safe to cooperate with you."

We argued about that back and forth before he finally agreed. He wouldn't charge her with being an accessory if she agreed to testify. Across the bullpen Frank stood from behind his desk and stalked toward me, shaking his head. Tuck thanked me for my help and I hung up feeling good about the call.

"You're just jerking my chain about the missing teens." Frank knuckled over the desk and stared at me as though he resented himself for being suckered as much as me for suckering him.

"The people doing this, they didn't seem to hesitate to kill my sister." I spoke patiently, as though reasoning with a stubborn child. "They were willing to kill Theresa for betraying them. If they haven't killed other teens, it's only a question of time before they do. You're the one with the big brain here. Think about it. According to Theresa, these kids all believe they're going to be made into movie stars. It's like a cult."

Frank stood bolt upright as though someone had just goosed him, and his right hand flew up to smack his forehead with enough force to give a smaller man a standing-eight count. "I'm an idiot! A moron, an imbecile, a blockhead, a cretin! A cud-sucking cow has more brains than I do."

"Tell me something new," I said.

He spun on his heels, took three steps parallel to the desk, then pivoted and took three steps back. "You're so smart, what did I just figure out?"

"That I'm always right."

He turned his head slowly left, back to center, then right, in a slow pantomime of negation. "You're so wrong you don't even know when and why you're right. You said the magic word."

"Please?"

"No. Cult." He whirled and paced. "Why didn't I see it before?" He unclipped the cheap plastic pen from the neck ring of his T-shirt, said, "Let me see those photographs again."

I lifted the proofs from the envelope and spread them on the desk.

"This is what we'll do." He circled an image of Theresa standing in the desert, looking forlorn, and another image of the warehouse at night. "These photos suck—no insult intended—but cults sell newspapers so we'll print these two below a story titled . . ." He flipped the proof to its blank back, chewed on the tip of his pen, and then wrote something, concealing what he'd written with his other hand. "You have to get me better visuals, something with more visceral impact, but I think the headline will sell the story well enough."

He pulled away the blocking hand and swiveled the proof sheet so I could read, right side up, the proposed headline: "Teen Terrorized by Celebrity-Bone-Napping Cult."

"What do you think?" he asked.

"Brilliant," I said.

"Cults, celebrities, terror, and teens," Frank said, nodding in agreement. "It's really got it all, doesn't it?"

TWENTY-THREE

A PENCIL of smoke drifted from the rail overlooking the lights of the city, then darted toward the mouth of a lean figure clad in a long black trench coat, the moonlit dome of Griffith Park Observatory looming above him. The stars above Los Angeles are pale and anemic things, gasping through the weave of smog and night, and the light radiating from the city long ago deprived the observatory of any scientific usefulness. If the view above disappoints, the one below doesn't. On the street the lights of Los Angeles do not cluster brightly or tower overhead but space themselves sensibly just above eye level, ordering the city into signs and signals devised for the passing eye of an automobile. Viewed from above the lights cascade down the hills like froth on the curl of a wave breaking upon a long, flat sheen of sand; streetlamps, arc lights, flashing and static neon signs, fluorescent office and incandescent house lights, and everywhere at every hour of night the bright heads and red tails of automobiles flowing through the freeways and surface streets like tropical fish in an aquarium of lights. Whenever the city irritates me I climb the hills and fall in love all over again.

"Enjoying the view?"

Vulch didn't turn when I spoke, his elbows propped on the metal railing, the cigarette burned to a nubbin between his fingers. At the opposite end of the observation walk teenagers huddled in small clusters, couples bound together in two-headed silhouettes, their chatter and laughter spraying down the hillside. "I like it here," he said. "Always have." The rigid line of his mouth creased into what might have been a smile. "I've always enjoyed the stars."

He was making a pun.

"Like a wolf enjoys sheep," I said.

"Not that way," he answered, his voice deep and serious. "I love celebrities. I love them like an arrow loves the target. They're my home." He ground the butt under the heel of a black cowboy boot and slipped a box of Marlboros halfway out the breast pocket of his leather trench coat. "Cigarette?"

"Don't smoke, thanks."

He pushed the Marlboros back into their leather sleeve as though thinking twice about lighting up. "Hate will motivate you only for so long in this business. You have to love what you're shooting or you'll sour like all the other homunculi we call our colleagues."

It was a sad fact of our business that the majority of paparazzi were offensively aggressive and dimwitted creatures with all the predatory charisma of hyenas hounding a lion. I was happy for the moment that Vulch excluded me from that lot even if the exclusion was falsely self-congratulatory. I wasn't sure I was all that different. "Thanks for loaning me the equipment," I said. "It's still in one piece, in the trunk of my car."

He straightened at the rail and turned, towering over me. Height is an advantage for a paparazzo, enabling one to shoot over the crowd, and Vulch had it. We circled the observatory, heading for the parking lot.

"You get your shots?" he asked.

"Nothing special," I said. "Big setup, no payoff."

"I know the feeling. Nothing like sitting in a duck blind all day and shooting nothing but the shit with yourself." A low, guttural sound that might have been a laugh stuttered from his chest.

"Too dark to shoot anything anyway," I said.

"What stock were you shooting?"

"High-speed infrared black-and-white, five-hundred-millimeter Zeiss optics, aperture wide-open. Normally that would have done the trick but backup security spotted me walking through the brush, one of them wearing some kind of night-vision device."

"A camera?"

I pointed to my forehead. "He wore it attached to his head. Only one lens."

"Head-mounted goggle, then," he said. "Passive IR system lit you up like a Christmas tree on the White House lawn. You have a night-vision scope?"

"I see well enough at night without that," I said.

Vulch sniffed the air, black Ray-Bans like wings above his enormous beak. "I smell dinosaur again. You're resourceful, I'll give you that, but your tradecraft is antique. This isn't the 1950s, when you can expect to hang by your heels from a balcony to snap Richard Burton canoodling Liz Taylor." He pointed his key chain at a big black BMW in the parking lot and the trunk popped open. "Night-vision devices, GPS tracking systems, body cams, covert cams—you have the same surveillance gear the cops use available to you, if you're smart enough to use them. I took your photograph tonight. You know when?"

He'd been smoking when I'd first seen him, standing at the rail overlooking the city, the cigarette worked down to a butt as though he'd been waiting there, smoking, for several minutes. I thought he hadn't noticed me until I'd spoken. "In the lot, when I got out of my car?"

He reached two fingers into the breast pocket of his trench coat and scissored out his pack of Marlboros. "Mind if I smoke?"

"They're your lungs," I said.

He palmed the pack into my hand and bent over one of a half-dozen equipment cases in the trunk of his car. The cigarette pack felt heavy, even for a full one. I turned it beneath the trunk light and spotted the lens poking from the flip-top. The thing was a camera. "Guess I'll have to take up smoking," I said.

"Nobody smokes in L.A. anymore so don't bother." Vulch turned away from the trunk, something that looked like a lens in his hand. "This is a generation three night-vision pocketscope with a military-specification C-mount lens."

"C-mount?" I put the viewfinder to my eye, saw the night flare into an alien world of bright greens. A young couple walking arm in arm across the parking lot looked like a two-headed Martian. "A standard thirty-five-millimeter mount? You mean I can attach this to my Nikon?"

"There's an idea." He lifted a metal tube from a small black case and flourished it beneath the trunk light. "The basic lens is wide-angle but with this adapter you can get up to seventy-five millimeters." He snatched back the pocketscope and nestled it into the case, latched the case shut, and handed it to me. "Give it a try. If it works for you, buy one of your own. Exposure times are hit and miss so remember to bracket like hell." He eased the trunk shut and followed me to the Cadillac.

"What do I owe you for the rental?" I asked.

"I don't want your money," he said.

That was good because I didn't have much, but it left open the question what he wanted in lieu of money. "People in our line of work are not known for generosity so forgive me for wondering why you're being so nice to me."

He flipped the case switches on the digital tracking device and checked the equipment with quick, sure hands, the kind of guy who could disassemble and reassemble blindfolded every piece of equipment he owned. "How old are you?"

"Thirty," I said.

"I'm fifty-five. It suits my vanity to have someone younger I can show off to, someone I can advise and to a limited extent protect. That someone used to be your husband. I liked Gabe. He was talented and funny. But Gabe is dead so now I like you. You're not as funny but you're talented."

My husband had left me little more than aggravation, heartache, and a skein of lies at his death. That I'd also inherited a knight—if a dark one—surprised me. If I harbored deeper suspicions about his generosity I suppressed them. I'm sentimental in my own cynical way and wanted to believe that loyalty to a dead friend motivated him. "I'm working on the Hollywood Forever robbery," I said.

"The theft of Valentino?" He sounded surprised. "There's nothing in that for me."

"That's why I'm telling you." I may have been sentimental but I wasn't stupid. One of the cardinal rules of my line of work is never to tell a colleague what you're doing until it's finished because we all steal shamelessly. My sister would have been a great paparazza. "You hear anything about people collecting the bones of celebrities, weird black masses, that sort of thing?"

Vulch lifted the case from the trunk of the Cadillac and set it on the pavement at his feet. "Nothing specific, no, but you should know that Satanism has deep roots in Los Angeles culture."

"There's too much sun and orange juice here for the devil."

His teeth flashed yellow beneath the parking-lot security lights. "The chamber of commerce would be happy to hear you say that. You ever hear of Aleister Crowley?"

I told him I didn't know the guy and shut the trunk.

"The most notorious Satanist and practitioner of black magic in the twentieth century. An Englishman. Was the grand pooh-bah of the dark arts until his death. Lived in Pasadena for a short time in the 1920s. It's been written that he inspired L. Ron Hubbard."

"The founder of Scientology?"

Vulch lifted a pack of Camels from the left flap pocket in his trench coat, shook out a cigarette, and lit it with an onyx black lighter. "For several months he supposedly belonged to a local chapter of Crowley's sect, Ordo Templis Orientis, got some of his ideas about Scientology from Crowley and standard concepts in black magic. The rumor goes the head of the sect, a guy named Parsons, conspired with Hubbard to produce a satanic child, with Parsons acting as the high priest to impregnate the girl and Hubbard acting as the seer guiding events in the spirit world, astral plane, whatever you want to call it."

"But Scientology is everywhere in Los Angeles," I said. "Some of the most famous actors and musicians belong to it."

"And they got successful pretty damned fast, didn't they?" He blew a thin stream of smoke out the side of his mouth. "Almost as if they'd sold their souls to the devil."

"That's a cynical thought," I said.

"We live in cynical times."

"You think the Scientologists are involved?"

"Not enough money in it," Vulch said. "That was just an example of how deeply Satanism is embedded here. And remember, it's not all pentagrams and goat's blood. The devil isn't a hideous creature with horns and a tail, not anymore. Who's going to fall for that shit these days? That's the devil people try to scare you with, but it's a false image. Lucifer began as an angel, the most beautiful of all of God's creations. Remember that." It seemed he spoke from personal experience. He spoke bitterly. "The devil is so beautiful and desirable you'll do anything, sell anything to embrace him. And when you do, he'll drive a stake through your soul."

TWENTY-FOUR

I R A N along the Venice Beach Boardwalk that night, the pump of muscle and blood a centrifugal force driving the toxins from my mind and body. I didn't believe in the devil but that didn't mean those who did weren't capable of great harm. The Rott patrolled ahead, fell behind while investigating one irresistible scent or another, then raced ahead again. I tried to let my mind go blank as I ran, meditating on the breath pumping through my lungs. If I didn't believe in the devil I did believe in the existence of evil and that was frightening enough. Evil done in the devil's name makes the devil's existence a moot point. A single idea flared in imposed calm of the run: I needed to do something decent to counteract the evil interjected into my life. No need to get carried away with thoughts of goodness—I wasn't about to volunteer at a soup kitchen to feed the poor, being close enough to poverty to join those in line—something small would suffice if it felt genuine. Handing out a few quarters to the homeless, always a cheap feel-good gesture, wasn't going to be enough. Then I realized what I needed to do, should have done the day I learned of my sister's murder.

I made the call after getting the number for the only Micklin family in Phoenix from directory assistance. A woman answered—a tired woman in her fifties by the strained sound of her voice. It was just past ten PM but still I heard the clatter of children in the background. I asked if Cassie was in.

"Who's calling?" A sharpness carried over the line, as though the woman suspected me of something just by the sound of my voice.

"Her aunt, I guess."

"You guess? What the hell do you mean? You are or you aren't."

"I didn't know Cassie existed until three days ago." I resisted adding an epithet to the end of the sentence. Swearing at the woman wouldn't help. "I'm her mother's sister. That makes me her blood aunt. But I've never even met the child so I can't claim more than that."

"You the mother's sister?"

"That's right."

"Then you know the girl don't have a mother no more, not that her mother was worth a damn to begin with." Her end of the line rapped sharply, as though she struck the receiver onto the tabletop, and she shouted a warning to a wayward child before her voice came back to me. "None of the kids I care for have parents worth a damn. That's why they're with me. Course it's a shame what happened to the girl's mother, does no good to talk ill of the dead."

"The police asked me to identify the body," I said. "That's how I learned I have a niece. My sister disappeared from my life when I was six. I don't want to interfere with the care you're giving. But it might do my niece and me some good to talk to each other, to get to know each other a little bit."

"What's your address," she said. "I'll send you a picture."

"I'd rather talk to her."

The woman said nothing.

"She knows about her mother? About what happened?"

"Cassie ran away from us two months ago."

Like mother, like daughter, I thought.

"I'll take that picture, then," I said.

The previous night had been sleepless and the run on Venice Beach Boardwalk had taken the last of my energy. I didn't have to worry about insomnia. Exhaustion silences the brain. Moments after hitting the futon I plummeted below the surface of dreamlike images to the dark and barren depths of sleep. Some sleeps you earn. When the Rott began to bark from his nest at my feet I kicked blindly from beneath the covers. It was like kicking a baby bull. The Rott leapt from the bed and charged the door, his bark harsh and percussive, no longer a warning bark but a signal of attack.

I bolted upright, my body quick but my mind still clawing through the smothering density of sleep. The door shuddered under a clanking blow that sounded like metal on metal. The wood splintered between the door and jamb near the base. I leapt forward to put my eye to the peephole. A figure cloaked in black swung a mallet toward the door, his back grotesquely bent in the parabolic lens. One step below on the exterior stairway another figure hurled his arm forward and something flickered for a moment before winging from view. The security-barred window to the right of the landing shattered a split second later and a breaking glass jar splattered liquid against the wall. The smell of gasoline invaded the room the moment before the air flashed with the ignition of flame on petrol.

The door whomped again, this time higher up the jamb. The Rott glanced at the flames over his shoulder and flung himself forward as though he could run through wood. I snatched open the closet door and wrapped my palm around a baseball bat. The Rott responded to my voice and heeled to my leg, trust stronger for the moment than fear. I stepped to the side, planning to fling open the door and follow the Rott's charge with the bat. The Rott skittered back, understanding what I was about to do when I flicked back the top bolt. I turned the bottom knob and pulled. The Rott charged forward on the movement of my arm. The knob didn't give and my shoulder pitched into the wood. The Rott thumped into the side of my leg and bounced back, his look recriminatory. I was human. It was my job to open doors. I thought one of the assailants held the door closed and put my eye to the peephole again to see both figures running down the stairs. The wood at the jamb above my head had splintered. I realized then the trap.

They'd spiked the door shut.

Smoke scudded across the ceiling in the kitchen and rolled down the walls. The Rott whirled to face the fire curling toward the kitchen, howled, and careened into the wall, the bookcase collapsing in a spray of books. I ran to the window and shoved at the security bars, and when they didn't budge I lifted a chair and threw it. The chair broke out the rest of the glass and bounced back to the floor. The bars had rusted shut long before I moved in. I didn't even have a key. The only other window, in the bathroom, looked onto a three-story drop into the alley. Within minutes we'd suffocate and fry.

Sweat from my palms slickened the smooth grip of the bat. I stepped up to the door, tapped the lower-left quarter panel, marked by decorative grooves in the wood, and swung. The shock of wood on wood nearly wrenched the bat from my hands. I cocked the bat and swung again, the solid crack of wood grain sounding my progress. I golfed the third swing. The head of the bat punched through the panel. I swung again and again, each blow splintering out chunks of wood, until the entire panel gave at the grooves.

The Rott cowered in the closet, howling. I pressed the neck of my T-shirt across my mouth to filter the smoke and hauled him out by his collar. The moment he saw the gap he dashed forward and bulled through it. I canvassed the room quickly and collected the things I'd need to stay on the job. I tossed jeans, leather jacket, and boots out the door, held my camera bag over my head, and squirmed through the hole.

Dr. James Whitehead labored up the stairs, his gray hair swirling like a storm above his head and a home fire extinguisher bundled under his left arm. The Rott barked from the sidewalk, bounded up the first set of steps, then hurried back down, torn between his fear of fire and coming to get me. I jumped into my jeans and boots. Dr. Whitehead yelled something at me. A firebomb, I said. Somebody threw a firebomb. He tried to yank open the door, his expression befuddled when the door didn't give.

Sirens wailed, blocks away.

I pointed out the spikes and we shouted back and forth about what to do. I wrapped my hands around the fire extinguisher. Dr. Whitehead gave it up willingly. I sucked a lungful of air, bellied down, and crawled through the hole. Flames ripped through the apartment from floor to ceiling. I pointed the hose at the center of the inferno and shot out the canister.

My neighbors lined the streets to watch the circus act of whirling lights, howling sirens, and ax-wielding firemen, but by five in the morning most decided the show was over and those who had beds— half my neighbors were homeless—returned to them. Dr. Whitehead's home fire extinguisher had slowed the fire, allowing the fire crew to contain the flames to my top-floor apartment. The apartment below mine suffered some water damage that I didn't regret; its tenant was a young executive with a preference for yellow ties and an aversion to dogs. His complaints about the Rott had led to my eviction. I thought of his ruined stereo equipment as a farewell present from the both of us.

I sat on the curb across the street from the building while the fire crew mopped up, the Rott's head in my lap, and drank an infusion of mint tea. Dr. Whitehead had given it to me, his own spirit-healing concoction, he said. I told him I was sorry to bring so much commotion into his life. He waved off the apology, said, "I saw trouble coming the day we talked. I'm just glad no one was hurt. If it's any consolation, your aura is looking much better." His eyes tracked up and over my shoulder and I knew by the movement that someone stood behind me.

"Are you the tenant of the top-floor apartment?"

I looked over my shoulder to the source of the voice, a tired-eyed man in his early forties, thin as a coat hanger, clad in a blue Los Angeles Fire Department windbreaker. He looked too pensive to be a fireman, his eyes distant, yet focused so intensely on the details of the moment I felt as though he could accurately describe my face and clothing after one glance.

"You're with the fire department?" I asked.

He looked at me like I'd just won the dumb-question-of-the-month award, then showed me his investigator's badge. "I'd like to ask you a few questions."

"Are we allowed up yet?" I stood and nodded toward the stairs. "I can explain things better if I show you what happened."

The arson investigator thought about that for a moment, opened the trunk of a sedan double-parked in front of the fire truck, and handed me a fire helmet. "Regulations," he said.

I put on the helmet and followed him up. Ash-blackened water trickled down the steps. The firemen had hacked their way through the front door with an ax, and what remained of it hung in shards from the hinges. Inside the apartment the fire had burned into the ceiling and blackened the walls. Another investigator squatted near the kitchen, his shoes wrapped in plastic. The lead investigator blocked the doorway, said, "I can't let you get any closer than this. It's a mess in there anyhow."

I knelt to examine the inch-wide head of the spike that pinned a chunk of the door to the frame. The spike, about six inches long, had gone through the frame and into the wall.

"I was wondering if you could tell me about that," the investigator said, squatting next to me.

"My Rott went into a barking fit about three this morning," I said. "Two guys wearing ski masks spiked the door shut and threw a Molotov cocktail through the window."

The investigator stood and edged across the landing to inspect the security bars. While climbing the stairs he'd slipped plastic gloves over his hands, and he spotted the lock with a penlight before probing it with gloved fingers. He glanced around the bars' edges, then brought the circle of light onto a rust-stained finger. "These don't look like they've opened in years." He spotlit the bolts securing the bars to the wall. "You didn't come out this way, did you?"

"No, sir," I said.

He clicked off the penlight and turned away from the window to look again at the door, glancing once at my face as though trying to read in my features the answer to a riddle. "Security bars rusted shut, door spiked—how did you get out?"

"I punched through a panel in the door with a baseball bat."

He leaned to look around the apartment without stepping inside and saw the bat, blackened with soot and leaning against the wall away from the door. "You're one lucky lady. You realize you could have fried to death in there?"

"It didn't escape my notice, no."

He pointed toward the window, his gesture short and sharp. "Those security bars are a violation of city safety codes."

"I just rent the place. You'll have to talk to the landlord."

"I'll do more than talk to him, I'll cite him. And you have grounds for a civil suit, if you're so inclined. Every year someone dies in a situation like this." He took a couple of steps down the stairs and turned to face the hole where the door once hung, then glanced toward the window. "The assailants wore their masks at all times?"

"I know who they are, masked or not."

He raised a dubious eyebrow, asked, "Did they speak to you?"

"No," I said.

"If you didn't see them and they didn't speak to you, you don't know who they are. That brings up a different question. Who do you think might have done this?"

"The same people who killed my sister."

He'd expected to hear the usual sordid tale of petty squabbles involving drugs or sex and stared at me with unflickering eyes as though waiting for me to admit a joke. Only when I began to tell him what I did for a living and how my sister died, complete with the details of how the detectives were handling the case, did he open a binder-style notebook and take notes. "I don't know this newspaper you say you work for." He glanced at his notes. "What is it, *Scandal Times?*"

"It's a gossip tabloid."

"And you do investigative reporting? I thought you guys made all that shit up." He asked where I could be reached over the next few days in case he had additional questions, which seemed a sure thing considering this didn't look like an ordinary kitchen fire. I gave him the number at the newspaper, said, "One other thing you should know about."

"What's that?"

"I'm currently on parole."

He stepped away from me as though I'd announced I carried an infectious disease, and the way he looked at me shifted from curious to clinical. "What was the conviction, arson?" His voice curled hopefully at the end.

"Manslaughter."

He grabbed my arm above the elbow and gestured toward the bottom of the stairs. "I'm sure I'm going to have some more questions to ask you once I've talked to these detectives you mentioned," he said. "Would you mind waiting for me in the car?"

TWENTY-FIVE

Lıke тне marked and unmarked police cars I'd been invited inside before, the rear seat of the arson investigator's sedan was screened from the front by Plexiglas and the doors could not be unlocked from the inside. Had I been a regular citizen I could have complained about illegal detention—either arrest me or let me go—but I wasn't a regular citizen. The arson investigator hadn't read my rights before guiding me into the car because I wasn't yet under arrest and as a parolee I didn't have the same rights as anyone else, except maybe bail jumpers. I did the only sensible thing possible, guided by my vast experience in similar situations; I carefully folded my leather jacket, lay back on the seat, and fell asleep.

A few hours later a knock on the window wakened me to bleached blue skies and the familiar smell of confinement—the sweat of past prisoners mixed with my own in a closed, airless box. The door at my feet cracked open and the long, thin face of the arson investigator poked into the compartment, the skin under his eyes purpled with fatigue. "You want to step outside?" He left the door open and stepped back onto the sidewalk to wait for me to comply. "Detective Dougan wants to talk to you." He flashed a yellow slip of paper scribbled in ink. "I promised him you'd drive over to the Hollywood station this morning."

He'd written Dougan's name, telephone number, and address on the slip of paper, just in case I'd forgotten. I struggled to find the inside sleeves of my jacket, told him I'd visit Dougan after the end of rush hour.

"I haven't managed to contact your parole officer yet, but I will," he said. "If I remember the terms of the standard parole agreement, you need a place of residence." He looked up the steps at my apartment, yellow police tape crisscrossing the plywood sheeting nailed over the doorway. "And it looks like you just lost yours."

As though I needed the reminder.

I collected the Rott from Dr. Whitehead's apartment and walked him to the public showers to wash the soot and smoke from our hair. If I was going to be homeless I'd have to learn how to soap up and hose down wearing a bathing suit in the open air. We dried off in the Cadillac, the heater blasting on high as we drove east on a line that would take us to Hollywood, though I had no intention of stopping at the Hollywood station to visit Dougan, not just then. I sipped a cup of take-out coffee and brushed my hair as I crawled forward with the rest of the traffic, calling numbers on my cell phone and steering most of the time with my knees. Rush hour in Los Angeles is an oxymoron squared: nobody rushes anywhere and it lasts not one but four hours. My parole officer wasn't answering her office phone yet, no surprise considering the hour. I didn't intend to talk to her anyway and left what I hoped would be the first message in a long game of telephone tag. Frank's voice mail picked up at *Scandal Times*. I tried his home and mobile phone numbers, left messages everywhere. Every now and then I glanced at my neighbors one lane over and most of them were no less busy than I, involved in everything from putting on makeup to shaving.

I reached Los Feliz by eight in the morning and parked the Cadillac down the block from the Palms, the apartment building Theresa had been taken to the night before last. Unless the driver of the van had warned everybody about the make of my car, Luce—the girl Theresa had met—wouldn't know the Cadillac by sight. I stepped onto the sidewalk and strolled past the underground parking gates, spotting the blue fender of her Tercel parked in its assigned spot. I needed information. Luce had an apartment, a car, and, according to Theresa, a blossoming career as a young actress; she'd be easy to pressure. I slipped back into the Cadillac, eyed warily by the Rott, laid out in the backseat. After his busy night he was even more exhausted than I, and the three donuts I'd fed him for breakfast finished him off.

The Tercel sputtered out of the parking garage and onto the street fifteen minutes into the stakeout, Luce bobbing her head behind the wheel as though listening to music. I waited for the car to clip by and then started the Cadillac. She kept to surface streets through Hollywood, turned south and then west onto the Miracle Mile section of Wilshire Boulevard. The indicators blinked conscientiously at every turn, the last one into a parking garage below a white-concrete and black-glass high-rise just across from Museum Square. The side pocket of my leather jacket chirped. I slowed to follow the Tercel, slipping the mobile phone from my pocket to check the caller. Terry Graves, my parole officer. I let it ring and ramped toward visitors' parking. The ringing stopped. Two lanes over, Luce reached a fringed and beaded arm out the window to insert a parking card into the monthly parking slot.

Her parking barrier raised first. The Tercel peeled to the right, the visitors' parking ramp routed me to the left, and I lost her. I followed the signs to a parking space near the elevators, jumped out of the car, and jogged up the stairs into the lobby, swarming at that hour with skirts and suits hurrying to report to work. Two security guards, red patches on the breast pockets of their blue blazers, staffed a desk at the street entrance. I walked over to study the building directory, angling my shoulders to keep the elevators from the parking garage in view.

Luce emerged from the nearest parking elevator a minute later, long, multiple strands of beads and pendants swaying beneath her black shawl as she bounced toward the bank of elevators that would take her to the offices above the ground floor. She looked like a happy young hipster in her long hair and granny glasses, smiling at the people she passed. It was difficult for me to imagine that she'd be involved in anything more sinister than a puff of marijuana before bedtime. I sidled through the crowd of workers waiting for the next elevator. The arrival bell dinged and the doors to the elevator to Luce's right slid open, disgorging a courier nearly trampled in the boarding crush. I squeezed in behind a suit and punched the button to the penultimate floor. The crowd inside the car dwindled with each stop. I wedged myself into the back corner, afraid not that the girl would recognize me but that she might later pick my face or figure out of the crowd as I followed her. She stepped out of the elevator onto the sixteenth floor and turned to the left. I rode the car to the next stop and took a U-turn back to the sixteenth floor. The hallway to the left ended abruptly in a door marked THEATRICAL ARTISTS GROUP. I decided against sticking my head through the door and playing lost; if Luce worked as a receptionist she might still be in the lobby.

I thought it through as I rode the elevator down to the parking garage. Luce had used a parking card and slotted her Tercel with the monthlies. That meant she worked in the building. If her schedule was the same as most office workers she wouldn't leave the building until lunch. I drove to the LAPD's Hollywood station and gave my name to the uniformed officer staffing the front desk. Dougan wanted to see me, I said, and stepped outside with the Rott to wait. The sun hovered low enough in the sky to cast a crisp, colorful light ideal for photography. I played around with the camera while I waited, taking images of the Walk of Fame–style stars embedded in the sidewalk until Dougan lumbered down the steps.

"Put your dog in your car and come inside the station," he said. "We'll talk."

I heeled the Rott to my side, said, "I'm on assignment this morning and this is the only chance I'll get to walk my dog. Be a sport and come along."

His face did not conceal frustration well, his brows furrowing above cheeks flushing such a violent red I worried about his blood pressure. "Somebody just burned you out of your apartment." He pointed a lecturing finger at my chest. "I'd think someone in your position would have a better understanding of her priorities."

"I understand my priorities just fine, thanks." The moment I stepped into the station he'd control me and I didn't have the time to be locked in one of his interrogation rooms. "I need to earn enough money to rent another place to live. I can't afford to turn down assignments." I knelt to leash the Rott.

"You want to walk your dog, okay," Dougan said. "I like dogs. I'll even walk the dog with you. But if I hear something I don't like or if I don't think you're cooperating fully we're going back to the station. No arguments."

I didn't want to impede an investigation into the murder of my sister. I tried to tell the truth while we walked but I couldn't tell the whole truth because it would mean spending the rest of the day in an interrogation room and perhaps the night in jail. I told Dougan that a street kid had offered to sell me information about the celebrity grave robberies. He stopped at the corner, beside a bright blue wall sign advertising Big Dog Bail Bonds, and prepared to jot a note into his binder. "This street kid, what's her name?"

"Theresa."

"I need a last name."

"She didn't say."

"That's not good enough."

"All I got. She's involved through her boyfriend. I suppose you want his name, too."

His moustache began to quiver like a wild and angry animal.

"A runaway from Indiana named Sean Casey," I said.

"Where can I find him?"

"New York City, last I heard."

Out of state and out of his jurisdiction. Dougan got through the first consonant of a curse before biting off the word.

"The girl wasn't happy either. That's why she offered to sell."

"Sell what?"

The Rott pulled on his leash, eager to cross to a fire hydrant across the street. "Her story to the tabs," I said, letting the Rott take the lead. "But she wouldn't give any names or addresses so we got into an argument and she did a runner. I followed her to a warehouse in North Hollywood." I described the journey the black van had taken to Wonder View Drive and the six teens I'd seen trekking over the hills toward Forest Lawn cemetery.

"And you didn't call us?"

"Of course I called. From a phone box. Check 911."

"And nobody responded?"

"Things got busy and I had to hang up without leaving my name."

"An anonymous call? From a phone box?" This time he didn't censor the curse.

"Kids go into those hills all the time to drink, smoke, and screw around." The Rott lunged forward again, pulling me in his wake. "I needed to confirm where they were going, what they intended to do."

"Don't bullshit me," Dougan said, hustling to keep up. "You

wanted the, what do you call it, the exposé. You wanted to photograph the break-in."

"Of course I did. That's what I do for a living and as far as I know it's not against the law, not yet. The minute something actually illegal happened I would have called you and 911 and every other law I could reach on autodial. You know why?"

"To keep your can out of jail," he said.

"Because of the lights."

"What lights?"

"The lights of the police cars swooping in for the bust. They make the most dramatic image. That would have been a front-page shot, but it never happened."

"Pull up your dog," he ordered, his face flushed red. He was having problems keeping up and the first few beads of sweat had popped from his forehead.

"I got a look at the driver of the van, recognized his face." I heeled the Rott and gave him a pat. I knew Dougan was about to yank me back to an interrogation room. I had to give him something to work with. "He works for Chad Stonewell. One of his bodyguards."

"Chad Stonewell the movie star? How do you know?"

"I'm a paparazza, remember? I've seen them together."

He wrote down the name, said, "The van license plate?"

"Never got it."

"Then you know what I can do with this?" He touched the tip of his right forefinger to his thumb, making a circle. "If you'd called us that night instead of placing an anonymous call to 911 we could have pulled them over, picked up the kids as runaways and sweated them. Somebody would have talked and we'd have made a case. What happens instead? You get firebombed out of your apartment and I got a big goose egg, zero, nothing to work on except your highly questionable word and the address of a warehouse that's probably empty now. You know what your problem is?"

"I'm not lovable enough?"

He didn't laugh.

"You're coming dangerously close to interfering with a police investigation and that's a violation of your parole. Do you want to go back to prison?"

I shrugged, said, "Beats getting killed, I guess."

He wagged his head as though disgusted with me. "I talked to your parole officer about you."

I couldn't help it. I rolled my eyes.

"Funny, she has the same reaction to you. Said in all of her years working for the Department of Paroles she's never had anyone give her as much work as you have. You're stubborn, borderline violent, and a pain in the ass to deal with. She also said that despite being basically honest and hardworking you have a genuine talent for trouble."

"A person's got to be good at something," I said.

"Let's hope you're good at staying out of jail," he said. "And at staying alive, too."

TWENTY-SIX

THE GIRL with the beads and pendants came swinging out the front entrance of the concrete and glass high-rise at thirty minutes past noon, flanked by two women barely out of their teens, both dressed in the tight-fitting spaghetti-strap tops and miniskirts popular among those in the workforce more interested in getting boys than getting promoted. I watched from behind the wheel of the Cadillac, parked at a meter down the street from the entrance. The Rott snoozed on the seat beside me, his head in my lap. The three crossed with the light at the next corner, swaying with chatter and laughter as they walked toward a strip of boutique fast-food restaurants next to Museum Square. I elbowed open the door, gently lifted the Rott's head from my lap, and slipped out of the car. The Rott gave me a look that suggested no more than passing curiosity about where I was going and went back to sleep.

Across the street, Luce and her friends filed through the door of a skinless chicken franchise. I walked past the winking chicken on the sign, peered through the front window. The choice was fine with me. The Rott liked chicken, too. The three approached the service counter and placed their order. I gave them time to collect their drinks, find a table for four, and sit. The two girls flanked Luce like bookends until they reached the table. I figured they worked together as receptionists or entry-level clerical. They looked excited and full of hope, the type of young women men love to exploit at work, in bed, or anywhere they can.

I ordered a half chicken for the Rott and chicken salad for me and moved to the drinks dispenser for a large cup of iced tea. When the cup filled I capped it and wandered toward the girls' table, turned my head sharply as though surprised, and called out, "Luce?"

She glanced up, green eyes treading water, not knowing who I was or what I wanted. Her face was too round for the camera to consider her classically beautiful and one eye looked slightly higher than the other, but an eccentric charm animated her features and emotions played across her face like images on a screen. She was one of a thousand young actresses all vying for the same few roles but I didn't have any trouble imagining her as the one who makes it. I stepped toward the table and pitched my voice to the high tones of giddy excitement. "I can't believe it's you!" I said. "We were just talking about you!"

One of the advantages of L.A.'s casual dress code is that nobody knows how important anybody is just by looking. The slob in a baseball cap, satin windbreaker, and ratty sneakers could be a television director, at least until he jumps into anything less than a BMW. I knew her name, sounded excited to see her. I could have been a production executive coming fresh from a casting meeting where her rightness for a role had been discussed. I could even have been the most important person on earth to an actor: a casting director. So she did what every other aspiring actress in L.A. would do. She smiled, a bit uncertainly, and waited for more information.

I slid onto the chair on the opposite side of the table. "I just saw Theresa yesterday and you remember that role she'd been cast in? The one where she plays a terrorized girl driven out into the desert and murdered?"

Even though I was nodding as though absolutely nothing was wrong, no reason to panic, the smile dropped from her lips and a look of sudden absence washed over her eyes, as though she wished to be anywhere but there, talking to me.

I gave a little wave of the back of my hand, said, "They hired another writer at the last minute and rewrote her part while they were shooting, if you can believe that."

"They did?" Her voice came out like a squeak and her hand went to her throat, just above a small pendant strung around her neck. The pendant, shaped like a cage around a grayish-white fragment, hung above multiple strands of swaying beads.

"The rewrite changed everything." I said it like a friend sharing good news with another friend. "Instead of taking a bullet in the back of the head, like in the first draft? She gets rescued while they're walking her out to get killed. That's the way they filmed it, too. She wanted you to know about it." I spun my fists in circles, pantomiming a fast run. "She's talking to everybody, you know, cranking out the publicity. Careers are so short these days you have to make the most of every break. But I don't have to tell that to a pro like you."

The girl next to Luce, her eyes sweetly crossed above a lipsticked smile, said, "That's so cool! You'll be next, Luce. Wait and see. I'm psychic about these things."

A number blared over the public address speakers and the girl next to me jumped to her feet, saying, "That's ours."

Luce dropped the hand from her throat, watched her friend trot off to collect their order, said, "In the first draft they were going to kill her?"

"Sure, anybody with any production experience knew that."

"Nobody told me." She tried to put the force of conviction behind her statement but her voice cracked and failed her.

I pulled a business card from my pocket, wrote the number of my cell phone on the back, pushed it across the table. "Remember what happened to Theresa if you ever get cast in a similar role."

She hid the card beneath her palm as though afraid someone might see her with it. Her head cocked to the side and she looked at me as though she wanted to ask something, then decided against it. "I'm glad it worked out for her."

"I like your necklace," I said. "Can I take a closer look?"

Her face stiffened and she covered the pendant with the palm of her hand. "It's kind of private." She smiled to hide her panic.

"But you're so proud of it," the cross-eyed girl said, trying to be helpful. Legs fluttered beneath the table and the girl flinched, her ankle kicked.

"It looks like bone." I reached for the silver strand on which it hung. "Is it bone?"

"No, it's just nothing, really."

The other girl slid two plastic trays laden with salad on the table, said, "It's a penis bone."

The cross-eyed girl laughed, leaning across the table with her hand

on her chest, and the other girl laughed even louder, still at the age
when all jokes about sex are funny. Luce's face pinked like a second-
degree sunburn.

"Go ahead, Luce, show her," the other girl said.

"Whose penis?" I asked.

The girls laughed again, voices bright and cheerful, keenly enjoying Luce's embarrassment but not understanding the true reason
for it.

"A dolphin." Luce pulled her hand away from her chest as though
defiant of contradiction.

A camera was not part of my act and I regretted leaving it in the
car. The fragment of bone was no more than a half inch in length and
jagged on both ends, as though recently splintered from a larger seg-
ment. The public address speaker blared the number to my order.

The cross-eyed girl leaned across the table, her voice a just-us-girls
whisper. "Dolphins are really sexual creatures. Luce is hoping it
helps her get lucky."

I suspected Luce hoped to get lucky in a completely different way
than the one suggested by the cross-eyed girl. Behind the wheel of the
Cadillac I listened to cell-phone messages while I tore the roast
chicken into bite-sized strips, fending off the Rott with my elbow.
Girls like Luce don't need to get lucky. They're born lucky. Luce
didn't need charms to enhance her sexual attractiveness. But in a city
populated by attractive young women all wanting the same thing,
she might want a charm to help her get it first and then hold it. The
message from my parole officer was brutal and short: call soon or
bear the consequences.

I piled the chicken strips onto the take-out container, using it like
a bowl, and set it on the seat. The next message was from Frank.
He'd tracked down the owner of the warehouse in North
Hollywood, a real estate speculator with an office in Beverly Hills,
and wanted to know if I was available for a little guerrilla journalism. The Rott inhaled the chicken and looked at me, disappointed
there wasn't more. I started the engine and pulled away from the
curb. I'd scared Luce but I didn't expect her to run that afternoon.
She might fear exposure and arrest but she wouldn't act, not until
after work. I even hoped that she'd call me and I'd be able to broker
a deal. She seemed genuinely shocked to hear that her coconspirators

had wanted to kill Theresa. The aspiring in Hollywood will often submit to any degradation and commit any act, criminal or not, that might further their ambitions. Her complicity in my sister's murder wouldn't have surprised me but she projected so much innocence and hope that I began to doubt she even knew anyone had been murdered that night.

Just inside the border of Beverly Hills I spotted Frank edging into traffic to wave me to a free parking spot behind his Honda Civic. A true friend, he fed coins into the parking meter while I collected my camera gear from the rear seat. I slung the bag over my shoulder, shut the trunk, and called above the buzz of traffic, "Hey, Frank, do dolphins have penis bones?"

He banked the meter up to two hours, said, "I've been waiting my whole life for someone to test my encyclopedic knowledge of sex trivia like this."

"That's why I asked. You seem like the kind of guy who'd know."

Frank pointed at a boutique courtyard building across the boulevard that looked like a cross between a Spanish hacienda and a minimall, the style of building that attracts lawyers, accountants, and others in the white-collar professional crowd. "The guy we're after, the guy who owns the warehouse, has a ground-floor office in that building." He scuttled toward the street corner, his eyes on the traffic light to cross with the next green. "His name is Daniel Sopwell and his company is called Sopwell Holdings. I've already done a walk-by. It's strictly small-time, a two-person operation. His secretary said he's at lunch. We'll ambush him when he returns."

I kept stride next to him, asked, "So do they or don't they?"

"Do they or don't they what?"

"Have a bone there."

"I thought you were kidding."

Sleek foreign steel knifed through the air in front of us, accelerating through the amber light.

"So you don't know the answer."

He stepped off the curb in front of a BMW straining to stop on the red, as if daring it to hit him, then half turned and flipped off the driver when the bumper slid over the white crosswalk stripe. "I've been asked some pretty arcane questions before but yours sets the record. Go ahead, ask me how big a whale penis is."

"I don't want to know that," I said, two steps behind.

"Fifteen feet."

I caught up to him, said, "Jealous?"

"Are you kidding? Of course I'm jealous. I know this might be confusing to someone with your lack of experience, but men don't literally have bones, no matter what the slang infers. We have something called erectile tissue, which is entirely a different thing. I can show you, if you'd like."

"No thanks." I followed him across the sidewalk and into the courtyard. "My interest is completely hypothetical."

"Then hypothetically I'd say a dolphin's penis is boneless too, and I don't even want to know why you're asking." He stopped before brass letters hung on an oak door. The letters spelled SOPWELL HOLD-INGS. "I told the secretary we're interested in profiling Sopwell as our land pillager of the month, so she expects us."

I opened up the aperture on the Nikon and slowed the shutter speed for low-light conditions. Frank knobbed open the door and stepped into the lobby. A permed woman in her mid-forties smiled cheerfully from behind the reception desk. "He should be back any second," she said, gesturing toward a couple of leather chairs at the far wall. "Please, make yourselves comfortable."

We sat, Frank bearing a pleasantly blank expression, as though he waited for the bus and not to ambush Sopwell. The light would be difficult to work with, fluorescents above and a smoked plate-glass window beside the door. I attached the flash and stopped down the aperture. A man dressed more for the entertainment business than real estate—Persol sunglasses, designer sport coat, knit cotton jersey, slacks, and sneakers—slipped through the door a few minutes after we sat and cast a sidelong glance at us as he moved toward a private office behind the secretary's desk.

"These people are here to interview you for a newspaper column about real estate?" The secretary's voice rose uncertainly at the end of her sentence. "Something about being the land optimizer of the month?"

Sopwell turned to greet us, making a show of flashing open his sport coat to slip his sunglasses into the inside breast pocket. Armani, the label read. From the top of his forehead to the crown of his head his hair grew in sparse clumps that looked like recently

planted tufts of crabgrass, the result of a series of hair-implant pro-
cedures. Except for the hair he was movie-star handsome, eyes gray
as granite and rugged chin adorably dimpled. The chin in particular
looked familiar and I wondered where I'd seen it before. With a
face that handsome he must have been really bummed out about
losing his hair. It must have seemed like a personal tragedy. I
stepped to the side of Frank's shoulder and put the Nikon's
viewfinder to my eye.

Frank stuck the tip of his pen to his writing pad and, pitching his
voice to a tone heard most commonly in district attorneys prosecut-
ing capital crimes, asked, "Could you comment on the current police
investigation regarding your involvement in the robbery-homicide at
Hollywood Forever Cemetery?"

His eyes blanked with the shock of the question and like he didn't
know what hit him he said, "What the fu . . . ?"

I squeezed off the flash.

"Sources tell us that one of your warehouses is the secret base of
the gang responsible for the crimes. Are you part of the gang or its
sponsor?"

"Who are you?" Anger infused his eyes with some life. He whirled
toward his secretary. "Call security!"

"Maybe I've made a mistake," Frank said, suddenly contrite.

"You bet your ass you've made a mistake."

"Records registered with the County of Los Angeles indicate you
are the owner of a warehouse located at . . ." Frank glanced down at
his notes, then back up again. "Nine thousand two hundred
Leadwell. Is that not your building?"

"I own a lot of buildings." He opened the front door and swept
his hand toward the opening. "Now get out."

"You don't deny owning that building in particular?"

"I have security on the line," the secretary announced. "What do
you want me to tell them?"

"You can tell them we're leaving." Frank nodded to me to take the
lead out the door. He followed me out but turned at the threshold.
"One last question. Do you expect to be indicted for murder or just
accessory to murder?"

Sopwell slammed the door so hard I glanced up to the roof,
expecting a few red tiles to come tumbling into the courtyard. "Great

work," I said. "You can print the text of that interview on the head of a pin."

"Take a shot or two of the exterior office," Frank said, and stepped back out of the way. "Did you get the deer-in-headlights shot?"

I crouched on the paving stones for a low-angle shot of the office. When questions come out of nowhere to surprise an interview subject his eyes widen and reflect the light. Frank was so adept at triggering the look with a shock question that we'd coined a phrase for it. "Like a deer in the headlights of a truck doing ninety," I said.

"That look alone will convict him in the eyes of the readers." He lit a cigarette, puffed it out the corner of his mouth while he jotted down notes, said, "I didn't need him to say anything. I'll write a basic denial-of-truth story."

"Headline: 'Suspect Denies Being Murderous Slimeball.' "

"Ninety percent of readers won't even register the denial."

I turned the lens on Frank, took a quick low-angle portrait, framed by sky. "Sopwell look familiar to you?"

"Careful, you'll break your lens," he said, his smile bitter, then shook his head. "Never saw him before."

"It's the chin, the dimple." I shouldered my bag, images clicking through memory like snaps in a slide show, and strode toward the street corner. I'm good with faces. Most photographers are. The stick-figure signal flashed red. Frank shouted at me from the courtyard, alarmed that I'd left him so quickly and wordlessly behind. I ran across the boulevard as the light turned amber and popped the trunk of the Cadillac. I plucked a copy of *Halliwell's Who's Who in the Movies* from a case of reference material I kept on hand to research and identify celebrities.

Frank wheezed up behind me, the cigarette still smoldering between his fingers. "I need the film before you go," he said. "You've been leading a high-risk lifestyle lately and it would be a shame to lose the pictures if the risks catch up to you."

"Meaning I get killed," I said, flipping the pages.

"I worry about it night and day." He took a drag on his cigarette and coughed, lungs sore from the exercise of running across the street. "Particularly if you get killed with next week's headline still in your camera."

Not many photographs run in Halliwell's pages but the book offers capsule biographies of most notable current and former movie stars. The capsules include date of birth, a filmography, and, if applicable, birth name and date of death. I paged to the entry for Chad Stonewell and underlined it for Frank with my thumbnail. Chad Stonewell was born in 1950 as Charles Sopwell.

"Thanks for your concern," I said. "But I don't think I've shot the issue's front page, not yet."

TWENTY-SEVEN

A FEW minutes before midnight Luce bolted from her Los Feliz apartment dressed as though she'd undergone a change of character from arts bohemian to film-noir dominatrix, a semisheer black cocktail dress, fishnet stockings, and spike heels peeking behind a flared ankle-length leather trench coat. The Tercel didn't match the new style but she sped and cornered as though she gripped the wheel of a Porsche. Los Angeles is not much of a late-night town and the streets clear of traffic as the clock nears midnight. Luce choked all the speed she could from the Tercel's four anemic cylinders, driving as though she thought the devil was on her tail or maybe just me.

She slowed midway into Hollywood and turned onto Las Palmas, cruised past a hipster-celebrity club of the moment named Bar Bar, and parked around the corner. I backed into a space down the street from the club and watched the corner, understanding then the change of outfit. She strode the sidewalk as though she owned it, past a rope barricade restraining a crowd of more than fifty stylishly dressed hopefuls waiting to gain admittance, glanced neither left nor right nor checked her stride until she reached the security guy working the entrance. He bent at his tapered waist, his bodybuilder chest and shoulders straining the seams of his black suit. Luce said something and he nodded his bald head once, eyes inscrutable behind chrome and onyx sunglasses. Some bouncers in the L.A. club scene acquire a celebrity to match the velvet ropes they guard and Luther had that glow, no mere thug but a thug with style. He'd turned me away at the ropes no fewer than six times, and five of those times I'd come disguised in borrowed Manolo Blahniks and Prada, the kind of person he'd normally admit. He stepped back, unhooked the rope, and let Luce enter.

I'd have a better chance of sneaking into heaven than Bar Bar with Luther at the door. On certain select nights the celebrity crowd partied there, not because the interior offered anything special—the decor wasn't any different from a thousand other low-rent clubs—but on a whim. The word goes out among a select group of people that this bar or that club is where the celebriati are going that month and so they all go. How the word spreads is a mystery. Homing devices implanted in their back molars, maybe. They didn't admit people they didn't know—except women who look desirable enough to interest the men inside—and they certainly didn't let known paparazzi anywhere near the entrance. That Luce had been admitted so readily meant that her name had been left at the door or that she was a regular, or merely that Luther thought someone inside would want her. Clubbing might have been in her plans for the evening before I'd talked to her or Bar Bar could have been chosen as the one place she could meet someone safe from my prying camera.

I accelerated from the curb and circled the block to the mouth of the service alley at the back of the club. Two stretch limousines idled midblock, light from an adjacent doorway spilling blue onto long, black hoods. I put the telephoto lens to my eye and opened the aperture wide. The back of the club had not been lit to encourage photography, and the limousines had parked close enough to the entrance that the doors, when opened, would shield those entering or leaving the rear compartments. I snapped the latches on the silver case Vulch had given me and attached the night-vision lens. The night blossomed fluorescent green when I lifted the viewfinder to my eye. The infrared lens wasn't nearly as powerful as the telephoto, but when I panned the lens to the back of the club the face of a chauffeur smoking a cigarette by the hood of his limo burst into light.

Five minutes after I'd set up the camera the rear door of the limousine nearest the exit winged open, gripped by a black-jacketed chauffeur. In the gap between the club and limo door I spotted a flash of hair that registered almost white through the lens, and a black spiked heel planted into the asphalt before it knifed into the limo and the door swung shut. Blond hair and stiletto heels are not rare fashion accessories in a nightclub—I'd been guilty of the same style on a few occasions—but the infrared lens was more sensitive to light than I'd thought. As the woman pivoted to enter the limousine the ghostly-green image of her face had veered toward the passenger window, visible in infrared through the smoked glass.

I ducked beneath the wheel as the limousine glided away from the back exit, the crack and roll of tires turning out of the alley toward Las Palmas. Maybe Luce had gotten lucky in record time, her quick exit a coincidence of good fortune, or maybe her friends intended to leave me out front, trying to gain entrance to the club while she slipped out the back. Anyone can rent a limousine and driver for the night, as legions of graduating high schoolers annually prove. Chad Stonewell wasn't the only possible occupant of the limo's passenger compartment—just the most likely one. More than once a changing traffic signal flagged me while the limo cruised ahead, rolling down Santa Monica Boulevard toward the sea, but I never lost sight of its taillights in the empty city night. When it reached the Palisades the limo turned parallel to the ocean and coasted to the curb. The chauffeur hustled around the hood and snapped open the door on the passenger side. Luce burst from the compartment as though pushed, indignantly straightened the line of her trench coat at the curb, and clicked on stiletto heels toward the pier.

I left the Cadillac at the curb and slipped onto the footpaths of Pacific Palisades Park, the narrow strip of green that hugs the cliffs above Santa Monica State Beach to the pier. The homeless crowded the park at that late hour, curled beneath their coats on the grass or wandering the paths with irresolute steps as they walked to stay awake through the night. Luce stayed on the sidewalk parallel to the park and skipped onto the pedestrian walk ramping down to the old carousel at the mouth of the pier. The video-game arcades that lined the south side had gone dark at midnight and the brightly colored bulbs of the Ferris wheel no longer spun in the night sky, but a few late-night revelers still weaved the wooden planks. Further down, where the pilings advanced from dry sand into the waves, a two-headed shadow leaned against the railing, joined at the lips. Luce skirted the railing at the base of the ramp and stepped onto the broad wooden deck fronting the carousel, hugging her arms to her chest as though nervous or merely cold.

I crept midway down the ramp to eye her through the night-vision lens. She stood too far away to allow me to read the expression on her face but at regular intervals she dipped her head toward steps leading to the beach as though she expected someone. I pulled the cell phone from my side pocket, paged through the list of recently called numbers, and hit call when the display lit Detective Dougan's. At that hour he wasn't around the station to answer his phone. I left a message on his voice mail. I knew he wouldn't be in. Like my game of telephone tag with parole agent Terry Graves I wanted the illusion of full cooperation and not the fact. I'd tracked down someone who might know something about the cemetery robbery, I said, wish you were here. I recited the time and my location and closed the connection.

I detached the night-vision lens from the Nikon and when I reached for the telephoto Luce straightened at the rail. I followed the line of her glance to the figure of a man jogging up the steps, sandy blond hair worn long beneath a black-brimmed baseball cap. He looked across his shoulder toward my position on the ramp and beyond. He couldn't spot me at that distance, crouched low behind the railing, not without night-vision equipment of his own. I didn't get a clear look at his face but from his build and hair he looked like Stonewell's bodyguard.

I mounted the telephoto to the Nikon and panned along the deck, searching out the bodyguard in the restricted circle of the telephoto until a pair of stiletto heels sliced through the frame. I tilted the lens. Luce was running. The bodyguard breached the top step and opened his arms. Luce rushed into the gap. I pressed the shutter, aperture wide open and shutter speed slowed to a thirtieth of a second, the big lens propped against the railing for stability. "Outlaw Lovers Embrace on Santa Monica Pier," ran the headline in my imagination. In the dim light leaking from the nearest streetlamp I had a clearer view of the bodyguard's boots, splayed out to the side, than I did of his face. Luce nestled her chin against his shoulder and closed her eyes. She'd met Stonewell in the limousine, I guessed. He'd abused her for speaking with me and kicked her out of the car to be consoled by the bodyguard, her lover.

The bodyguard stroked her head and though I couldn't see his face it seemed from that distance that he spoke to her. If he intended to calm her he failed. Her eyes snapped open and she pushed away, chopping at the space between them. His hands flew palms up as though he wanted no part of the argument. She chopped the air again, her head darting sharply forward as she spoke, then she wrapped her arms around her chest and angrily wiped something from her eye. The bodyguard opened his arms again. Luce moved into him, reluctantly this time, but after he held her for a minute her arms encircled his waist and she laid her head on his shoulder. He stroked the crown of her head with his left hand, drew his right elbow back and thrust it forward. The muscles along Luce's brow contracted and her mouth jutted open in a soundless scream as though she had been struck mute. Her hands writhed against the bodyguard's back like the scalded wings of a bird, then flailed against his shoulders in a failing attempt to push away. He clutched her tightly to his chest, his right hand working something between them, and she sagged against his shoulder.

I stood and screamed. I screamed for Luce because she couldn't. The bodyguard gently lowered her to the planks, his head cocked away from the ramp to hide his face. He knew I was there. He knew I was the one who screamed. I put the telephoto lens to my eye and took the shot. He wrapped something in a black cloth pulled from the pocket of his windbreaker and walked away from the body. I tapped out 911 for the emergency operator and sprinted toward the pier.

Luce's skin had grayed to the color of bone in the thirty seconds it took to reach her. She lay curled on her side, hands clenched over her abdomen to keep the wet mechanics of her intestines from spilling out, her body trembling in a black slick of blood. The couple I'd seen kissing ran up from the far side of the pier, the woman trying to hold back sobs of panic with the palm of her hand. The drunken revelers had vanished. I put my hand on Luce's forehead to let her know someone was there even if I was at a loss about what to do for her. She told me she was cold. Help was coming, I said. The man stripped off his jacket and draped it over her. You'll make it, he said. Just hold on. She was cold, she repeated. We tucked the jacket around her.

"Night," she said. She repeated the same word over and over, her voice fainter and the word more abbreviated at each repetition, until she whispered no more than the first two letters, as though the word she spoke was swallowing her as she spoke it. Then the word changed, subtly, and she repeated it twice. *Nike.*

The man who'd given her his jacket leaned closer, said, "Don't talk now. Don't worry. Just hold on."

But Luce didn't hold on.

She fell.

TWENTY-EIGHT

DETECTIVES DOUGAN and Smalls entered the suspect and witness interview room of the Santa Monica Police Department after I'd given my statement to the local detective who caught the case, a tanned and tired-eyed woman with chopped brown hair and lipstick the color of dried blood. She'd introduced herself as Detective Dabrowski, her handshake as brutal as her lipstick. Before she asked her first question I informed her that I was on parole, not because the law requires such disclosures but to save the time and trouble of additional questioning when she found out later. She led me through my eyewitness statement briskly, then cross-examined me as thoroughly as any prosecutor. Satisfied that my account was consistent in repeat tellings, both in content and with the facts on the ground, she called in Dougan and Smalls.

They did not look happy to see me, not at that hour in the morning and under the circumstances of a cross-jurisdictional murder. They may have headed the investigation into my sister's murder but Luce died in Santa Monica, an independent city with its own mayor, city council, bus service, and police department. Both departments belonged to the Los Angeles Superior Court system. That made inter-departmental cooperation necessary. More time. More meetings. More paperwork. More mess. Worst of all, more time wasted in traffic, commuting from one city to the other.

"I should have arrested you yesterday," Dougan said when he walked through the door. He brought coffee for four and that mattered more than civility. He sat directly across the table from me, Smalls to my right and Dabrowski to my left. If they wanted me to feel trapped, they succeeded. "If I had arrested you, maybe this girl would still be alive today."

I'd been thinking the same ever since the shock of watching Luce die had diminished to trembling hands and a persistent wrenching behind the shield of bone above my heart. Had he arrested me I never would have met her. Had I never met her she wouldn't have sought out Stonewell and his bodyguard. Had I given Luce's name and address to Dougan the day before, she might still be alive and I wouldn't be facing the possibility of arrest. I was guilty not of any criminal offense but of being blind to the consequences of my acts.

Dougan checked the notes on the top page of a legal-sized pad of lined yellow paper. "Lucille Ryan, eighteen years old, employed as a receptionist by Theatrical Artists Group." He pinched the bridge of his nose between his thumb and forefinger. "I pulled her DMV photo. Good-looking girl."

"She wanted to be an actress," I said. "The one time I met her I thought she might be a good one."

"Doesn't look like she'll get the chance, does it?"

I said, "No sir," and bit the inside of my lip until I tasted blood. Physical pain distracted me. Physical pain was easy to endure.

Dougan pushed a cup of take-out coffee halfway across the table, asked, "When did you meet her?"

I peeled the plastic lid from the cup and inhaled the steam like a drug. "After I left you. I knew where she worked, followed her and a couple of co-workers to a skinless chicken place across from her building."

"Was she the assignment you talked about, the one you had to do to pay the rent?"

I nodded.

"Son of a bitch," he said. "Here I was thinking you were running off to photograph Mel Gibson or somebody and instead you were planning to compromise the investigation of your own sister's murder while lying to my face."

"I didn't lie to you," I said. "I never lied."

"You just didn't bother to tell the truth."

"Why were you following Ms. Ryan?" Smalls asked, his voice so soft he might have whispered.

I turned to look at him, knowing that line of questioning could lead me to a withholding-evidence charge. "I suspected she was one of the kids who tried to rob Forest Lawn cemetery the other night." Smalls's expression betrayed little except watchfulness. I squared my shoulders to face Dougan on the opposite side of the table. "I told you about that yesterday. I never got a clear-enough look to be sure but I thought I saw her at the warehouse in North Hollywood, the one owned by Chad Stonewell's brother."

"And you recognized her?" Smalls asked, like he didn't believe me. "She'd only been in, what, a couple television shows, a small role here and there in films. How did you know who she was?"

"It's my job to know faces," I said.

Dougan stopped me with a raised forefinger and flipped back through his notepad. He underlined a penciled entry with his thumb. "The listing you gave me belongs to Sopwell Holdings, registered to Daniel Sopwell."

"Chad Stonewell was born Charles Sopwell," I said. "I can show you his bio in my film encyclopedia, if you want."

Dougan's walrus moustache fluttered above the gust of an exasperated sigh. "I hate movie-star cases," he said.

"Why?"

Dougan shrugged, glanced at Smalls.

"Juries never convict," Smalls answered. "We know more about celebrities than our relatives. You'd do better to ask a jury to convict their own brother."

"Maybe you can cut a deal with Stonewell's bodyguard, get him to testify, convict Stonewell that way." I'm no cop but it seemed like a reasonable suggestion.

Dougan pressed steepled fingers to his lips, his stare aggressive and pitying, as though he both hated and pitied me. "Stonewell's bodyguard has an alibi for the night of your sister's murder."

"Alibis can be faked."

"He accompanied Stonewell to a film premiere that night and later to a private party."

"You know how Hollywood types stick together," I said, angry that he wasn't seeing it. "And Stonewell can't be considered a legitimate alibi. He's just as guilty as his bodyguard."

"How about Hugh Hefner?" Smalls's voice bumped up an octave, as though amused. "Is he guilty, too?"

Nobody likes to be laughed at. The chair squeaked against the floor when I pushed back from the table. "I don't see what's so funny about that."

"Stonewell and his bodyguard were at the Playboy mansion the night your sister was killed," Dougan said, watching me. "The bodyguard lost his head, tried to pick up one of Hef's girlfriends."

Dabrowski snorted into her coffee, said, "Which one? I hear he had seven so-called girlfriends at last count. The man must order Viagra by the ton."

"Stonewell and his bodyguard were both at the party," Dougan said. "I have a dozen witnesses. So maybe we should go over your statement again, see if we can figure out the difference between what you saw and what you think you saw." He walked me through the events of the previous night, starting with the limousine at Bar Bar, Dabrowski dipping her head at each declarative point to check that this telling conformed with the previous statements. He flipped back through his notes, asked Dabrowski, "Do you have confirmation on the time of attack?"

"One twenty-eight," she said from memory. "One of the witnesses looked at his watch just before he heard screaming." She glanced at me. "That screaming would be Ms. Zero here, reacting to what she saw through the camera."

"Twelve minutes difference," he said to me. "You called and left a message at the station at one-sixteen. Why did you call me then and not before? Did you know she was going to be killed?"

"When else was I going to call you? She went to a club, slipped out the back and into a limousine. I didn't know where she was going, who she was with, or what she was doing. Young, attractive girls go to clubs and get laid by famous, rich men. That's the way this town works."

"You thought you'd photograph her with Stonewell," Smalls said.

I shrugged, a gesture that confirmed his suspicion without specifically admitting it. "I'm a tabloid photographer. I make my living photographing celebrities. When she went alone down to the pier I thought I should call. She had to know my sister was murdered. She had to know what she was doing was dangerous. I was afraid what might happen to her."

"Why not call 911 then?"

"Because she welcomed the guy like a lover."

"Who you identify as Stonewell's bodyguard."

"That's right."

Smalls asked, "How do you know it was Stonewell's bodyguard?"

"I'd seen them together. At a restaurant in Santa Monica."

"And on the pier, did you get a clear shot of his face?"

I said I didn't think I did, that he was too distant, the light too dim, and he wore a baseball cap. As I spoke Smalls watched me above hands clenched at his lips. The hands were fastidiously manicured and his eyes gleamed, sharp and mechanical as a pair of scissors.

"Then how do you know it was Stonewell's bodyguard?"

"The way he moved, his hair, his clothes—"

"Describe them."

"Black windbreaker, blue jeans, Timberland half boots."

"But the girl said Nike." Smalls dipped his head at Dabrowski.

"Nike, that's right," she said. "We have two other witnesses to that. Sounded like she was saying night at first, but then she said Nike."

"Why would she say Nike if he was wearing Timberland?"

"Maybe Nike, then." Maybe they just looked like Timberlands.

"Last words are meaningless," Dougan said, fingers thrumming the tabletop in a riff of exasperation. "You know the most common last words in all of recorded history?" He tipped his head back and gurgled—his imitation of a death rattle.

"He's right, even if someone talks, it's nonsense," Smalls said. "Case in point, why would she mention his shoes?"

"Her eyes were closed when I got to her. His shoes might have been the last thing she saw."

"That's pretty pathetic, don't you think? Beautiful young girl like that, whole world, bright future ahead of her, and the last thing she sees before she blinks out is a pair of Nikes? Doesn't that strike you as pathetic? Or do you have celluloid and cheap newsprint for a heart, don't feel things like normal people?" He dropped his hands to the table with a sharp slap.

I flinched. Dabrowski and Dougan didn't.

"Show her the photograph," Smalls said.

Dougan reached toward the back of his blue notebook. I expected a crime-scene photo showing Luce's death in all its ugly anguish. Dougan flicked his wrist and a color printout of a DMV photograph skittered across the surface of the table. The face in the photo—a muscular, thirty-something white male—looked vaguely familiar but I couldn't place it, not immediately.

"Do you recognize the man in this photograph?"

"I've seen him before but I don't know his name, who he is."

"Look again." Smalls's voice cracked across the table, sharp and contemptuous. "You don't remember where you've seen him before?"

I stared at the photograph, mapping the features of the man against the men I'd seen recently but not coming up with a match. "I've seen him, I just don't remember where. Maybe it will come to me later."

Smalls shook his head, said, "Be sure to tell us if it does."

I looked at Dougan, confused why the man in the photograph was suddenly so important, asked, "Who is he?"

"Stonewell's bodyguard," Dougan said.

TWENTY-NINE

A FEW hours before noon I walked into the church around the corner from what had once been my apartment and beneath the smiling portrait of St. Anne lit one candle for my sister, one for my mother, and one for Luce. The photographs I'd taken the night before, developed by a police technician, had provided basic corroboration of the story I'd told to Dabrowski, Dougan, and Smalls, but little else. The limousine shots were badly exposed because of my unfamiliarity with the night-vision lens; I'd never gotten close enough to clearly photograph its license plate. The man who killed Luce had kept the brim of his cap low over his forehead and never turned his face fully toward the camera. The shots I'd taken of Luce's fatal dance with her murderer were front-page images worthy of a Pulitzer in tabloid news reporting—if only such a prize existed. Publication would have solved my money troubles for months had Dabrowski not confiscated the negatives as evidence pertaining to an ongoing homicide investigation. The lawyers at *Scandal Times* would fight to get the negatives released. I wouldn't. Sometimes it's better to go hungry.

I knelt before the altar to say a short prayer for my dead. I felt odd kneeling and I didn't say much of a prayer, rest in peace and all that. After I finished I stepped back and noticed a candle burning before the next altar down from St. Anne's. The candle cast a flickering, amber light upon two objects mounted to the wall behind a protective guardrail. The object on the left was a portrait of an old woman praying, her haggard and sorrowful face framed in the black-and-white habit of a nun. Beside the painting the convex glass of a gold oval frame bowed over an aged heart. The heart had been shaped from rolled, gilded paper and pearls set on a red velvet background. On the front rail a worn brass nameplate read in a cursive script, *Santa Monica.*

"That's not what she really looked like," said an old voice behind me. "St. Monica, that was more than fifteen hundred years ago."

The old priest shuffled one pew over. He waved a brown, rootlike hand at the painting. "This is just what the painter, what he thought she looked like. But he got it wrong."

"How do you know?"

"Because I've seen her," he said.

I said, "Oh."

"I know that must seem strange for you," he admitted.

"A little. How did you see her?"

He pointed to a spot on his forehead, a few inches above the middle of his brow. "Like this." He smiled at me, as though knowing I didn't have a clue what he was talking about but it didn't really matter. "St. Monica is very special to me, you see. She helped me find God."

I remembered our conversation from before, asked, "So she's your patron saint?"

"She's the patron saint of many troubled people. Alcoholics, those in difficult marriages, widows, victims of abuse . . ."

"Sounds like my kind of saint."

He nodded his head as though he agreed.

I leaned over the railing to inspect the sculpted heart behind the convex glass. Gilded paper had been cut and rolled in a floral design to encircle the heart and at the base the flowers swirled around a grayish-white object no larger than a fingernail. I'd never seen anything like it before. "What is this?" I asked.

"A reliquary," the old priest answered.

"That thing at the bottom?"

"A relic."

The old priest shuffled toward the front altar, his back bent, the palm of his hand cupping the back of each pew for support. He looked at least ninety years old. Maybe he meant he'd seen St.

Monica in person. When he turned from the pews and tottered toward a confessional along the side wall, I followed, stooping into the black-curtained booth opposite his. The sweat smell of penitents clung to the curtain, wood-paneled walls and ceiling like the ghosts of sins confessed. The grayish-white thing at the base of the frame beside the portrait of St. Monica, what the old priest called a relic, had looked like bone. I said, "I'm not Catholic."

"Tell me what's on your heart," the old priest said. "That you are sincere of heart is more important right now than being Catholic or not. We call this the sacrament of penance. If you sincerely confess your sins the forgiveness God grants is sacred."

I could smell his breath through the slot, musty and sweet as an old closet. I asked, "How can one confess a lifetime of sins?"

"A good question. How can one climb a mountain?"

"One step at a time?"

His silence confirmed the answer. And so I began. The old priest wouldn't live long enough to hear me recite all my sins and so I concentrated on my most recent ones. I wasn't sure what properly constituted a sin in the Catholic sense so I talked mostly about my regrets. Most of all I regretted not saying good-bye to my mother and I regretted my part in the web of events that had led Luce to her death. Things I'd done that most people would consider sins but that I didn't regret I didn't confess, no matter how violent. Maybe those sins would keep me forever from the grace of God. Maybe my chief sin was not being sure such a grace existed. "This girl I saw killed, she wore something around her neck encased in silver, a bone, I think." Luce's pendant still troubled me. "Could it have been something tied to her religion?"

The priest said, "You mean a relic."

"Can bone be a relic?"

The old priest was silent so long I feared he'd fallen asleep.

"You still alive in there?" I asked.

"This doesn't sound like part of your confession."

"Maybe it's part of my penance," I said.

The yellow palm of the old priest's hand flashed across the vent as he made the sign of the cross. "You must demonstrate your good faith before God," he said. "That will be your penance. To begin to demonstrate your good faith, you must pray."

I said, "Okay."

The priest hole flashed shut. I felt like I sometimes do in the movies, when I don't know if the film has really ended yet or one last bit remains to be played. When the priest didn't speak again for a minute or so I stood and stepped out of the confessional.

"You want to talk to a man named Gregory Cherubin," the old priest said from behind the curtain. "He'll tell you what you need to know about relics."

My parole officer was leaning against the hood of her brown Chevy sedan when I stepped out of the church. She didn't bother to nod or look at me as I approached, the tip of her blue pen flicking as she reviewed a case file from behind sunglasses impenetrable to the outside eye. "Since when did you get religion?" she asked.

"What makes you think I've got religion?"

"Calling to meet here, a church, of all places. Just don't think it scores any points with me. Every other con in prison claims to have found God but that doesn't mean we should let them out onto the streets again." Her eyes slit a glance above the rims of her shades. She wanted to make sure I was paying attention. "I'm agnostic, myself. After what I've seen, it's hard to believe whatever planned things has much intelligence."

"I like churches," I said. "Maybe I'd do all right in a convent if it wasn't for the parts about sin and belief. The solitary life, you know, it suits me. Those little rooms they give the nuns, it wouldn't bother me at all."

A distressed bark sounded behind me. I glanced over to the Rott, locked in the car. I nodded to Graves, walked over to let him out. I don't think he shared my acceptance of solitude in small places.

"I talked to Detective Dougan." Graves snapped shut the case file. "He suspects you may have violated the terms of your parole by withholding evidence. Normally, a charge like this is difficult to prove but the evidence you withheld pertained to a murder investigation. He's not disposed to be merciful."

"Will I have enough time to find a place for my dog?"

It took her a moment to get what I was asking.

"He's not against copping you, not for now," she said. "And no, when I come for you, you won't have time to do more than wave good-bye to your dog. Maybe that will encourage you to be a little more responsible."

I straddled the Rott's back, something he liked me to do as long as I didn't sit on him. *Cop* was parolese for *continue on parole*. She meant that Dougan wasn't demanding that parole be revoked, not yet.

"Let's review the situation." She crossed her arms over her chest and glanced up to the sky, as though calculating sums. "In the past two weeks you've filed a police report for assault—"

"That wasn't my fault," I said.

She tipped her head in my direction, and even though I couldn't see her eyes through the optical camouflage, I knew she was glaring at me. She made me wait a good ten seconds before she continued. "You filed another police report when your sister kited one of your checks, and that same sister was murdered after following a tip meant for you. Then someone torches your apartment while you're in it. Last of all, a young girl you're following, a potential witness you didn't bother to tell Detective Dougan about until the last possible moment, is murdered right in front of you." She flashed five fingers for five charges and asked, "Is that everything?"

That was everything I'd confessed to and I wasn't going to admit anything additional, not just then, when the hole I'd already dug was too deep to crawl out of. "I think that's all," I said.

She let me wait another ten seconds while I supposedly thought about the error of my ways. "What does this tell you?" she asked.

"I shouldn't go to Vegas because my luck isn't running too good?"

She held up the forefinger on her opposite hand. "Oh, almost forgot, six, you don't have a place of residence, as required by your parole agreement. I could refuse to cop you right now, do you know that? I could take this to a judge tomorrow and get your parole revoked. You are involved in five separate criminal investigations. Five! Are you trying to set some kind of record?"

I said, "No, ma'am."

"Where are you going to live?"

I glanced back at my Cadillac.

"No way," she said. "You need a fixed address. I'll give you seventy-two hours to settle somewhere. If you don't have a place lined up by then, you'll need to register with a flophouse." She reached out to give the Rott a pat, a smile cutting through her icy expression like a blowtorch. "One that accepts dogs."

THIRTY

GREGORY CHERUBIN greeted me that afternoon outside UCLA's Bunche Hall, easily picking me out among the students clustered below the steps, most of them dressed in the casual California style sold by stores like the Gap and J. Crew. I guess I didn't look too much like a UCLA student; the closest I came to wearing an earth tone was the paving stone below my boots.

He carried a black briefcase in one hand and a blue sport coat slung over his back on the hook of his forefinger. His pale arms stubbed from a short-sleeved white shirt, top unbuttoned to reveal the collar of a white T-shirt. I'd caught him by appointment after a lecture on Catholicism to students of comparative religion. He seemed to wear his hair whichever way the wind blew it, wispy red strands spraying from a case of male pattern baldness that gave him a natural tonsure. He clenched the briefcase between his elbow and ribs to shake hands. His handshake lingered without being cloying and he measured me with eyes that seemed to combine priest with cop.

"You've seen Father Morales today?" Cherubin asked. "How does he look?"

"Old," I said.

"He always looks that way," he said. "I don't know why he referred you to me but I'm happy to help."

We got something warm to drink at a student café across the lawn and found a free table in the mild February sun. The students around us chatted and studied at tables piled high with books. They seemed happy. I'd managed two years of junior college while working forty hours a week. I always wanted to go back to school, never made the chance for myself. Cherubin sipped at a cup of herbal tea, asked, "Are you interested in first-, second-, or third-class relics?"

"I'm mostly interested in bones," I said.

"Bones are first-class relics, a category that also includes hair, fingernails, anything that formed the corporal body of a saint. Plus pieces of the Passion."

"What's that?"

"The Passion?"

I nodded.

"You're not even Christian?" He sounded surprised.

"My religious education is a little thin."

"No matter. Father Morales must have sent you to me for a reason." He cleared his throat and glanced at his watch. "The Passion refers to the suffering of Jesus on the cross. Most commonly, pieces of the cross on which he was crucified, called the True Cross, are considered first-class relics."

"Are there a lot of those?"

"Probably enough to build Noah's ark several times over." His smile was brief and severe. "That's why Father Morales mentioned my name. I research the provenance of relics, trying to prove the genuine and expose the frauds."

My time in prison had exposed me to two types of cons serving time on fraud, the pro and the prankster. "There's money in this? Or do people do it just to prove they can?"

"People have been selling relics since the death of Christ. Fakes have been around just as long. St. Augustine wrote in the fourth century about swindlers impersonating monks to sell spurious relics." He raised the cardboard cup to his lips and sipped, his glance wandering to the surrounding students as he measured what he wanted to say next. "I'm sure a few well-intentioned believers have created fakes with the intention of inspiring the faithful and many have been gullible in their certainty that a set of otherwise anonymous bones found near an ancient church are the bones of a saint. But the overwhelming majority of the time it's about money.

The Church has fought the sale of all relics, even genuine ones, since the reign of Theodosius. It's part of the canon law against the sins of simony."

I started to feel like I do in this dream I have every now and then, of finding myself back in high school, taking the final exam of a class I forgot to attend. I felt the side pocket of my camera bag for a pad and pen. "Simony? How do you spell it?"

My ignorance must have been obvious, from the lost sheen of my eyes if nothing else. Cherubin took pity, spelling it out for me, his tone indulgent. "Simony is the purchase of the spiritual with temporal things, such as the purchase of relics. A relic is considered an object with spiritual value, particularly first-class relics."

"What I don't understand is, why? What's the purpose in worshipping an old bone?"

"First, the Church expressly forbids the worship of 'old bones,' which are more appropriately called first-class relics when discussing the remains of a saint." He held up a single, warning forefinger. "*Non colimus, non adoramus; honoramus.* We do not worship. We do not adore. Instead, we venerate or honor the relics of the saint as part of our adoration of God. If I told you that people have been healed by touching a garment worn by a saint, or by kissing a fragment of bone from the body of a saint, would you believe me?"

That seemed like a trick question so I thought carefully before I answered. "I'd like to believe it but I'd have to wonder about the mental state of the person getting healed, whether or not it was all in their head."

"If the crippled can walk, does it really matter?" He slapped the table, a gesture of impatience, and stared at me as though he might make me understand by the force of will as much as reason. "If healing the spirit heals the legs, are the legs any less healed?"

"Fair enough," I admitted.

"Catholic doctrine states that inanimate things can be instruments of divine power, though they are not in themselves divine. That's why we honor but do not worship relics, which would be idolatry. But when something becomes the instrument through which God works His will, people sometimes mistake the instrument—the relic—for the cause, which is God. This results in people putting the cart before the horse, so to speak." He smiled, pleased with this explanation as though the use of a common metaphor had just occurred to him and made the whole more readily understandable.

"Are Catholics the only ones who venerate relics?"

"The veneration of relics probably extends back to the days of the Stone Age. Almost every culture has one variant or another. The body of Buddha was supposedly divided into relics. The Greeks honored the bones of their heroes. Ancestor worship in several cultures involves the veneration of bones or ashes."

"Do people ever wear a relic, say, as a necklace or pendant?"

"That was one of the abuses." He nodded as though I'd finally given him a correct answer. "Because secular jewelry was forbidden at times during the Middle Ages, the rich would encase a small relic in gold and decorate it with precious stones, making it a reliquary, and wear that."

"Have you ever heard of someone making reliquaries from the bones of a movie star or celebrity?"

Cherubin's skin flushed to the tips of his ears, which glowed such a violent red they seemed about to ignite in flame. "Someone came to me with similar questions about relics a couple months ago. A dealer in movie memorabilia. He'd run across something someone claimed was the relic of a movie star. Wanted to know what I thought of it." He waved the back of his hand through the space between us as though dispelling a wasp. "I told him I thought it was sacrilege."

"Why would somebody wear something like that?"

"Probably from the belief that the relic has magical properties. That it will work miracles." His eyebrows contracted sharply. "Black miracles, I'd say."

"Black miracles?" I'd never heard the phrase before, but it reminded me of something Vulch had said. "Does that have anything to do with the dark arts?"

"Whoever blasphemes the Church—and making reliquaries from the bones of movie stars is blasphemy—is a practitioner of the dark arts, whether consciously or not." The look he gave me, his brow furrowed and the frown lines around his mouth deeply scored, served as warning that this was a subject of dire importance to him.

"The person responsible is either a Satanist, purposely perverting the rituals of Catholicism, or a renegade."

"A renegade what?" I asked.

"Priest," he said. "Every now and then a priest goes bad. The Church will only rarely disown one of her sons. But sometimes, a priest rejects the Church, not just to lead a pleasantly temporal life but to fight for the other side." His finger inscribed a hundred-and-eighty-degree turn onto the tabletop. "A renegade."

THIRTY-ONE

THE SHELVES that lined the walls of Mad Mack's Movie Memorabilia spilled over with the detritus of thousands of film and television productions, some famous and others known only to aficionados, but each having created a series of artifacts that fans and collectors considered indispensable to their well-being, such as a vintage Han Solo and Chewbacca plastic 7-Eleven *Star Wars* cup or a genuine gorilla soldier vest and matching ammo strap from *Beneath the Planet of the Apes.* Costumes took up two entire walls, each item wrapped in clear plastic and marked with a tag describing which star, starlet, starling, or stunt double wore what, or, in the case of a swatch of Spock's uniform from the original *Star Trek* television show, framed behind glass with a certificate of authenticity, testifying to its impeccable value as a collectible.

The remaining wall and aisle displays were packed with scripts, press kits given to members of the media—who promptly sold them—and props that ranged from the keys to the Aston Martin driven by James Bond in *Thunderball*—not the car itself, just the keys—to a prop gun stolen from the unforgettable Stallone starrer *Stop! Or My Mom Will Shoot.* Near the top of the ceiling, where the shelves could stretch no higher without imminent danger of toppling, signed photographs of stars dating back to the silent-film days crammed every available inch of wall space. The sensory effect of so much memorabilia of questionable cultural importance packed so tightly together was like entering an archaeological exhibit organized by a ragpicker.

Mad Mack presided over the shop from behind a sales counter piled shoulder-high with products that he hadn't yet bothered to squeeze onto the shelves. He kept an eye on customers through an archer-sized notch cleared beside the cash register. As I was his only customer, that eye was free to wander over the pages of *Variety*. "You Max Perlstein?" I asked him.

"Was last time I looked at my driver's license." Long gray hair spiraled from his head like smoke. His eyes, shielded at the corners by thick, black-plastic-framed eyeglasses, didn't stray from the page, as though he'd sized me up as a nonbuyer from the moment I walked through the door.

I poked my head into the gap beside the cash register, said, "Gregory Cherubin said you might know something about people who collect the bones of dead celebrities."

The *Variety* turned to an oblique angle and he rubbed his right hand across the chest of his red-checked shirt. "Are you buying or selling?"

"Neither. I'm asking."

Mad Mack swiveled the stool to get a direct look at me, the glance of his blue-gray and bloodshot eyes both wary and curious. By the way I was dressed, the flicker of his eyes said, I looked more like a seller. "I still need to know who you are, why you're interested."

"I'm a freelance photographer for *Scandal Times,* the gossip tabloid," I said. "Might be good publicity for you."

"You wanna show me some ID?"

I dug the press credential from the side of my camera bag and placed it on the counter. He craned his neck to read the print and to check the photo against the original, took a moment to rummage beneath the counter, then slapped the previous week's issue of *Scandal Times* next to the cash register. "Lucky for you, I'm a fan." He plucked a felt-tip marker from a *Toy Story II* commemorative cup and presented it to me like a knife, blunt end over his forearm. "Would you mind signing this one?"

It took me a moment to realize he wanted me to sign his copy of *Scandal Times*. Nobody had ever asked me to sign anything except checks and my parole-release agreement. I took the pen and swirled my signature over the front page, said, "I doubt this will make it worth anything more than the price of the paper."

"If it's got a signature, it's collectible." He wrapped the issue in protective plastic. "You said Cherubin sent you?"

I nodded, said, "A couple days ago I met this girl, this young actress, and she was wearing something around her neck that looked like bone. Told me it was the penis bone of a dolphin."

"I don't collect those," Mad Mack said. "But if you want a life-sized plaster replica of John Holmes's private parts, cast from the original himself, I can get you that."

"I don't think she was telling me the strict truth," I said. "I suspect it was another kind of bone, maybe stolen from the grave of James Dean. Would you know anything about that?"

"James Dean, you said?" His eyebrows shot above his eyeglass rims. He was impressed. "Not directly, no. But I know things like that are for sale to the right people at the right price." He inserted the paper into a previously invisible gap in the clutter atop the desk and waved toward the aisles behind me. "Just about anything connected to the movie business is collectible. You want Jerry Lewis's little red hat from *The Bellboy,* well, I got it on the shelves here. You want something a little more risqué, two shelves down from the hat you'll find the athletic supporter worn by Nick Nolte during the filming of *North Dallas Forty.* But some things just aren't meant to be collected, in my opinion, and the bones of film greats are one of them." He ducked his head below the counter and was gone for a good thirty seconds before reappearing with a small white box. "This little sucker cost me five grand."

I waited for him to open it. He didn't.

"First we gotta come to a mutual agreement. You can take a picture of my beautiful mug if you want." His smile was lurid and singularly unattractive, perfect for *Scandal Times.* "And you can take a picture of what's in the box, but for legal reasons you can't identify it as mine and you can't take a picture of me and it together in the same shot, do you dig me?" He pried off the top of the box. A silver and glass locket rested inside, the glass framing an off-white fragment about the size of a finger bone.

"What is it? Or should I ask, who is it?"

"Montgomery Clift." He said the name with awe, as though enough of the actor still resided in the fragment to command respect and reverence. "I was eight years old when *The Search* came out. You see it?"

"A little before my time."

"Clift played a soldier who befriends a concentration-camp survivor, a little boy. A Czech Jew." He stroked the glass case above the bone fragment. "The film meant a lot to me then. This is the only thing of his I have." He lifted the reliquary out of the box and held it in the palm of his hand as though he cradled a sacred egg. "I'm meaning to give it back to his family. Still, five grand is five grand, so I thought I'd keep it a while."

"You're supposed to wear it around your neck, that the idea?"

"That's what the guy sold it to me said." He lifted the locket by its chain and then separated the strands to form a neck-sized gap. "Said it was supposed to have mystical, sacred powers, only it didn't work so well for him because he hadn't been cast in anything since the day he bought it. Said he wasn't supposed to sell it to outsiders, risked the wrath of the Church of Divine Thespians by selling it to me."

"The church of what?" I said, thinking I'd heard wrong.

"Divine Thespians. You never heard of it?"

"Does it sound like something I should have heard of?"

"I agree, the group is a little out of the ordinary, but with you working for the tabloids, I thought if anybody would know, outside the circle of cognoscenti, that is, it would be you." He guided the locket to a soft landing on the cotton padding inside the box.

"You're right, I have heard of them, though nothing more than the name." The macro would get me close enough to make out the bone behind the glass. I switched lenses. My sister had mentioned the group the day she came to my apartment. "This church, where's it located?"

"No idea," he said. "No idea if they've even got a building. If they do, it's not public information. They don't maintain a Web site. You find them mentioned here and there on the Internet, but nothing specific. Just rumors. I didn't even hear about them until a few months ago. Another crackpot group, right? Only about a thousand of those in L.A. But the name attracted my attention and then I noticed that my high-end business started to drop off."

"What you got here that's high-end?"

I didn't mean to be offensive. I was just ignorant.

"I take it you're not a collector."

"Just parking tickets," I said. The macro lens magnified the locket enough to see the bone behind the glass for what it was. I tipped the box toward the light and propped it up with a wedge of paper.

"I can see how it might strike an outsider as a little odd that some-one would pay a couple grand for something that most would con-sider secondhand junk, but that's the nature of my business," he said. "Stuff that the stars actually owned or wore, clothing, accessories, personal things, that's high-end in my business."

"Kind of like second-class relics," I said. "You know, things the saints touched."

"Never thought of it that way." He dropped his head to counter level to better appreciate the way I was setting up the shot. "That makes bones first-class, right?"

"That's what Cherubin told me."

"Hate not to carry first-class merchandise, no matter what it is. Maybe I should reconsider my decision. The hard-core fans, they still come in or buy stuff on the Web site, but a big part of my business comes from actors who want a little something special from a per-former who inspired them. You know, a hat Barbra Streisand wore in *Funny Girl*, a script signed by Marlon Brando, that kind of thing."

I kept my eye to the camera, clicked the shutter, asked, "Chad Stonewell ever come in?"

"The stars themselves, never. They send their personal assistants. Young women mostly, snappy dressers, kind of harried-looking, don't know anything about collecting but know exactly what they want." He watched me intensely while he talked and, being more than a little myopic, edged so close to the work that I nearly got his nose in the shot. "Sometimes they drop a hint who they're shopping for, you know, let me know only the best will do. Then about a year ago the number of personal assistants I see in the store started to decline and I heard my first rumor that people were finding some-thing else to collect."

I swiveled the camera to frame an extreme close-up of his face, from the top of his glasses to the bottom of his lips. "You mean they were collecting celebrity relics, like this locket."

He stared at me dead on. I clicked the shutter. Perfect.

"That's exactly what I mean," he said. "If you're an actor and you got some coin in your pocket, why would you settle for a second-class relic if you can buy first-class? Why settle for James Dean's toothbrush when you can have his teeth?"

THIRTY-TWO

FRANK ATTACKED his midday breakfast omelet with a combination of anger and appetite, as though intent on killing each bite before swallowing it. "I can't believe you gave up the film," he said for the third time. We ate at a sidewalk table outside a hipster café called Kings Road. Just beyond the curb, noon traffic whooshed down Beverly Boulevard, heading toward the mammoth Beverly Center mall and beyond. Across the chest of Frank's sweatshirt graffitilike letters scrawled THEY CAN TAKE MY SMOKES WHEN THEY PRY THEM FROM MY COLD, DEAD FINGERS. His usual pack of Winstons lay at the corner of the table, not more than six inches from his left hand, the reason we ate outside. "You never give up the film," he ranted. "Never. Never. Never. It's one of the cardinal rules of tabloid journalism."

"I didn't give it up," I said. "The police confiscated it."

"Of course they confiscated it!" Fluffy bits of egg flew from his mouth with the protest. "That's not the point. You should have known they were going to confiscate it and ditched the film somewhere I could find it later."

"Do you want me to go to jail?"

"Who said anything about jail? Of course I don't want you to go to jail. I want the film and because you gave it to the cops like it was some kind of goodwill gesture I don't have it."

"Goodwill gesture? I'm a convicted felon on parole. They would have thrown me in jail."

"On what charge?"

"Withholding evidence in a murder investigation."

He stared at me, a forkful of egg lifted halfway toward his gaping mouth. "Withholding evidence? We would have given them prints after we developed the roll." The fork finished its journey and returned to the plate for more.

"And said what? Look what fell off the back of a truck? They would have thrown me in jail, absolutely no doubt about it."

"What do you think we have lawyers for?" he asked. "Their sweet personalities?"

"You mean you would have hired a lawyer to get me out of jail?"

He nodded, chewing away. "You get arrested on company business, yes, that's right, *Scandal Times* pays the ticket."

"If the lawyers can't get the film released, why should I think they'd have better luck with me?"

"All this doubting, all this lack of trust." Frank shook his head and sighed as though his faith in human nature had been wounded. "Not to mention that you've seriously fucked up the Stonewell story."

"Me? How?"

He raised an eyebrow.

"You mean the bodyguard? So maybe I was wrong about that. But it doesn't mean Stonewell isn't involved. His brother owns the warehouse in North Hollywood, remember?"

Frank glanced toward the street, where a sun-yellow H2 Hummer pulled into a parking space painted blue for handicapped parking. "This is about to get interesting," Frank said. "What would you say to Stonewell if you saw him again?"

"I'd ask him who he was meeting the day I tried to take his photograph," I said. "You were right when you said Stonewell should have been grateful for the publicity. But he wasn't, and the reason he wasn't, he either didn't want to be seen with the guy he was lunching with or the guy himself didn't want his picture in the tabs. You get what I'm saying."

"Sure, you're saying we don't have a story." He stared over my shoulder. "But it looks like we're going to have one hell of a photo op."

I turned in my chair and when I saw what he was looking at I reached for my bag, wishing I carried a gun instead of a camera. Chad Stonewell had stepped from behind the wheel of the Hummer and circled the back bumper to meet a walking tree stump on the curb. I stripped the lens cap from the Nikon and focused first on Frank because I wanted to document the guilty look on his face.

"I got a call about an hour ago from his personal assistant but I never dreamed he'd actually show up." Frank mopped the last remnants of egg, potato, and jam with the butt end of a piece of toast and stood to shovel it into his mouth. He stared down at me as though waiting. "I'm only the intermediary. He's actually here to meet you."

"Thanks for warning me, or should I say, setting me up." I offered him the camera. "Maybe you should take this so we don't lose any photographs when he throws me across Beverly Boulevard." Frank didn't move to take the camera. I swiveled the lens toward the Hummer. The tree stump carried a plastic bag as he walked toward our table. I panned up from the bag and recognized the face from the DMV photograph Dougan had showed me the day before. I closed my eyes and studied memory like a series of snapshots, the black-suited chauffeur striding around the hood of the big Mercedes on the day I'd tried to photograph Stonewell, the restaurant door swinging open, and the first face popping out to scope the scene, a face I now recognized as the one I'd just seen through the lens. I dipped the viewfinder to frame his shoes. Adidas. The other guy, the one standing near the street corner, had smashed my camera and later killed Luce. I'd assumed—wrongly—that he worked for Stonewell.

"Should I say cheese or do you prefer sex?" Stonewall called, his adorably dimpled chin cleaving the air like a star trailed by his retinue. I checked the number of exposures remaining on the roll of film and strode toward the Hummer. Stonewall slowed and opened his arms as though he wanted to hug me. I skirted him on the sidewalk and framed the Hummer, its obscene blaze of yellow steel dwarfing the blue wheelchair sign that reserved the space for the handicapped.

"What, not even a hello or a fuck you?" Stonewell said. "Are you a photographer for *Scandal Times* or *Car and Driver?*"

I lowered the camera, gave him a look. "Last time I checked, stupidity was not an officially recognized handicap in the state of California."

Stonewell dropped his arms, a hug out of the question for the moment. "I got a sticker, see for yourself," he said.

"Tell that to the next heart patient looking for a parking spot."

"What are you busting my balls for?" His arms came up again, this time in the classic palms-up gesture of innocent victim. Almost all actors can play charm. It's difficult to stay angry at an actor because the moment they laser their charm in your direction you just melt. But Stonewell wasn't playing his charm just to me; he included Frank, the craning necks in the café window, and the cars cruising past on the street. He said, "I came here to apologize."

"For what?"

He grinned sheepishly and his eyes rolled once to the sky. "I really fucked up with the camera that day. I never should have allowed that guy to smash it. I should have stood up for you. I've regretted it ever since." He crooked a finger at his bodyguard. "Here, I've brought you something to kiss and make up."

The bodyguard held out the plastic bag as though reluctant to give it to me, said, "I should make you eat this."

"Right," I said. "And if you tried I'd kick you so hard in the balls you'd be flossing your teeth with pubic hairs."

Frank slid around me, snared the bag, and put his arm around Stonewell's shoulder. "How's the Bruiser from Brewster, Texas, my favorite action star? Hey, Nina, take a picture of us together, would you?"

Stonewell looped his arm around Frank and beamed. "I'm glad someone around here doesn't think I'm poison."

"Just at the box office," Frank said.

Stonewell's smile drooped, the crack reminding him too sharply of the financial failures of his past films, but then he laughed, deciding to be a good sport. He wrapped Frank's head like a walnut in the crook of his elbow and pulled it toward his chest, faking a punch and then knuckling the top of his head, a boy thing I remembered was called a noogie. Whatever I thought of Stonewell I had to admire his pipes; most weight lifters look like cuts of beef but his biceps looked sculpted from marble. The photo was too good to pass up, staged or not. I snapped the shutter and called, "Who were you meeting the day you broke my camera?"

Stonewell straightened his arm to release Frank, who grinned, seemingly as happy as a schoolboy. "Hey, big guy," Stonewell said, "this photographer of yours is a real terrier, isn't she? Does she ever let go?"

"Once she's locked her teeth onto you she'll never let go," Frank said. "You could cut off her head and she'd only bite down harder. That's why you're here, isn't it? Because you beat her up and burned her out but she's still got her teeth in your butt and it's starting to hurt. Am I right?"

Stonewell's forearms crossed and flashed apart as though waving off the question. "Wait a minute, I haven't beaten anybody up since the last time I was in production, and that was strictly for camera. I haven't even seen her, not once, not since she tried to ambush me outside that restaurant."

"Ambush you?" I said.

"You should have kissed her feet for taking your photo," Frank said. "But instead you smashed her camera. Why?"

"I already apologized for that."

"Sure, but you never bothered to explain."

"Who were you meeting?" I asked again.

"My agent," he said.

"My ass," I answered.

Stonewell crooked his neck to the side as though looking at the part of my anatomy I'd just mentioned. "Not bad," he said, and smiled. "You work out, don't you?"

I'm sure his charm worked for some people.

"Who's the guy you ordered to break my camera?"

"Never saw him before," he said, still smiling. "I assumed he was a bystander. Never even got his name."

"I saw him kill a girl named Lucille Ryan, did you know that?"

"What's that? Killed who?"

"A young actress," I said. "He knifed her to death on the pier. Same guy you ordered to smash my camera."

"An actress? I didn't know her." A tremor ran though his voice as though the news shook his confidence. "I mean, I heard someone had been killed, it's all over the news, but the cops, they never told me anything." He glanced at his bodyguard. "Did they tell you anything?"

"Not a thing." The bodyguard pointed his chin at me. "I knew it had something to do with her, that's all."

"What do you know about the trade in celebrity bones?" I asked, setting the camera to rapid-fire. "Are you a member of the Church of Divine Thespians?" I watched the light reflect from his eyes as they glazed over. The deer-in-headlights look. He knew. "Luce was tangled up in the cult. That's why this isn't going away. That's why you need to be watching your ass more than mine."

Stonewell looked to his right, out to the street, and then his gaze swept past the lens to fix against the impassive stare of his bodyguard. I don't think he understood until then how deep the river of blood he swam in, or how fast.

"Is your brother part of the cult?" Frank asked, notebook in hand.

"My brother?" Stonewell asked, shocked again. "My brother is in real estate."

"He owns a warehouse frequented by known cult members," Frank said. "Bet he wants to be an actor just like his brother."

Stonewell stepped back and nodded to his bodyguard, who moved in front of Frank and held his hands up like a fence. "That's all Mr. Stonewell has time for," he said in a rehearsed voice. "Thanks for your interest."

"Who did you meet that day?" I called. I moved toward the curb to dodge the bodyguard but he slid over to block me. "Who's the guy in the black suit?"

Stonewell gave a cheery wave and dove behind the wheel of the Hummer. His bodyguard gave me a different kind of wave, one with his middle finger poked like a stake on his fist, and strutted toward the passenger side of the vehicle.

"I think he likes you," Frank said.

I dipped my head toward the bodyguard, said, "You mean him?"

"No, he hates your guts. I mean Stonewell."

"He did say I have a nice butt."

"And he gave you this, too." Frank lifted a boxed Nikon from the plastic sack. I glanced at the model description. A top-of-the-line digital SLR camera. The sticker on that model ran three grand, and that didn't include the lens.

"It's a bribe, Frank. I don't take bribes."

Frank poked a cigarette into his smile and lit it. "That's one of the reasons I like you."

"You mean because of my integrity?"

"No." He tucked the camera under his arm. "Because I get to keep the bribes meant for you."

THIRTY-THREE

THE PREVIOUS owner of the Montgomery Clift reliquary worked in the showroom of a Chrysler dealership on Santa Monica Boulevard. The showroom was a flagship, big enough to park eight display models, from a low-slung Prowler the color of egg yolk to a staid Town and Country, and even at that dead hour for car sales, between the end of lunch and the beginning of happy hour, the sales staff busily attended to customers. We spotted our guy near the Viper. We knew he was our guy because he was the only employee in the room under thirty-five and looked uncomfortable in the role of car salesman, as though he had other ambitions in life. This is not that uncommon a look on the West Side, where every other man or woman under the age of thirty is doing one thing while aspiring to something else entirely. He was a slim, dark-haired man with long, sensitive fingers and a wounded look, just the kind of guy I expected to identify with Montgomery Clift.

He turned to greet us when Frank called his name, Scott Bartlet, a practiced smile bounding to his lips. His glance flicked to our feet and back again, judging by the way we dressed our intention and ability to purchase a new car. Frank pressed a few of the multiple wrinkles from the sport coat he'd pulled from the trunk and walked toward the center of the showroom. He figured the coat and tie would make him look more like a real customer, and though I don't think he entirely succeeded, Bartlet stepped forward to meet us.

"A friend of ours recommended you." Frank thrust out his hand. "We'd like to take a look at the new PT Cruiser."

"Then I'd love to show it to you," Bartlet said. "Can I ask you what car you're driving now?"

"A Honda. With all these SUVs on the road I feel like a rabbit in the middle of a buffalo herd."

Bartlet laughed like a good salesman and said, "I know exactly what you're talking about." He stepped up to a metallic-blue PT Cruiser parked on a pedestal. "What you'll like about the PT is that it doesn't drive like a truck but because of the beautiful throwback design you ride higher in traffic, almost as high as most SUVs."

The cell phone in the side pocket of my leather jacket chirped and vibrated. I pulled the phone to check the caller. The number was an unfamiliar one, but then, most of my tips come from phone boxes. I walked away from Bartlet's sales presentation, cell phone pressed to one ear, finger plugged into the other, and said, "Hello?"

"What happened to your apartment?"

Female voice. Young voice. Theresa's voice.

"How did you hear about my apartment?"

I must have shouted. Heads in the showroom turned.

"I didn't exactly *hear* about it," she answered.

I glanced around for the door and strode toward it. "Tell me you're not back in Los Angeles," I begged. "Please tell me you haven't seen the apartment in person."

"But I passed the audition!" From the background hiss of surf I guessed she called from a phone box on the boardwalk, her voice a wail of protest against my lack of understanding and a shriek of delight at the possibility of being cast in anything.

"What audition?"

"A film. *Mischief at Malibu High*. I auditioned before I left."

I counted. Three days ago I'd put her on the bus.

"How far did you get? Because you sure as hell didn't have time to make it all the way back home to Indiana."

"Don't get mad," she said, as though that would help. "This could be my big break. You should be happy for me."

"Where are you?"

"At the pay phones by the beach, the ones down from your apartment," she said. "And you don't have to yell. I can hear just fine, thank you."

I thought it entirely possible she'd just landed a role in a porn film—or a repeat performance with the Church of Divine Thespians.

Theresa would walk smiling off the edge of a cliff if someone told her it would make her a star. I told her I'd pick her up as soon as I could and disconnected just as Bartlet led Frank out of the showroom, a driver's license I took to be Frank's clipped to a clipboard. Frank dangled a set of car keys at me, winked, and said, "You ready to take a test drive, honey?"

I sat in the back while Frank drove, camera bag zippered open on the seat beside me. Bartlet twisted sideways in the front passenger seat to talk up the technical specifications of the car, gallantly addressing his comments to me as well as to Frank. "Notice all the looks you get driving this car," Bartlet said. "Let me tell you folks, if you don't want people to notice the kind of car you drive, if it makes you uncomfortable having people admire your wheels when you pull up at a stoplight, then I suggest you look for a different car."

"Like a Honda," Frank said, a smile cracking out the side of his mouth.

"Nothing wrong with a Honda. A Honda is a reliable car," he observed, in the way that he might say a girl has a good personality.

"You never did ask who sent us," Frank said.

I put the viewfinder to my eye and checked the exposure.

"I sell a lot of these cars so I assumed it was a happy customer." Bartlet glanced back at me, realizing something was up but not knowing what, expecting a joke or a message from a friend.

"The Church of Divine Thespians," Frank said.

"Stop the car right now." Bartlet bit the knuckle of his fist, his cheeks blotching scarlet. "No, turn the car around and go back to the dealership."

"Relax, Scott," I said. "We're not from the church itself." I was afraid the guy might implode right there on the front seat, wanted to put him more at ease. "But we know about the church and your former affiliation with it."

Frank scissored a business card from the breast pocket of his sport coat, said, "Frank Adams, features writer for *Scandal Times*. You ever read us?"

"Oh God." Bartlet sank low in his seat. "You're the tabloids."

"That's right, Scott, the big, bad tabloids." Frank sounded gleeful, as though he enjoyed terrorizing car salesmen. "You can choose to cooperate with us, either for attribution or as an anonymous source, or you can tell us to fuck off and find a photo of your mug in next week's edition above the headline 'Former Actor Accused in Dog Molestation Case.' "

"Oh God," he repeated, his voice a low moan.

"He's kidding about the dog molestation. At least, I think he's kidding. You're kidding, aren't you, Frank?"

"I've printed worse."

"He has," I admitted. "I've read it."

"Let's start with the locket, the one with Montgomery Clift's bone inside it, the reliquary." Frank had trouble pronouncing the word, asked, "Did I get that right?"

"If I'm caught talking to you, it's not just that I'll never work in this town again." Bartlet shaded his face with the palm of his hand. I think he wanted to hide his face from the camera, didn't know the hand made him look like a criminal being led into the courthouse. "I was told that I couldn't sell the thing. I was told all kinds of terrible things would happen to me if I ever sold it or talked to anyone about it outside the church. I mean, it was like I sold my soul to the devil when I bought it. It was that heavy. The friend who brought me into the Thespians, he won't even talk to me now that I've gone apostate, as he calls it."

"Tell me what happens when you and other Thespians get together, where you meet," Frank said.

"This has to be off-off-off-record. You can't print my name with this. You can't mention my name at all."

"You're a former member of the Thespian cult. You heroically escaped the brainwashing techniques of a dangerous organization and now you're rightfully fearful of retaliation." Frank glanced over to see how the car salesman was taking the extemporaneous pitch. "You can't reveal your identity for your own protection."

"We'll do one of those face-in-shadow portraits to run with the story," I suggested. "You know, like an undercover cop."

"Or Mafia informant." Bartlet wiped his mouth and stared out the window. Looking for a way to escape, probably. "Oh God, how did I ever get into this?"

"That's a good place to start," Frank said. "How did you get into this?"

"I want to be an actor. I mean, I am an actor. I just don't work very much. I received fabulous notices back in Maryland, where I got my B.A. in theater arts, but the competition here is just killer. I mean, everybody here was a star in whatever Podunk little town they come from."

"It's the big leagues," Frank agreed.

"There's so much competition, it's hard to get a decent audition. Just cattle calls, you know, where you show up with a hundred other people to audition for a one-line part in something that turns out to be a student film."

"You wanted an edge." Frank knew how tough it was to find work as an actor. He'd heard it hundreds of times. Every struggling actor told a similar story.

"Anything. An edge, a break, a little freaking hope. This friend of mine—"

"What's his name?"

"No names. You want to make a right turn here, take Wilshire back. I can't be gone too long."

Frank showed he was a good sport and turned.

"This friend, he gets cast in everything. I mean, television, feature film, even a freaking music video. So we were drinking beers one weekend at the Whiskey Bar. You know the Whiskey Bar?"

Frank nodded and turned again to circle back. The Whiskey Bar was a hotel bar where the rock-and-roll set and certain actors hung out, actors who had perfected the twenty-four-hour hangover-with-a-suntan look, a common look among those who party nonstop in L.A.

"We were just chilling, you know, the bar was rocking and six or seven beers into the night I was bitching up a storm about how hard it was for me to find work when my friend, he pulls this necklace from under his shirt, points to the case at the end of the chain, and says, 'Fredric March.'"

"You mean, the actor, what did he win that Oscar for, *Dr. Jekyll and Mr. Hyde*?" Frank was grinning. Despite his lampooning the stars for a living, he loved to display his knowledge of trivia. "And one other one, *The Best Years of Our Lives*, right?"

"Starred in *Anna Karenina*, too, opposite Greta Garbo," Bartlet said. "He was in the original filmed production of *Death of a Salesman*, played Willy Loman long before Dustin Hoffman."

"You're right, I forgot that one," Frank said. "And your friend, what did he mean by the name? That he had a little piece of bone from Fredric March's body inside?"

"This is too weird to believe." Bartlet shook his head as though he didn't believe it himself. "He started laying down this rap about how the locket and bone inside were his magic talisman, that he'd been struggling like me to find work until six months before, when he'd met this guy from the Church of Divine Thespians. After that, after he'd bought the relic, his luck magically changed."

I asked, "Did you meet Sven?"

When he turned his head I snapped the shutter.

"You know about him?"

"A little."

"Then you should know that no one meets Sven. Sven talks to you over the phone." He put his hand in front of the lens to block the next shot.

"You met the other guy, then, the one with the good build, sandy-blond hair worn over his back collar." I cranked the focus to his palm, lit in a shaft of light from the side window, the top of his head and one ear visible but blurred in the background. I hadn't been looking for that shot but the image was perfect for what we needed. I took it.

"You mean Eric. He's the one who sold me the locket."

"Last name?"

"Never knew it."

"Phone number?"

"He called me." He kept his hand in front of my lens and turned to Frank. "Can you ask her to put away the camera? It's not that I don't trust you guys, but I don't trust you guys."

I capped the lens.

"What did Sven talk to you about?" Frank asked.

Bartlet pulled his hand back to his lap but kept his eye on my camera. "He talked a lot about what he calls the Hidden Mind Principle, that we all have a higher mind other religions have sometimes confused for soul, and if we learn how to tune into the higher mind through certain exercises, then it will direct us toward our chosen fate, which is what we most want for ourselves. He says the hidden mind is like the homing instinct in certain birds, that if we can tune in, it will lead us to fame and fortune as certainly as a homing pigeon will make it back to the roost."

"Let me guess." Frank made a humming sound in the back of his throat, the theme song to one of those television quiz shows. I never saw him happier than when a tabloid story was breaking and it was his to run with. "The exercises you need to reach your higher mind involve the purchase of one of these lockets, supposedly with the bone of a dead celebrity inside it."

"You already knew," Bartlet said, surprised. He didn't understand how obvious the scam looked to an outsider.

"Just a lucky guess," Frank said. "How much did you pay for it?"

"Ten thousand." He mumbled the sum into his fist.

"Dollars?"

"I know. Pretty stupid." Bartlet clasped his hands together, thumbs toward his chest, as though he was about to pray. "You're supposed to hold the relic between your palms like this, close your eyes, and concentrate on the Hidden Mind Principle. The relic is supposed to act, I don't know, like some conduit of higher energy, because the person it came from was the living embodiment of the hidden mind, you understand? Only it didn't work for me."

"Why not?"

"Probably because while I was holding on to the thing, trying to get my thoughts tracked onto the higher mind, I kept thinking, this is really stupid, I've just spent my entire life's savings on a piece of Montgomery Clift's tibia."

The pole sign marking the Chrysler dealership loomed ahead. Frank turned into the lot. "But I'm sure the Thespians offer some kind of support group to help you get over the resistance, other people like yourself trying to channel fame and fortune and feeling a little less certain that kissing a celebrity's bone instead of some producer's ass is the right way to go about it."

"I wish," he said.

"No meetings, no coffee klatches, nobody you can call when you're sweating with doubt?"

"Nothing like that. It's not AA. It's private. You're not supposed to know who else belongs, it's all supposed to be supersecret because it's offered only to the chosen few. Sven says other people aren't necessary. Just the basic teaching and the instrument, which is what he sometimes calls the relic, because no one can find your higher mind for you, only you can do it. And if you can't find it, then you aren't meant to find it, understand what I'm saying?"

Frank understood. The structure of the Church of Divine Thespians could have been inspired by a revolutionary group, the lower tiers broken into discrete cells that had no direct contact with each other and no traceable access to those higher in the organization. The PT Cruiser rolled to a stop. Frank killed the engine, trying to think of another angle.

"What about a shrine?" I asked. "Did you hear anyone talk about a sacred place, maybe where the bones were stored?"

"Sure. Steve Reeves Ranch, somewhere in the hills near Canyon Country. But that's just a rumor. It's strictly inner-circle stuff, reserved for the special few, the high priests and big stars. Not even my friend has been invited." He elbowed open the door and stuck one foot outside, then leaned across the seat as though giving a confidence. "Sven supposedly conducts rituals there, where he channels the energies of the bones, what he calls higher-mind triangulation, which is supposed to help you focus into your own higher mind."

"Higher-mind triangulation?" Frank asked, not sure he'd heard correctly.

"Sure. You're holding on to one fragment of bone that's supposed to help you find your higher mind, right?" He waited for our uncertain nods and then continued. "He's conducting a ritual with the main set of relics, helping you to focus. It's like you're the first point on a triangle, he's the second point, connected to you at the base, and where your lines of energy converge out there in the cosmos, that's where your higher mind is. Only one problem."

"Only one?" Frank asked.

"It didn't work for me. Maybe my higher mind left the galaxy." Bartlet pushed out of the car and circled the hood to get the keys from Frank. "So what do you think?"

The question confused Frank and he thought a moment before he asked, "About what?"

"The car," Bartlet said. "With your good credit, I can cut you a really sweet deal."

THIRTY-FOUR

I SPOTTED Theresa rummaging through a rack of T-shirts at an open-air vendor's shop on Ocean Front Walk, not far from the block of pay phones where we were supposed to meet. She looked in need of some new clothes, wearing the same slacks, bare-midriff blouse, and calfskin jacket that she'd worn to Café Anastasia the day I'd met her. She'd put a lot of miles on those clothes since then. I stuffed into my camera bag the mail I'd collected from the box below my burned-out apartment and heeled the Rott. When the girl heard my voice she dashed from the rack and wrapped her thin arms around my waist. She was happy to see me, it seemed. Just when I thought I'd need to get the crowbar from my car to pry her off she pushed away and announced she was hungry, if I didn't feed her within the hour she'd starve to death. Not only is it surprising that most of us find a way to survive our teenaged years, it's a miracle that those living with teens survive, too.

I bought a take-out pizza from a stand on the boardwalk and took it down to the sea to eat and watch the sun descend toward sunset. The conversation would involve some yelling and crying, I figured. We needed privacy to work through the problems that confronted us, first and foremost her return to Los Angeles. The Rott sat at attention on the sand beside me, big brown eyes mournful at the sight of any bite of food heading to a mouth not his own. I tore small chunks from my slice and fed them to him. "How far did you get before you turned back?" I tried not to sound sarcastic or ironic. I was curious.

"Denver." Her cheeks bulged with the bite of pizza she'd just taken. The bite was so big she looked like a snake trying to swallow a hedgehog. She managed to get it down without choking and smiled. "I should have checked my messages in Las Vegas when we stopped, but I guess I was kind of tired and didn't wake up in time to get off the bus."

"Checked what messages?"

"Sean and I, we got voice mail at one of those places rents mail boxes, you know, so we'd have a callback number to leave at auditions." The setting sun lit a black smudge near the top of her forehead and the breeze blowing off the ocean tossed her ash-blond hair into tangles behind her back. Dirty, hungry, broke, and a runaway, she seemed completely content to be where she sat. "And I got called back. I was lucky to make it here in time. They want to see me tomorrow. Can you believe that? I'm going to be in a movie!"

"How did you get back? I'm only asking because I put you on the bus with my last dollar and I don't remember you having any money to help pay the fare."

"I hitched a ride." She shrugged as though it was that simple.

"You're a sweet young girl, Theresa. Do you have any idea how many people out there would rape you given a closed door and nobody watching? Do you know how many sweet, attractive young girls are killed and buried by the side of the road they hitched on?"

She took another bite of pizza and shook her head, unable or unwilling to conceal a smile, a smile that said I just didn't get it, she was different, those things didn't happen to her. "I was careful. I didn't just stick my thumb out and take what pulled over. I went to a truck stop, found a nice trucker going all the way to Long Beach, you know the big harbor there?"

"You're fifteen years old," I said. I wanted to make it clear to her. "You don't know the evil people are capable of. I'm thirty, and it still catches me by surprise."

"I know it's dangerous. That's why I decided I should come straight to see you when I got into town, not try to stay on the streets by myself again."

"They killed Luce," I said. I hadn't planned to tell her so quickly. I wanted to give her time to eat, time for the food to settle. But more than that I wanted to impress upon her the dark consequences of running wild in the world.

She swung her head toward me, another bite of pizza bulging her cheek, disbelief sheening her eyes. She remembered to swallow but the food went down hard, and in the golden light of the low sun, her face crimsoned.

"It happened two nights ago," I said. "One of the guys who took you out to the desert did it, the one called Eric. He stabbed her to death."

"No." She shook her head, stubborn in her disbelief.

"I'm sorry. It happened on Santa Monica Pier. I saw her die."

The swell rose to six feet that afternoon and the waves crashing to shore muffled Theresa's sobs. I watched the surf, something I can do for hours without pause, my arms around the Rott's neck, and waited for her to stop. I didn't offer to hold or hug her. I didn't want to soften the blow. I wanted her to hurt. Pain helps us understand how closely our lives hew to tragedy, that whatever we have can be ripped from us, our friends, our relatives, our lives, and our dignity taken without notice or apology. She began to eat again while the tears still streamed down her cheeks, chewing slowly and swallowing with effort. I knew by that one gesture that she possessed an unconscious strength of will. Nobody's will is indomitable. We can all be damaged and broken. But Theresa seemed more determined than others to survive intact. She asked, "Did the police catch him?"

"No. He's still out there." I picked up a slice of pizza, thought about eating it. "Did you remember the shoes he wore, you know, when he took you out to the desert?"

She finished the slice and licked her fingers, her expression perplexed, as though she couldn't understand why I asked but trying nonetheless to answer. "Hiking boots, I think. Why?"

"Because Luce said the word *Nike* just before she died and I can't figure why. Nike doesn't make hiking boots. Not like the ones I remember seeing."

"Nike? She said Nike?" Theresa eyed the pizza box, measuring the remaining slices against her hunger. "Isn't that Japanese or something? I mean originally. Before it became a running shoe. Like Seiko probably meant something in Japanese before it became a watch."

"It's not Japanese." I stared out to sea, trying to remember. "Nike is Roman or Greek. It means *winged victory*."

"You're kidding. You mean it's one of the gods they had? Like

Zeus? Why would she be thinking about that? Gotta be a running shoe."

"Maybe the police will figure it out." I had my doubts but didn't want Theresa to know. "You'll have to talk to them, now that you're back."

"The police? Why?"

"Because you're at the center of two murder investigations." I heard parole officer Terry Graves in my voice and shuddered. I was beginning to understand how Graves felt having me as her charge. I wasn't sure I liked that. "At a certain point, you have to obey the law. You can skirt it sometimes, if you're quiet and lucky, but you can't run headlong against the law and expect to be the one to survive the collision. Let's say you get this part you're talking about. Would the film crew come do your scenes in a juvenile detention center, you think? Because that's where you're headed if you don't correct your course. Once you start to get work, particularly in a high-profile job like acting, you won't be able to hide anymore. People looking for you, you'll be easy to find. That means you have to make it right with everybody. Do you understand what I'm talking about?"

Theresa puffed her cheeks in glum exasperation, asked, "Can we talk to the police after the audition?"

I didn't want to negotiate with her but I wasn't her mother or a cop. It wasn't my responsibility to make her decisions. "That's up to you." I offered her my cell phone. "But if you want to stay with me tonight you have to call your mother."

"I called her from Denver." She dug her hands into the sand and looked away. Her face was like stone. Either the conversation hadn't gone well or she was lying. I suspected she was lying.

"Call her again."

She made no move to take the phone.

"If you want to stay with me, you have to trust me a little bit," I said. "Otherwise, it's not going to work."

"I don't have a mother." She spoke so softly I barely distinguished the words from the wind and waves. "I was lying to you. She ran away when I was two. Sends me a card on my birthday and on Christmas, no return address."

I didn't put away the phone. I said, "I'm sorry for that. But you must have somebody taking care of you. Call your father."

"I doubt he even knows I'm gone." The tears that sprang to her eyes came from anger more than self-pity. "I live in a trailer park, all right? I'm trailer trash. My dad is drunk most of the time he's not at work and 'cause he never lasts more than six months in any job he's not at work all that often, you know? It was fine, I was living with it, but he's got a new girlfriend who drinks as much as he does and we don't like each other. If he realizes I'm gone, which is extremely doubtful, he's probably pretty fucking happy about it."

I took her hand and held it. We watched the ocean, each thinking our own thoughts. Then I replaced my hand with the cell phone, said, "Call your father."

She nodded, not resentful about it now that I knew the truth, and dialed an eleven-digit number. She said a sullen hello into the mouthpiece and asked for her dad, then stood and walked a few yards down the beach to talk in private. I tore the last slice of pizza into bite-sized chunks and fed them to the Rott. Theresa wandered back, nodding and saying, "Yes, dad . . . yes, dad." She handed the phone down to me. "He wants to talk to you."

I pressed the phone to my ear.

"You taking good care of my little girl there?"

Even through the tin-can acoustics of the cell phone I could hear the booze. He wasn't just drunk, he was twenty-years drunk, his voice a cheerful rasp. "I don't think you understand the relationship," I said, phrasing each word carefully. "I'm your daughter's friend and I'm happy to help her but I'm not taking care of her, not in the way you seem to think."

"I'm happy you're happy," he said. "And don't think your help is going unappreciated. She's told me all about you and your work out there in Hollywood."

I looked up at Theresa. Hope and fear worked her face into an expression of anxiety, as though her fate hung in the balance at that very moment. I wondered what she had told him about me. I said, "Theresa is fifteen years old. She needs to go to school."

"I couldn't agree more. Lemme think a second." I heard a long, liquid swallow lubricate his thinking. "By God, when she gets that part she's talking about, we'll hire her a tutor. And then maybe I'll come out there. That's what parents do when their kid hits it big, isn't that right?"

"Sometimes," I said.

"I'm not proud. I won't stand in my little girl's way." The man sounded precariously close to tears. "I'll do everything in my power to support her."

A sudden screeching sounded in the room where the man spoke, loud as a car locking tires and skidding through the room. Several distinct words emerged from the shrieks. *Bastard, I'm not gonna, you don't, fuck you, then . . .*

"Don't you yell at me like that when I'm talking long-distance!" The shout was muffled, as though he'd cupped the phone against his chest. His voice returned, low and ragged, to the mouthpiece. "Gotta go now."

"I'll give you back to Theresa to say good-bye."

I held the phone up. Theresa snatched it, held the receiver against her ear, said, "Hello?" Then again, "Hello?"

Her eyes misted.

He'd hung up.

We did our best to clean the dirt and stains from Theresa's clothes in a 1950s-era courtyard motel a few miles inland. I didn't mind sleeping in the back of the Cadillac and the Rott wasn't all that particular either, but I couldn't sleep rough while supervising a fifteen-year-old girl, not in good conscience. The motel's swaybacked roof looked one Southland trembler away from collapse and rust pitted every metallic surface, from the sign advertising rooms to rent to the bathroom fixtures. The room didn't have cable, a telephone, or air-conditioning and the furnishings had the wounded look of life in the company of transients, but they allowed dogs, the sheets were clean and the water hot. I didn't ask for more than that, not at the price.

Theresa sat on the edge of the bed, working on her calfskin jacket with a toothbrush and bottle of stain remover. She wore a sun-yellow T-shirt with the words *Venice Beach* emblazoned on the front, each letter a different color, and looked up from her work every now and then with a dizzy smile, her greatest worry whether or not her clothes would dry in time for her audition the following morning. I'd bought a hair dryer at the drugstore, along with the hand wash and stain remover. The clothes would dry, I assured her, even if we had to run the hair dryer over the fabric half the night.

When Theresa closed herself into the bathroom to shower I worked the cell phone. Detective Dougan wasn't at his desk. I hadn't expected him to be. I left a voice-mail message that I'd tracked down someone who knew Lucille Ryan and hoped to bring her by the station tomorrow afternoon. I figured Dougan would take her statement and call her father. When he could establish the girl wasn't a runaway he'd cut her loose. I left another message with my parole officer and thought about calling Marshal Tuckman. With the three-hour time difference it was past midnight in Fairmount. I didn't think he'd appreciate a call to his cell phone at that hour telling him his witness wasn't showing up.

I lifted from my camera bag the sheaf of mail I'd collected before meeting Theresa and tossed it onto the covers beside me, thinking about what I was going to tell Tuck, then made a call to his office line. Most of the mail was junk. I sorted through it while the answering machine picked up, announcing that I'd reached the Fairmount marshal's office. One envelope had been personally addressed to me. The postmark read Phoenix. I slit open the envelope and shook out a letter and photograph. The photograph fell facedown onto the bed. On the blank back someone had penned *Cassie, 9th grade*. The letter was from my niece's foster mother. I flipped the photograph to look at the face on the opposite side.

Sometime later a long beep signaled that I'd reached the end of the time allotted to leave my message and the line disconnected. The bathroom door opened to a plume of steam and Theresa stepped out, wrapped in a towel. She glanced down at the photograph in my hand, said, "I never figured that girl out. She wants to be an actress? As though she thinks anybody's gonna cast her with a look like that. Maybe if they're casting for a TV movie about Columbine."

I closed the cell phone. I hadn't left a message. The girl in the photograph was one of the kids I'd seen in the warehouse owned by Stonewell's brother, part of the gang I'd followed that night to the mountain behind Forest Lawn cemetery. The barely teenaged girl with multiple piercings and hair as black as my own. "Did you meet her?" I asked.

"Not really, not like we got to know each other. She was just around, with the others. Sean did most of the talking anyway."

"What did she seem like?"

"Angry. Really angry."

That made sense. Anger ran in the family.

"What are you doing with that anyway?" She plucked the photograph from my fingertips and examined it beneath the light of the bedside lamp. "You didn't shoot it, did you? It looks like a class picture."

"Did my sister ask about this girl?"

"Her? No, not specifically." She looked again at the photograph, then returned it to me. "But like I said before, she wanted to know who ran in the gang—ages, personality types, looks, that sort of thing. That's why I thought she was a journalist. And yeah, when I mentioned the Goth girl, she wanted to know more about her. But I thought it was just because, you know, Goths make good villains and she needed one for her story."

I slid the photograph back into the envelope, tucked the envelope into my camera bag, and stuffed the rest of the mail, all junk, into the trash can beside the door. "I'm going to take the dog for a walk," I said. The Rott bounded to the door, his eyes riveted on the knob like a bird dog. "Don't open to anybody except me. I won't go far and I won't be gone long."

"What's wrong?" Theresa clutched the towel more tightly around her, took a small step forward. She knew I was upset and it panicked her, because she didn't know how I'd react. She had to fear that I'd abandon her, because in her experience that's what people did to each other.

"I can't tell you yet," I said. "I need to think about it some. But it has nothing to do with you, not really, don't worry about that." When I glanced back to close the door behind the Rott, Theresa looked like she didn't believe I'd be coming back.

I walked the Rott from the motel into borderline gang turf near Oakwood, blankets hanging as curtains in apartment windows and random tufts of crabgrass sprouting from dirt lawns. As I walked I thought about how my sister may have been a liar and thief but she had also been a mother searching for redemption. Greed hadn't been her sole motivation. Desperation played its role, too. She had been broke in a strange city, looking for a daughter whose deeply troubled life mirrored her own, a daughter taken from her because she had lived her life so badly the system had declared her an unfit mother. Had I been broke she probably would have confided in me rather than conned me. My money made me a better target than confidante. The thought made me want to cry. I rarely had more than a month's rent in my bank account. My sister reappeared in my life during one of the few times I had money.

Not that I could cry for my sister. Not that I was capable of crying for anyone. Not that I'd even think about crying in that neighborhood. Too many men lounging near street corners, too many cars cruising the streets, the long arms of multiple occupants hanging below rolled-down windows. I turned toward the next commercial avenue, the size and seeming ferociousness of the Rott my pass through the neighborhood. Perhaps my sister had maintained some kind of contact with her daughter. When I considered how deeply my sister seemed to care for her daughter, I thought it likely that they weren't completely estranged. She might have known that Cassie had run away to Los Angeles. Cassie would have called to tell her that much. Cassie might have bragged about her criminal life, trying to impress her criminal mother. My sister easily could have known that her daughter was in Los Angeles, involved in an enterprise that involved robbing graves.

That knowledge would have led her straight to me. I had always assumed that my sister hadn't known who I was or what I did for a living when we met in the room that held our mother's body. She may have known far more about me than I ever suspected. The day she showed up at my apartment with a copy of *Scandal Times* she had pretended not to know that I had changed my name and asked what had seemed at the time casual questions about the story I had been working on. I hadn't realized until then that she had been pumping me for information. She'd certainly learned her craft well during the years she'd spent kiting checks, robbing banks, and conning the foolish out of their life savings. We're all good at something. My sister had been good at conning people. She'd conned me out of more than just money. She claimed kinship not out of any deep feelings of rediscovered sisterhood but to use me to help find her daughter. Her skills had failed her at the end. She hadn't found her daughter and lost her life.

The people I passed looked at me like I was a crazy woman and it wasn't until then that I realized I was shouting. Even the Rott was looking at me like I'd lost my mind. I'd been shouting at my sister. For her dishonesty. For her thievery. For her years of silence. For her ease in forgetting me. For her failure to give a little big-sister advice that might have made all the difference. For her attempts at manipulation, which continued after her death. So what if she'd been looking for her daughter? So what if she'd sinned against me for a greater cause? She'd still lied and stolen my money. Even dead and laid out on a stainless-steel slab in the morgue, unclaimed by friends or family, she was trying to manipulate me. She stared at me from the dark hole of family, a family that had abused and disowned us, and pleaded with me not just to forgive her but to recognize that we were bound more inextricably than ever because I knew who she was behind the false masks and fast cons and I was the only one who could or even cared to help her gain the redemption she'd failed to achieve in life.

THIRTY-FIVE

THERESA CHATTERED nonstop about actresses and roles that had inspired her during the morning rush-hour drive to her callback audition in Hollywood, obsessively smoothing invisible wrinkles from her slacks. The young Laurence Olivier would vomit before stage performances, so I counted myself lucky that Theresa's nervous energy expended itself in talk. The audition was scheduled for nine AM in a bungalow complex north of Hollywood Boulevard. After we parked I told her to wait in the car with the Rott and circled to open the trunk, where I kept the crowbar. The complex had originally served as bungalow apartments, early-twentieth-century clapboard and shingle units constructed around a central courtyard. Its first tenants had worked for the studios. The bungalows had been converted to office use when the tenants moved with the studios to Burbank. I zippered open my camera bag and placed the crowbar inside, careful to secure it against the padding.

"What are you doing?"

Theresa stood behind me, her voice shrill with adolescent panic. She'd moved so quietly I hadn't heard her.

"Just making sure it's safe," I said.

"You can't go in there with a tire iron!"

"I thought I told you to stay in the car."

Her face flushed bright red and her breath fluttered with the first stages of hyperventilation. I couldn't remember when anything had meant so much to me as this audition meant to her. "I'm not going to walk in swinging," I said. "Sven has connections in the film business. What if he knows you're going to be here? It's not like your first audition was a big secret. Your ex-friend Sean knew and you probably told Luce. So get back into the car and wait."

She opened her mouth as though about to continue her protest but spun on her heels in tacit admission I was right and returned to the car. I shouldered the camera bag and crossed the street. Theresa had been crying the night before when I'd returned to the motel from my walk. She had pretended nothing was wrong but by the changed position of my camera bag on the bed I knew she had found and read the letter from my niece's foster mother. "I understand that you couldn't really help yourself," I'd said. "I understand you need to know what's going on, but in general, you should never go through someone else's stuff. You understand me?" I thought she was going to lie and deny. That's what I would have done at her age. But she nodded, a little too easily, and hopped into bed. She tossed a few times, then fell still with sleep long before I did.

The casting agency occupied a double bungalow at the end of a brick walkway flanked with pink lawn flamingos. I put my eye to the brass nameplate on the door, noting from the oxidized corners that the plate hadn't been screwed on that morning. I opened the door to a harried redhead tapping at the keys of a laptop and talking to herself. A black cord dangled from her ear. She was speaking on the phone. I glanced over the padded folding chairs and framed posters that lined the room, not looking for anything in particular but trying to sense whether anything looked or felt out of place. Bad things rarely come out of nowhere. Bad things usually come from bad places. The redhead lifted a hand from the keyboard long enough to press the disconnect switch on the cord and glanced up at me as though about to ask what I wanted.

"I'm here with Theresa," I said.

The redhead glanced at a list on the corner of her desk and nodded. "She's our first girl this morning. Bring her in and she can get started reading the sides." The phone played the first few bars of Tchaikovsky's *1812 Overture*, without the cannon fire. She reached back to the cord hanging from her ear to connect again. If she was giving a performance, it was a convincing one.

Theresa paced the sidewalk outside the bungalow complex, a

compromise between my command to wait in the car and her impulse to follow me into the casting agency. When she glanced up and spotted me walking down the brick path she darted forward and might have run me over had I not braced myself for the impact. The hug she gave me was short and fierce, something taken for confidence.

"What's a side?" I asked.

"Pages from the script they give you to read for the audition," she answered, her voice quick and a little surprised that I didn't know already.

"They don't give you the whole script?"

"Not if you're auditioning."

"Then how do you know you'll want to do it?"

She glanced up at me like I'd just asked the dumbest question in the world. "Because it's film," she said.

From the sides I discerned that *Mischief at Malibu High* was a teen comedy. I didn't laugh at the jokes, but then I wasn't the intended audience. Theresa was auditioning for the role of Daisy, the daughter of the new janitor, recently moved to Malibu from Oklahoma. When we read the lines together she tried a few with an accent that sounded dead-on Oklahoma to my ear. "One of my dad's girlfriends was from Tulsa," she said. Then the door behind the front desk opened and the production assistant called Theresa's name. I told her to break a leg and she smiled at my attempt to sound like show business. She told me that the average audition lasted between ten and fifteen minutes; anything over that was a good sign.

I used the time to step out onto the lawn and call Marshal Tuckman at his office. He greeted me with a terse question about the location of his witness. "We have a little problem here," I said, and proceeded to tell him about Theresa's return, the audition, and her appointment to talk to detectives Dougan and Smalls.

"You said she'd be on the bus," Tuck said. "She wasn't. And now you tell me that in addition to her legal problems she wants to be a movie star? This kid is in a heck of a lot of trouble and I don't have the time to play games." I strained to hear the easygoing, friendly country marshal in his voice and failed.

"I put her on the bus once already but she did a U-turn," I said. "She's in the middle of the audition right now. I couldn't break the kid's heart. I couldn't put her back on the bus. She would have jumped at the next stop anyway."

"You could have given her to children's services."

"Sure, I could have cuffed and gagged her and tossed her into the trunk, because that's the only way she would have gone." I kicked at one of the pink flamingos with the tip of my boot. "Then I could have just forgotten about her and continued about my business, right?"

"Better going about your own business than interfering with the law's. I know who this girl is now, understand? I know her name, where her father lives."

"And why do you know her name?" I tried to keep the anger from my voice. "You wouldn't even know she existed if I hadn't identified her. You'd still be watching surveillance tapes from every McDonald's within a fifty-mile radius."

Ten seconds of silence confirmed the truth of that, a truth Marshal Tuckman might not have appreciated hearing. He cleared his throat away from the receiver, said, "You get that girl back on the bus by tomorrow at the latest, then we still have a deal about not pressing charges."

"What if she passes the audition?" I asked. "She isn't guilty of anything more than bad company. If you keep her from taking the role you'll kill her dream."

"You're checking in with this detective, what's his name, Dougan?"

"Right after the audition," I said.

"Let me know how the audition goes," he said. "I'm not gonna deal in hypothetical situations. You tell me what happens and I'll tell you what I want you to do from there."

I hung up feeling okay about the call. Tuck didn't sound like he was going to play the heavy with Theresa. I was beginning to hope that everything would work out for her. If she didn't get the part, I'd put her back on the bus, sadder but wiser. If they wanted her for the film, we'd find a way to make it work, at least during the time it would take them to shoot her scenes. I knelt to straighten the flamingo I'd flattened and checked my watch.

Thirty-two minutes after Theresa began her audition the door behind the production assistant opened and a short man with bristly salt-and-pepper hair and matching goatee stepped with her into the anteroom. By the tear tracks running down her cheeks I figured the audition hadn't gone well enough. The director introduced himself and shook my hand, said how much he'd enjoyed working with my daughter. I thought to correct him about the relationship but a smile burst across Theresa's face when he spoke and I didn't want to blunt her happiness. The way she'd chapped and reddened her skin was perfect for the part, he said. He was surprised to find such advanced method-acting techniques in a young performer. He was auditioning several girls for the part. It would take the production a couple of days to settle on a choice. Then the front door opened to another child actor, herded by a woman with a stress-pinched face, and the director retreated behind the closed door. The woman gritted her teeth toward us. She might have meant it to be a smile.

The February sun hung just high enough in the morning sky to ride through Hollywood with the top down. Theresa bounced in the passenger seat, the Rott at her feet. "He asked me to work on another scene with him," she shouted. "That's why it took so long." She beamed through the wind-whipped tendrils of her hair, her face incandescently bright in the morning sun. I could never tolerate being an actor, waiting around for someone to tell me whether or not they wanted me, but she seemed not to mind. She talked about the scene and recited some of the lines she remembered—and she remembered most of them. The casting director had read the other parts so it wasn't like doing a real scene, but still, she felt she connected with her character. She liked the director. He was very adult. She'd heard that some directors could be difficult, more like angry little kids than adults. But this one was good. She wanted to work with him.

"You gave it your best shot," I said. "We'll go somewhere nice for lunch to celebrate after we talk to Detective Dougan."

The light on her face did not measurably shift but still she darkened, as though lit so clearly by the emotions inside that changes in her mood played like light upon her skin.

"You never know when you're going to be cast in a cop film," I said, trying to sound sage. "Think of it as research."

Detective Dougan walked out of the Hollywood station five minutes after I gave my name at the front desk, gravity tugging even more than usual at the bags and folds that pieced together his face. Cops work long hours, I'd noticed, and they can age quickly. He thanked me for dropping by, his manner so unexpectedly polite I suspected he'd forgotten that I was an ex-con. He was probably just tired. It takes energy to be rude. I introduced him to Theresa, who stared up at him with a mixture of suspicion and awe. If the girl's age surprised him, he didn't show it. He wanted to talk to the witness alone, he said. Theresa's panicked glance told me what she thought of that.

"Don't worry, he's a good guy," I told her. "He's interviewed me a couple of times, didn't hit me once."

I'd wanted to reassure her, make her laugh, and failed on both counts. Dougan raised the drawbridge to the side of the front desk, used for the station's walk-in trade. I gave her a hug and told her I'd be waiting in front of the station when she was finished. I watched her disappear down the hall and stepped out of the station, thinking I'd take the Rott for a walk while I waited. Dougan lumbered down the steps behind me before I reached the sidewalk.

"What's your relationship to the girl in there?"

"Complicated." I thought it was a trick question, an attempt to trick me into admitting I'd withheld evidence. "Right now I'm taking care of her."

He folded his arms across his chest, said, "Well, she's under arrest."

"What do you mean she's under arrest? I brought her to you in good faith! She's not a runaway, not anymore. She has her father's spoken permission to be here to audition for a movie. I heard him say so last night. She hasn't done anything wrong here, she hasn't committed any crime except being under eighteen."

Dougan raised his palm like a stop sign and his gaze, patient at first with the anger in my voice, hardened until it reflected no give at all. "I'm not the one who issued the arrest warrant."

"Then Smalls?"

He shook his head again, said, "The arrest warrant is coming out of Indiana. Madison County. The fax came into the station less than twenty minutes ago."

THIRTY-SIX

My SISTER'S body had been found on granite steps that descended to a pond in front of the Douglas Fairbanks memorial. Marigolds in fluted brass urns lined the staircase, framing the view of the pond from the top step, and just beyond the far end of the pond, partly obscured by jets of water pluming from the fountain at its center, the white marble crypt of the Fairbankses themselves gleamed beneath the late winter sun, father and son nestled side by side behind a patinated copper medallion depicting the senior Fairbanks's famous profile. A low wall of granite block shielded the landing of the staircase from the street, and it was there that I imagined my sister had lain in wait with my little point-and-shoot. As I stood where she knelt, looking toward the stodgy gray mausoleum where Valentino's coffin lay stacked with hundreds of others like files in a drawer, I concluded that despite all my efforts to learn how and why she had died I knew no more than the few facts grudgingly dispensed by Dougan and Smalls the night they had taken me to identify her body.

She had died from a broken neck, they'd said. I remembered the blue-gray pallor of her face framed by the green plastic of the body bag that sheathed her, remembered the single cut bisecting her eyebrow. The steps were steep and the boughs of a eucalyptus shielded the staircase from the ambient light of the city at night. She had crouched behind the low granite and waited, but for what? A glimpse of her daughter? Or a tabloid-worthy photograph of the theft of Valentino that might score her twenty grand to add to the nineteen grand she had stolen from me? Had she been foolish enough to fire off a shot the flash of light would have revealed her position. She might have taken the shot and turned to run. Her pupils would have contracted at the flash of light and when she bolted she might not have seen where one step dropped to the next. Maybe she hadn't even been murdered. She could have tripped, her brow splitting on the granite step as she fell, the awkward splay of her body as she tumbled down the steps cracking her neck.

I trotted down the steps and looked toward the Fairbanks memorial. Water lilies scudded across the surface of the pond and poplars lined the back of the memorial like sentinels. She might have thought she could escape by running through the cover of trees. Or maybe she stood her ground to confront whoever came to investigate the source of the flash. They argued and he hit her. Maybe he hadn't intended to kill her. Maybe all he wanted was the camera. Under other circumstances her death might be considered manslaughter but she had been killed during the commission of a felony. Whoever pushed or hit her could be charged with first-degree murder. I glanced back up the staircase and saw Frank staring down at me.

"I have something to show you," he called. He set two cups of take-out coffee and a box of donuts on the low granite wall. When I reached the top step he flashed a photograph faceup beside the box. "Ever seen this guy before?"

The man in the photograph looked fit and well fed within the sleek confines of a dark gray suit, good-looking but not so good-looking somebody would suggest he make a living from his face. "Never seen him before," I said. "Who is he?"

"Stonewell's agent."

When I laughed my lungs opened as though surfacing from a long stint underwater. "You thought Stonewell was telling the truth about Sven being his agent?"

"I didn't think anything," he said. "I'm just desperate because a story moves or dies and this story is starting to look like a lizard stuck in the middle of six lanes of traffic." He dealt a second photograph onto the granite. "How about him?"

I didn't recognize him either.

"Stonewell's manager," he said. "I'm running out of ideas here.

You remember Bartlet said he'd heard rumors about a shrine at Steve Reeves Ranch in Canyon Country?"

"Families fuck you up," I said.

Frank stuffed a donut into his mouth, said, "What?"

"I don't know." I really didn't. I didn't know anything.

"Are you talking about your family? Or families in general? What's going on with you anyway? You never swear, not once have I ever heard you say the F word." He looked at the staircase and his head snapped back with the realization of where we stood. "Isn't this where your sister bit it? It is, isn't it?" He pointed his chin toward the pond. "Here at the base of the stairs."

"She's only fifteen years old," I said.

"Who?"

"Theresa."

"I thought we were talking about your sister."

I struck off across the lane, away from the steps where my sister had died, toward the mausoleum that rose, like an acropolis, from the island in the middle of the lake. My attention shuttled between my dead mother, my thieving sister, Theresa's arrest, and the dread that not only couldn't I properly grieve, I couldn't comprehend what had happened or why. Frank chased after me, donuts and coffee clutched against his chest. "I'm sorry about the girl," he said.

A spray of wildflowers attracted my eye and I glanced down at a very simple headstone marking the grave of John Huston, then over to a towering, rocketlike spire beyond the lake. Huston's films were his legacy; he didn't need a big memorial. "She trusted me," I said. "And now she's in jail because I was a fool and believed the law. Can you believe I was stupid enough to take her in for questioning? They haven't even told me the truth about my sister's death—just half-truths. The law screwed me so many times I should know better, I should have known they'd play me both sides against the middle."

"You've been a real model citizen, no doubt about that," Frank said. "Two months ago you wouldn't have given snaps of a killing to the cops. No way. You would have swallowed the roll first."

"I still owe my lawyer for the last time he got me out of jail and now I have to take care of Theresa's legal expenses, too. Where's that money going to come from? Her dad is a drunk who thinks she's going to be his ticket to riches. It's my fault she's in jail. I walked her right into a cell and slammed the door." The law wasn't my friend and never would be. I gazed across the tombs of Cecil B. DeMille and Janet Gaynor to Jayne Mansfield's cenotaph across the lake, then picked out the memorial to Hattie McDaniel not far from the steps where my sister had died. "All these dead people, maybe they have the right idea. No worries when you're dead, no disappointments either." I grabbed a donut from the box and bit down, the glaze swirling around my tongue like the sugary froth on a wave. At least I could eat. At least I could still do that. "Maybe the shrine doesn't exist," I said. "Bartlet said it was only a rumor. I feel like we're chasing ghosts here."

"I don't know about ghosts but I do know Steve Reeves Ranch exists." Frank settled into the grass next to Huston's headstone. "He took up horse ranching when he retired. Only two problems. Mr. Reeves was very much alive until this year and the ranch is near Escondido, in San Diego County. Bartlet said Canyon Country."

"Then why him? Was he an actor or something?"

"You don't remember?" He shielded his eyes from the sun and looked up at me. "He was the first Arnold Schwarzenegger."

I sat on the grass opposite the headstone and took one of the coffees, asked, "What do you mean?"

"A bodybuilder who turned to acting. Won all the big competitions. Mr. America, Mr. World, Mr. Universe. As though he was competing against muscular space aliens for the Mr. Universe title, right?"

"Didn't he do those sword-and-sandal flicks?"

"That's right," he said, chewing and nodding. "Lots of muscular, sweaty guys in togas. Got his break playing Hercules. Did a bunch of sequels that practically invented the genre, became so popular they named a missile after him."

I looked at him like, you're kidding.

"No, I'm serious," he said. "The Hercules, one of the first antiballistic missiles. Okay, maybe they named it after the original Greek myth, too. But the first Hercules missiles were deployed the same year the movie came out so there was a connection. They had a bunch of them stationed in silos up and down the coast."

"Is that the same thing as the Nike missile bases, you know, the ones in the mountains around here?"

"Sure, same thing," Frank said. "The military abandoned them years ago, in the 1960s, I think. Sometime after they discovered missile defense systems don't work against other missiles." He pantomimed pointing a rifle to the sky. "Like a bullet hitting a bullet."

"What are they now?"

He shrugged, like he couldn't speak for all of them. "They're all different. Some torn down and paved over entirely, like the one in, where is it, Long Beach, I think. Some taken over by the forest service. Others leased out for television and radio transmission towers, you know, because the bases were generally built on mountaintops."

"Could someone lease the entire base, maybe buy it from the government?"

"Sure, I think that's been done, but why are we talking about this? I know you're looking for a place to live and personal security is important, particularly after someone burned down your last pad, but a Nike missile base? Isn't that a little extreme?"

I swallowed the last of the donut, wiped my hands on the grass, and stood. "Luce said the word *Nike* when she died. Everybody thought she was talking about running shoes."

"Nike? That was the missile before the Hercules." He stared up at me, piecing together the connections. "You think it's called Steve Reeves Ranch because it's a former missile base?"

I held out my hand to help him up. "Can you think of a better place to set up a shrine to dead celebrities?"

"You mean because it's remote, out of the way?"

"No," I said. "Because rockets shoot toward the stars."

THIRTY-SEVEN

THE ROUTE to the abandoned Nike base came back to me as Frank and I drove the granite slope of the San Gabriel Mountains some thirty miles north of Los Angeles. On the penultimate night of her life my sister had talked about the times she had slipped out the bedroom window to drink and kiss boys in the weird isolation of the base. At the time it seemed my sister had wanted to say more but held back out of what I thought to be reticence. Maybe she had already known about the role the base played in the Church of Divine Thespians or at least suspected it. I felt as though she had known things at her death that I had yet to discover, that I still trailed her, just as I'd followed in her footsteps when I too slipped out the bedroom window at the age of fifteen to play adolescent games involving boys and alcohol in the abandoned landscape of the Nike base.

We swung off the freeway at Lost Canyon Road and wound through sharp-backed ridges to clusters of oak and wild-grass fields below Angeles National Forest. I'd always ridden to the base by the light of headlamps and in daylight almost missed the faded red graffiti on the roadside oak tagged to mark the dirt road branching up the hill to the base. Frank talked to an editorial assistant on the phone as I drove, jotting facts into his notebook. I steered to the side, left wheels down the ridged center of the dirt road to keep the Caddy clear of rocks.

"The site is no longer owned by the government," Frank said.

He'd dispatched the assistant to research Nike missile bases. "It was bought years ago by a communications company to use as a microwave relay site, then sold again. Current owner unknown, but we're working on it."

NO TRESPASSING signs appeared on the oaks to the left of the road just before it split again. A V-shaped gate swung across the fork heading up to the base, metal bars padlocked to a post. I parked the Cadillac at a turnout a quarter mile up the road. "How do you want to do this?" I asked.

"I thought I'd walk up and ring the bell," he said.

"I don't think there is one."

"No bell? Then what's up there?"

I laid it out for him, the way it had been when I was a teenager, dirt road leading to a chain-link fence topped in barbed wire. Not much remained on the surface of the base back then, just a few pad-locked outbuildings, a radar tower, concrete launch pads, and welded-shut doors descending to the munitions magazines. We'd snuck through gaps in the chain-link fence cut by a previous genera-tion of teens. A private owner would have patched those gaps. Frank levered open the door and stepped outside. He lit a cigarette and stretched out the kinks the ride had put in his back, asked, "Are you coming with?"

"You're going to walk up there, just like that."

"That's the way you get a Pulitzer Prize." He puffed his cigarette a little too vigorously, smoking and smirking through his nerves. "If you're too chicken to come with me, I understand."

I opened the trunk, fished the boot cam from my camera bag. "They know who I am. I show my face, they might shoot us both on sight." I handed the point-and-shoot camera to Frank. "You, they might not recognize."

Frank slid back the lens cover and pointed the viewfinder at my head. "You plan to stay here?"

"Don't worry, I'll call 911 if I hear shots."

He lowered the camera. The expression on his face, he didn't look all that confident. "You'll help scatter my ashes too, I bet."

I pointed to the right of the barred road. The base had been built where the ground leveled out below the crest of the hill. "There are some trees up there, if I remember right." I pulled the telephoto lens from my bag and attached it to the body of the Nikon. "I'll cover you with the telephoto from there. It's going to make a more dramatic shot in telephoto, the courageous journalist braving death alone."

Frank smoked his cigarette down to the filter, his smirk fading to a grimace. "You have cell-phone coverage up here?"

I checked my phone for a signal, nodded.

He crushed the cigarette beneath his heel. "Battery charged up? Remember how to dial 911?"

I strung the crowbar through a belt loop and affixed a pair of wire cutters to the opposite side. "Smoke another death stick, give me time to get in position for the shot." I called the Rott to my side and struck off between a couple of NO TRESPASSING signs, glancing back once to see Frank dip into his pack of Winstons like a condemned man offered a second last cigarette.

I skirted the perimeter of the base, my trail screened from the casual eye by a line of oaks standing fifty yards distant. The San Gabriels to the north are different from the Coast Range, enough rain falling to support oak, buckeye, and walnut trees among fields of wild grains and grasses. The occasional prickly pear cactus breaks through the soil, a reminder that the desert is never distant in Southern California, but thickets of chaparral and sagebrush are absent and the hills are easy to hike. I put the telephoto to my eye and scanned the wide swath of land, cleared to chickweed and thistle, that separated the line of trees from the perimeter fence. Fresh razor wire topped the chain-link and the fence stretched taught, uncut. Orange and black PRIVATE PROPERTY signs alternated every dozen yards with those declaring NO TRESPASSING. I'd never before seen an unguarded fence in the hills that hadn't been cut by hikers and wondered who guarded this one.

The Rott loped ahead, where he found the scent of old horse droppings so irresistible he rolled in them, wriggling on his back as though he bathed in ambrosia. I looked for a tree with an unobstructed view of the base and selected an oak at the edge of the field. Camera strapped around my back, I boosted myself on a knothole to the lowest branch, then vaulted to the next, which hung, thick as a dolphin's torso, over the field. I straddled the branch and aimed the telephoto down the road. Frank marched into view a minute later, not-so-discreetly scanning the trees in an attempt to spot my position. The Rott hunkered low in the grass. I was all but invisible at that distance, shielded by the branches and dry, barbed leaves of the oak. Frank stepped up to the chain-link gate blocking the road into the base and shook it. A length of steel chain looped both sides of the gate, secured by a thick padlock that looked Kalashnikov-proof. He wasn't going to break through the gate by shaking it.

I panned across the base looking for surveillance cameras. Rubble from the base's decommissioning and the refuse of teenage beer busts had been cleared from the grounds and the cylindrical-roofed out-buildings glistened with fresh green paint. A giant satellite dish hung from the radar tower. No cameras, dogs, or security guards in sight. If Sven had set up operations here, he counted on the remoteness and innocence of the location—and a good security fence—to keep out intruders.

I ran off a few frames of Frank at the gate and slid down the trunk. The Rott jumped to his feet, relieved to have me closer to eye level. I gave him the hand signal for *down* and he reluctantly obeyed. He was a good dog but I didn't need him bounding around the grass, not where I planned to go. I signaled him to stay and crawled toward the fence on my belly. The Rott thought that was a peculiar thing to do. He watched, intensely curious while I covered the first dozen yards, then, conflicted between the needs to obey and to see what I was up to, crawled after me. He'd done that before, technically obey-ing one command while ignoring another, thinking maybe I wouldn't notice.

I slipped the tin snips from my belt when I reached the fence. Frank shouted his name and profession as he aimed the lens of the point-and-shoot through the chain-link. If he saw me, he didn't give any indication. I trapped the bottom wire between the blades and squeezed until it popped, moved to the next link and the next. A slim black figure stumbled from the outbuilding nearest the gate. I twisted the camera toward my eye, distracted by a rustling to my right and then the flick of something warm and wet on my arm. The Rott. His glance imparted more than a little worry, as though he feared I'd scold him. I repeated the signal for *down* and twisted the focus ring until the figure of a thin young girl dressed in black came into clear view, walking toward Frank at the front gate. A girl whose skin looked powdered white and whose eyes and lips had been painted in shades as purple as a bruise. A Goth girl. Cassie Bogle. My niece.

My finger stilled above the shutter release.

She stopped a few feet short of the chain-link fence, her hands wedged into the back pockets of her black jeans and her eyes fixed to the ground at her feet as she listened to what Frank had to say. I couldn't take a picture that exposed her face not only to the readers of *Scandal Times* but to a legal system that cared little for the welfare of juvenile offenders. In California, a killing committed during the commission of a felony is first-degree murder, and anyone participating in the original felony can be charged with murder, whether they hold the weapon, give the order, or merely go along for the ride. If the police obtained evidence that she'd been at Hollywood Forever Cemetery the night of the grave robbery, they could charge her with the murder of her mother. The state could even try her as an adult. I couldn't trust the law to treat her leniently. Theresa's arrest proved that. I couldn't risk the same happening to Cassie with far more serious consequences.

I auto-dialed Frank's number and watched through the telephoto while it connected. He ignored the rings, lacing his fingers through the chain-link at his shoulders while he talked. Cassie shook her head, shrugged, and turned toward the outbuildings. She was sorry, the gestures said, but she couldn't help him. Frank shouted something as she walked away, then thought to answer his phone.

"Call her Cassie," I whispered.

"Why would I want to do that?" He scanned the trees again for my position. "She says she's the daughter of the caretaker. Nobody's home except her."

"Don't fight me on this. Her name is Cassie. Call her name."

He shrugged and shouted her name. She turned a long and suspicious look over her shoulder. Her high, thin voice wafted through the receiver. "How do you know who I am?"

"Look back behind you," I whispered. "Toward the car." I didn't want him to glance toward my position. I wanted Cassie to think whoever called spoke down the hill from them. "Tell her you have a message from her mother. Not her foster mother, but her real mother, Sharon."

I snipped higher up the chain-link fence while he repeated my message, then folded the sharp edges away to make a gap in the fence about two feet high. "Tell her that you're talking to someone who knows her mother, that her mother sent me to Los Angeles to talk to her." I held my hand flat toward the Rott's snout, ordering him to stay, and slithered through the gap in the fence. "Keep looking behind you, like you expect me to come that way."

"I don't know what's going on here," Frank whispered, turning toward the road so the girl wouldn't hear.

"The girl is my niece," I whispered, moving silently forward.

"Wait a minute, you mean your sister, the one who was—"

"Do not mention anything about her mother's murder. She may not know anything about it. But keep talking. Keep her distracted."

I wedged the cell phone into the hip pocket of my jeans. Frank pretended he continued to talk to me, gesturing so wildly he looked like a crazy man. I closed enough distance to hear her voice as she questioned him, a voice thin and scratchy, much like her mother's. Her jeans hung low over hips so thin the twin bones of her pelvis jutted out like wings, and the skin of her lower back, visible in the gap between her jeans and bare-midriff top, stretched emaciation-taut around the vertebrae. I said, "Hi Cassie."

She turned and backed toward the fence, her hair short and blond at the crown but dyed black and worn long at the bangs, like the tonsure of a rebellious priest. Her eyes flicked from my boots to dyed-black hair, judging not just my style but also my speed in case she decided to bolt. She asked, "How'd you get in here?"

"I cut through the fence," I said. No reason to lie. "I'm your mom's sister. That makes me your aunt."

She blinked hard, jolted.

"It was news to me, too," I said.

"You're Mary?"

"A long time ago, when your mom lived at the house." My sister had told her about me. That surprised me. I glanced back at the Rott. He'd crawled through the gap in the fence. My glance caught him creeping forward again. I slapped my thigh, the way I called him to me. "I go by Nina now."

"I've seen a picture of Mary. She had blond hair." She looked at the dog running up and shifted her feet, uncertain what effect the dog would have on a decision to run.

"I suspect you and I get our hair from the same bottle." The dog bounced against my leg. I told him to sit and he obeyed. "I talked to your mother a week ago. She asked me to get you out of trouble, so you should know that's what I'm here to do."

An adolescent voice called out behind me, the tone uncertain of its authority or maybe just afraid of the dog. Two more voices, young and male, screeched a second challenge. The Rott let out a low warning bark. I didn't turn, brought the palm of my hand toward his head, a hand signal I'd taught him to stay put.

"You got three behind you," Frank said.

I took a step closer to my niece, carefully measuring the distance between us in case I had to do what I had to do, and told her, "You're in a bad situation here."

"You're the one outnumbered." She wanted me to go away. She owed her allegiance to the crew she ran with far more than to an aunt she'd never seen before.

"You remember Luce?"

She nodded, willing to give me that much.

"Eric murdered her. On Santa Monica Pier. The people controlling this little gang of yours, they're killers."

I watched the realization flash through her eyes. "You're lying," she said.

"I saw him kill her. Through my camera."

The challenge sounded again behind me. I reached down and grabbed the Rott's collar, aware that he was close to going into attack mode. Two of the boys carried iron bars and the third one a knife. They looked as evenly spaced in age as brothers, none of them over eighteen. "Looks like we have to make some fast decisions," I said. "Tell your friends to back off. Tell them we're family. I need to talk to you alone."

She shook her head as though the prospect of being alone with me frightened her. "I don't believe anything you're telling me. I don't believe you're my aunt. You should leave now, before you get hurt."

I nodded, as though agreeing that was the most sensible option. I released the Rott's collar and gave him a single command to protect. He launched from my side, his bark deep and vicious as a chainsaw ripping wood. Cassie's eyes followed the dog. I hit her with a right hook, the blow striking her flush on the jaw where a smile might normally go. She went down without a word of complaint, no more than a sharp exhale of breath on impact.

"What the hell are you doing?" Frank said.

I stepped to the fence and drew the wire snips, working the blades as fast as a pair of scissors. The Rott stopped just beyond the range of the weapons, his bark alone ferocious enough to keep the boys at bay. I told Frank to pretend he was calling the police, try to scare the boys into backing off. The Rott charged the young one on the left, who had tried to slip around the side, and the move exposed the dog's flanks to the older boy in the middle, who swung and connected against his right haunch. The Rott yelped in pain and snapped at the boy's forearm.

I pushed out the gap in the fence and grabbed the collar of my niece's blouse just as the middle boy shouted that the dog had no teeth. I pulled her through the cut-hole and shouted at the Rott to come. He skittered aside to dodge the next swing and dashed toward the fence. I pried back the jagged ends of the chain-link so the Rott could see the hole and he shot through it without hesitation. The boys charged the gap, thinking they'd squirm through behind the dog. I drew the crowbar from my belt loop and whacked it high against the fence.

"This is a family affair," I said. "The first head that comes through that hole gets separated from its shoulders. Cassie is my niece. I'm taking her home." They were brave boys and I sympathized with their instinct to rescue a fallen friend but I didn't intend to fight them all the way back to the car. It was better for them to understand the situation clearly. They needed to realize that I'd hurt them. They clustered on the opposite side of the fence, glaring through the chain-link but curious too, as though they lacked people willing to stage a commando raid to rescue them and they wondered what such a relative would be like. I wanted to help them, if I could.

"Eric murdered Luce," I said. "He'll kill you too, soon enough."

"Eric wouldn't do that," the oldest boy said. "He wouldn't hurt Luce. They were hooking up together. They were tight." He glanced at his two companions, whose nods confirmed the opinion.

"She's dead all the same," I said. "And even if you're not afraid of Eric you should know the cops can arrest you on charges of robbery and murder."

"What are you talking about? We didn't kill anybody!" The middle boy's voice broke with adolescent outrage.

"A woman was killed the night you took Valentino."

"We weren't anywhere near her," the oldest boy said. "We didn't even know anything happened."

"Doesn't matter. They'll charge you with murder anyway, just because you were there, the same way they charge the driver of the getaway car in a bank robbery." I turned away from the fence. If they were smart, they'd put it together and run.

Cassie tried to sit up, couldn't quite get there, and rolled onto her side. Frank asked if she knew where she was. She tried to sit up again and this time she made it. "You hit me," she said, resentful and rightfully so.

I crouched, slung her arm over my shoulder, and lifted her upright. "I'm not sorry I did," I said. "Come on, I'm taking you somewhere we can talk."

Her legs wobbled when she tried to walk. Frank took her opposite shoulder, the Rott scouting ahead. I glanced back at the fence. The smallest boy, the one who had held the knife and seemed most determined to get around the Rott, slithered through the gap in the fence. I ordered the Rott to sit and asked the boy his business. He dropped the knife and jogged up to us.

"Give me a ride down the hill with you?" he asked.

THIRTY-EIGHT

HE CALLED himself Jason and said he'd lived in Portland before hitchhiking to Southern California six months before. From the way he quickly took the responsibility of supporting Cassie from Frank I guessed he favored her in some special way. He appeared to be her age or a year older and sported a look that mirrored hers, hair worn long and black in front and shaved blond in back. He wasn't a big kid, except in the face; his neck and shoulders seemed too frail to hold his oversized head, his lips swelling beneath a massive brow as though he hadn't yet grown into his features. Cassie latched onto his hand in the backseat and didn't let go during the ride down the mountain. I didn't know the exact nature of their relationship and didn't ask. Jason cared enough for her to risk throwing his lot with hers. I couldn't ask for a more genuine sign of his loyalty than that.

Frank and I booked two rooms in a chain motel close to the freeway to clean them up, feed them, and get their story. Frank had wanted to take them to *Scandal Times* and worry about where to put them up later but I didn't want my niece to feel any more kidnapped than she already had the honest right to feel. We met on the walkway outside our adjoining rooms while the two kids showered, Frank using the break as an opportunity to smoke. "We can't use their names in the paper," I said. "Are we clear on that?"

"They're minors. We'd have legal issues if we tried." Frank blew his smoke away from me, a rare show of consideration.

"Let's break them up," I suggested.

"I'll talk to Jason," he said. "I've got some pot in my bag. After I loosen him up with a few joints he'll tell me everything he knows."

I stared at him.

"Just kidding," he said, showing the palms of his hands in a don't-hit-me gesture. "But I need to know how far to take this. Are we going to put them up here for a few days or what? Will it offend your sense of morals if I bribe him to tell me about the shrine? If this guy Sven really has a bunch of celebrity bones up there this is front-page stuff."

"I need to talk to my niece, figure out what to do, how to get her out of this. If I put her on the bus back to Phoenix, she'll skip at the next stop, just like Theresa did."

"What about her father? Can he help?"

"Her stepfather? He's in the joint, serving time on a bank-robbery conviction," I said, remembering what Dougan and Smalls had told me. "Her blood father is a double murderer, executed last year in Texas."

Frank smoked and thought about that for a moment. "Con-artist mother, bank-robbing stepfather, death-row daddy, and an ex-con paparazza for an aunt." He whistled in mock admiration. "The girl has lots of role models."

Like any other talent crime runs in families. My niece, at thirteen already implicated in theft and murder, was looking like a prodigy. I didn't know how to alter that course. I wasn't all that convinced it was my responsibility. I jogged down to the car to pull from the trunk a change of clothing and a few back editions of the *Los Angeles Times*. My niece was too young to take care of herself but old enough to make taking care of her without her consent impossible. I returned to the room to sit on the corner of the bed and wait for her to emerge from the shower.

"How's your jaw?" I asked when the bathroom door opened. She scuttled around the far side of the second bed in the room and wrapped her arms around her thin chest, eyes fearful but curious, like a small predator watching a larger one. Hitting somebody isn't the most endearing way to introduce yourself to a relative. "I had to get you out of there," I said. "I'm not sorry I hit you. But I regret the pain it caused."

"Where's my mother?" she demanded. "You told me you'd take me to my mother."

"Your mother is dead."

I hadn't planned to say it that way but it needed to be said and that's how it came out. I laid on the bed the issue of the *Times* that headlined the robbery from Valentino's crypt and next to it the two-column follow-up story identifying the murder victim by name. Then I sat back on the bed to give her time to read.

Cassie wasn't the fastest reader. I tried not to mark her progress by watching too closely. We looked physically similar, enough to guess at a glance we were related, though she was going through her rebellious stage about ten years before I'd gone through mine. She dyed her blond hair black, just as I did. Our eyes were the same color of brown, so dark they could pass for black in dim light or when shaded by rage. Like me, she didn't seem much disposed to tears. The shock of seeing her mother's death in print twitched the corners of her eyes but she did not cry out or weep. Maybe life had already burned the tears from her.

"I thought she was still in prison," she said.

"She was paroled a couple of months ago."

"It wasn't like she came to visit me all that often." The scratch in her voice cut so deeply the words broke up as she spoke. She sounded thirteen going on forty.

"When was the last time you saw her?"

"When I was nine. The day before she was arrested on that bank robbery thing." She braved a longer glance at me, starting to believe that I wished her no harm.

"You close to your stepdad?"

"Which stepdad? The one in prison or the one they fried in Texas?"

"Texas? I thought he was . . ." I didn't finish the sentence.

"My real father? Define real." The scratch running through her voice hardened and spiked out like a barb. "You mean someone who holds you in your arms when you're a baby and helps you do your homework and other shit like that? I don't know what real fathers do because I never had one. Or do you mean the sperm bag who knocked up my mom and nine months later out pops yours truly?" Her hands flourished, palms up at the shoulders, and she clowned a smile. "Mom lied to you, I'm sure. Mom lies to everybody. She sure as fuck lied to stepdad number one, telling him I was his kid."

"Did she tell you who your biological father is?"

"You mean the sperm bag? A con artist is all I heard. Some guy who took her money and left me as the deposit. You think he cares? Or are you thinking blackmail?" Her eyes flashed at the thought. "Like maybe he's got a nice little life now, a nice little family, he'll pay something so I'll stay away?" She examined my boots, jet-black jeans, and black leather jacket as though seeing possibilities, as though she imagined we might embark together on a life of crime. She asked, "You've been to prison?"

"Does it show?"

"You look like you've done some illegal shit. But maybe you're smart, didn't get caught."

"I'm smart enough," I said. "And I still got caught. You'll be caught too, unless you change the way you look at your life."

Her lip curled and her glance turned sullen. "Is this the part where you talk about how I have to adjust my attitude, stop fucking up so much?"

"I don't have the right to tell you what to do," I said. "I have the responsibility to care what happens to you. That's all. And part of that is letting you know what I think about things, to share a little hard-earned wisdom about the way life can cut the legs from under you. But I can't tell you what to do."

"So if I get up right now and walk out the door, you won't stop me?"

"I'm not your guardian. I may be your blood aunt, but that doesn't give me some moral authority over you, not unless we both agree that's what we want."

Cassie threw down a defiant stare and strode toward the door. I clasped my hands together to hold back the urge to tackle her. It was her choice, not mine. The girl was damaged, maybe irreparably. Thirteen is old enough to run away. Thirteen is old enough to go bad, if the determination is there. She paused when her feet crossed the threshold. "Just one question." She leaned against the door frame, waiting for me to look at her before she asked it. "What the fuck was my mom thinking? Why was she even at the cemetery that night?"

I couldn't judge when my sister had spoken the truth or lied, and if confronted with the need to guess which was which I'd put my money on the lie. My sister may have been desperate and like most criminals blind to the consequences of her actions but she wasn't stupid. She had to realize the stigma attached to being the daughter of a convicted murderer. And so she had told her daughter a little fiction about the identity of her father, I supposed, inventing a figure just enough of a rogue to render him untraceable. Not all lies are hurtful or self-serving. "Your mom started looking for you the moment she got out of prison." I didn't know whether or not that was true but maybe by saying it I could make it true for Cassie. It was a hard thing to have to call your own mother a liar. "She loved you more than anything or anyone else in the world. She was looking for you at the cemetery that night because she thought you were in trouble."

My niece hovered at the doorway, trying to construct a psychological defense against the assertion that her mother had loved her despite the lies and absences. A mother's love is among the most powerful forces in all of life, no less potent withheld than given. Breath shuddered into her like wind through broken glass and her hand, draped insolently against the door frame a moment before, trembled. She dropped to her heels and hugged her chest as though violently ill, short gasps breaking from her body until tears swelled her eyes shut. I don't know whether kinship sings in the blood or merely speaks to the brain but that thin and trembling body called to something vital in me. My life was no worse than hers. Why hadn't I been able to cry? What had so jammed my heart that such simple emotion seemed forever blocked? My sister had failed at nearly all the basic requirements of parenting, but still, Cassie cried for her. For all her faults my mother too deserved to be properly grieved.

After some time Cassie's trembling ceased and she stared dully out the open doorway, all thought of escape vanished for the moment. "What happened that night?" I asked. When the question did not move her to respond I said, "Did you know someone had been killed?"

Her brow creased sharply and her face reddened, as though the question wounded her and she might cry again, but she shook her head to will away the pain. "Rumors. Some of the crew, they said something bad happened, but nobody knew anything. Gunny said he saw news of it on TV. He likes to go to Circuit City, watch television on the sets they got displayed there."

"Who's Gunny?"

"Just a fuckhead." She shook her head again, a short, disdainful gesture. "One of the crew. Nobody believed him. Gunny lies a lot."

"Nobody saw anything? Nobody heard anything?"

"We knew something happened," she said. "But we didn't know what." She grasped her head, palms winging from her eyes like blinders. "Maybe we knew. Maybe we were just too afraid to admit it. I was in the vault with Valentino. I didn't see anything. But I heard. One of the crew said somebody was out there. I was helping pry away the stone, you know, the marble protecting the coffin. Eric ordered us to stop, to shut up. He told us not to move. And he went outside, outside the vault. We didn't know if it was the pols or not. We were scared. We thought we were all gonna get busted. So I crawled toward the door. Hands and knees like a dog. Getting ready to jet, you know? In case it was the pols. I was gonna be the first one out, jump the fence, escape. Then I heard a shout." She nodded to herself, as though confirming something remembered. "It was a woman. A woman shouted. But it wasn't like a scream or anything. And I did see something. I saw a flash of light."

"From a flash camera? Could it have been that kind of light?"

"Fuck," she said. "Everything's fucked." She pushed off the floor, her legs unsteady as she moved into the bathroom to wash the salt from her face.

My niece's language didn't shock me. I didn't like it, but it didn't shock me. She spoke like a lot of women I'd known in prison. I once thought people swore to sound tough, but I've since learned that just as often it's the nearest they can come to articulating despair. "Why was she looking for me?" she cried from the sink. "Three years I didn't see her, three fucking years. And she shows up there? I mean, what the fuck? Did she have radar or something? Was it some criminal thing, like she wanted part of the action?"

"You ran away from your foster home." I met her glance in the mirror above the sink. My sister didn't deserve much, but she deserved the good truths that could be spoken about her. "Nobody knew where you were. She was worried about you. That night, it was the first solid tip she'd received about how to find you." I began to doubt my words as I spoke them. She'd ripped me off for nineteen grand and taken my point-and-shoot. Why take my camera if she wasn't intending to photograph the robbery and sell the snaps to the tabloids? I didn't intend my sister's death to turn her into something she wasn't—angel or demon.

Cassie heard the doubt in my voice and turned to better read the shifting lines of my face. She needed to believe something. At thirteen we are aware how our parents fail us but still we need to believe in their essential benevolence, that no matter how hard they beat us they beat us from love, that their criticisms no matter how sharply worded are meant to improve more than wound us, that their many and inscrutable punishments are meant to goad us to success and not to drive us to failure and misery.

"Your mother was not perfect," I said. "In many ways, she was a terrible mother. But she loved you. Her failures had nothing to do with that."

"Mom was a fuck-up," she said. "Fuck-ups run in the family. Are you a fuck-up, too?"

"I'm a recovering fuck-up," I said.

I heard the pounding of feet in the hallway before Frank's face jutted through the doorway. I turned toward him, already shaking my head. Now was not the time. Go away.

"You have to turn on your TV." He lurched toward the remote control and pointed it at the set. A diamond of light burst into the center of the screen and a face surfaced from the black, a young man's face, blond hair worn unfashionably long in back. A face I recognized from the day my camera had been smashed on a Santa Monica sidewalk.

"Fuck, that's Eric," Cassie said. "They busted him?"

A walking hairdo with a microphone stared into the camera in front of Santa Monica City Hall and announced that at one PM that afternoon Eric Noet had walked into the 2nd Street station of the Santa Monica Police Department and confessed to the murder of Lucille Ryan. Frank simultaneously worked motel and mobile phones while the report played. The on-scene reporter, who had mastered the difficult skill of staring seriously into the camera without wrinkling her brow, called the victim a stunning young starlet and her murder, at the hands of her estranged boyfriend, a crime of passion.

I shouted in protest.

"His lawyer all but copped him to voluntary manslaughter," Frank reported. He held the motel phone cupped against his chest. "Rumor is they hope to plea-bargain him down from first-degree murder."

The screen flashed to a live feed of Eric's lawyer, his face as familiar as the celebrities he frequently represented. Two young lives ruined, he said. A tragedy for everyone. No one regrets what happened more than my client.

"We told you they were hooking up together," Jason said. He sat next to Cassie on the bed, their hands an inch from touching.

I'd been in and out of the so-called criminal justice system often enough to know the drill. The defense would contend Luce had died as a result of a lovers' quarrel. The knife is a common murder weapon among wronged lovers, the phallic thrust of steel serving as a coup de grâce for the relationship. Because of my criminal record the prosecution wouldn't be eager to let me testify and the state wouldn't want the case go to trial. Eric would cop to losing his head in a moment of passion and plea-bargain down to a few years in prison. I still believed that Sven had ordered her death, motivated by the fear that she would talk, but I couldn't prove it and probably never would. I lifted my camera bag onto the bed and rifled through the compartments, checking equipment and film stocks. "How do you think he got the lawyer?" I asked.

"That guy, he loves cases like this." Frank held the motel phone close to his ear while he waited for follow-up information. "A high-profile case, a Hollywood murder, lead story on the five o'clock news, it makes sense that he'd want to get involved."

"So you think Eric just called him up, said he wanted to confess, please represent me? You think that's what happened?"

"What are you thinking?"

I shouldered the camera bag, considered taking the motel key, decided to leave it behind. If they caught me, the key would lead them back to the motel. The Rott jumped from the floor, alerted by the signal of shouldering the bag that we were about to go. "I'm thinking we don't have any visuals for the story you're going to write."

"So we'll stage something," he said.

"A front-page story needs a front-page photo."

"I'm on a call," he said. "Wait up, I'll go with."

I walked out in the middle of his sentence.

"You're not going out there alone," he called.

"Of course not," I said. "I'm taking the dog."

I jogged down the stairs and cranked open the passenger door for the Rott. Cassie vaulted down the stairs as I circled the trunk, Jason two steps behind. Anywhere she went, he'd follow.

"Take us with you," she said.

"I have to do my job and I do my job best alone," I said, and slid behind the wheel. "But I'll come back for you, I promise. And when I do, we'll work out together what we're going to do, you and Jason and I." When I shut the door and started the engine she rapped a silver skull ring on the window. I powered it down.

"If you're looking for Sven you won't find him," she said.

"Why not?"

"Nobody finds Sven," Jason said.

"I've already heard that from somebody else," I said. "But if nobody can find him, how did you find him?"

Cassie shook her head once. "I didn't find him. He found me."

"Me too," Jason said.

"How did he find you?" I asked.

"He sent Eric to Arizona to get me," Cassie said.

"He sent for all of us," Jason said. "He found us all."

Frank pounded down the stairs, cell phone pressed to his ear. I put the Cadillac in gear and spun out of the lot.

THIRTY-NINE

I RETRACED in the skittering beam of my headlights the route we had taken that afternoon, the boughs of oak trees looming over the road like the limbs of giant ghosts. The layout of curves and straights came back to me as I wheeled through the hills, girlhood memory refreshed by that afternoon's drive, and I anticipated sighting the red scrawl of graffiti marking the road to the base moments before the headlights picked it out of the darkness. The Rott stood on the passenger seat beside me, paws shifting for balance when the Caddy heaved onto the dirt road. Dogs are not keen-sighted animals, and I doubted he recognized the terrain until I edged the car off the side and let him out to smell it.

The Rott threaded us through the oaks in darkness, picking out our previous path by scent. I followed in the light of a curved blade of moon, tuning my ears to the soft fall of the dog's paws and the snuffling of his muzzle held low to the ground. I wasn't sure what I'd find at the base or if I did find something what I'd do with it, but I knew that before long the perimeter fence would be mended and fortified by someone more daunting than four scrawny teenagers armed with iron bars. Sven had counted on secrecy to defend the base and our appearance breached that secrecy. If the shrine existed he would either defend or move it.

The Rott nosed up to the tree I'd climbed before and glanced back at me as though afraid I'd pull the same stunt twice and abandon him to the ground. I knelt and hugged his head, to reassure him, yes, but also to gather courage from his stout heart and physical strength. I put a forefinger to my lips to command his silence and caught the attentive look in his eye that meant he understood. The crowbar twisted in the belt loop of my jeans when I stood. I straightened it and struck off across the clearing between the oaks and the fence at the perimeter of the base.

The taut sheet of chain-link slackened near the cut, the break in the cross pattern visible even at distance in the dark. I squeezed through the gap, then pulled back the flap of chain-link to allow the Rott to slip through. The ground leveled inside the perimeter, the wild grasses trimmed to ankle height. Three cylindrical-roofed out-buildings, once used for administration, lay twenty yards ahead, arching side by side into the ground like half-buried cans. No light showed in the four-pane windows nor anywhere else on the base. I listened carefully for sounds and watched the Rott, whose weight shifted to his forepaws as his ears pricked forward. His hearing was far keener than mine and if I watched closely his behavior would reveal what he heard. He turned his head to me, waiting for my next move, the same as saying he heard nothing that threatened us.

I stepped to the first building, careful to plant my feet softly at each shift of weight, the stubble of weeds cracking beneath my boots. By the lack of light and noise I guessed the two remaining boys had fled. I reached for the doorknob, bright stainless steel shadowing at the approach of my hand. I gave it a turn. Locked. I veered toward the window to the side of the door. The reflection of my face in the glass appeared brighter than anything behind it.

The knob on the door of the second building turned freely. I thought back to my encounter that afternoon. I hadn't seen which building Cassie had emerged from, and later, when the other kids had charged out to confront me, my back had been turned. But I had to assume, perhaps wrongly, that the center building had served as living quarters for the crew. I nudged my shoulder against the wood. Nothing blocked the door. I twisted my shoulders away from the building and brought my fist to my chest, the signal I'd taught the Rott to watch my back. He whirled away from the door, his atten-tion focused on the ground stretching toward the front gate. Even though he imperfectly obeyed them, the Rott liked getting commands and he always responded with a sense of excitement to the ones that did not order him to sit or stay. I pushed the door fully open and stared inside.

The moonlight from the open doorway spilled a dozen feet into the room and pooled against a darkness so deep it seemed solid. To my left a row of cots, white top sheets lipped over green blankets, extended three cots into that darkness, the fourth cot no more than an outline in shadow. I kicked at an empty bag of potato chips to the side of the door. Beneath the first cot a can of cola rested on its side. I reached into my bag for a flashlight and spotted the beam to the far corners of the room. Twelve cots lined to my left, all freshly made, and beyond them, the beam picked out the white porcelain of kitchen facilities and a half-open door revealing a toilet, lid raised, all looking to my eye like a photo ready to be taken. I hung the Nikon around my neck, stepped forward, and scanned the flashlight beam to the right over a long, wooden table, the door swinging gently shut behind me.

I heard the spark of electricity firing the overheads before the first flash of light sharded into my eyes. I jerked the crook of my elbow toward my face and pivoted, the fingers of my opposite hand groping for the crowbar at my belt. In the near corner of the room a sunglassed man in a black, cassocklike suit sat within reach of a wall switch. The man's hands rested palms down on his thighs, his skin glowing bloodlessly white against the black thread of his suit. Midway between the two hands a 9mm Beretta automatic protruded like a deadly phallus.

"Welcome to the shrine, dear sister," he said.

The lenses of his sunglasses curved like teardrops, thick bottoms tapering to sharp points past the far corners of his eyes, their sleek black surface a stark contrast to the ghostly white and deeply lined brow above the rims. He wore his black hair slicked back, the hairline cutting straight across the top of his brow as though stitched. His face looked like a trick of makeup and stage light, so pale and white—except for a bright and sumptuous bloom of red at his lips— that he looked more vampire than living, bleeding man. We regarded each other in silence, his glance cloaked and mine naked. I thought again about the sunglasses and about the light inside the room, what he could see and what he couldn't. Outside, the Rott barked twice, then twice again, unsure of the danger.

"Yes, I'm a good shot," he said, answering the question I had just silently asked myself. "I'll certainly shoot you before you get to me. But I really don't want to do that. Violence is the first resort of inferior minds."

"Like Eric?"

"Like Eric's exactly," he said.

I can't explain how I knew that behind his sunglasses his glance shifted to my camera, not rationally, just that I felt a subtle warming of my arm where it rested against the lens. I moved my hand from the crowbar and laid it across the top of the camera, in position to lift the viewfinder to my eye.

"I wish to make a proposal to you." The Beretta jumped into the palm of his hand as though commanded and he pointed the gun at my chest. "I won't shoot if you won't." He smiled like a magician disarming the audience with a joke. "Remove the camera from your neck by the strap and set it on the floor with your bag. Maybe it would be a good idea to leave your crowbar behind, too."

I eased the camera strap from my neck, set my satchel on the floor, lowered the camera into the bag, and propped the crowbar against the side. He still held the gun, I noticed. "You're free to shoot me anytime you want," I said.

"My dear girl, I don't want to shoot you." He laid the pistol on his lap again. "I want to enlighten you."

"Like you wanted to enlighten Luce? Or maybe like you wanted to enlighten my sister."

"Oh dear, I can see we're going to have to talk about Eric." He steepled his fingers beneath his chin and sighed. "Eric lacks emotional control. He's a good disciple. The younger ones respect and obey him. I thought for the longest time that he had transcended his emotionality, that he had learned to calm and channel the darkness in his soul." The corner of his lip lifted, a sad and ironic expression that failed to become a smile. "I was mistaken. He never should have fallen in love with Luce. By the time I knew about his feelings for her, the damage to his self-control had already been done, although I didn't see it then." His lips tightened to a straight red line. "I didn't believe he would hurt her. I knew that she wanted to break with him, but I never imagined that he'd revert back to the crude and violent boy he'd been when I harvested him. I thought my training had taken deeper root than that. It's my fault. He was my first. I waited too long. He was too old when I took him. I never imagined he'd hurt her."

"The night she was murdered, that was you in the limo outside Bar Bar," I guessed.

The question stilled him for several seconds, and I imagined he wondered what I'd seen, what I knew about the encounter. "No," he said, his voice heavy and sad. "That wasn't me. I won't tell you who occupied that limousine with her—I prize confidentiality above all else—but you don't strike me as being unintelligent. You can imagine the type of person who would have instant access to such a car, the type of person who might be attracted to Luce and to whom Luce would want to attach herself." Something glistened beneath the right lens of his sunglasses, cutting a straight line down his cheek.

The man was crying.

"Luce was my star. Lucid, luminous, Luciferian, Luce." The words fell gently but heavily from his lips, like velvet-wrapped stones. "I didn't have the opportunity to name all my children, but I named her and the name proved prescient. Even at birth she glowed. She was going to be a wonderful actress, a major star. The famous and powerful were already falling in love with her. She was my brightest hope, the brightest of all my children."

"And my sister?" Tears can be faked. Actors fake emotions for a living and their fakes are more vivid and convincing than the real emotions of most of us. "Was her death also a so-called crime of passion?"

Sven dipped into an inside pocket for a white handkerchief and brushed his cheek with the folded corner. "Sharon was always a schemer and a cheat, though I have to admit a very sexy one in her youth." He returned the handkerchief to his pocket and straightened his jacket. "She always had a little more daring than brains, which helped her to excel at the small cons but blinded her to the big ones."

His glasses shielded the direction of his glance but still I felt the heat of it on my cheeks and brow, as though he stared at those points with particular intensity to gauge my reaction to the admission he'd just made.

"You knew her," I said, sounding stupid to my own ears.

"Intimately, but only for a short time." He rose from the chair, his balance and grace almost magisterial, and tucked the pistol beneath his belt. He had me then and he knew it. He didn't need the pistol anymore. "What was she doing at the cemetery that night, do you think?"

"Looking for a daughter who'd joined your cult, or whatever you want to call a gang of ignorant kids who dig up graves for you."

He nodded slowly, as though thinking deeply and carefully about the accusation. "Then why was she carrying a camera?" The question hung taut in the air between us, unanswered because I refused to answer, and he knew by my refusal that we both suspected the same answer. My sister was angling for advantage up to the moment of her death. "Was it blackmail, do you suppose?" He spoke slowly, his voice deeply pensive, as though he wasn't taunting me, as though he sincerely wished to know. "I thought at first the two of you were working together, that you'd sent her to the cemetery that night. You were already hunting me, I knew that from Eric. I figured it had to be blackmail." His smile was warm, paternal, persuasive. His smile forgave. "I've been just as suspicious of you as you are of me. But now that I've met you, I don't think so. Either Sharon figured it out on her own or she ripped you off. She wasn't smart enough to put it together herself but she was just amoral enough to abuse the trust of her family. She ripped you off, didn't she?"

"Stonewell wasn't the one objected to having his photo taken," I said. He didn't have the right to hear his suspicions confirmed. "It was you who objected. You didn't want your photograph taken."

"I'm photo-sensitive," he said, pale skin glowing like paper in the dark corner of the room. "Please understand that you terrify me with that camera of yours just as much as my gun scares you. The picture-in-the-paper style of celebrity is for my disciples. I want none of it."

He walked toward the door, his steps slow and solemn and his wrists crossed at his waist as though he moved at the head of a procession. I stepped back to give him space, realizing as he neared that though he had seemed a large and physically imposing man while seated in the corner he stood no taller than I. The impression of size came from his weight, from the slow dignity of his movements, and his supreme poise. I could have clocked him before he reached the gun but I didn't. I was too curious to know what he seemed only too willing to tell me. He swept a hand toward the door. "I'd like to show you something," he said. "Would you control your dog, please?"

He opened the door into his body like a shield. The Rott barked once and skittered to the side, uncertain of the danger. I stepped through the doorway and slapped the side of my leg, commanding him to heel. Sven waited until the dog sat at my feet and then, satisfied that he posed no risk, stepped from behind the safety of the door and walked a raked dirt path toward the rear of the base, each step carefully placed and ponderous as the beat of a kettle drum. He took no precautions to protect himself or to prevent me from running. Beyond the outbuildings rose a hump-shaped mound fronted by twin recessed doors.

"How long did you know my sister?" I asked.

"I've known Sharon off and on for just over fourteen years."

I thought about the timing of their relationship, said, "No."

"No what?"

"Not Cassie."

"Are you asking whether or not she's my daughter? You already know the answer. I saw it in your face, when I told you I knew Sharon." He looked across his shoulder at me. In that dark night, eyes cloaked in sunglasses, he shouldn't have been able to see anything. "I see it in your face right now."

"You're the sperm bag," I said.

His feet scuffed against the dirt and his pace slowed as we neared the mound, which sloped above the surface of the ground as though designed to withstand a bomb blast.

"That's what she calls you," I said. "What she calls her biological father. The sperm bag." I wanted the words to wound him. "She doesn't know it's you."

"None of them know." A silver key appeared between his fingers and he stuck a waist-high lock on the steel door and then second and third locks at the base and top. "The light switch is on the right." He pushed the door open to a steel-grate landing and stairs descending into pitch-black. "Please be careful of your steps."

The landing rattled with the weight of my boots. The light switch glowed green beside the door. I flicked it up, igniting twin rows of dim amber lights not much brighter than the illumination strips in a darkened movie theater. The lights descended a stairwell lined in concrete. "None of them know what?" The clang of my boots on the metal stairs carried my question down the well to a space that sounded cavernous.

"Why do you ask a question when you know the answer?" His voice sounded softly behind me, as softly as his steps on the stairs.

"If I knew the answer I wouldn't ask the question."

"You know the answer but you won't admit it."

"If you're trying to say something, just say it."

"I'm not trying to say anything. Instead, you're trying to listen but you're not yet tuned and so you improperly understand."

We stepped down to the next landing, the amber illumination strips dipping to another sharp-angled turn. "How much further down?"

"Two more flights." He laughed, soft and low. "To a place safe from nuclear attack and prying paparazzi."

"Eric is your son, your biological son."

"If you want to call it that, why not?"

"And Luce?"

He sighed more than spoke. Yes.

"Did you tell them they were brother and sister?"

"It's implied in the teaching. Sexual contact between special disciples is forbidden."

"Didn't work so well, did it?"

He didn't answer.

"You can't put teenagers together and not expect them to screw around. Look at Cassie and Jason. They're inseparable and not in a healthy way for brother and sister. And what about Theresa and Sean? Did you tell them before they came out here or were you saving your special teaching for when it was too late to do any good?"

"Theresa? Who is Theresa?"

I glared over my shoulder. He pursed his lips and shook his head as though genuinely puzzled. "You mean the little girl from Indiana? The one who came out with Sean? The interloper?"

"Sean is one of yours but she isn't," I guessed.

"Sean is destined for greatness once he finds himself."

"Sean is destined for juvenile hall, but I'm sure you don't care about that." My boots rang against the final stair and settled on ground so solid I supposed it to be concrete, like the walls. "How can you possibly justify calling them your children? You abandoned them. They were raised by their mothers. And my sister wasn't even capable of caring for her child. Cassie was being raised by foster parents. You gave these kids nothing except genetic material. And you stole from most of them the chance of having a real father."

"I didn't grow up any differently," he said. "And look at how I turned out."

"You turned out a monster," I said. "Where are we?"

"In the shrine." His pale hand flicked toward a switch glowing green on the wall, fluttered as though about to throw on the lights, and fell back. "Conventional fatherhood was never my intention, but I didn't abandon them. I planted the seed, let it germinate. When they were ready, I returned for them. And you're wrong to say I've given them nothing. I've given them this." His hand flicked forward again and this time struck the switch.

FORTY

THE FIRST lights brightened gradually, scattered through a ceiling that vaulted fifty feet overhead, the increase in illumination like a breeze thinning the mists to a night shot through with stars. A spotlight flared to my right above a twenty-foot-tall portrait of Mary Pickford, depicted sitting on a bench, legs demurely crossed beneath a black satin dress, a single rope of pearls hanging white to her waist. She stared at the camera with a look both brave and unbearably sad, as though the one who took her photograph was slowly breaking her heart. As the spotlight's intensity peaked another glowed to life on the wall to its left, illuminating the camel-humped crown of a cowboy hat and the grimly determined face of William S. Hart glowering above drawn six-guns. Then Harold Lloyd dangled from the minute hand of a town clock, Theda Bara vamped behind kohl-lined eyes, and Rudolph Valentino held a cigarette in profile, smoke flaring beneath eyes as heavily kohled as Theda Bara's. A waist-high mahogany display case topped in glass fronted each portrait, the lights reflecting off the glass to hide the contents of each case behind a shield of glare.

Sven strolled down the line of portraits and paused beneath one of Douglas Fairbanks Sr. as the Thief of Bagdad, his head wrapped in a bandana as he scampered along a wall, grinning like the devil. "Families re-create themselves in their own images, I've found," he said. "The children of violent, abusive fathers in turn beat their children. The children of the famous become famous themselves. Not always, of course, but the child of a movie star is much more likely to become a movie star than, say, the child of a class-three sex offender." He pointed to the portrait looming above him. "It's easy enough to see theatrical talent runs in families. The Fairbankses, the Barrymores, the Carradines, the Curtises, the Coppolas. Criminals beget criminals. Genius begets genius." His head cocked to the side as though he watched me for some reaction. "Makes you think about your own family, doesn't it?"

"My mother was a hardworking, decent woman," I said.

"Your mother was beaten as a child. That's why she chose your father. Because he beat her. But you already know that, don't you?"

Did I? Did I know that?

"Sharon knew. She knew and she ran. Where did she run? To men who beat her. They all beat her, except me. And where did you run?"

"I didn't run," I said.

"You killed a man, didn't you? Put another into a coma, if the newspaper reports are correct. No, you're not the type to run. You won't allow anyone to beat you, not anymore. You'll beat them instead. To death, if you have to." His smile gleamed in the spotlight. "I haven't been able to find out anything about your sex life. Don't you have one?"

I stepped up to the display case beneath the portrait of Valentino as the lights continued to flare one by one above the portraits of the stars, with those who had become cultural icons—Marilyn Monroe, Charlie Chaplin, James Dean, and John Wayne—lighting up the far wall. "I'm not a breeder," I said. The display case was shaped like a casket, a set of gray bones laid on red velvet beneath the glass. "And what are you re-creating? A family of con men and false prophets?"

The reflection of his face appeared in the glass above Valentino's bones. "Beautiful, aren't they?"

"They're just bones," I said. "Not beautiful. Not ugly. Just dead."

He jerked his arm around the room, fully lit now in portraits and reliquaries from Mary Pickford to James Stewart. "The dead are beautiful. And powerful, when you know what to do with them. But you have to know what to do with them. You have to know how to work the magic. And that's what runs through the veins of my family. The magic." He reached beneath the case as though pushing a button, then slid back the glass top shielding the bones. "Fifty years ago two men and a woman intended to create a very special child, the incarnation of the spirit world. A moonchild." His fingers wrapped a bone near the base of the reliquary. The bone was long and thick but still he gripped it tenderly, as though he held something as fragile as eggshell. "The man was a high priest of the Ordo Templis Orientis and the woman a volunteer. The two men chanted and conducted an intricate series of rituals for eleven days, and on the final day, the man and the woman engaged in a sacramental act of sex while the other man, the seer, guided all our spirits on the astral plane."

Three deep lines scored his forehead like red ink on parchment and the skin below his chin sagged to jowls. I guessed his age at mid-fifties. I asked, "*Our* spirits? You trying to tell me you were there, seeing this warped your poor little mind?"

"It didn't warp my mind, no. I was the star of the show. It formed my mind." He lifted from the case the twin to the bone in his hand, long bones from the leg, Valentino's left and right femur. "I was the one being conceived. My biological father was a disciple of the most powerful magician in the world, and the seer who guided us went on to create the most powerful new religion of the twentieth century."

"Scientology?"

"I'm happy to hear you're not completely ignorant." He carefully positioned the bones into a *V*, the ball-and-socket heads at the base. "You might say that creating religions runs in the family."

I backed toward the center of the hall, framing in the eye of my mind a shot of Sven and his bones before the giant portrait of Valentino, the smoke from Valentino's cigarette pluming above Sven's head. "You're a devotee of that English Satanist guy, what's his name, Crowley?"

"Would you like to see me triangulate the power of the stars?" The lines in his forehead creased bloodred with sudden concentration. He raised both bones high above his head, then as though struggling with terrible forces that threatened to cast him to the floor he crossed his trembling arms and brought both the bones down to his chest like ancient scepters. His stance steadied and he stood motionless for seconds, the spotlights mysteriously brightening to halo his head and shoulders. He tilted his head toward the ceiling and the drone that poured from him sounded barely human, as though he channeled vibrations from the depths of the earth, and whether caused by fear or a simple trick of theater the hall trembled beneath my feet. "All men shall be my slaves!" he chanted. "All women shall succumb to my charms! All mankind shall grovel at my feet and not know why! I and all my children shall be immortal!"

Sometimes you go to the shot and sometimes the shot comes to you. When you have only one or two chances to get it right, you wait for the shot to come to you, and Sven bathed in light, the femurs of Valentino crossing his chest while their original owner looked on, wreathed in smoke like a demon, was the shot coming to me. I gripped the corner of a pack of Marlboros in the front breast pocket of my leather jacket, lifted free the fake flip-top to expose the lens, and pressed the shutter.

"What in hell's name are you doing?" Sven's head snapped forward as he shouted, the change in angle casting his face into shadow.

"Thought I'd have a smoke," I said. "Do you mind?"

"This is a shrine!" His shout shook the hall. "Would you pull out a pack of cigarettes in the Sistine Chapel? Would you smoke before the tomb of St. Francis?"

I stepped back, pressed the shutter again.

"Sorry, wasn't thinking," I said. "I'll go outside and smoke."

I turned and walked toward the stairs.

"I could shoot you for this blasphemy!"

I glanced back over my shoulder. The bones of Valentino still crossed his chest. No actor likes to be walked out on midperformance, but he'd have to set one of the bones down to pull the gun and shoot me. "Your inferior mind is showing," I said.

He strode forward, his skin flushing slick and red. I thought he was going to brain me with Valentino's femur. "I'm trying to make peace with you," he said. "I brought you here to show you what we've created, what you can take part in, if you choose."

"Bones aren't my thing," I said.

He stopped a few feet distant, said, "But celebrities are."

"Do you expect me to believe you had nothing to do with my sister's death, with Luce's murder, that you didn't know Eric was going to take Theresa out to the desert and execute her, that he planned to firebomb my apartment?"

He suddenly didn't know what to do with the bones in his hands.

He couldn't continue to hold them across his chest, like King Tut preparing for the sarcophagus. He lowered first the left femur, then the right, until they dangled from his waist like skeletal images of his own legs. "True believers sometimes go to unwanted extremes, particularly in the early days of any religion," he said. "But even so, Eric was not going to hurt that little girl. He planned to leave her out there to walk back, true, but what's the worst that could have happened to her?" He shrugged and smiled. "A few blisters, that's all."

"What about Stonewell? Is he a true believer?"

"A recent convert."

"His brother, then."

"His brother has been very helpful."

I glanced around at the setup, said, "He's your financial backer?"

"Just one of many." He stepped closer to me, close enough that I could smell the sweat on him. "Many rich and famous people believe in the sacramental power of celebrity relics and in my powers to tap them, more than you might imagine. Why fight me? You can become the photographer to the stars, if you wish. I can make that happen for you. No more hanging around the bushes, ambushing celebrities." A drop of sweat sloped down his forehead and disappeared into the abyss behind his sunglasses. He swept his forearm across his brow, the bone in his hand flashing beneath the lights. "I've asked around. You're a good photographer. Why be stuck on the outside when you can be inside? One phone call and I can set up photo shoots with a dozen movie stars. Why be an outcast when you can become a member of the club? You could be the next Bruce Webber or Richard Avedon. You could be shooting for *Vanity Fair.* I can make you into the next Annie Leibovitz!"

"You can set me up with star-sanctioned photo ops?" That sounded like one of those once-in-a-lifetime opportunities people talk about—or a deal with the devil. "What do you want in return, that I get the paper to drop the story?"

"I have something a little more grand in mind." He edged another half foot closer. "You're really beautiful, you know that? You try to hide it because beauty attracts men, and relationships scare you because all you've ever known are lies and abuse. But you can't hide, not from me. Your beauty is only a small part of your value. You have talent and courage. And something else. You have a certain darkness of the soul, just like me, just like all my children. You're just what I've been waiting for all these years. A woman of determination and dark fire. A woman strong enough to share the vision. A woman wise and ambitious enough to make the vision her own."

"You want to make a deal with me?"

"That and much more." He edged another half foot closer, so close I could feel the heat of his breath on my neck. "I want to make love to you. Cosmic, triangulating love. I want to have children with you."

I kicked him in the source of so much trouble in the world, the source of a pack of kids let loose on the world like scavenger dogs, the source of my niece, yes, but also the source of my sister's death and Luce's life and death. His knees knocked together and the air vacuum-sealed in his lungs, but he didn't go down, so I uppercut his gut just beneath his rib cage. The blow dropped him to his knees. I waited for him to reach for the pistol under his belt and knew if he did I'd make him eat it. I didn't hate him. I just wanted him exposed for the demon he was. But he didn't reach for the gun. A single tear tracked down his cheek. Maybe I'd broken his heart with his balls. I left him kneeling on the floor, ankles splayed out like broken wings.

"You're a loser," he shouted when I neared the top the stairs. "You're all losers. You and your whole fucking family!"

I realized something when I shut the doors behind me.

He was right.

FORTY-ONE

WE BURIED my sister at a cemetery in the foothills of the San Gabriel Mountains, about a half-dozen miles from where she'd been born and one hundred yards from the ashes of the woman who had birthed her. We buried her in a simple blue dress from the suitcase the police had pulled from the trunk of her car, found two days after her death on a side street near Hollywood Forever Cemetery. We felt better consigning her to the earth wearing something a little more personal than a body bag from the morgue. My mother's ashes lay shelved in the mausoleum down the hill, near the cemetery's entrance. I tried to believe she was as close to us in spirit as her earthly remains and failed. I couldn't feel her anywhere. In truth, I couldn't feel much of anything.

We met at the cemetery gates and drove toward the grave site together, a funeral procession of three cars, five people, and one dog. Just past the gates we passed a nondescript Chevy sedan parked outside the office of the funeral director. I didn't know that particular vehicle but I could recognize a government-issue detective's car when I saw one. I noticed Cassie also eyed the car as we cleared the gates. She rode in front, Jason and the Rott in back. We'd almost lost Jason at the motel when I explained that Sven was their blood father. He was quick to figure that meant he and Cassie were brother and sister and ran off into the night, not to return until two in the morning, drunk and weeping. Cassie had taken care of him. The news hadn't seemed to distress her; to the contrary, she said she was glad to hear it because it meant that Jason would always be part of her life. Boyfriends come and go, but you're stuck with family.

The bargain plot we'd bought for Sharon lay in the far corner of the cemetery, overlooking a junkyard-scramble of scrapped oil derricks to the north and the Antelope Valley Freeway slicing across the base of the San Gabriel Mountains to the east. The grave was cut into a hillside so steep the casket would slide into the hole like a drawer. An advance from *Scandal Times* saved my sister from a county-financed cremation, the modern equivalent of a pauper's grave. The casket had been cobbled together in unlined, rough pine—the best I could afford. Cassie and I brought flowers stolen from the yards of houses we'd passed along the way. Sharon would have preferred stolen to store-bought, we figured, the way she'd preferred most things in her life. Ben and Frank had opted to acquire flowers the more traditional way. Neither had known my sister but both volunteered to help me put her to rest. They were more family to me than she had ever been.

The five of us stood around the hole in the ground and stared at the casket set on rollers beside it. We said nothing, the late-winter sky bleaching from crayon blue to bone white near the sun, the traffic hissing from the not-so-distant freeway, the hole at our feet swallowing our thoughts before it swallowed my sister. We hadn't hired a rental-pastor to read Scripture. We didn't think Sharon would have wanted one. It was Jason who finally broke the silence. He said, "What do you remember most about her?"

"That she was never there," Cassie said.

"But she wanted to be there," I said. "She just couldn't."

"Even when I was little I'd look at her like, what's wrong? What's the matter, Mom? Why are you crying? And she'd like, scream at me. Then my stepdad and her, they'd get into these, like, screaming fights, and she'd come into my room and scream at me again."

"The good things," Jason said. The wind blew his dyed black bangs and his hand darted forward to protect his eyes.

"She read to me when I was little," Cassie said.

A memory flared across the years, of my sister sitting at my bedside, reading. "She read to you?" I tried to remember more, how she'd looked, the name of the book, anything.

"Every night. And she liked to dress me up, you know, real girlish." Her laugh was small and nervous, almost like her mother's, and she reached down to finger her black T-shirt. "You can see how well that took. I didn't even have to change clothes for the funeral."

"*Green Eggs and Ham*," I said.

Cassie's expression pitied me, as though I'd suddenly lost my sanity and spouted nonsense, but then she too remembered. "She loved that book. Read it to me a hundred times. How does it go? 'Do you like green eggs and ham?' "

I closed my eyes, saw her face in my mind like an old Kodachrome print, long hair straight down her back, eyes scrunched together as she read. " 'I do not like them, Sam-I-am. I do not like green eggs and ham.' "

Cassie nodded along as I spoke. "That's right. Then it goes something like, 'Would you like them here or there?' . . ."

" 'I would not like them here or there. I would not like them anywhere. I do not like' . . ." Midway through the line I heard Frank's and Ben's voices to my left, and Cassie's off my shoulder, and next to her Jason's voice, less steady than the others but still there, and it was like we were singing a hymn. ". . . 'green eggs and ham, I do not like them Sam-I-am.' " Then Cassie thought to say "Amen," and I guessed that meant the service was over. I tossed my ragged bouquet of flowers—daisies, a rose, and the first wildflowers of spring—onto my sister's casket. Cassie stepped around me and dropped her bunch like a rock onto the pine. "G'bye, Ma," she said. "Hardly knew ya."

I wrapped my arm around her shoulders and stepped toward the car. She pulled away. "I think I'll stay behind a few minutes, with Jason." Her glance, hard and scared, pinned a spot on the horizon. I turned to observe Detective Dougan lumbering toward our vehicles, parked along the access road. Given her family history, she could spot a cop at distance. I couldn't blame her for avoiding the police, certainly not after I'd told her what happened to Theresa.

"Think I'll stick around, too," Ben said. "Enjoy the view a while." In his own taciturn way he was volunteering to watch her while I was gone, like he watched the Rott. He got along with the dog. I didn't know how well he'd get along with my niece.

"I'll walk you up," Frank said.

I knew that cops liked to go to the funerals of murder victims. Not to mourn the deceased but to see who showed up to gloat or peep on the ceremony. Dougan slipped something from beneath his armpit when we got close to talking distance. The latest edition of *Scandal Times*. He spread the front page open on his chest, face out, as though we hadn't yet seen it.

"How much of this is fiction?" he asked. "Ninety-eight percent? Or only ninety-five?"

The front-page photograph spread across the upper-left quarter of the page. The lens on the Marlboro-cam is about as clear as the bottom of a Coke bottle and the exposure time is hit-and-miss, but I'd hit. Sven stood in the photograph as though spotlit, two very human-looking bones braced across his chest and the giant face of Valentino staring down at him, his nostrils streaming smoke like an angry demon's. "Celebrity Bone-Napping Cult Exposed," screamed the headline. "Exclusive Photos and Story," shouted the subhead. I'd briefed Dougan on what I'd found at the old Nike base the night I'd left it. I'd expected him to use the information to request a search warrant. He hadn't believed me then any more than he seemed to believe the story now.

Frank leaned forward to examine the text, pointed to the byline. "They spelled my name right, at least."

"Mine too," I added.

"That has to count for two percent right there," he said.

The corner of Dougan's walrus moustache lifted to a flash of teeth, as though he might lurch forward at any moment to bite a chunk out of Frank's skull. "Two percent accuracy is about average for this roll of toilet paper."

"Sometimes they don't even get my name right," Frank said, playing along. "If they spell my name right, I'm happy."

"Speaking of names, I forget, what was this guy's name again?" Dougan stubbed his forefinger against the front-page photograph. "I thought it was Sven but funny enough when I looked him up in the computers I didn't find a social security number or driver's license. You don't happen to have a last name, do you?"

Frank had traced the ownership of the former Nike base to a company registered in the Bahamas that was in turn a subsidiary of companies registered in Belize and the Cayman Islands, a corporate shell game played to conceal the identity of an owner who probably wouldn't turn out to be Sven anyway. "We're still looking," I said.

Dougan folded the paper in half and for a moment I thought he was going to fling it across the grave markers, disgusted, but instead he wedged it back under his arm and folded his arms across his chest. "When you get a name, give me a call." He nodded at Frank to include him in the comment and turned to walk away.

"What about Theresa?" I said.

His foot scuffed over a grave marker and he looked down to read the name. "She'll be extradited. Only a matter of time." He looked up from the headstone and slapped at his coat pocket. "Almost forgot to give this to you." He fingered a thin, white envelope from his side pocket. "We found the enclosed item in your sister's personal possession, put it in the case file for purposes of identification, and forgot about it until today. Should have been with the effects given to you when we signed over the body. My fault." He scuffed a shoe over the headstone again after I took the envelope, then walked away, not looking back.

"Well, hell," Frank said.

"What?"

"The story will be dead in a week if he doesn't investigate."

"Let it die, then." I moved toward the trunk of the Cadillac, planning to take a quick look at the envelope's contents and toss it into Sharon's suitcase. Neither Cassie nor I knew what to do with the few personal things she owned. Give them to Goodwill, probably. My nineteen grand had vaporized. Maybe it would turn up later in her bank account. If it did, her will bequeathed the money to Cassie.

"I didn't get it onto the front page to see it die in a week." Frank followed me to the trunk and pulled out the keys to his Honda. "You know the story this bumped from the lead?"

I didn't answer.

" 'The Sex Life of Stars: A Tragic Tale of Lurid Loves Lost.' "

"Sure," I said. "I'd read that."

"See what I mean? The competition is tough." He keyed the door to his Honda. "Gotta work hard if you want to stay on the front page of *Scandal Times*."

I gave him a little wave, thanked him for coming. He shrugged and called out the window, "Sorry about your sister."

I returned the shrug and watched the Honda until it crested the hill and I couldn't see it anymore. Then I keyed the trunk and pulled forward Sharon's suitcase, a battered gray Samsonite knockoff made in China. Just looking at it, I should have known my sister's story about her life as a successful real estate agent was a con. I flipped the latches. I recognized the gray pantsuit she'd worn the day I met her, in the viewing room where my mother lay coffined, and the jeans and cotton blouse she'd worn the night we'd gone for Mexican food. I gently brushed aside her underwear, neatly folded into thirds. Six plain-white cotton panties and one black lace. The sight of them felt like an intrusion.

Dougan had lick-sealed the envelope. I stuck the tip of the trunk key under the flap, sawed it open, and shook a small color photograph onto the pantsuit's gray rayon. Four figures stood in front of a one-story wood and stucco family home built in the 1950s, a thin and balding lawn at their feet and the right front fender of a late-1960s Chevy pickup truck in the drive. The smallest of the four, a young girl about six years old, wore a dark green jumpsuit short enough to show her scraped, red knees. A teenager with strawberry-blond hair draped her arm casually over the little girl's shoulder and smiled at the camera with the desperate kind of happiness seen in last-place beauty pageant contestants, her smile a grimaced demand to love her rather than a true expression of pleasure. A woman in her mid-forties stood next to the teenager, her permed hair rising from her head like a bubble and her hands at her sides as though she did not touch people easily. The click of the shutter had caught a crease of lines across her brow and again at the far corners of her eyes. An outside observer might suppose she squinted at the lens, unable to see it, not recognizing the look as the wince of a woman perpetually distanced by pain. The face of the barrel-chested figure on the far right of the composition had been blacked out by ballpoint. Sharon had tried to blot him from the photograph but he was physically so much larger than the other figures that she had instead transformed him into a shadow looming over us all.

The emotion, when it struck, was not rage. I know rage. I'm comfortable with it. Rage is an old friend. Rage animates me, for better or worse. This emotion crippled me, rooting my legs so heavily to earth I couldn't move from the back of the trunk, away from the car, away from the weight of pain. I leaned forward, too weak to stand upright, and gripped the rim of the trunk to brace myself. Grief rolled through me like a storm surge that takes everything with it, and yes, I cried, but I didn't cry with just my throat or eyes, I cried from every muscle and organ of my being; every cell within me writhed as though drowning. I cried for the hurtful things I'd said and done to my sister and to my mother and for the compliments I'd neglected to give them, the good deeds left forever undone; and I cried from love for my dead husband and for my hatred of my father and for the deaths of those I'd known and loved but never grieved except through rage. Seven years of pain surged through me, seven years of crying for no one, not even myself. I cried for all that had been given to me and all that had been taken away, yes, but most of all I cried at last for me, because though I tried to believe I cried for all my lost loved ones, they left voids when ripped from me and so I mourned the dead spots in my soul where they once had thrived.

My niece said, "Your dog is howling like he's dying in there and you don't even let him out?" The car rocked with the opening of a door and a moment later the Rott thudded into the back of my leg. I'd left him locked in the car for the service. When he looked up at me I wondered whether the empathy of dogs was real or imagined. Cassie peered around the edge of the trunk, fear guarding her glance. "Are you okay?" she asked.

"I'm fine," I said.

And then, I was.

ACKNOWLEDGMENTS

THE NOVELIST'S ability to convincingly render the most arcane subjects is often due to the guidance given by persons truly knowledgeable about things novelists only pretend to know. The experts whose advice guided me in the preparation of this manuscript included priests, parole agents, lawyers, filmmakers, and photographers. Special thanks are owed to Meredith Murray, who kindly shared with me details of a petty crime that are mirrored in this fiction. Thanks also to Allen Plone, who always seems to know the answer to everything I ask. This book and the two novels that precede it owe an intellectual debt to *City of Quartz* and *Ecology of Fear*, urban and environmental histories of Southern California by Mike Davis that have helped to clarify my vision of Los Angeles as a city of unbearable beauty and dread.

This manuscript was edited by Amanda Murray at Simon & Schuster, who proved an ideal reader.

I owe a debt of hospitality to the inhabitants of the city of Prague and the Catalan village of San Pol de Mar, where this book was written. *Děkuji Vám, přátelé. Gràcies, amics.*

ABOUT THE AUTHOR

A graduate of the University of California at Santa Cruz and UCLA, ROBERT M. EVERSZ pounded the pavements of Hollywood for a decade before fleeing to Europe to write his four novels about Nina Zero and the American obsession with celebrity culture: *Shooting Elvis, Killing Paparazzi, Burning Garbo,* and *Digging James Dean.* One of the leading literary voices in Prague, the setting for his novel *Gypsy Hearts,* he helped found the Prague Summer Writers' Workshop, now the Prague Summer Program, where he currently serves on the faculty. His novels are widely translated and have appeared on critical best-of-year lists from Oslo's *Aftenposten* to *The Washington Post.*